❧ The Enchantress ❧

The Enchantress
by Han Suyin

BANTAM BOOKS
TORONTO · NEW YORK · LONDON · SYDNEY · AUCKLAND

THE ENCHANTRESS

A Bantam Book / February 1985

Book design by Ellen S. Levine.

Library of Congress Cataloging in Publication Data

Han, Suyin, pseud.
  The enchantress.

  I. Title.
PR6015.A4674E5   1985   823'.912   84-41585
                ISBN 0-553-05071-0

Published simultaneously in the United States and Canada

Bantam Books are published by Bantam Books, Inc. Its trademark,
consisting of the words "Bantam Books" and the portrayal of a rooster,
is Registered in the United States Patent and Trademark Office and
in other countries. Marca Registrada. Bantam Books, Inc., 666 Fifth
Avenue, New York, New York 10103.

PRINTED IN THE UNITED STATES OF AMERICA

DH   0 9 8 7 6 5 4 3 2 1

❧ Acknowledgments and Thanks ❧

This book is fiction, but the historical events it describes are as accurate as research can make them. The unstinted help of the writer's many friends in Switzerland, China, and Thailand is hereby gratefully acknowledged.

In Switzerland:

His Highness Prince Sadruddin Aga Khan;
Madame Madeline Morin, of the Municipal Library of Lausanne;
Mr. and Mrs. Guido Reuge, of Sainte-Croix;
Monsieur Andre Mamin; Monsieur and Madame Maurice Bridel; Madame Edouard Givel; and many others.

In China:

The historians of Beijing University, of Hsiamen University, and the curators of the Overseas Chinese museum in Hsiamen; the scholars of the cities of Yangchou and Cuanchou; the Peking National Museum of Art; the Committee for the restoration of the Yuanminyuan palace; the Chinese association for friendship with foreign countries; the abbots of many Zen Buddhist monasteries in South China; my friend Rewi Alley, who lives in China and has helped me in many ways.

In Thailand:

Sir M.L. Manich Jumsai, CBE., M.A.;
Dr. Didja Saraya, Director, History department of Chulalongkorn University, Bangkok;
His Excellency Kukrit Pramoj;
Mr. Seni Pramoj;
Mrs. Pornsri Luphaiboon; Mrs. Ankana; Mr. Gregory Meadows of the Oriental Hotel.

Special thanks to His Excellency Tula and Madame Chamcham Bunnag, for the stories of his eighteenth-century ancestor, a Persian grandee in Ayuthia.

Mr. Bill Hwa, Mr. Liu Zhenting of the Bangkok Chinese newspapers, and my sister Teresa, whose interest throughout was a mainstay in writing *The Enchantress*.

HAN SUYIN

⊰ *One* ⊱

Anno Domini 1752

LIKE A GREAT CAT, the lake lay purring in the May sun. The buds stirred after the passing of the Saints of Ice, and the *morget*, the cheerful romping wind of spring, brushed the sky blue, shouldered small clouds away from the mountains, and played among the fishing boats on the bright water.

"Look at my eyes," said Bea.

"Blue, the pretty *morget* makes them blue," I told her.

"And now?" She tilted her face towards me and the sun.

"Now they are green, like blown glass."

"The gale will blow from the northwest tonight," she said.

Bea's eyes. The gates to that other world, the world of mindless joy, of knowing the speech of trees and clouds and the song of the lake.

Bea is my twin, half an hour older than I. I follow where she leads, for without her there is no entry into that kingdom of ardent night, of burnished days, which is hers and our mother's.

Another world, turning this one—the apple and linden trees, the neat houses with their capelike roofs, the babble of women at the well, the vineyard battalions assaulting the slopes towards the city of Lausanne—into shadowland. Another world, where the great oaks stir, and bones are fleshed again, and I no longer know what is, what is not, since all things become other.

Bea knows.

1

We play games, Bea and I, that other children do not play. We play at calling the winds and uncoiling the clouds; and in autumn we make the fireflies dance around us, studding our clothes with their star bodies. Bea's eyes change color with the temper of the lake. Blue, green, slate grey, dark slate after rain. She speaks to me with her mind, needing no words. We have always been able to do so. "It is our secret," she says. "Do not tell anyone. Only Mother knows."

Father does not know, nor does Valentin, our elder brother. But is he our brother? Bea says, "No, he is not, he is other," and her mind is fierce. Valentin is several years older than we are, and when he comes home from the forge where he is apprenticed, Mother becomes uneasy, disquieted in front of his questioning smile. For he smiles a good deal, Valentin, asking us to love him, and I think he would like to love us. But Bea says, "No, Colin," when I try.

Mother. She is not like the other women of our hamlet of Vidy. Not like Madeleine, the wife of Pierre-Thomas Griot, the carpenter, or like Louise, the wife of the baker, Andre Paluz—women with many children, who come to her for remedies and balms. Others, with no children, come to her to have them. Still others, huddled in their shawls, whisper their torment or hope.

Nor is Mother like the great ladies of the city of Lausanne, their panniered skirts stiff with hoops, their befeathered hats high upon their wigs, so that they can scarcely enter their coaches. Once a month Mother brings to the market, on the stairs of Lausanne Cathedral, the mantillas and fans, ruffs and sleeves of lace that she makes, and the ladies press around her to buy. "Madame Duriez, you have a fairy's fingers!" they say.

The Vidy women do not come to babble with Mother or spend time with her as they do among themselves. Only when they need her do they enter our house, crossing the garden with its apple trees and lilac, looking round with avid eyes. They exclaim over her linen, the whitest; her lace, the best; her weaving, fit for the walls of a castle; the fine cakes she makes of candied fruit and honey. But they do not want her with them, and this we know, Bea and I. Mother is beautiful and smells sweet, and washes with soap of Naples, which

Father brings back from Lausanne as he brings pomade from Florence and cocoa from the Caracas. Her clothes, though sober, look dainty upon her, so that even the great ladies stare, and stare again.

Only Marie-la-Folle, the crazy one, comes to our house at dawn, standing on the threshold with her hands beneath her apron. She is a girl whom no one wants, least of all her father, the basket weaver, who beats her when he is drunk, and even, it is said, uses her in more terrible ways. The children throw stones at her, and sometimes her belly waxes big with a child, unwanted. No one knows who the father is. Pastor Burandel's wife, Agathe, takes the baby to the orphanage in Lausanne, to be raised in piety and repentance for its birth.

Marie scours our slate floors, washes our clothes, takes our goats to the common pasture, or sits quietly, watching Mother. She weeps when she has to leave at night, but her father does not let her sleep in our house.

Father is well liked. On Sunday after chapel and Pastor Burandel's sermon, men come to him to talk. They do not smile, since smiling on Sunday is sinful levity, but they touch their caps and pass comment on the weather. Pastor Burandel also talks with him, asks him to have a pitcher of wine on Monday and wonders whether the vine will ripen well this year.

Sometimes coaches stop at our door with English gentlemen and gentlemen from France or Prussia, because Father makes automata and androids, and they are all the craze in Europe now.

WE WERE NETTING THE SPRAT, which we use as fishing bait, when something began to stir.

Bea, who was splashing barefooted among the rocks, turned back to the gravel shore. She let her skirts drop and put on her clogs. Then I knew again that I had not really heard anything; it was through her mind that I had heard.

"Someone is calling us, Colin. One of ours."

She began to run, and I followed prudently, always looking where I set foot, for I dislike stumbling and hurting myself. Not so Bea, who runs like the uncaring wind.

We reached the top of the slope and saw them in their redingotes of grey and black and their somber tricorn hats: the bailiff, Monsieur de Crozay, and other notables, large with meat and wine, living in the fine stone houses with walled gardens on the crags topped by the Cathedral. The fields and vineyards of Vidy are theirs; many of the men in our hamlet are their day laborers.

Six of these, with picks and mattocks and shovels, stood by a freshly dug trench, bringing out of it a marble coffin. As we watched, they lifted the lid. In it lay a dead Roman's body, so well preserved that he had all his hair and teeth. "What a beautiful corpse," shouted Bailiff de Crozay. "Is it not a wonderful specimen, Doctor Combelle?"

Now the workers were extracting bowls and saucers of silver from the coffin. Each time the gentlemen exclaimed, handling these objects with reverence. Though many of the laborers still crossed themselves at the thought of digging up the dead, it was now the fashion among the burghers and the nobles of Lausanne. In several places along the lake they had been discovering the tessellated mosaic floors of Roman villas, as well as pillars and graves of their own lands.

"Aye, a well-preserved specimen," said Doctor Combelle.

I recognized him because the *Limping Messenger*, the once-a-year almanac that my father bought, which gave news of the whole world and of all the new discoveries, had a description of him and his finds of Roman relics. Doctor Combelle was well known, though not as much as Doctor Tissot. From all the countries of Europe, the wealthy and the noble, even monarchs, came to Lausanne to be cured by Doctor Tissot.

Bailiff de Crozay read aloud the inscription on the stone lid of the coffin: HONOREM D. DEO APOLLINI CA . . .

"Now we must really have a museum in Lausanne to house these finds, Combelle," de Crozay said. "It is a Roman of quality we have uncovered today—a great discovery."

"This merits a peg of white, Sir Bailiff," exclaimed a French nobleman in a pink satin coat and tight white culotte, with an abundance of white lace ruffles at his neck and slashes of gold upon his cuffs. "I confess I have fallen in love with your *fendant* white wine. It is pure as crystal and goes down like water. What about it? Have we not done enough for one day?"

"An excellent idea, Monsieur le Marquis! Wine for all, then," cried Bailiff de Crozay, with a large gesture that included the vineyard laborers. "In truth, the sun will set in another hour or so, and we have labored well. Come, let us take our Roman away where Doctor Combelle can gaze upon him at heart's will."

They left, the laborers carrying the objects and the body wrapped in a burlap sheet. Afterwards we heard that, exposed to air, the Roman had begun to shrivel; his hair came off, his teeth dropped out, and he was no longer beautiful to look at.

Bea's mind whispered to me, "There's one of ours beneath the Roman grave."

We walked home toward the click of Mother's lace bobbins. Mother was making a fan of blond silk, so fine she had to keep it damp with her oil-lamp carousel, whose goblets were filled with water blued with copper sulfate, with the lamp to vaporize the water. Mother had learnt lace making from the French Huguenots, the lace makers of Neuchâtel, whose lace was even finer than that of Malines, finer than anywhere else.

As we entered the house I heard Bea's mind: "Mother, Mother, I heard one of ours call," and Mother's responding: "Yes, my children. We shall go tonight."

Bea and I sleep in a wood alcove, a large bed with linen sheets. Mother weaves all the linen we use, as well as our woolen coats. Our parents sleep apart from us, in a bedroom of paneled oak. Mother gave Valentin his own bed, partitioned from ours, because Bea told her that Valentin had pulled my bad foot. I was born with a club foot and move prudently, and many games I cannot play; but Valentin had pulled it only once.

I always thought, *When I grow up I shall marry Bea, as Father married Mother;* until Pastor Burandel taught me that it was a great sin to marry one's sister. Yet in that other world, it was not.

DARKNESS LAY THICK UPON us as Mother, Bea, and I left the house. Father did not stir.

Moving surefootedly, Mother opened the house door and we walked into the night. Outside, the other world now held sway: forests of oak instead of vineyards, and the beasts of the forests slithering and grunting, yet all of them kind. Their eyes watched us. Among tall oaks was the grave which had been opened that afternoon.

Mother stooped over the mound of freshly dug earth.

The angry gale had risen as Bea had predicted. Mother began to dig with the shovel she used for the herbs in our garden. She and Bea and I dug under the stone coffin, struck a ridge of baked clay, and found the heaped bones and the clay figure: the Soul-Keeper, Mother-Goddess, Protector of Birth and Death.

Mother took the clay doll and wrapped it in her shawl. I heard her sigh of relief in my head. "Let us go back," she said, peering at the sky, which had begun to flake with silver.

But as we moved away there was loud barking and the noise of dogs, and a voice: "Stop thief, stop thief!" I knew that voice, yet did not know it, for in this world all the landmarks and signs, indications and warnings we lived by lost clarity.

We ran. Bea and Mother held my hands, pulled me. The hounds' voices neared, the man's shouts edging them on: "Hophop, at them, at them!"

I stumbled. Bea dragged me up. "Quick!" She panted. "Quick!"

We were home.

Father had not awakened despite the noise, and this was strange. Mother whispered, "Sleep now, all is well." She went to the attic and placed the clay figure with the others in the cache she had made, ensconced in an angular space where the beams came down. Nine of them. Now there would be ten. Had we really been out ten times to gather the Soul-Keepers?

When morning came it was hard for me to wake, but I

went to milk our five goats, and Horace the ram nuzzled me and sniffed as I hugged him. Horace was so beautiful, so fleet on his four hooves. I wanted to be Horace. He looked at me with his brown eyes and butted me playfully with his horns. I walked down the road to carry goat cheese to the wife of Baker Paluz. She went to the city every week to sell the cheeses she made, and also Mother's. The women at the well talked of the diggings. "They found gold coins and basins of silver. . . . There were thieves a-prowl last night. . . . Antoine the Preacher was up with his dogs."

On the way back, I saw Antoine the Shepherd, called the Preacher. He was a man who appeared to me immense, perhaps because of his hair, his beard, and his hands. He tended no flock, grazed no cows. "I tend the flocks of the Lord God," he said. He was dressed in a thick brown mantle, his head covered with a large black hat, and he held a tall crook in his hand. I had often seen him watching our house, looking at Mother. When Mother went into her herb garden, amid the phlox and *marjoram*, the thyme, parsley, and witchhazel, or stood by the bush of whortleberry gathering its fruit, I had seen him stare, unmoving, and go on staring even when she had left.

One morning, her arms raised, Mother was hanging the clothes to dry on the line that ran between the apple trees and the linden, near the fence, and he stood by it, and put out his arm with its clawlike hand and ripped the fine lawn from round her throat, above her bodice, shouting, "Whore, whore . . ." and Mother fled into the house, bolting the door, and sat down trembling a little. Bea rushed out, crying, "Villain, don't touch my mother!" We saw him leave, and then Mother came out to continue hanging the clothes. Bea and I stood by her side, in case Antoine returned.

Now, legs spread under the great mantle he wore like the wing of night, Antoine stood on the climbing pathway to our house, muttering and mumbling. "Devil's spawn, incubus, God will strike thee in His time. . . . Behold He hath already put his mark upon thee," he said, grinding out each word. My heart beat wildly but I did not run. I could not do so without awkwardness and sometimes falling down. His voice was the one I had heard in the night. I knew he had two

7

mastiffs, which he kept in the barn where he lived. Antoine preached there of a fierce and terrible God, who had doomed His creatures from the beginning of time. And some of the vineyard laborers and a few men and women from Vidy, and even from Lausanne, would gather to listen to him. I had seen them come out of the barn, looking transfigured, or swaying, drunk with the passion and fury of his words. One of the women had begun to scream and throw herself about while he preached; it was the Devil in her, which Antoine exorcised.

My brother Colin has dark shadows under his eyes today. He has seen Antoine and he is afraid.

"There is nothing to fear," I say.

I take his hand and walk across the meadow sprinkled with yellow daisies and blue cornflowers down to the lake, and we watch the small ducklings ferry themselves, serious as pastors.

"Last year, the ravens got some of them," says Colin. "I don't like ravens, Bea."

"I am their queen, they'll never harm you," I reply, and he grips my hand very hard.

Many centuries ago our people lived on the shores of this lake. They raised stones to measure the course of sun and stars, and named the winds, rivers, and springs. They built the villages on stilts, stockades on high ground, and called the place Lug's city, in the name of the Great Lug, who is all things to all men, the sun's light and the night's darkness. And they honored the raven, symbol of Lug, whose blackness is the other face of light. Their priestesses sat in the councils of war and peace, and the Earth Mother presided over those two gates of life, Birth and Death.

They went by many names: Celts, Gauls, Wals. They honored the oak tree; immense were the oak forests then, so enormous that as their angled roots came out of the soil they formed great arches under which chariots of war could drive. Elm and nut tree and mountain ash, companions of the oak, peopled the land and made it fruitful.

All kinds of beasts thrived in the forests: droves of wild boars fed on acorns; their meat and hides gave us food, mantles and shoes, belts and shields.

In summer our people lit fires upon the hill crests to celebrate the sun, joyful fires which purged all evil. But in winter, Taranis, the Evil One, Lord of Storm and Cold, would seek to murder the sun. He had taken a branch of the mistletoe and given it to the Blind Old Man, Death, who made a javelin out of it and threw it at Lug to kill him. And so at the winter solstice, when daylight is eaten by night, our people went to the grove of the sacred oaks and cut down the mistletoe with gold sickles, catching it in sheets of linen cloth.

And the priestesses smeared the blood of a boar upon themselves, singing fierce songs to wake the sun. All the beasts of the forest came out of the shadow woods to listen. And the sacred three-horned ram came running and leaping out of the sky and danced around the sacrificial stone. Our priestesses healed the sick, led the chariots of war, divined men's thoughts, and talked to one another without words. Of these priestesses is Mother descended. When such a one died, she was buried with a clay figure of the Earth Mother, who presides over the soul's great voyage to the land of the golden-haired gods.

Then the Roman legions came. Our people burnt down their stockades and four hundred villages; they moved twelve thousand strong in chariots to join other Celts battling against the Roman, Julius Caesar. Eight thousand of our people died, among them many priestesses, who slaughtered themselves rather than be exhibited in Rome as playthings.

The Romans then built their city on the lake and named it Lousonna. A beautiful city, with temples and villas. They perched a fortress on the molassic crags about the lake. For three centuries the city prospered, for it was on the main Roman road from the Inland Sea to the confines of Germania. The citizens grew olive trees and planted vineyards, and felled the oaks to build barges to sail the rivers as far north as Hyperborea, where the sun rises at night.

After the Romans came the Vandals, who destroyed the city, and after them came Christianity.

Lousonna was rebuilt, with a cathedral and churches, many of them on the sites of the ancient altars of Lug, the Sun God, for the people knew the sacred places and would not abandon them. The Christian priests changed our gods into their saints, as they had used the stones of ruined temples for their churches. Thus three-headed Lug became their Holy Trinity, and our Earth Mother their Virgin Mary. The Christians also took our Sacred Rite of Winter and made it Christmas, and our summer fires now burnt in the name of Saint John.

Nothing really dies. All is reborn, in a different time, under a different name and shape. The old passion, the knowledge, remained, passing from mother to daughter through the centuries. Mother told us many legends and tales as Colin and I sat with her by the hearth, while Father read and did not hear; for Father was ever absorbed in his book learning and his mechanical devices.

She told us of the Priestess-Queen, Boadicea, who warred in the isles of Britain against Rome; and of Guinevere, who saved Paris; and of Morgan, the Queen of the Woods, who loved Merlin the Enchanter; and of Ysolde, who taught the world to love; and of Joan of Arc, who saved France. And Mother told us the time was coming when the dead would stir into life. My grandmother, Grisolde of the Forest, had taught her to search for the Soul-Keepers, who guard the souls of the dead against the Great Wind of Nowhere blowing them away. We find them when they cry out aloud to us. I hear them, as does Mother. Colin does not, but his mind receives mine.

Very few of us are left with the gift. The Christians have hunted and killed us for many centuries. Witches, we were called, destroying cattle, bringing plague, consorting with demon-lovers. They turned our Lug, Lucibel, into Lucifer—Satan. Ram and raven became the Beasts of Evil.

Yet so many of those who were killed for witchcraft, broken on the wheel, their flesh torn off with red-hot pincers, burnt alive, were merely trying to heal others, to redeem misfortune.

Millions have died because of this Christian hatred of us. But a small number continue to live, able to decipher thunder and rain, to greet the sun and the moon as kin, knowing that passion, whether hatred or love, is more powerful and earthshaking than any other strength in the world.

"Use your gift well, my daughter," Mother says to me. "It is so easily lost."

She is losing it because of Father. Her love for him, an outsider, takes away her power.

She loves Father, and so turns deaf to herself, blind to that world *within for fear of hurting him. She cannot tell him of the gift. "And Valentin must never know," she says to me.*

Valentin, whom my mother loves and loathes. Son from her womb, foisted upon her brutally, in the dark and against her will.

I hate him, and grow strong, learning to hate.

⠀

FATHER GOES OFTEN TO LAUSANNE, taking automata he makes for Lord Kilvaney, the English nobleman who lives in the big house on the Rue du Bourg and who comes to see Father at his work.

In Father's workroom off the kitchen Lord Kilvaney spends a good deal of time, talking of the androids made by the Frenchman, Vaucanson. "You would not know they're but a machine; why, they breathe! I almost fell in love with one of them until I was told she was but a replica, not a real human being."

Thus Lord Kilvaney speaks to my father, laughing uproariously and waving his great plumed hat. Vaucanson the Frenchman, once a pastor, was now addicted to making androids; he had created a duck that quacked, and ate, and drank, and was so much a live duck that no one could tell the difference. And a man who played the flute, his fingers covered with leather so fine it was like real skin. As wealthy men wanted clocks and watches to measure time, and music boxes for delight, so they now wanted moving figures—on their banquet tables, in their salons and gardens, to amuse and astonish their guests.

Father wore his light coat of blue cloth and his red waistcoat with silver buttons. His shirt and lace jabot were snowy white. He looked so fine, entirely like a gentleman, not like a farmer, not at all like the people in our village of Vidy. He smiled at Mother and said:

"I shall hurry back as soon as the sale is done."

And she smiled up at him, her face smooth and young, and said, "I hope your Englishman will like his toy."

He had fashioned a couple perched upon a music box. The

11

man was dressed in pale green satin and held a flute that he brought to his mouth. The lady pirouetted and also curtsied. Mother had chiseled the faces out of wood and painted them, and stitched the clothes—the gentleman in a coat of pale green satin, the lady in pink, with panniers and a high powdered wig upon her head. Pierre-Thomas, the carpenter, had made the box, and Master Blacksmith Chavenaz the coiled spring, the cylinder, the cogwheels, and the spiral fuse, which made movement possible. The cams going into the limbs of the automata were of wood jointed with fine screws. The couple danced, and music came from the box.

It all had to do with time, I thought, looking at Father wrapping the box carefully. Androids ran on clockwork, as did automata. They ran down if one forgot to wind them. Supposing time stopped? Or supposing one could go backward in time?

Then I thought Father exceptional, wondrously skilled. Now I know that he was good, a fine craftsman, but hamstrung by living in the hamlet of Vidy and seeing few others like himself. For apart from Chavenaz, the blacksmith, and Griot, the carpenter, Father worked alone. He did not have the means to travel to Paris or to London and was too proud to ask Kilvaney's help. Yet in those places philosophers and mathematicians were studying the laws of nature, speculating on the stars and the cosmos, and trying new devices. In Lausanne, however, high society was too much bent on amusement, on literature and art, and looked down upon science; it was in German or in English that scientific books were written or translated; novels and plays and poetry were in French.

Lord Kilvaney had told Father that in Paris a machine had been invented that would make a boat travel on water without sails or oars, and that such a machine could also be made to travel on land. "I am afeard that man's mind will seek to become godlike, and to master the universe," he said. "Should this day come to pass, I only hope we may use well the knowledge we shall have acquired. I'm half-afeard, looking at your automata, at Vaucanson's androids, that we treat science with casual frivolity."

I helped Father; twisted cotton and hemp threads, previously soaked so that they would not stretch, into the strings that pulled the cams; adjusted the cogwheels upon which were affixed the toggle joints. It was a matter of trying out the distances, making sure of the exact second at which the joints would snap into the cogs, thus compelling the limbs or head of the creation to move. It was a matter of skill and patience, for I had little learning.

I too wanted to create androids. Life-size, lifelike. So lifelike that no one would tell the difference between them and a live being. I would make a Colin, to look like me; he would walk straight, run well, never stumbling. He would be indestructible, invulnerable—and Valentin, my brother, would be in awe of me and would never pull my foot again.

Father left, as usual making a cross upon our foreheads with his thumb. "God preserve you from evil," he said. Mother stood, her grey eyes still as the lake, watching him sit in the horsecart and shake the reins. "Alexander, off we go," he shouted, and Alexander stepped smartly, and we waved to Father, waved until he was out of sight.

Father returned from Lausanne as the sun slipped behind the mountains of Savoie and the lake turned pink and green. Colin, reading aloud the tales of mariners at sea—for it had been reported in the almanac that a siren had been perceived by temperate sailors in the ocean—said, "When I grow up I want to sail the ocean in which the sun goes to rest." For Mother had told us the story of the Argonauts, who had sailed to find the sun. And if one set out from our lake and followed the river running out of it, one came to that ocean at last.

Father was in high spirits. Lord Kilvaney had entertained him with great courtesy and told him of James Cox in London, who made clocks and watches for the kings of Hindustan and the Emperor of China. Mother helped him to remove his blue coat and put on his ordinary brown one and to change his shoes to the wooden clogs he wore at home. "The English are truly mechanic-minded," said Father. "They have a great talent for invention. Why, he tells me that in London they are searching for the power of electricity!"

"You should *go to London, then," said Mother.*

"*Perhaps . . ." said Father.*

He had brought back books, as usual. He could not pass a printer without entering, standing to watch the machine turn out the pages, the sheets falling on top of one another as the engine clattered back and forth. All the master printers knew him, and there were many settled in Lausanne, descendants of those Huguenots who had fled France when the evil Catholic King, Louis XIV, had crushed the Reformed Church by revoking the Edict of Nantes, which had tolerated the teachings of Luther and Calvin. More than a hundred thousand of their followers, the Huguenots, had been put to death, and another two hundred thousand had been sent to row the galleys of the French King. Some ten thousand had fled France, to reach Neuchâtel, Geneva, and Lausanne, cities that adhered to the Reformed faith.

"*It was bad for France, but good for us," Father said, his hands reverently touching the books. "They brought us much learning. The making of lace, clocks, watches and jewelry; the arts of the printers and engravers, builders and weavers—all came to us then."*

"*You seem to think it was preordained by God, to bring us skill and money," Mother said, teasing.*

"*Perhaps," Father said. "Now all the French nobility come here to see our automata and speculate on making androids."*

Philosophers wrote about automata; stories and plays were produced about some of them coming to life, or falling in love, or destroying and killing human beings. A circus was going round Europe showing three dancers, two men and a woman, whose arms rose and fell, who scattered flowers from baskets attached to their waists, and glided about on a platform to the sound of music.

"*I hear they're coming to Lausanne—we'll go to see them," Father said happily. "And here are some drawings of the fashions at the Court of France." Father collected these drawings, which were engraved in Lausanne, where many ladies bought them—though Their Excellencies of Berne, who were our overlords, frowned on this frivolity. Mother would make fashionable clothes of silks and satins for Father's automata; although she herself wore only a long skirt without the usual many-layered underskirts or pillows, and a simple square-cut bodice of black velvet over a shirt of fine lawn.*

There was a thumping on the door. When Father opened it, there in the dusk stood a small group of men: some vineyard workers,

Baker Paluz and Carpenter Griot, and the father of Marie-la-Folle.

"Good day, good day, my friends," Father called. "What fine wind brings you here? Come in, do not stand outside. I have a pitcher of wine cooling, let us share it."

"Jean-Francois," said Andre Paluz. "I did not want to come. But Master Antoine, there, he is saying, he says . . ." Helplessly he gestured.

Antoine the Preacher, who stood behind the others, strode forward and stretched a finger towards my father. "Woe to you, woe to you who traffic with Satan," he chanted in a loud strong voice. "Woe to the followers of Satan who by night do his work among the graves."

"In the name of God, what is this?" said Father.

"All evil-doers will be chastised," Antoine raved in his resonant voice. "Jean-Francois Duriez, you, who gave up the service of God to marry this woman, know that she goes at night to dig up graves and work spells with the bones of the damned; she takes your children with her, to teach them to serve Lucifer as she does."

"You're having nightmares, Antoine," Father replied. "Or the foehn, that hot wind, has blown your wits about."

"A snake's glib tongue, that you've always had," Antoine went on chanting. "To protect the harlot who makes spells and conjurations and lays a plague upon us."

In the gathering night I could see the white faces of women come out of their houses, standing beyond the pathway, listening. All color drained, the lake was now lighter than land or sky, a stretch of shining silver.

"Nonsense," Father said, raising his voice. "Andre, Pierre-Thomas, it is unworthy of you to come here with this madman. Why, Andre, only a month ago your wife was cured of a running of the bowels by mine."

The workers muttered, shuffling their feet, and Andre said, "Jean-Francois, it's true that Mistress Duriez gave Louise something to make her well, and we did not see anything, but . . ."

"You help her with her magic, your dolls, yea, dolls which walk and talk—incubus, succubus." Antoine raised his voice.

Father laughed, a high, clear laughter; and it was as if I saw him for the first time: short, slim, with the round head and brown eyes of the people of this land and the light, singing voice. He walked easily towards the men, who stepped back, even Antoine.

"Madman, troublemaker," Father said. "Go and tell Messire the

15

Bailiff, who digs up graves in the open day, what you have told here. Go and ask my Lords of Berne, who like my dolls, go, go. . . .''

At this mention of authority the knot of men loosened, and soon they shuffled away. As a coiled spring suddenly undone, the tight group fell apart, some of the vineyard workers touching their hats before sidling away in twos and threes. Antoine also walked down the path, his back still fierce, still intoning, "God is not mocked. I have delivered God's message." Only Andre, the baker, remained, moving his feet unhappily, saying feebly, "I didn't want to do harm."

"Come in, friend," Father said. Mother put out the pewter goblets and also goat meat, bread, and soup, and we all ate together. Andre was loquacious, wishing to be forgiven.

"That Antoine, he can make one feel as a cherry tree in the storm, all blown about. We did not mean to harm Mistress Duriez. . . . Pastor Burandel has told us no one can accuse a woman of witchcraft without some proof. That is what my Lords of Berne have laid down. They are our rulers, aye, for they are strong and impose their laws." He drank thirstily, becoming ever more slurred in his speech.

Father put a hand on his shoulder. "Andre, stop listening to that madman. Times have changed. Even the bailiff is no longer afraid of old pagan bones."

Andre laughed and emptied his tankard. "The bailiff . . . Nevertheless, it is not good to meddle with the dead."

➥➤

THAT NIGHT WE HEARD THEM, Bea and I. Or rather she heard. I listened to her.

Father spoke, and the pain he carried under his smile and gaiety was like a hairshirt he had worn many years now. "Oh, Daout, Daout, you promised . . . you promised that you would not go out at night on these mad searches for souls, and you have taken the children with you. Have you no heart, no concern for them and for me?"

And Mother sighed and said, her words dragged heavily from her, "It called out, it woke and called to us—"

"Us? Do the children also hear these voices you hear?"

"No, no, only me."

"Then why did you take them with you?" There was anger in his voice, but also pain and fear. "It is fancy, hallucination, it's almost . . . a sin. How can you believe these bits of clay hold life, hold a soul?"

Mother wept quietly. "Oh, beloved, I do so wish I could not hear them. Then all would be well, and I would not be forced to save them. But they are my people. . . ."

Father said, "Daout, you must never again go out at night. Your people are as dead as the Romans. When will you stop this dreaming? And the children, what have you told them? Can they believe in your dreams, your voices? They are Christians, Daout, as I am, and now I am afraid it is indeed the Evil One trying to harm them, and you."

"No, no, husband. It is not. It's Good. To learn to read wind and water, to understand the talk of bird and beast, to know there is life beyond this living, that death is but another kind of living—why, even your Holy Book says there is life after death."

"But only God can bring life back to a body, Daout. Our souls are in His hands. Your clay Watchers will never come to life. The dead are dead, and Resurrection is in the hands of the one God, Daout, oh, Daout. . . ."

And Mother sighed.

I heard no more; Bea had withdrawn, shut her mind to them, to me, as she always did when Father and Mother came together in love.

Early the next morning I went out to the stable as usual. Horace was there, and I hugged him tightly and whispered in his ear, "Horace, I'm not afraid, Horace." Horace's throat shook with a deep chuckle. He knew I was afraid, and he was laughing at me. I hooked my hands around his horns and pulled his face to mine, and told him, "My mother is not a witch, Horace, she is not . . . she is . . ." But there was no word for Mother.

When I came back from milking the goats and putting the foaming milk in the cheese vat, Father was dressed. He said, lightly and cheerfully, "Colin, we're off to Pastor Burandel today. You will have schooling, now that you're going into your eighth year."

"Yes, Colin, you must go to school," Mother said. She was fingering the torque round her neck; it was of twisted gold with the head of a ram at each end.

"But I can already read," I said. Father had indeed taught us, Bea and I. We could read the books he brought back, we read aloud to each other and to Mother. "If I read too many books I shall forget to read wind and water and the souls of men," I went on.

"Who told you that?" Father asked sharply.

"I . . . I don't remember."

Father looked at Mother with anger, and Mother said, "There are many ways to become wise, my son."

"Will Bea come with me?"

"No," Father said. "Pastor Burandel teaches only boys."

"I don't want to go to school."

"Nonsense," Father said. "You will have to learn Latin and Greek if you wish to go to the Academy."

I dressed slowly, putting on my hose and shoes and my best coat, brown with scarlet slashes. Bea came to help me. "Bea, will you come to school with me?"

"Yes, Colin, I'll be there."

"Still, I don't like going by myself."

"I'll always be with you, Colin."

I went to Mother to kiss her, and she hugged me and stood waving as I followed Father out; already he had saddled Alexander. He would take me up the slope, along the Flon River's climbing shore, to Montoie where Pastor Burandel lived, near the Chapel of Bon Secours.

✦ *Two* ✦

PASTOR BURANDEL LIVED UP the slope of Montoie beyond the Flon River. He was in his garden when we reached his gate; his hawthorn hedge blossomed mightily, his pink and white tulips from Holland stood delicate and straight, and his cherry trees shed their petals upon the lawn. He came forward when he saw us, hands extended.

"Jean-Francois, I was thinking of you. Only yesterday, someone came up from Vidy, and I was saying to Agathe, 'It is time to go to see the Duriez, to see their lovely garden.' Your wife grows the juiciest apples. Well, I am deceived with pleasure at your visit." This was Burandel's way of letting us know that he had heard of the incident caused by Antoine. Pastors have a way of knowing all that goes on in the villages under their care. They are responsible for reporting to the bailiffs, who report to my Lords of Berne.

"Fernand, I've brought you Colin to teach. To begin Latin and Greek."

Pastor Burandel cocked his head and patted my hair. "I baptized you, Colin, and your sister, aye, I remember. And now that you are seven—almost eight—years old, it is time to be earnest about learning." He was a stout man with a bald head, and when agitated during predication he removed his wig and waved it about. With his fine voice, he sang hymns so loudly that the windows of the chapel vibrated, and in the

Easter chorals at the Cathedral of Lausanne his choir had taken first prize. "You've done well, Jean-Francois, to bring your son to me. One is never too young to study and also to become a good Christian."

"My daughter also can read," my father said.

"Oh, aye, it is pity we have no instruction for girls," Pastor Burandel replied. "I shall come tomorrow to see your wife and your house—yes, I feel it needful." Burandel sighed. "But I babble on. One hears things. Women have many fancies, but there is no evil in them, no evil."

Agathe Burandel entered, smiling and exclaiming in a sweep of skirts and shawls and a large hat upon her black cap. She was thin, sharp of voice, and older than Pastor Burandel. They had no children, but Agathe gave instruction to the orphans and the children of unwed mothers, and in church these unfortunates sat, apart from everyone else, singing their hearts out. "Stay and have some chocolate to drink, and some of my almond cake, Jean-Francois." Her smile lifted her mouth almost to her ears. We sat and drank the chocolate, and Pastor Burandel took down a book and made me read, and said, "Good, good." Then Father and he went into Burandel's study to talk, while Agathe chatted at me and made me sing a psalm with her.

"Now, does your mother sing hymns with you?" she inquired.

"Yes," I said.

"And your sister? Do you pray morning and evening, as good Christians do?"

I knew Agathe wanted to know about Mother, Mother who was so different, but I would not tell her.

When Father came back with Burandel, Agathe insisted that he drink a little of the previous year's *fendant*, the soft white wine that makes our land famous. "Of course, you drink hydromel at home," she said, cackling a little. Burandel frowned at her. "D'you know it was the French Huguenots who brought the vine shoots here? The Lord indeed guided them to safety among us and has rewarded us for our charity. We have prospered since."

It was decided I would attend school every morning, going

home before three of the clock in the afternoon. And so each morning Father took me there, but I walked back by myself, for it was downhill and reckoned easier than climbing.

PASTOR BURANDEL'S SCHOOL HELD twenty boys. Some were the sons of Prussian burghers sent to Lausanne to learn French. All of educated Europe spoke French, and the countries of the Reformed religion sent their children to us in this land of Vaud, to Lausanne, where they would not be contaminated by Catholic teaching and yet learn excellent French.

The children bullied me and pushed me about because of my club foot. "He hath the Devil's foot," they said. "The Limping Messenger," they called me. And once, two boys started kicking me so that I fell; they went on kicking me downhill, edging me towards the Flon, intent on throwing me into the water. But suddenly Bea was there, mounted on Alexander, a whip in her hand, with which she lashed at them so that they cried and fled in terror. "I told you I would be with you," Bea said, and we rode back together.

Pastor Burandel was happy because I learnt very fast. "He must go to the Academy," he told Father. "Your son could become a teacher or a pastor."

Father smiled. "Colin is also good with his hands," he said.

I could now put together all the parts of a clock, and I was beginning to build simple automata, making some of the parts myself, out of wood, as so many craftsmen still did. But Father now preferred metal—iron, copper, or bronze—and for these metal parts we had to go to the forge of Master Chavenaz for his help.

Once a month Father would take me with him to Master Chavenaz's smithy, whose ensign was a mallet and cauldron. As our horsecart climbed the road we could see Lausanne, the city, so proud and lovely on its rock, and all around it, like a belt, the vine-covered city walls with their gates and towers.

Chavenaz's smithy was near the tower of Ale and its postern gate. Le Chauderon, or Cauldron, this area was called;

there were many ironsmiths here, and also leather workers. Here the servants of noble gentlemen brought horses to be hooved.

The forge of Master Chavenaz was a great cave lit by splendid fires. He kept five anvils going at once, which blazed and spurted in the wind from the bellows manned by young boys. The cave was filled with the music of metal as his apprentices brandished the hammers and brought them down on pieces of red-hot iron, held in pincers by other apprentices. "Vulcan," my father called Chavenaz, and Chavenaz, hearing my father call out to him, emerged from the darkness and came towards my father, arms extended to embrace him.

He was a large man, with a face shadowed by thick brows and capped with dark hair in ringlets. He had such a chest and shoulders upon him that he appeared as wide as he was tall. Chavenaz wore a leather apron and boots; the veins in his arms stood out. I was not afraid of him, I who am timorous, easily frightened, for he had stooped down to me the first time we had come and said, "Now, little man, what is thy name?"

"Colin Duriez, son of Jean-Francois Duriez, of Vidy, Sir Blacksmith," I had replied politely, and he'd nodded, pleased.

"Colin. A good name upon thee. Thy father tells me thou art good with thy fingers. Come, I'll show thee something."

He led the way through the forge, and I saw Valentin there, with an apron of leather, standing tall and handsome, the fire glow making his face ruddy. Here in the forge he was not the sad, gangling almost-man he was at home when he came back on Sundays. Here his head was straight upon its muscled neck, and he lifted the heavy hammer easily and brought it down sharp and clean and true upon the molten iron, beating it into shape. Chavenaz put an arm affectionately round him. "Valentin will be a great master blacksmith one day," he said aloud, and I could see my brother's face radiant with pleasure, though he tried to look as if he did not care and went on working.

Valentin was happy at the forge, happier than he was at home; but then, I thought, Sunday was the gloomiest day of the week anyway, the day when my Lords of Berne, in their great zeal to uphold the Religion, brooked no infraction of their commands. It was forbidden to sing, to dance, to play cards or any game; to run or to shout or heave a ball; to draw water at the well or to light a fire. All one could do was to read the Holy Book, and go to chapel, and listen to sermons, and sing hymns. And in the evening there was chapel again, and exhortation, to which my father went because he took turns with Pastor Burandel reading the lesson from the Holy Book. Valentin was happy at the forge, and Father was more at ease with him there; as if the preying disquiet that infected us when we were together in our house vanished in the glow of the smithy's fires.

Blacksmith Chavenaz led us to the back of the workshop, across a courtyard, and into his own kitchen. On a long piece of wood he had traced with chalk a delicate scroll—the design for a main gate of a mansion to be built in Lausanne. On another small anvil, with its own fire, he was forging, leaf by leaf, petal by petal, the stems and spirals of the design; nothing soldered, all the pieces dovejointed together by his skill. With his big hands he now lifted part of the scrollwork, and Father exclaimed:

"How beautiful, Vulcan. Thou art indeed an artist."

"Thou shouldst know . . . thy grandfather had the most beautiful gates in Neuchâtel," Chavenaz said.

"I have forgotten," Father replied, suddenly stiff, and I knew he did not want me to hear what Chavenaz had just said.

The latter laughed. "Sooner or later little ones grow, and little ears hear even what's not told. It is not good to bury family secrets like skeletons, Jean-Francois." Then he turned to another work table, where with his fingers, which looked like sausages and were so skilled and delicate, he picked up the minute cogs and gearwheels, so small it was a wonder he could hold them—they were like snowflakes. He showed us the cogwheel and the fine chain he had soldered. "For the next android thou'rt building. I have used a different metal, not so much iron, which rusts; I've melted copper to alloy it, it is brass, Jean-Francois." Then he went to a tall cupboard, rummaged in one of the drawers, and came out with a small cock of beaten bronze and handed it to me, saying, "For thee, Colin, remember always to look for the sunrise."

Mallet and cauldron. They were the emblems of the Great God Lug. This I knew from that lore gathered between sleep and dreaming, Mother's otherworld reality. Every time I went to Master Chavenaz's forge I felt whole, sound, undivided, as if he had soldered my worlds together.

For now, learning the Good Book with Pastor Burandel, I was at times sorely distressed, an anguish that I concealed from everyone, even from Bea.

I am the Lord thy God. Thou shalt have no strange gods before me.

Pastor Burandel was eloquent on the Uniqueness of the True God, the heinous sin of setting up other gods, of heathenish or popish practices. The Unique brooked no challenger; in His hands was Redemption or Damnation. For God decided who was redeemed and who was not. So the great Calvin had said: God hath not created all to the same condition, but some to eternal life, others to eternal Damnation. One could only hope and pray, not knowing the decision taken aeons ago in God's mind. And Master Calvin was the elect of God; he had made Geneva, Bern, and Lausanne the strong fortresses of the Reformed Church.

But this was the horror which preyed upon me: that God was to be worshipped in fear and trembling, for He was Pitiless; He had all Eternity and the fate of all mortals in His hands—Past, Present, Future. He knew them all, and He had predetermined the fate of our souls before their birth. He had put the mark of Satan upon me, my club foot, and nothing I could do would mitigate the torments of Hell to which, perhaps, I was destined.

We were enjoined to pray and to repent. Perhaps, in His Infinite Goodness, the Only God would save us.

No strange gods. The nights, and Bea and Mother bending over the graves, finding the Watchers . . .

"Cast out the Prince of Darkness," Pastor Burandel and his choir sang cheerily.

Mother, Bea. I loved them, yet they honored the darkness in which all things grow bright. Dimly, fitfully, I heard Mother talking without words to Bea of the enchanted forests of the night.

"For centuries they have hunted the memory of us, because they are afraid . . . afraid of us," said Mother's mind.

> *I have been multitude,*
> *A raindrop,*
> *A star,*
> *The glow of a flame,*
> *For nothing is truly what it seems,*
> *But also something else,*

Bea sang.

Witches. Witchcraft.

"Mother, will your people live again and move, as do Father's automata?"

Mother laughed.

"Your father's automata are artifices; but yes, perhaps one day a spirit will enter one of them."

When I spoke to them without words, they heard me, but only faintly, turning their faces to me inquiringly. I still had dreams of the forests of oak with their wild singing, and of my mother in white, with a crown upon her head and round her all the beasts of the forest, all come together in this marvelous beauty that was Evil, which God would destroy.

I saw Mother and Bea, both of them opening their hands, and blood flowed in a stream from their hands, a great stream, a river of blood, which poured towards me and carried me away. . . . I screamed and Bea was there.

"Hush, Colin, hush, it's only a nightmare."

"Bea, Pastor Burandel says we are damned."

"God does not damn His creatures."

"Oh yes He does. He has damned some of us for all eternity."

"No, Colin. We can only damn ourselves."

"Bea, I love you, stay with me always."

"I'll never leave you, Colin."

And at those times I felt that all I learnt was but a parody, unreal. Pastor Burandel, Agathe—they were automata, dressed and painted; I saw the lake shimmer, and the sky came down to meet it. *I am multitude,* I thought. *Everything alive is also me.*

ONE SUMMER AFTERNOON, JUST before the Fires of Saint John, Father and I went to the forge, and Chavenaz came to us, grinning and holding a contrivance in his hand.

"Colin, I have made thee a good leg," he said.

In his hand was a foot of wood shaped to my measures, with a joint in the middle so that it bent. A half-leg, hollowed, with leather, went like a glove over mine. Chavenaz made me sit down and take off my hose and shoe, and then slipped the contrivance over my leg. It fitted well, and my stump rested on the leather pad. Now I could walk almost without limping, both my legs like those of other people.

"Now thou canst walk upright, and no one can tell. Why, I know a German prince who has the same club foot as thou hast, and I made him a new foot, and now he can dance all night with it."

"Thou'rt a good friend to us, Vulcan," said Father, beaming. Father never referred to my club foot; but I knew he hoped that somehow I would grow out of it.

"It is your brother, Valentin, thought of it," said Chavenaz.

I said shyly, "Thank you, Valentin."

And Valentin smiled and jerked his head, and went back to work. For he too was shy, knowing himself unloved. But from that time on he was really my brother, and I thought, *Next Sunday when he comes I shall sit with him, and perhaps we shall read together, or talk.*

But then Bea would be angry with me.

On Sunday when we went to the service, I wore my new leg and everyone noticed. Mother sat holding the book of hymns in her hand. Valentin and I sang together. He knew the hymns by heart, and that day he wore a new coat. Father put his arm round his shoulders and round mine. Afterwards I read Valentin my favorite tales of voyagers to the New World, of Robinson Crusoe and of Pinto the Portuguese. But Valentin yawned and said he would go walking awhile.

"Do not forget it is Sunday," my father called after him, watching him go.

Valentin was much grown, almost a man, sixteen years old, and as tall as my father.

SO WENT THE YEAR. It was spring again; our cherry tree burst into blossom, and in the pond some ducklings were born. The ravens came, and with a great swoop of wings plucked them off the water to eat them. Bea and I shouted and flailed the air with our arms to beat them off.

Now I could make an automaton all by myself, from chiseling the face and limbs, hands and feet, to inserting the mechanism within the hollowed body and joining the limbs, the face, and the neck. I had my bench next to Father's in his workroom, and my own set of tools, which Chavenaz had made. I toiled to perfect the mechanism so that there would be no jamming, so that the cams and levers fitted as smoothly as do the joints of a human body. Now I wanted to study the inside of the body. Perhaps someday I would be able to make a perfect android, one with a life of its own, a will of its own.

Father took me everywhere with him now. He was, I knew, fighting for something in me; to wrest me from that torment which hung heavy between us. But this also meant to break the link between me and Bea.

Father read from the Holy Book every night, and brought more books for me to read, in Latin, and also on theology. For he seemed convinced that I would go to the Academy, where much theology was required, and become perhaps a pastor. "Vaucanson, who made a most perfect android, was a pastor," Father said.

I never went up to the attic to look at the Watchers now. And Mother no longer rose at night, so that slowly I began to convince myself that I had dreamt it all. "There is nothing in the attic," I told myself.

Antoine the Shepherd-Preacher had gone away, taking his mastiffs with him. We heard tales of an itinerant preacher who exorcised demons and uncovered witches in some villages.

The diggings went on at Vidy. The city of Lausanne had celebrated, on April 7, 1739, the discovery of her Roman name, Lousonna, in the Roman ruins at Vidy—an inscription upon marble, an invocation to the sun, protector of the city, and to the moon. And since then much more had been found. Lausanne was proud of its Roman past. I could hear Bea's mind, contemptuous, as Father read aloud of the finds in the

27

Limping Messenger. "Lausanne is older, so much older than the Romans," her mind said.

More frequently now Father and I went by horsecart to the city. Alexander knew the way and I knew blindfolded the three districts of the city, the Bourg and Saint Laurent, with the Palud and its large marketplace. Each of these had its own banner, but one wall, with its many postern gates and towers, girdled them all.

We went because Father's automata were becoming known, although he was not alone in making them. Throughout the land of Vaud were such craftsmen—carpenters, clockmakers, forgers—whiling away the long winter nights, making clocks and watches, and figures dressed and painted to look like soldiers, or acrobats, or magicians, or music makers with vielle, trumpet, or drum.

At the great fairs, three times a year, they would assemble and compare their work. On those days stalls escalated up and down the slopes from the Palud, where a statue of blind justice presided over a fountain up the stone stairs to the Cathedral. Each stall was for certain goods, so that order should prevail. And so I knew where grain and flour were sold, shoes and leather, butter and cheese, herrings and sausages. The best stalls of all were those selling lace, silk and velvets, and damask from China, porcelain and spices, and of course clocks and automata. All the world, it seemed, wanted automata, and spoke of androids, which are automata so perfect they seem alive. To reproduce the appearance of life, if not life itself, is a dream as old as mankind; I too dreamt of creating an android, as I have said.

Father's passion became mine, as his gifted hands were also my inheritance.

As we left in the cart, with his creations carefully wrapped in cambric, Father would brighten, grow taller. In the city many men hailed him.

"Messire Duriez, what good things do you bring this time?"

"A fair lady for the nobles of the Rue du Bourg," he would reply, and everyone would laugh with great good nature.

We would go from stall to stall, looking, sometimes buying. I remember one year when cotton was in fashion, all the ladies wanted to wear it, cotton so fine one could see through it, or heavy as linen. And one day, as we lingered, we saw ten men from China, with plaits down their backs, in tunics and trousers and round hats and soft cloth shoes. They were here to paint the walls of noble mansions recently bought by wealthy Prussians and Frenchmen. In France for many years the custom had been to send for workmen from China, some twenty at a time, to paint the walls of castle rooms with birds and flowers and landscapes—only the Chinese had the art.

It was at one of those fairs that I discovered Chinese cardboard, and papier-mâché, lighter than porcelain or clay or wood, which could be moulded to make the faces of our automata. I pressed Father to try, but he hesitated. "People may not like it," he said.

And once we went to the city to carry Marie-la-Folle's new baby to the orphanage. Mother had delivered the child, for no one else would help; when questioned as to the father, Marie would only laugh, her hands upon her belly. But after she had nursed the baby for some months, her father would not let her keep it, and Agathe Burandel said it must go to the orphanage to be raised Christianly. Mother wanted us to keep her, for she was a pretty little girl, but "the whole village is against it," said Pastor Burandel. So we took her away to the city, while Agathe came to sing some hymns with Mother, for it was Agathe's habit to sing away all woes.

IN THAT YEAR OF 1754 there were more foreign visitors than ever in the great houses of the Rue du Bourg—English broughams and French carosses, German berlines, Spanish light calèches, and some elegant landaus in which the ladies drove, chatting with the sound of bluetits. In bonnets of gauze and ribbons, in velvet capes, in pelisses and muffs when the weather turned cold, the ladies took the air. Sometimes a French duke with powdered wig, holding in his hand a perfumed handkerchief, went at a gallant pace in a lacquered coach-and-four.

It was not only the beauty of our lake and our mild climate that played its part in enchanting the visitors to our land of Vaud. Most enchanting of all, they said, were our people, with their reputation for civility and exquisite manners. Thus, while war raged between England and France, English and French gentlemen and ladies here would meet and converse, play chess or whist or bezique, dance the minuet, and discuss poetry and philosophy. And though they might detest one another, yet they seemed to delight in one another's company, for there is much delectation in being able to say malicious things about one's friends in a witty manner—it is an indispensable amusement of high society.

This high society we visited, Father and I, though we were not a part of it. Here assembled the great, the talented, the beautiful, the witty, surrounded by the best that the arts could offer. Here they came to be amused, for to escape boredom was their life's purpose.

Others came to consult our famous Doctor Tissot, who seemed able to cure every known disease. Crowned heads of Europe stayed some weeks, some months, and the houses of one or another of Lausanne's aristocrats were ever at their disposal.

"Without the rich foreigners, many a noble family would be penniless," Blacksmith Chavenaz said. "Their Excellencies of Berne do not leave us any political power. Hence we try to amuse ourselves, and create amusement for all our visitors."

Their Excellencies of Berne were not too happy with us in Lausanne, with our propensity for dances, plays, and gaming. Indeed, they suspected deep plots beneath the gaiety; fulminated against amusement as ungodly, decadent, perverse, destructive of public morality. But the pastors of our land eagerly assured their masters of faithful compliance, although they were aware that the foreigners spent money in Lausanne because they were satisfied and diverted; and that many a great and good family—the de Chandieu, de Mezery, de Bottens, de Saint-Cierges, d'Aray, de Villardin, Madame de Prelaz, and so many others—provided houses, apartments, delicate food, and excellent servants, which brought prosperity to the city and employment to many.

Behind this facade of play and social graces there was also intellectual stimulation. The Lausanne Academia was renowned. Youths from the patrician families of Berne, from Prussia and Westphalia and from the Netherlands, and also from England, flocked to the Academia to learn French, for the French spoken in Lausanne was said to be the best, save for that spoken at the Court of France itself. Hence the Lausanne schools and boarding schools were full of foreigners. One family had fourteen English and twelve Muscovite youths to lodge and feed.

The result was that even our masters, the Excellent Lords of Berne, were losing their German, which became studded with French phrases and French words. Despite the sumptuary laws, which prohibited extravagant finery, the ladies of Berne all wanted to be dressed as at the Court of France, and in 1752 a great ball had been held in Berne, with many fireworks, for the birth of the French Dauphin. "They danced the whole night through," our people said gleefully.

All this I learnt by going with my father to show our automata in the fine houses of Lausanne. I also learnt good manners; how and when to bow, to take off my hat at sight of a lady, and to half-curtsy, which my club foot made difficult. Father encouraged me to learn how to behave in society. He wanted me to go on to the Academy. And though I was greatly afraid of school, and of being tormented by the other boys, I tried not to think about the hurt but saw myself becoming a master in philosophy, or perhaps a doctor, renowned as Doctor Tissot, and at the same time a master craftsman, making watches and automata and androids. One day I too would travel, showing my androids in the courts of kings and sultans, travel as far as China, the Ottoman Empire, or the Indies . . . and come back with great wealth and marvelous tales.

ONE SPRING DAY IN 1754 when the apple trees were in flower and the chestnuts burst with the effort of sap and bud, Father and I went to the house of Isabelle de Thunon.

In that society of sprightly people whose greatest love was the display of good manners, elegance, and hospitality, Isabelle de Thunon's salon was held to be one of the most refined. There congregated many of the celebrities who came to Lausanne.

La Tramontoire was on the sunny flank of the Rue du Bourg,

where the large mansions succeeded one another, all of them with ornate gates of iron lace and gardens surrounded by walls.

The Rue du Bourg was the center, the heart of the upper city. Its northern side had four inns, always full of people from many lands. It was past the Three Crowns that La Tramontoire was to be found, with its green sward sloping to the honeysuckle-covered walls of Lausanne.

I saw a woman, her hair powdered and adorned with pansies and violets to match the violet taffeta of her dress, come down from the colonnaded porch towards us.

"Jean-Francois, my dear, dear cousin, how glad I am! It has been so many years." And she threw herself into Father's arms.

Father, holding her lightly with his hands, was also smiling. "Dear Cousin Isabelle, I too am happy. This is my son Colin," he said.

"Colin." She bent towards me, and I could smell her perfume. She had much powder on her face and a *mouche* on her right cheek. Her hair fell in well-coiled ringlets on her neck. "He is adorable, so sweet!" she cried in her high voice. "But come, let us have tea. You must be starving."

When we went in, Father rubbed his hands and looked around, as if the place was somewhat familiar to him. We sat on chairs covered with tapestry. Gold and gilt were everywhere. There were many cakes, and tea in a silver teapot, milk in a silver milk jug, and sugar and honey and three kinds of jam. The cups were transparent; it was the fashion, copied from England, and Aunt Isabelle raised her little finger when she lifted her cup to her lips.

Father watched as my plate was filled, perhaps to see whether my hands were clean. "He has *such* good manners," Isabelle de Thunon said as I bowed when she again filled my plate with cake; there were also macaroons, and *brisselets*, crisp to the tongue. "Lord and Lady Mansard, who are staying with me, love them," said Isabelle. "Take some more of the chocolate cake, Jean-Francois; it comes from Vienna, Lady Toogood brought it this morning." She chatted, sometimes putting in an English word, for now with many English nobles it was the fashion to speak English. Then she was pleading with Father.

"Now, Cousin, if I've asked you to come, it is because of Theodore. He is not well, that is why I wrote to you. Methinks, after all these years . . ."

"After all these years . . ." Father said, a little mockingly, "does Theodore wish to see me?"

"Jean-Francois, do not be hard. It is time for you to return to Neuchâtel."

"Ah, the prodigal son. Theodore will kill the fatted calf," Father said.

I had never heard of Theodore, nor indeed of any of Father's relatives. All I knew was that Father came from Neuchâtel, and Mother from the Jorat. Whereas other children had grandparents and cousins, uncles and aunts, Father never talked about his family to us. Not so Mother. She told us of Grisolde of the Forest, her mother, and how she dwelt in the Raven's Nest, beyond the Lost Stone, in the oak forests of the Jorat. Once a year, Father would take Mother in the horsecart to the Jorat to see Grandmother Grisolde.

Father would not let us go with her. He would come back the same day, with Alexander all in a lather. Then he would go to fetch Mother a few days later. I vaguely remembered being taken there once—but I was not sure whether I remembered or whether Bea had told me. . . . This was the unreal, dim world I was beginning to forget.

And suddenly I could not understand what Isabelle and Father said. They began to speak in a way which was devised by the nobles so that others might not understand them. It was done in England among the aristocracy, adding a *fi* or a *do* between the syllables of each word, so that they could converse with each other as in an apparently unknown tongue.

At length Father rose and drew from the pocket of his coat a music box, which he gave to Isabelle.

"Oh, how beautiful, how beautiful, everyone will be jealous of me," she cried theatrically, in understandable French.

I was angry. I had made the clock's inside, using a cylinder with nail studs, which, turning, set in motion the cams. We had pored together, Master Chavenaz and Father and I, over many diagrams before making the box. And now Father had

33

given it to this woman without a word to me of explanation. . . .

We returned home. An apple-green light lay in streamers upon the lake, and the last gulls went screaming and wheeling overhead.

"Who is Theodore, Papa?" I asked, bold and yet fearful.

And Father, looking straight ahead, replied, "Your uncle Theodore was my father's younger son. One day, Colin, when you grow up, perhaps I shall take you to him."

PASTOR BURANDEL TOLD MY father that I should study theology. "Colin is gifted. He has a retentive memory and he writes well. Consider seriously, Jean-Francois, what you would wish him to be, for he is now ten years old." Pastor Burandel still hoped I would become a pastor. Pastors were an aristocracy of their own; they had influence. They were teachers, they helped bailiffs keep records of births and deaths, of good or bad behavior. Since the Reform, the spoils of the Catholic Church had been confiscated. The sale of the gold and silver had provided for the construction of bridges and highways, the repair of houses ruined by the flooding of the river, and the sustenance of pastors of the Reformed Church.

The city was prosperous, for the Huguenots who settled in our land had brought many crafts. But the countryside was starkly poor, with heavy taxes and levies imposed upon the peasants. Many who lost their lands left to become mercenaries in whichever army would employ them. Thus the land of Vaud supplied officers and men to England and France, to Prussia and Sweden and Rome, to the Muscovites, and even to Acadia and New Amsterdam. These men fought in every war, and sometimes fought one another. And because so many young men went off to hire themselves to foreign armies, out of seven thousand people in Lausanne there had been only thirty marriages that year, for there were no young men to marry.

"You *are* a man of Neuchâtel, Jean-Francois, you could send your son there," Burandel said. The pastors of Neuchâtel had great power in the land, for Neuchâtel was rich, prosperous, a well-ordered city, and not under my Lords of Berne, but distantly controlled by the King of Prussia.

My father looked at me. In those months of working together, as my fingers grew clever, our silences also spoke, more comforting than words, which sometimes hurt.

"It will be what Colin wants," he said lightly.

After meeting with Cousin Isabelle, Father had taken to walking along the lakeshore, staring at the lake, forever renewed in its untiring vanity of colors and moods. I watched him and knew him sorely beset, thinking of me and what I would do. I knew that as a poor man's son it would be difficult for me to enter the Academy or the better schools. We were not wealthy, but neither were we as poor as the laborers of Vidy, most of whom had lost their lands, parceled out to the big families and to the new landlords from Berne, and could only sell their toil for daily bread. We had a house of our own, five goats and a ram, a horse and cart.

I was impressed by the welcome my father had in the great houses, and also by his cousin Isabelle de Thunon, remembering the mansions with their sparkling windows, the rooms splendid with gilt and crystal, with paintings and silks, the women and men who talked to my father as an equal, neither high nor low, but as one of them. Yet Father's clothes were sober, the buttons silver, not gold studded with precious stones as those of some of the gentlemen who spoke to him, whose jabots of snowy lace flowed upon their embroidered doublets, whose hose was fine silk, used only once or twice and then discarded. I returned from these visits yearning to be part of this world where all was easy and gay, or so it seemed.

Yet Lausanne smelt bad. There were great heaps of manure in the backs of many fine houses, and through the summer, swarms of flies invaded the rooms—keeping them away needed a host of domestics.

But our house was clean. Lavender and thyme, gentian and verbena, heather, camomile and blackcurrant; the healing herbs my Mother brewed scented the rooms. Mother made balms for the fever, draughts for the ague and sore bones, cataplasms for wounds, sorrel at end of summer, and saponaria for the cough; hawthorn for women out of their youth, and

Saint John's herb, the fire grass, Artemisia, for girls with belly discomfort, mint and rosemary for bone aches and angelica and pale roses and black radish. She went with Bea to pick myrtle and the bark of willow, and meadow saffron for the gout. She brewed dandelion and gave it to us to drink, and it kept us healthy.

"Mistress Duriez," said Louise Paluz, the baker's wife, "all these brews—who taught you them?"

"You will grow sick with all that washing," Marie-la-Folle said to my mother. "Why, everyone else washes their linen but once a year."

And somehow, all that Mother did for our cleanliness was evil in the minds of others.

But I hid these thoughts as houses conceal themselves under their overhanging roofs, wrapping them and keeping them warm in winter. I hid my turmoil of questions with no answers. I knew Father was sorely tempted, for my sake, to visit his brother, my uncle Theodore.

But Uncle Theodore wanted nothing to do with Mother.

This no one had told me. I knew it.

ONE DAY PASTOR BURANDEL came and walked with Father, talking, in the garden.

Mother sat weaving at her loom, and Bea was stitching herself a bodice; I could feel them talking to each other.

"Neuchâtel . . . if he goes there, I shall die."

"He will not go, Mother."

"He may, for Colin's sake. He is taking Colin away from us."

"Colin is with me."

Mother sighed. And then Father came in from the garden and went to Mother, his face radiant with love. We would not go to Neuchâtel.

❧ *Three* ❦

Anno Domini 1755

IN THIS YEAR OF grace the harvest was so good in our land that
even Bailiff de Crozay came down among the vines to sing
with the vine workers trampling the fruit in their wooden
vats, and everyone was drunk with the crude new wine. The
workers took off their clothes, for the sun darted its blessed-
ness upon the vineyards, and women too had to help, carting
away the barrels of new wine. Because Pastor Burandel knew
this was God's blessing, when he found the naked workers
trampling the vine and the women singing he did not chas-
tise them, for he too loved wine and saw nothing ill in the
rejoicing.

But Their Excellencies my Lords of Berne viewed this with a
different eye, becoming much concerned about the public
morals of their domain, and Pastor Burandel had to explain
himself. "It was hot, they took off their clothes," he said. But
Berne decided it was grievous immorality, and Burandel was
warned that on no account, however hot the weather, must
the vineyard workers be anything but decently clad.

Pastor Burandel came to see Father, who comforted him
with friendship and *fendant*. The autumn was indeed a wine
autumn, the lake rosy at dawn and parading a riot of colors
throughout the day.

"It is hard to be a pastor," said Burandel. "Little money,
and at the beck and call of Berne." Father was concerned

about this matter; I think this also made him decide that I would not be a pastor.

But the core of his unease was Mother. Of this he never spoke, and only when events took their fatal course would I know how much he loved and worried about Mother.

Of a sudden, Father announced that he and I would go to Geneva. It was Lord Kilvaney who had counseled him, "Go to see Abraham Hirsch in Geneva. He is a Jew, but a good one, and farsighted. The world is changing, Jean-Francois, and though we need scholars, yet I've seen wealth come through tradesmen and inventors." Kilvaney had an attack of the gout, because of his great consumption of excellent port wine. Doctor Tissot was making him well with colchicine, but his foot pained him exceedingly. "I'd go with you, except for this damned toe of mine. But it is my view that your son is too bright to be a mere parson. Go to see Hirsch. He will know what to do.

"I hear that Frenchman, what's his name, Voltaire, the fellow who's always trying to stir trouble, is trying to get a watch factory working, and Hirsch is his banker. He did me a good turn, did Abraham—rescued my rascal brother from his gambling debts. Abraham has a cousin in the bank in London and another one in Amsterdam. Half the nobility of Europe owes money to the Jews. I don't hold with looking down upon a man because of his birth. Or looking up to him, either."

It was through Hirsch that an English factory, owned by James Cox, was established in Geneva. It was a difficult feat, for the Council of Two Hundred of the City had, in 1696, restricted the right to trade or make timepieces to the citizens and burghers of Geneva. The Council had also proclaimed a division between "master craftsmen" and "artisans," or ordinary craftsmen; and though a great number of craftsmen from other lands were settled in Geneva, working in watchmaking and in jewelry, in gold- and silversmithing, and in the textile factories, they had no hope of ever becoming masters, owning workshops in their own right and freely buying and selling what they made. "But Hirsch can establish you," Kilvaney said. "Believe me, Jean-Francois, you'll make money, and your son will be well provided for."

And so we left early one morning, Alexander stepping smartly, a horse of some age, but whose sinews were still good for many years. We had had him reshod some days before, and he seemed very proud to be going along the good road that my Lords of Berne had built. That was one thing our Berne masters did well. Like the Romans, they made roads sound, and safe from highwaymen. Some years before, Their Excellencies of Berne had hanged twenty-three high-waymen, after breaking them on the wheel; this hanging had been a prolonged festival for all the people of the land of Vaud.

We passed the Chapel of Lepers and the executioners' field where malefactors were broken on the wheel and quartered. All along the road to Morges were the gibbets, one of them still occupied with a stiff corpse wrapped in black; around it wheeled a cloud of ravens.

We traveled all day, stopping only once to water Alexander, to eat our bread and goat cheese and drink the wine in our gourds. When night fell, we halted at Coppet and found a hostelry. The innkeeper gave us a bed in a room with three other men. "They are mercenaries back from the wars in Holland," he told us. "They have money in their pockets, and try to spend it quickly." He served us large slices of venison, with cabbage and tankards of beer.

I slept fitfully, woken by the comings and goings, laughter and screaming, and once by a man who vomited in the bed next to ours. My father muttered about lice and fleas; we rose before dawn and set off.

From quite a distance we saw Geneva within its high grey walls, a good-looking city, crowned by its tall-spired cathedral. Large, well peopled, its streets were dirty, with the refuse of the tall houses on both sides. There were thirty thousand people in Geneva, but unlike Lausanne it was a city of staid grimness. People walked about with black umbrellas to preserve their clothes, and never a smile upon any face. My father, querying the way politely, was given directions in a melancholic, punctilious manner by a man who first looked at us long and thoughtfully, cogitating whether he should vouchsafe us the information.

Geneva was the city of Calvin the Reformer, the Protestant

Rome, and therefore behavior was far more strict than in Lausanne. Here the pastors relentlessly pursued pleasure seekers. Women caught in frivolity were whipped publicly. Vigilantes kept lists of those who failed to attend the Sunday services. Sundays were even gloomier than in our land of Vaud. It was a whole day of preaching and praying and denouncing the sins of all and sundry. Sumptuary laws limited the color and cut and material of all vestments. "But Geneva is a powerful city, Colin, because it has factories and trades, and makes many beautiful things, and sells them. . . . Money and godliness go together," Father said cheerfully.

Geneva's great sources of revenue were clock- and watch-making and textiles. The French had imported "indiennes," Indian cotton cloth—printed and woven, gingham and madras—through their East India Company until 1686, when imports of painted cloth from India and also the making of these in France were prohibited. As a result, the French ladies wanted indiennes at any price. These were now made in Neuchâtel and in Geneva. There were many workers in the factories: designers, engravers, printers, colorists, and *calandreurs*, who gave the cloth its ultimate firmness by passing it through hot cylinders.

Geneva's clocks and watches went everywhere, to Russia and to the Ottoman Empire, to India and China, to Japan and New Spain. Almost half the citizens of Geneva were employed in watchmaking; and jewelers, enamelers, engravers, and gold- and silversmiths vied with one another to create for kings and princes timepieces studded with gems, exquisite to look at, with wonderful inner mechanisms. Half the Council of the city were merchant watchmakers.

We reached Place Chevelu, below the ramparts, the center of the *fabrique*, or factories. Here was a great din of people; stalls and shops with small windows; steps going down into dim rooms where people toiled fourteen hours a day, many of them children of my age, selected for their perfect sight. In the narrow streets were many strangers: Arabs in long robes, Persians, Spaniards, Germans from Bavaria, Muscovites with great fur bonnets and boots

Geneva's crowds were unlike the travelers who came to Lausanne to enjoy the sun and the lake, to make music, to see comedies and plays, to discuss art and philosophy, or to be cured by Doctor Tissot. Here all was trade and money; merchandise going to all parts of the world and also coming in. Yet, with this profusion of wealth, the burghers of Geneva staunchly maintained their lugubrious deportment.

There was new building going on, tall new houses with wide windows and fountains in the squares. The ramparts were being made higher, as if another assault upon the city was feared. For in December 1602 a vengeful Duke of Savoy, eager to seize again what had once been his domain, had tried to recapture Geneva. It was defended by its citizens, including the women, who threw boiling soup and their cooking pots upon the invaders. And since then Geneva had continued to behave like a beleaguered citadel of goodness, surrounded by evil and corruption.

We went up the sloping streets to the High City, past the Rue des Granges, stopping just beyond it in front of a large house of fine stone, whose facade held that air of gracious secretiveness which is the hallmark of the wealthy. Father spoke to the liveried servant who opened the door. As we entered the hall, the master of the house was coming towards us. "Jean-Francois Duriez, Lord Kilvaney wrote to me. . . . You are most welcome," he said.

Abraham Hirsch was dressed in dark garb; his hair unpowdered, tied with a black ribbon as was the custom in Geneva. He had piercing eyes, with heavy brows.

My father saluted him and said, "It is good of you to receive us, Sir."

"And this is Colin." Abraham Hirsch smiled at me. "John Kilvaney wrote to me about him. I am glad he came with you. And since you cannot stay in the house of a Jew"—Abraham said this so smoothly that it passed before we realized what he'd said—"I have taken lodgings for you in a mansion nearby, an excellent family, the de Graniers. They are hospitable and well thought of, and the house is comfortable."

In Lausanne, behind the Castle Sainte Marie, was the quarter of La Barre where Jews lived. It was said that at their festivals Jews used the blood of small children, and that they had killed Our Lord the Christ. Some women crossed themselves when the word *Jew* was uttered. But neither Father nor Mother had ever said a word against them, and Father was easy in his manner with Hirsch, as if talking with a Christian.

"We thank you for your great kindness, Monsieur Hirsch," he said.

The servants brought in our travel bags, Father's leather valise, and the box in which he had packed the automata he wanted to show Hirsch. As Father unlocked the box, in came a boy, slightly older than I.

"This is my son Jacob," said Abraham Hirsch.

Jacob bowed to Father and then came to me and extended his hand, in the English manner. I bowed as I took it.

Father set the automata on the table. It was a coach and four horses, with a coachman and two postilions behind, and inside a couple, a lord and a lady. He wound the spring, which was concealed within the carriage, and the horses advanced, pacing and waving their heads. The coach rolled forward and the coachman waved his whip. The lady nodded, and the gentleman took off his beplumed hat and put it back on his head.

"My son Colin helped me to build this," Father said proudly. Father always mentioned that I helped him, and Hirsch threw me a shrewd look.

"It is good to start young. Look at our musicians, they begin at the age of three . . . and Jacob has been peering at the stars ever since he was five years old."

Hirsch seemed delighted with the coach, while Jacob bent his head and examined the figures closely. "This century of ours is one of much thinking, of many new discoveries," Hirsch said. "All this is going to change our lives, and more quickly than we know. I have in mind a factory for making androids. Nay, do not shake your head, Messire Duriez, listen to me. Stay a few days, see for yourself. You will not regret it; why, even the English are setting up their factories here. It is easier than in England because there are so many skilled workers in our city."

Madame Hirsch came in, dressed in emerald taffeta, with a collar of Malines lace which flowed over the bodice and large bouffant sleeves of the same delicate fabric. With her was their daughter, Sarah, who wore a beautiful dress of blue velvet and had blue ribbons to match in her dark hair.

"Sarah," Hirsch called fondly, and she ran to him to be kissed. She had the most lovely black hair, and a face like porcelain; when she smiled back at me, I blushed crimson and turned my eyes away.

We were somewhat travel-stained, and Hirsch sent us in his coach to the house of the de Graniers. I kept telling myself, "Colin, you have been in the house of a Jew, an infidel, worse than a heathen," but no indignation, no awe or guilt invaded my soul. On the contrary, I felt a freedom and ease with the Hirsches that I had not encountered in some other great houses, despite the merriment, the gaiety, the light talk, words like butterflies hovering over roses.

The de Granier house was a genteelly disguised hostel. Money was not mentioned, but the guests paid for whatever they used. Monsieur de Granier was melancholic; he never smiled. Every night before our dinner he would read the prayers out of a Bible of enormous size, black and leather bound, which had been in his family since 1556. He did not utter a word throughout dinner, nor look at us. Madame de Granier inquired suspiciously whether we belonged to the True Church or the free one; a certain libertarian movement, begun by one Pastor Bridel, was causing comment in Geneva. Father reassured her, but she did not appear entirely satisfied.

The next morning, back at the Hirsch house, Hirsch told his son, "Jacob, take Colin and show him the garden. He may like to play quoits or croquet." Jacob smiled and took me by the hand, and we walked to the garden. It was at the back of the house, lovely with very large English roses, the last of the season, for the best roses are the October ones, just before the first winter gale.

There was a croquet lawn and also a gallery for playing quoits.

"Which would you like?" Jacob asked.

"Croquet," I said, thinking of my leg. I had my contrivance on, and no one seemed to have noticed it, but I doubted that it would enable me to bowl down the quoits.

Jacob and Sarah and I played croquet, then went back to the salon, where Father was still talking with Hirsch, sipping chocolate. The previous day Hirsch had offered us no collation when we arrived, because some Christians considered eating in the house of a Jew sinful.

"Come and see our books," Jacob said, and led me to another large room, their library.

Books, books, so many books! Rows and rows of them from ceiling to floor. Jacob went about the shelves. "What would you like to read, Colin? I prefer mathematics and philosophy, but there are other books too."

"I like stories about other countries and people and their customs."

"As my father does. He traveled a good deal in his youth, not by choice, but because we Jews are forever being thrown out of so many cities. Here we are: *Sinbad the Sailor*, the *Arabian Thousand and One Nights*, the *Chronicles, Marco Polo's Voyages*. . . ." He picked out books, a dozen of them, heaping them on a massive oak table. "But perhaps you had better choose them yourself. My father does not mind so long as the books are well cared for and put back in their places. D'you read English, German, Italian?"

"Only French with a little Latin and Greek," I said. Jacob was thirteen, two years older than I, but I felt he was very learned compared to me.

"I will show you my spying glasses," Jacob said. He took me to the top floor of the house, I following as nimbly as I could, and there was a room, with a large window, and a long tube propped on a stand to look at the stars; and a table with instruments on it, one like a ship's sextant; and on a stand a round ball covered with drawings. "This is our earth, our globe," he said. "Look, here is where we are, spinning around the sun."

The earth was round, and went around the sun, and we did not fall off it because there was something called gravity. I had never seen a globe, and now, staring at it, I felt the immensity of the universe.

In the twelve days that followed, two things happened. The first was that I grew to love Jacob with a love whose strength was untainted by any grief, or doubt, or dread. I loved Bea, and Father and Mother, and also Valentin, but always there was something in my love which also hurt me, so that the more I loved them, the more I also dreaded to love them overmuch. Bea I loved so dearly, yet dreaded to care for her too deeply, for it was sin. But with Jacob I did not need to fear. Nothing would go awry, dismantling love, revealing a leprosy of the soul.

Jacob was what I wanted to be. It was he who furnished my mind with the method of true learning; not the learning by rote, which was Pastor Burandel's method; nor the unsystematic, haphazard though ingenious ways in which Father contrived to create his automata, without much knowledge of mathematics and the principles of mechanics. With Jacob, all was method and logic, a relentless reasoning that pushed on and on, pushed back the limits of the mind and uncovered a boundless universe of knowledge to conquer. And that was the second marvelous thing which happened to me.

Jacob had read Newton's *Principia* when he was seven years old. He spoke to me of Leibnitz, Newton, Galileo, so many others. His mind saw links, connections, between all things. He would read a book and then give me the core of its meaning, and go further, taking the argument to pieces, showing its flaws. Thus he would speculate on the color of roses, which would lead to a discussion of the rainbow, and how light was fractured in the crystal prism upon his table, and what was light made of?

I peered at the stars through Jacob's telescope and saw Mars and Venus, and beyond them, fiery wonders with marvelous names. And Jacob wondered how it had come about, and how many myriad worlds existed, and whether people lived on them. "Or another kind of life, Colin, life in shapes and with souls, animae we have not dreamt of." This led us to a great argument about the soul and God, and I was both appalled and delighted by our daring. For what was soul? And if God was in us, then how could He ever damn a fragment of himself? And where did evil come from?

I learnt from Jacob how navigators sail by the stars and the compass, and read the speculations that agitated the astronomers as to the composition of the universe. Jacob queried how old the earth was. Had the moon once been part of it, wrenched from its side by a great collision? He set my soul and my brain on fire.

So many things I learnt in those twelve short days. I learnt the history of the automata that I was making. Suddenly they were no longer mere toys, but were linked to the Grand Design of the universe itself, part of man's search and hunger to recognize himself. "As God created man in His image," said Jacob, in his calm reflective way. I also began to apprehend Jacob's infinite torment, for at age thirteen he was racked by doubt about the nature of God. . . .

Automata were forty centuries old. They began with the moving dolls of Egypt, where it was thought some of the secrets of life could be discovered by thus imitating the shape and movement of living beings. Anubis, the dog-god, had a mobile jaw and could bark. The statue of a dead man, by the very magic of image making, possessed the power of the dead, waiting for the soul to reenter it. And living statues, being the undead, could read the future, give oracles in Egypt, in Greece, in Rome.

The Watchers, the Soul-Keepers. My mother's obsession became logical, fell into place. Her search was mankind's search for his own eternity. And for the first time I talked to someone else about Mother, and the night with its magic, and my nightmares. Jacob nodded. "I do not know enough of this, Colin, but it seems to me that all human beings want reassurance. Want infinity, eternity. What do we *mean* by time? Here we make clocks, Colin, perhaps because it makes us feel less impermanent, to measure the days, the hours. But we do not really know what time and space are, although Newton seemed sure they were fixed values. I do not know, I do not know. . . ." Thus Jacob, suddenly transfixed, peered through his telescope and muttered, "I wonder how much time it has taken a star to send us the light I see." That night he was searching for the Pleiades, a cluster of dim stars which that night was above and to the moon's right.

In the ninth century the Arabs had delighted in putting figures of people on their water clocks to announce the hours and half hours with movement, and also music. A treatise in 850 A.D., written in Byzantium by al Jazari and Ridwan, explained how these hydraulic automata worked. After the

Crusades, the French kings had installed such water-driven devices in their gardens.

In 1601 a Jesuit who was also a mathematician and astronomer, Matteo Ricci, had brought watches and clocks to China. But because no one knew how to wind or repair them, his efforts to convince the mandarins of his technical felicity were defeated, although he went on to be greatly honored for his ability in predicting eclipses.

In 1640 another Jesuit, Magellan, had constructed for the Emperor of China a statue with interior springs, which walked for fifteen minutes with a spear in his hand. And in 1737 Vaucanson the Frenchman had built a satyr playing a flute, with a face of wood and arms of cardboard imported from China. His fingers had bits of real skin on them, blocking the holes, so that the satyr really played the instrument. Vaucanson had also invented a weaving machine for making damask cloth and cloth with inset flowers, using a cardboard roll pricked with holes, the holes creating the pattern.

Now I knew myself heir to a great tradition, one which was not the making of childish toys, but a search for the prime forces of nature.

"You see, Colin, that nothing in life is mysterious, all can be explained," Jacob said.

Could *all* be explained? Was all knowledge accessible? But man's original sin was his disobedience, tasting of the fruit of the Tree of Knowledge, wanting to know. "Ye shall then be like gods," Satan had said. Was this true?

Was this search for knowledge a challenge to God?

I said this to Jacob, and he sighed and walked about a little. "I do not believe the Lord God, the One, Eternal, wishes anything but to make man like Him, for He created us in His image and rejoices when we discover His greatness—otherwise why should we be endowed with thought? Yet sometimes I imagine He became bored with all this perfection of His, this total harmony without a scratch, which meant absolute Stillness, and He had to create man, and also to create evil, since He is the Creator. Out of this warp, this defect, this voluntary flaw, came everything that is around us. God must have known that man would sin, otherwise He would not be God, containing both the past and the future for all eternity.

47

"Do you think, Colin, that what man does *amuses* God? Are we His automata? If Calvin is right, then we are indeed automata, since everything is predetermined, but I don't believe that. I believe that we fashion ourselves and the future, and that God has left it to us to conquer the universe He created and to make what we can of it. I feel He needs us to become whole, as we need Him."

On fire. I was on fire. I tossed all night with these new, strange thoughts.

Oh Jacob, how I loved you when you asked me, "What is light? How does it get to us, and what time does it take? And as for sound, see how much time passes between lightning and the thunder that is its passage in the skies. As for our thoughts, are they like light or sound? How much time between pricking my finger and knowing pain?"

And so I opened myself to him and told him of Bea and me, our minds talking to each other; and the undead screaming, which she and Mother heard, and I through them.

"My people too have such tales," Jacob said. "We have the golem, that strange creature fashioned of clay, made for revenge, who will arise and destroy our enemies." So we let our minds roam, and Jacob asked himself whether insubstantial substance exists, as it must, "for should a man receive a blow on the head and go insane, his soul is thereby affected."

Sarah loved music and dancing, and teased me, saying that I was turning into a bookworm like Jacob. She would drag me with her to play in the garden. And now I did not wear Master Chavenaz's contrivance, and no one queried my club foot. Mrs. Hirsch set on a course of feeding me cakes made with almonds and milk, and was perturbed that I remained thin.

Abraham Hirsch took us to the fair to see the Chinese porcelain which had come to Geneva that year, a trade with much profit. A company in Holland had imported Chinese porcelain in the past. "But now Holland makes its own, at Delft, albeit not as beautifully as the Chinese do, yet it is pleasant enough," Hirsch said. In France were cast the gilded bronze pedestals, the rims and bases in which the large vases from China stood. There was scarcely a noble house that did not boast at least a pair of these, some as tall as a man.

And then one night as we all sat together, Abraham spoke of witches and witchcraft, bitterly, for, he said, the same fear, blind fury, had led to the persecution of witches and wizards, and of the Jews.

Torture, the stake, burnings—in all the lands of Christendom.

"From 1575 to 1700, a million people were denounced as sorcerers, wizards, witches in France," Abraham said. "And two hundred witches were burnt alive in Geneva in the last century. The last man to die as a wizard was a Jesuit, in 1731." And in these same centuries a million Jews had been persecuted, tortured, burnt alive. The Spanish Inquisition had driven away the learned Jews of the University of Toledo, who had been the translators of the Arabs, and had brought Arab knowledge in astronomy and mathematics to Europe.

"But," said Father, "it is no longer so. Our century is enlightened, Abraham. Surely these things will never happen again."

"Do you think so? Our age is one of enlightenment, you say. True and also false. Here in Geneva many come to me who need money, or letters of finance, but they do not know me when they meet me in the street, and never would they invite me to their house. For I am a Jew, and though I can help you, I cannot help myself."

Suddenly Abraham Hirsch smiled and turned to his wife, patting her hand. "Enough of sad matters," he cried. "Tomorrow I have a treat for you, to go to see Monsieur de Voltaire—doubtless you have heard of him?"

"Who has not?" Father said. "Lausanne buzzes at mention of him, and he is having his books printed there."

Many a book hunted, burnt, sequestered, or refused publication in France or Prussia was given birth by the small, clickety-clackety printing presses of Lausanne, presses set up by the fleeing Huguenots.

"A personage," Hirsch exclaimed, slapping his thigh with recollected amusement. "He is never taken short. He talks— how he talks! Always ready to flatter the great, to make people laugh at the unready and at the foibles of others. He has a great ire for anyone standing in the sun as tall as he does, and he does his best to denigrate our great man Rousseau."

Jean-Jacques Rousseau of Geneva had been received with honor at Dijon, but his books shocked many people and the Council in Geneva frowned upon him. "Rousseau is an idealist, a man who would have us all perfect, and thus near to a Heaven of his invention. I read him with pleasure, even if, at times, he goes far beyond ordinary morality," Hirsch said.

"As for Voltaire, he was imprisoned at the Bastille in Paris for publishing his *English Letters* praising the liberalism of the English as compared to the French system. He is an extraordinarily gifted man, both mean and enlightened—and with great sense for making money."

WE DROVE TO LES DELICES, Monsieur de Voltaire's mansion, in the black coach with one coachman which Hirsch affected. Because he was a Jew, he was careful to give no cause for envy, and therefore in public appeared, if not penurious, at least not endowed with much wealth. "In Venice and Genoa people like me live crammed into ghettoes, shut in by iron gates imprisoning them from sunset to sunrise," he told Father. "Here, at least, no one insists on my wearing a tall hat and a long robe with yellow stars upon them."

Hirsch was impassioned by inventions; but whereas Jacob pursued knowledge for its own sake, his father also reckoned the gains and advantages man would derive from them. As the coach swayed on the road to Les Delices, Hirsch told us of the Frenchman who, ten years before, had created a vapor machine for boats, so that the boat went forward without sail or oar, "but the machine was destroyed, at the boat's first attempt, as it sailed up the River Seine, by some enraged and foolish people.

"Throughout history men who sought to know nature, the workings of our universe, have been rejected, even persecuted. Yet science is the key to mankind's deliverance, and that means using the energies of vapor and electricity and magnetism—in England philosophers talk of understanding the forces of nature and using them."

At last we reached the house of Francois Arouet de Voltaire. Hounded out of his own country, he had taken refuge with

Frederic II, King of Prussia. But then he had fallen out with Frederic, who thought him amusing, nothing more. Now he was in Geneva, living in an imposing house with his niece, Madame Denis; three lackeys; eighteen other servants; and a majordomo.

The grounds were indeed delightful, a French garden with a well-laid-out drive that led to the stone mansion with its many windows. Voltaire's study was a large room with silk-damasked walls. An enormous table was littered with volumes bound in morocco leather, sheets of paper, three quills in inkstands of chased silver, and five aligned bottles of medicine of different colors.

Sitting at the table, looking like one of those bright-colored parrots from New Spain I had seen, was Voltaire, with a turban of many-colored silk upon his head and his gnomelike body wrapped in a fur-lined robe of crimson and gold velvet. "I am dying, my dear Abraham," he proclaimed, as he rose unsteadily and then sat down again. "Doctor Tronchin has just been to see me and peer at my urine. You have come in time to hear the last words I shall utter."

Then he glared at my father and me. He was thin, so thin that his pointed face and nose looked like one of those grimacing masks that the peasants at festivals wear to dance in the roads, with bells round their ankles and on their caps.

"Monsieur Duriez and his son are from Lausanne," Abraham Hirsch began.

"Lausanne, ah!" Voltaire sprang out of his armchair, his face contorted with delight, pathos, and calculation as he bounded towards my father and seized his arm. I noticed his beautiful hands, the skin with brown spots but the joints undeformed by age, the fingers delicate. "Lausanne is where I want to rest this old carcass of mine. I have rented a house there to die in peace in that beautiful city. At last I have obtained the assent of Their Excellencies of Berne. I am leaving in a few days, when all this"—he swept an arm towards his table—"is done."

The eternal moribund, as he was nicknamed—for indeed one could believe him frail, save that he generated energy as a waterfall generates sound—now paced up and down, holding my father by the shoulder and arm and declaiming at such speed that we were carried away by the torrent of eloquence poured upon us. "Lausanne is the home of a poet of talent, Albert de Haller, a patrician of Berne. I shall meet him—I am going there, I intend to acquire a small property there. Doubtless you know of my correspondence with Berne. At first they were perturbed that I address them simply as Messieurs, instead of Excellencies—but at last they have seen the benefit of my presence in their territories. Doubtless you, Maître Duriez, occupy a post in your city. . . ."

"Nothing is left to us but to amuse ourselves," my father replied. "My Lords of Berne give us naught else to do, Monsieur de Voltaire. They do not trust us overmuch."

"But nowhere else does literature flourish as in your magnificent city," Voltaire cried. "Now we shall have the pleasure to meet often, Monsieur Duriez. Tell me, are there any small properties available? Oh, no great domain, only something like this"—his arm swept the sixteen-room mansion around him. "I am a man of modest taste and means. Do you know the bailiff? He appears an excellent man. Tell him that you have seen me, and that I need the air of Lausanne. I am a dying man, eager to lay my bones in a civilized city. . . . I know of a house on Montriond. . . ."

My father extricated himself from Voltaire's grasp and replied, "Monsieur, I rejoice that Their Excellencies of Berne, our overlords, have granted you what you so earnestly desire; I know that your presence in our small city will add greatly to its renown."

Voltaire glowed. "I shall present a play there, it is all arranged," he said. "It's called *Genghis Khan,* or the *Orphan of China*—a Chinese tragedy, based upon an old Chinese play. Do you know Mr. de Gentils? He will lend me his castle for my play, and the actors will be the gentlemen and ladies of Lausanne—"

"Mr. Duriez," Hirsch interrupted, "creates automata and androids. He and his son would like to set up here in Geneva and seek your counsel, Monsieur de Voltaire. Indeed, as your friend Monsieur Diderot has said, he who is passionate of knowledge, '*C'est chez ceux qui pratiquent les arts mechaniques qu'il faut aller chercher la sagacité de l'esprit.*' It is among those who practice the mechanical arts that one must seek for sagacity of the spirit."

Voltaire stopped talking, looked stung, glared at my father, and perhaps noticed his clothes, which placed Father not quite in the category of fashionable society. He frowned, a very slight frown, almost imperceptible on his wrinkled face, but then with exquisite politeness called for wine.

"Ah, my friend Diderot," he exclaimed, "have you read his *Letter on the Blind*? It is from the English Saunderson and Locke he got his inspiration. Diderot is quite incapable of any original thought. But I am enamored of the East, of China; all wisdom comes from it, and true virtue. The Jesuits, who have been there some decades, have translated Confucius. . . ."

"Monsieur Duriez," Hirsch said patiently, "could make automata for China. I hear they are much valued there."

The verbal fireworks, the mental pirouettes, stopped. Voltaire was now the man of money, shrewd as a banker, his brain agile with louis, livres, ducats. He inquired of my father about the automata and offered to buy one. "I know it is the present craze. You must show me your pieces when I am in Lausanne." But he made the offer with an air of condescension, and Father merely bowed and said:

"My workshop is open to all visitors, Monsieur."

Voltaire now expatiated against the Prussians. He had received letters, he said, that showed to what an extent the "Tudesques," as he now called them, were uncivilized, rude, and could not appreciate his writings (he had forgotten how the King of Prussia had saved him from his own country, France).

Back in the coach Hirsch chuckled. "Now you have seen our local phenomenon. He looks as if the smallest wind would blow him down, but he will outlive all of us, for his malice and his verve in insulting others keep him alive. Tomorrow he will say evil things about me, should the whim seize him. He can turn the smallest coin into profit; he's worth a hundred thousand livres a year, and he already owns several houses, four carriages, and eighteen servants. He intends to set up a textile factory and is looking for land. But he quarrels with his wine merchant for the paltry sum of six louis, and with his carpenter for even less. Why, he even tried to cheat me!"

Hirsch convinced my father to set up in Geneva. "I shall assemble for you some craftsmen and apprentices, for I am convinced that the making of automata on a large scale could become a lucrative enterprise. It is not enough to call them playthings. I can imagine one day an android, a mechanical worker, being taught to spin and weave, to thresh and harvest; all heavy toil done by them. What a boon for mankind!"

Father promised to let Hirsch know when we would come. Spring was the best season to move, Hirsch said. Meanwhile, let Father make some automata that could be shown to the Council. . . .

I was very happy. In Geneva I would see Jacob often.

As we left, Sarah burst into tears, and Madame Hirsch gave us a great parcel of comfits and candied fruit and two cashmere shawls for Mother and Bea.

"I'll see you in the spring, Colin," Jacob said. "Meanwhile, perhaps you will write to tell me what you think of Spinoza."

We had spent the last evening talking, Jacob and I. It was a mild early October, and Father and Abraham Hirsch sat over their wine in the salon. I could hear the murmur of their voices, but I did not strain to listen. Being with Jacob was more important. That afternoon we had peered at a drop of water under the new microscope that had come from London for Jacob, and I had seen the animalcules swimming in it, transparent life, wriggling and squirming with ferocious energy. Jacob had packed for me a small bag of books, sighing that I knew no English, "for it is the English who are our masters in science and mechanics," he said. "You must read Bacon, and Newton, and Bradley—who discovered the aberration of light—and Jonathan Swift's *Gulliver's Travels*." He gave me Montesquieu's *Lettres Persanes*, and a treatise on mechanics by Euler and Spinoza, and of course Diderot, Diderot the Frenchman, who questioned everything, who was writing his *Encyclopedia*, who praised passion, for only passion can lift the soul to great things. And Jacob had inscribed a play by Shakespeare, *The Tempest*: To my friend, Colin Duriez, for tempest inhabits our souls. "Perhaps we are all the same stuff, man, animal, worm . . . all of us the same substance, all of us in perpetual flux," he said as we left. "Let me know what you think."

My throat was tight. I knew I would not write to him about Spinoza, being quite incapable of it. But I would learn. I would even read *The Tempest,* in French and then in English. I would hoist myself to the level of Jacob.

It was night as we approached our house. We had gone swiftly, Alexander eager for his own stable. The house with its heavy cape of roof seemed to stare at us out of its luminous windows.

Mother sat weaving a cloth of scarlet wool. She rose with gladness as my father went to her, and love sprang between them and I was happy. She hugged me and said, "Oh, Colin, how you've grown in these two weeks."

And Bea came down the stairs: "Colin, I've missed you. What was Geneva like?"

I told her. I told her about Voltaire, and Jacob, and our going to Geneva in the spring. I wanted Jacob and Bea to meet and to like each other. Then my happiness would be complete.

"And you, Bea, how has it been with you?"

She looked at me, the smile fading from her mouth and eyes. "Antoine the Preacher is back. Mother and I are afraid," she said.

➻ *Four* ❧

Anno Domini 1755

ANTOINE THE PREACHER was back. He was now called Antoine Voice-of God—and he preached every evening in a derelict barn beyond the fishermen's hamlet.

November was the empty season of small catches; an early winter greyed the water, and the fish went lower, down to the warm heart of the lake. The fishermen and their wives, and the vine laborers, now out of work, flocked to hear Antoine. And though Pastor Burandel had warned his people against "strange heresies," yet a growing number from Vidy, from Montoie, from as far as Saint Sulpice, came to listen to Antoine Voice-of-God.

There was a pervasive apprehension in the air. The lake was muffled in mist, its waters leaden. A boat capsized for no reason, and a fisherman drowned. Old men felt much pain in their bones and could not sleep.

One night a baby choked and died. His mother came knocking at midnight, crying, tugging at Mother's sleeve. "The medicine—it choked on it. . . ." Mother had given the infant a soothing mixture two days previously. She went with the mother to see the child, but it was too late.

And within three days another baby died, just as suddenly. Yet Mother had given it no medicine, had not seen it. "It is a contagion," Pastor Burandel said, and comforted the bereaved. The chapel bell tolled for the souls; the upturned earth in the cemetery showed two fresh mounds. Pastor Burandel preached that death stalks each of us, and its coming was God's will.

Five days later Marie-la-Folle did not come to our house; at nightfall Pierre, the son of Andre Paluz, came running and screaming. He had seen her body in a thicket. She had been savaged and then strangled.

Who had done this terrible deed? The Lausanne gendarmerie came, but nothing could be found. It was known that some returned mercenary band was about, and the militia hunted for them. A shudder, a whisper began. Valentin had been seen walking in the woods, precisely on the day she had died. . . .

There was also a report of a witch, a woman dressed in black with eyes like coals afire, come down from the gloomy Jorat forests of the high land. Evil dwelt in the Jorat. In the previous century many sorcerers, witches, and spell throwers had been burnt alive there. Now my Lords of Berne had forbidden the killing of witches without a legal inquiry. And woodsmen from the Jorat, bringing in their carts the felled trunks of oaks—timber for houses, stools and tables, cupboards and beds and coffins—no longer boasted of having seen Satan walk or dance with a cohort of sorcerers. But still the talk went on, of witches flying silently by night, flying down chimneys when the fire had died, and killing the children. . . .

Father was much grieved by Marie's death and forbade us to go out when dusk swallowed the path. "There is a murderer about," he said. And indeed a week later a man was apprehended. He had broken into a farm and stolen some clothes and money, and under torture he confessed to the killing of Marie.

But the whispering continued. There was witchcraft about and some women had fits, and asked for Antoine Voice-of-God to tear the demon out of them. Father blithely ignored all this. He was preparing for our removal to Geneva. He must sell the house and spoke about it to Master Chavenaz. "It is a good piece of property; Sir Bailiff might like it," Chavenaz said. But only when spring came did the burghers buy house or land, never in winter.

"You'll sell well in spring," Chavenaz said.

On Sunday we went to chapel with Valentin, who had returned as usual from the forge. After the service, on the steps outside, the men grouped together, looking at us, their hands behind their backs. Valentin did not think there was anything untoward; he smiled good-naturedly, his blue eyes candid as a summer sky. After the service no one shook Father's hand.

"What is the matter with them?" Father asked.

And Mother replied, "Perhaps jealousy . . . because we are going to Geneva."

Pierre-Thomas, the carpenter, came to our house to make boxes for Father's books. But he was slow, moving stiffly. "Some people are lucky, and some are unlucky," he said, addressing the air around him as he assembled the planks, nails in his mouth. "Now you're going to make much money, Jean-Francois, but it was my work that put you on the way."

"I won't forget you, Pierre-Thomas," Father said. "As soon as I am established, I shall send for you."

"I have been thinking that making these moving dolls is sinful," Pierre-Thomas replied. "It is against the will of God."

"Who put that idea in your head?" Father asked.

Pierre-Thomas shrugged and changed the subject. "Times are not good, and there's a bad spell upon our village. It's time to think of one's sins and repent. Evil does walk about in winter nights."

"Now he talks like Antoine," Father said, when Pierre-Thomas had gone.

I would have liked to tell him, "Mother is afraid, and some are saying Valentin killed Marie-la-Folle." But Mother did not want us to disturb Father, and I kept silent.

IN MID-NOVEMBER, ON A grey afternoon, an English hansom stopped at our garden gate. Isabelle de Thunon, in black with a large fur muff, her maid by her side, walked up to our house.

"You are Jean-Francois's wife," Isabelle said when Mother opened the door. "I am his cousin. It is a pleasure to meet you at last."

"Jean-Francois has told me about you," Mother said. "I shall call him."

Father had heard the carriage; he came out of the work-room where he had been putting his books in boxes and pecked Isabelle's cheek. "What happy wind blows you here, Cousin Isabelle? Daout, let's have some of the good China tea I brought back from Geneva."

Already Mother had guessed and taken out the tea in its black lacquer canister and also some cakes she had baked. She was setting the table, putting down the pewter plates and the big milk jug. I thought of Isabelle's delicate silver and porcelain, her lace tablecloth, the satin-covered chairs we had sat on in her house.

Isabelle sat on the bench along our table. "Jean-Francois, I hear that some bankers in Geneva want to finance you to open a factory for making your toys. It is a splendid occasion to leave this place." Her eyes went round the house, her glance sweeping across Mother, taking in the weaving loom, the spinning wheel, and Mother herself in her grey skirt and white apron. "Perhaps I can help you. I know some families in Geneva. But you know them too, Cousin—the Doumas, the Givel, the Gillieron. . . . I have also had news. From Neuchâtel. Your brother Theodore would be happy, I think, to receive a word from you, Jean-Francois. Merely to tell him you will go to Geneva . . ."

Father sat back, waiting till Mother had poured the tea, letting silence settle. And then in that easy and graceful man-ner he had, which I now knew was that of the patrician families: "Dear Cousin Isabelle, is Theodore proposing to invite us to Neuchâtel?"

Isabelle touched her hair. She had it done in a high pile above her head, powdered, and upon it perched a hat of black velvet. "Dear Cousin, I think Theodore wants to talk business with you. As you know, there is an estate and you are the heir."

And Father, still sitting well back in the chair, his hands upon its arms, stared at her.

"Dear Cousin," he replied, his voice very quiet, "if we go to see him, Daout and our children, all *three* of them, come with me."

Isabelle reached for a biscuit. She chewed upon it, her face suddenly unguarded and angry. Then I saw that she was older than Mother, despite the high hair and the powdered face with its painted eyebrows.

And Mother, in her silken way, said, "Cousin Isabelle, will you have some of my *brisselets*?" And passed a plate to her.

Isabelle ignored her and went on, "Theodore's health is precarious, Jean-Francois. He is quite unable to entertain many people. It is seemly that you should write to him. That is why, at the risk of angering you, I have again to plead for him. . . ."

Father sighed, looking away. Isabelle took a sip of tea delicately, and I saw she was a forlorn woman, a sad woman, under the brittle gaiety. So that the silence should not be too heavy, and because she was well bred, she said:

"But I forgot . . . what a head I have . . . Suzanne, fetch the packages."

The maid went out and returned with parcels. A doll for Bea, who did not play with dolls but nevertheless curtsied and thanked her, and a doublet of velvet with silver buttons for me.

"Your children have such excellent manners," Isabelle said.

She had also brought a pair of boots of fine morocco tooled leather for Father. "Cousin, I thought you might like these." And for Mother she had brought some satin ribbons and a length of muslin.

Mother smiled her thanks, went to her loom, and cut off the piece of linen she had woven; it had a pattern of leaves and would serve for a bedspread or a curtain. "It is both warm and cool," she said in that manner of hers which left people puzzled, wondering what she really meant.

"It's lovely work, I shall certainly find it most useful. But enough of chatter, I must go." Isabelle shook her front skirt free of invisible crumbs, and held up the watch that hung suspended round her neck—it was studded with small rubies and looked well against the black velvet. She held it up a long time, longer than needed.

Then came the ceremonial of departure, I bowing and Bea curtsying, Isabelle patting our cheeks; and not kissing Mother but clinging to Father's hand longer than necessary, saying,

"I only want Theodore and you to be reconciled. Jean-Francois, for your own good, think about it."

NIGHTMARE: A WOOD, WITH OAKS towering overhead, gripping the sky. A clearing, and round the stone in its center, people in white, singing. Women in white, crowned with the Golden Bough, the mistletoe, whose fruit is the color of sun-and-moon.

One of the white-clad women held a curved knife and with it cut the throat of a buck; it was Horace, his blood poured, went on pouring. It became a river, endless. The killer turned. It was Mother. The blood was upon her dress, swallowed her feet, took her away. . . .

I woke up screaming.

Bea was up and hugged me. "Colin, hush, hush . . ."

But there was noise, and Mother's voice was saying, "I must go, I must go, oh do let me go. . . ."

And Father: "Daout, Daout, but it's only a dream. . . ."

Mother wept, and Father was angry: "How can you have heard anything? It's your foolishness once again."

Father lit the lamp in its sconce upon the wall at their bedroom door. Mother was dressing and she saw us.

"Children, my mother is dying, I have to go."

Grisolde of the Forest, who lived in the Jorat.

"Bea, how . . ." I whispered.

"She called, Colin. I also heard her."

"We've received no message, it's only a dream, Daout." Father's voice was both angry and frightened.

"She spoke to me. I heard her." Mother's voice was obstinate.

I stepped forward. "Father, there was a call. Something has happened to Grandmother. . . ."

"You . . ." Father stared at me in bafflement.

"It is not strange, Father. God allowed it in His Prophets, to see visions and dream dreams."

Father walked downstairs to stir the hearth fire. The flames rose in sonorous music. He placed the soup pot on the hearth and set the milk jug and the bread upon the table.

"I shall go with you, Daout," Father said wearily. "But

someone must look after the house, the animals. Colin, Bea, you will remain here. I'll go to Chavenaz now, to get Valentin. He'll stay with you two."

Father saddled Alexander and set off. Mother and Bea made themselves ready.

"I am going too," Bea said. "Grisolde has also called me."

Valentin, still disheveled with sleep, came back with Father; he and I would stay to care for the animals.

They left in the cart, the three of them, Mother telling Father that Bea was going with her, for Grisolde had called her. Father shrugged.

"Colin could not climb the Raven's Nest," he said.

Grandmother Grisolde had not called me.

Pierre-Thomas came out of his house and stood looking after the cart. "Where are they going?" he asked Valentin.

"To the Jorat. My grandmother is ill," said Valentin.

"To the Jorat," Pierre-Thomas repeated. "Well, well." He folded his arms, spat on the ground, and walked back into his house.

VALENTIN HELPED ME WITH the goats and patted Horace; he shifted some wood logs for the fire, and we settled down to a game of chess. Now that Marie-la-Folle was no longer with us we did everything ourselves. At mid-morning we sat down to our meat and cheese and drank some wine. And Valentin, in his slow way, said:

"Colin, all of you are going to Geneva next spring, but what about me?"

"Father will certainly bring you there too, after you have done your apprenticeship, Valentin."

"I shall have done next year. Five years. I too would like to see the world, Colin. I've heard Geneva's a great city. There will be work for me there."

"Surely, Valentin. And then we can all stay together."

He looked at me. "You'll want me—with you?"

"Assuredly," I said. "I'll teach you science, Valentin."

"Methinks I would like to be soldiering, Colin. Then one

goes to many countries; I could be looking after the weaponry. I know muskets and I could learn how to make cannon."

"Only master clockmen are entrusted with cannon," I replied.

"I'll learn, Colin."

Soldiering. Hiring himself out in mercenary regiments. There were Swiss soldiers and officers everywhere, even in India, in the service of rajahs and nabobs. And the French King trusted no one but his Swiss guards. Fifty-four thousand Swiss men, said the *Limping Messenger*, were in armies abroad.

"Then I could come back and settle down after making a fortune," Valentin dreamt aloud. "I am no scholar, as you are, Colin. My legs always want to be moving, and my arms. But I could make a fortune in the wars and come back."

Valentin was simple and strong and would always remain so. He was also very good-looking. It was a pity Bea hated him so much. Why did she? Because of Mother. Because . . . But here my mind went blank.

We strolled into Father's workroom. Its window streamed light. The room was also mine, my bench and tools at a smaller table; and Father had made a chair for me with a rounded back. "A sea captain's chair," he had said, "since Colin likes sea tales." But it was for my foot, I knew, so that I could balance better. And there was my *Robinson Crusoe*, next to my tools—fine pincers and saws, drills and compasses, wedges and pluckers, and small screws and minute cogwheels I had made. On Father's table were the mechanisms of the two androids we were building for Geneva: a drummer and a trumpet player, life-size. Their bodies, already partly limbed, were in a corner; Bea and Mother had carved and chiseled their faces of fine wood and painted them; the heads lay on the table, near the "souls," as I called the mechanisms we put into the bodies.

"They'll walk a few steps, then stop; one will flourish his trumpet and blow, the other beat a drum," I explained to Valentin. "And it must be set so that they are both on time. How can two apparently separate androids be made to step in time together? They're really attached twins, Valentin. Look, a rod, concealed by their clothes and the drum, so that the mechanisms will synchronize . . ."

"Like you and Bea," Valentin said. He grew sad. "Bea does not like me, though I love her."

"I love you," I said. "And Father does, too, just like another son."

I showed Valentin how the coiled spring inside the mechanism was wound, and the way the cogs and wheels fitted, and the art of the cams, the lever action as they lifted or dropped.

Then we went to the well to get water. When the women there saw us, they turned their backs and hurried away.

"Why, they seem to think we have the contagion," Valentin said in his simple way.

Something queasy started in my belly. I knew danger, and as I turned back with the pail a stone hit me. Christophe Griot, the carpenter's son, had thrown it at me.

"Devil's spawn," he cried, "go back to Hell, you and your horned-beast foot!"

Valentin would have hit Christophe, but I held him. "It is nothing, take no notice." As we walked back, I could feel the eyes behind the window. I could feel the women putting their hands on the crosses at their necks. When I reached home I bolted the door and put the big beam across it.

"Why do they hate us so much?" Valentin asked.

"They have gone mad," I said. I knew where the madness came from. Antoine.

The day was soon eaten up by darkness; a sour wind began and scattered snow. I heard the bell. It pealed unevenly; its sound carried in the silence. It was not the bell of Pastor Burandel's chapel, which he rang on Sundays and holidays, at Matins and Angelus; this was another bell, calling, calling. Ominous. It went on pealing for a long time.

Then I saw them through the window, coming out of the houses, the women and the men, and some children too, trudging towards the bell sound, towards Antoine Voice-of-God's barn.

We heard her, Mother and I, calling, "Daout, Bea, I am dying. Come, come quickly, my child and my grandchild."

Colin woke up with a nightmare. Mother woke Father. Father did not want to let us go, but Colin said, "I too heard her." But he had only had the nightmare, he had not been called.

We left Vidy and I could feel the hatred, though we saw no one except Pierre-Thomas coming out of his house.

Mother had been happy that we would go to Geneva. Antoine would not reach us there. Now he had waxed powerful, far more so than before. The whole village went to hear him preach. He would say:

"Death to the witch and her brood, Satan's children."

"Death to the Whore, who seduces all men."

We drove past desolate vineyards, past the cemetery, down the road through pastures with thickets, and then began to climb towards the Jorat. The oak forests were about us, great trees like pillars, and Alexander paced smartly. A woodcutter stood by the road shouldering his axe. "God be with you," he said, and so did we. We passed The Children's Place, where, it was said, fairies came of old, and changelings had been found. We went on, sinking now in the shadows under the oaks. Father muttered that it was not yet two of the clock and already darkening.

We reached the foot of Raven's Nest, that rock twenty cubits high jutting abruptly out of the slope, which went on, on towards Mount Jorat. Colin could never have climbed the Nest. I wished that he were with me, and sent my mind to meet his. He was with Valentin, and happy, and saying, "I love you, Valentin."

I could only hate Valentin, because of Mother. Mother's secret, open to me. Her mind unguarded one day when she watched Valentin come walking back from the forge, and as usual was both wanting to hold him in her arms, and at the same time remembering the man who had come suddenly upon her and forced her, here at the foot of Raven's Nest, while Grisolde, her mother, was away delivering a woman long in childbirth, in the hamlet of the Chapel of Bones.

And tongue-tied Father, so skillful at evading the boulders of pain locked within his head, he had known of this when he married her. He had not sent Valentin to the orphanage, but had taken him as his own.

Valentin—I had to hate him since no one else did. Hate is power, and strength.

We left the cart at the foot of Raven's Nest and followed Father, who led Alexander by the bridle up the pathway crumbling with small boulders. The clay house with its tiled roof stood in the small clearing. The door was ajar. Mother pushed it open. On the bed lay Grisolde, the light of the hearth fire flickering upon her. There were fresh logs piled by it. Someone from a neighboring farm must have come in to help her, and gone before we arrived.

"Daout, Bea"—clear and strong came Grisolde's message to our minds—"child and grandchild. You have come."

Mother went to the bed and said aloud, "Mother . . ."

"Jean-Francois." The old woman's voice was but a whisper, shockingly weak when her spirit's voice was so powerful. Father approached, removing his hat, believing now that Grisolde was truly dying.

Grisolde extended a feeble hand towards him. "Thank you, Jean-Francois, for bringing them to me."

And the magic began.

Suddenly the room with its floor of dark tiles was not, nor the smell of firewood and pine resin. It was a palace of light and fire; splendid flames glowed within crystal walls. The bed was a canopied throne, upon which sat Grisolde, goddess of the forest, clad in gold, not an old woman, but eternally young, a queen. And Mother stood by her, in a flowing dress of white and a crown upon her hair.

"Daughter . . . Bea . . . Death will come for me now, but you must stay here. There is danger if you return too soon to Vidy."

Mother turned, distressed, to look at Father, and at that moment her image wavered, like smoke; my eyes could no longer discern her crowned head. The glory left her as she said, "Jean-Francois, my mother would like us to stay here awhile. She says there is danger."

Father said, "Daout, if there is danger at home, what of Colin? And Valentin?" He knew now that we spoke to one another without words.

Grisolde said haltingly, gasping, her breath labored, "My son, 'tis you and my daughter who are in danger, great danger. Nothing will happen to Valentin or to Colin."

Father said, "Let me get a good doctor for you, Grisolde. I can fetch one from the Chapel of Bones."

The dying woman rolled her head on the pillow. She squeezed my mother's hand, her mind streaming out at us, "Daughter, do not go back, do not let him go back, there is danger for him and for you."

Mother said, anguished, "But Colin is there."

"Yes, but he will not be hurt." She closed her eyes. "The Gift, the Gift must go . . . to you, to Bea after you. . . ."

My father saw an old woman lying in a bed with the firelight dancing on her, and his wife wiping the sweat off the wrinkled brow, lifting a cup of water to the parched mouth. He said, "I beseech you, if indeed God is calling you back to Him, to let me get a pastor."

"No, no."

His body tensed. "Then, Grisolde, I implore you, let my loved ones go. Do not hold them bound to your strange world of darkness. They are Christians. Only Jesus the Christ can give eternal life."

And the old woman said haltingly, "There is no darkness. Only . . . living."

Night seemed to pour into the room as the vision faded, and Father whispered, "Daout, Daout, let us pray for your mother."

And Mother turned to him, a slim, slight woman turning to her love, abandoning strength and power for love. . . .

And in that moment I knew Mother had chosen him, chosen love. The old woman groaned, and I heard her very clearly: " 'Tis thus. My daughter. The Gift will be Bea's, then."

"So be it, Mother."

I heard the great wings of the Raven, beating, and saw the sun obscured by its blackness, and the power coming to me.

The power filling me, like music.

Grisolde died then, and Mother did not weep but knelt with her husband to pray, and then rose to straighten the body.

I went out to the small shed, and as if I had an owl's eyes found the potter's wheel and the clay. Fresh clay, which I moistened from the water trough. The shed was warm with Grisolde's spirit. In the dark my fingers knew what to do.

When I returned, Mother had covered Grisolde's face and sat in the chair to keep watch. Father was piling bedding for us on the floor. I sat on an oaken stool by the hearth. It was Grisolde's stool. My hands were cunning, and the mould I had begun I perfected: the Watcher, for Grisolde of the Forest.

And when I had done, my hands brown with clay, her spirit told me that there was another one to make. Obediently I went back to the shed and made a mould, and my unwilling fingers stuck in the clay like claws, until they had etched another face.

And then I knew what would happen, and my spirit cried out in agony. Yet, for the sake of the power that was to be mine, it had to be.

THE BELL STOPPED. Valentin and I shuttered the windows and fed the hearth. Night pressed upon us, came through the walls, a miasma of fear. Even Valentin felt uneasy. "They've gone to listen to Antoine," he said. "Colin, when will Father be back?"

"I don't know, Valentin. But do not worry. We'll be safe together."

A monster was rampaging outside. When I went to the goats I was afraid, and told Horace so, digging my fingers into his shaggy coat. On the way back from the stable I heard the rumor of the crowd returning from Antoine's preaching.

Valentin said, "I'd like to go and have a mug of wine with Pierre-Thomas." He rose, and his shadow with him. He had a lithe, strong body with good shoulders from the forge.

I said, "Pierre-Thomas and the others, they listen to that mad preacher. He talks such nonsense. For instance, about Marie-la-Folle."

"What about her?"

"Because she worked here, they think it's our fault she was killed."

"Poor Marie"—Valentin shook his head—"her father came to the forge the other day, shouting and swearing. Master Chavenaz threw him out."

"Valentin . . ." I got up and hobbled to him. My leg felt very painful. "They caught the man who did it."

But Valentin was thinking of himself. "It's unfair. I know Father only bears with me, because I am not his son."

Awkwardly, he raked the hearth fire and helped me up the stairs to bed. I listened to the silence wrapping our house. Would I dare to sleep?

Perhaps Father would be back tomorrow. I lay on my bed and listened; I called in my mind to Bea, but she did not reply.

❧ ☙

The ground was covered with bright frost. The sky was a high blue. Snow had fallen on the Jorat, and spicules of ice blew in the air. It would be a cold, hard-ground day; but on the morrow the foehn would come in suddenly, like a mad dog on the heels of the cold.

Father rose. In shirt and hose he stirred the embers, then put on his coat and went out for more logs. Mother lay, awake but still dozing, among the blankets on the floor. When Father returned he said to her, "I must get the pastor, Daout, to bless your mother's grave."

Mother pushed back her hair. "Why not bury her ourselves in the forest?"

"She must have Christian burial," said Father. He was set on doing all things seemly. While he went out to find the pastor of the Chapel of Bones, we made things tidy. Grisolde lay in the bed as if asleep.

Mother said, "The Gift is thine, Bea."

"The Gift is also a curse. As thou knowest."

"There are no more Watchers. My work is done."

She had brought the last ones we had found.

The previous night, while Father slept, Mother and I had risen, and on wind-borne feet reached a clearing among the oaks as light as day. There stood the great stone with its scooped surface, pocketed for the holding of blood. Grisolde was there, clad in white, splendid in the glory of the newly undead. And round her the ten shades Mother had brought, ten not-quite-bodies, faces turned to her. They sang for the sun, and for that speck of darkness within the sun, the blackness in a deluge of light through which life manifests itself.

They sang for the sun, that it would not die, and Grisolde of the Forest lifted her golden sickle.

The mistletoe fell from the sacred oaks that sheltered the clearing. And the ten Mother had saved, whose shapes wavered between being and unbeing, caught it in the linen sheets Grisolde had woven. And I was crowned with the Golden Bough.

All the beasts of the forest were there; weasel and fox, badger and marmoset, the antlered buck and the prowling wolf.

A fire was lit. Grisolde of the Forest walked into it. The flames bent back before they wrapped her round and consumed her.

Beyond Raven's Nest, the hamlet called the Chapel of Bones possessed a ramshackle, uncared-for presbytery. The roof shingles had fallen from it. Some stray bricks and tiles strewed the ground. The man who opened the door of the chapel was thin with blazing eyes, his clothes in a wild state of disarray, and from him came a sour smell of wine. Within the chapel was a cross of hacked wood; a man's shape hanging there and on it a face dreadful to behold. At its foot—empty bottles of wine.

My father began, "Pastor, I come to tell you of the death of an old woman, Grisolde of the Raven's Nest."

"Dead! The witch has died at last!" the pastor clarioned, his hands clutching my father, his breath fetid. "Satan has taken back his own. . . ."

He dragged Father into the chapel. "Come, let us give thanks to Jesus Christ our Lord and drink a cup of wine to praise Him. Let her bones be picked by the crows and she burn in Hell with her demon-lovers. Listen . . ." Again he gripped my father's coat. "This place is full of them. Witches. Sorcerers. The hand of God has forborne until now, but it will come heavy upon them."

Father walked out, leaving the man to his frenzied shouting. There would be no holy burial for Grisolde of the Forest.

Mother said, "The big oak chest at the bed's foot; let us place her in it and bury her under the oak trees. That is how she would have it."

We buried Grisolde's body in the great oak chest with its strange carvings of serpents and three-horned bucks. By nightfall we had done. We ate the last of the smoked meat we had brought. Mother placed Grisolde's Soul-Keeper by her side. I kept the other one I had *made in my cape pocket. A storm blew to shake the house and sparks flew off the hearth logs, like shooting stars.*

We who live by the lake are the creatures of its climate; its moods are ours. It is at times a great sheet, mauve and green, mauve and lilac, green and turquoise, rippling with small foam; at others it is a solid silver plate, almost white. And when the winds blow, the lake answers them, as its myriad birds wheel and turn in the gales.

When the foehn, *more treacherous than wine, sweeps hotly down into our valleys, even the Lords of Berne do not sit in council. Judges and bailiffs, complaining that the* foehn *disturbs their minds and reason may be impaired by the caprices of the weather, stay at home. In the forests the oaks and beeches vibrate to its insidious warmth. Mountain avalanches thunder down, burying villages, people, cattle.*

The foehn *blew as we came down from the Jorat. We should have awakened early, for Father, always exact, with his gold watch strung on a chain across his scarlet waistcoat, had announced that we must be back before dark. But we had slumbered late. The sun was high when we woke, and we felt the threatening stillness that drove men to violence and women to fits of weeping.*

Grisolde had friends among the women of the surrounding hamlets. She had helped them, giving them potions, caring for their children. Wrapped in her shawl, one woman came to weep for Grisolde. "Who will listen to us now? They said she threw spells. But they were good spells, which made us well."

In the forest, pig herds were rooting and grunting in their winter coats, disturbed by the sudden heat. And when we reached the Abbey of the Cistercians, the scarcening trees spread darkness within their branches. The sun reddened to its daily death. We hurried, but night was upon us as we reached Vidy.

And all the way the message came to me strong and urgent. Danger, danger . . . dreadfulness. But Mother sat with Father, and I behind them all the way, silent. Their love was a tight mantle, a high wall around them, closing them to everything else.

"Danger, danger . . . I do not want the Gift . . . I do not want to know . . . Colin to care for . . . I must tell them . . . but they will not believe me."

Mother turned her head to me. "We'll soon be home, Bea." Her smile was happy.

I said, "I'm afraid, Mother. There is evil in Vidy."
But she smiled that blind and glowing smile of hers. "All the
more reason to get home quickly. Colin is waiting for us."

➵ ⋐

ALL DAY WE HAD WAITED, Valentin and I, for their return. I
went to see Horace and nestled by his side. His tongue nib-
bled my hair and ears. I told him everything. He seemed to
understand, his eyes on me golden with tranquil wisdom.

The sky became red, and the people came in procession up
the pathway. All of them, it seemed, the women too. The
fishermen and the laborers. In a black cape, holding a cross
in his hand, Antoine Voice-of-God led them. They stopped at
the garden gate and began to sing an exorcism:

> *Go back, Satan, to thy den in Hell;*
> *Monsters of evil, flee before the Holy Word.*
> *We are the Army of Christ.*
> *With God's Word we shall purify our land.*

Antoine was at our door, the cross in his hand. "In the
name of God, succubus and incubus, children of the Devil,
come out."

Valentin, my tall, strong brother, as if hypnotized, went to
the door. I sprang at him. "Valentin, don't open, don't open."

The haunting, obsessive voice, the voice of Antoine, came
through the closed door, punctuated by the shouts of the
men and women.

"Open, open, you cannot resist God and His command."

Valentin pushed me aside and lifted the thick bar I had set
across the oaken door.

They were upon us then, seizing us, dragging us outside to
make us kneel before Antoine.

And Antoine bent the cross upon us and chanted, "Behold,
ye vampires, ye evil-doers, who drink the blood of the innocent and feed upon carrion, the judgment of God is upon
you. Tie them to the gate posts," he shouted.

They had brought staves with them and axes and sickles. And some of the boys I had played with tied me to one of the poles of our fence gate, and Valentin was tied to the other by the men; it took four of them to knock him down and bind his hands and feet. I recognized Madeleine Griot, Louise Paluz, Marie-la-Folle's father—all of them chanting now, signing themselves, as they followed Antoine into our house.

"Lucifer, Satan, Beelzebub, monsters and devils, show yourselves in the name of Almighty God."

And then a cry of triumph, as Antoine discovered Father's androids.

"Monsters of Hell, the demons have entered these!"

I screamed, "No, no, don't touch them, they're my father's!"

Antoine raised the cross and said, "God hath spoken: 'Destroy this den of evil. Purge it with fire.' "

Valentin cried in anguish. "Please don't burn our house, we've never done any harm."

Antoine stood on the steps of our house, his arms extended like Christ on the cross, while the men and women of Vidy ran to our pile of winter logs and started to carry them inside. Others went to the grange and came out with the forage. All were shouting and singing, "It is God's will. Burn the sorcerers, fire, fire."

Antoine walked to us; now it was so dark he looked immense, the moving darkness itself. "Valentin, child of evil, of the filth that walks at night, this day judgment is come unto thee."

And there was Pierre-Thomas and others with torches, and Antoine blessing the torches. They set fire to the grange, and to the house, running and touching their torches to everything, and breaking the windows with their axes.

Antoine pointed a finger to Valentin: "Child of evil, offspring of Satan, born in shame and sin, thou shalt burn in Hell for all eternity."

And a woman cried, "He raped and killed our Marie."

"He threw a spell upon me at the well."

"He burns," Antoine chanted. "Then our land shall be purified."

Pierre-Thomas and Christophe and some of the men rushed to untie Valentin and started dragging him towards the house.

73

Already flames were licking from inside; I could see Mother's loom, the kitchen table, burning.

Valentin screamed, "Colin, Colin. Mother!"

And then I heard Mother's voice high and clear: "Colin, Colin," and Father shouting, "Stop! What are you doing? Stop!"

Suddenly the grange burst into a great blaze, and fire licked its tongue into the stable.

"Horace," I cried, "Horace!"

Father was there, grappling with several men who, abandoning Valentin on the ground, had thrown themselves at him. Mother reached me and threw her arms around me.

Flames came out of the top window and the attic. Father gasped, "My androids!" He shook the men off him and plunged into the house.

And Mother, screaming, "Jean, Jean," left me and went after Father into the burning house.

Now the wood shingles of the roof caught fire, the house roared, and sparks blew into the trees and upon the crowd so that they fell back. Only Antoine stood there, holding the cross to the burning house and chanting:

"Demons, Satan, Beelzebub and your cohorts, burn, burn. . . ."

Out of that fire came a running blaze; a monster of fire, a horned beast, terrible to behold, screaming, running straight into Antoine. Antoine's cape was caught in his horns, and Antoine rolled on the ground, and Horace trampled him, and both became one agonizing scream, one whorl of fire.

The men and women around us, seeing Antoine burn, fled in terror. "The Devil has taken Antoine!" they cried.

Then Bea was there, releasing me. And Valentin, stupefied, staring at our burning house. On the ground beneath the linden tree, which now was catching fire, what had once been Horace tangled with Antoine. And the odor of burning flesh was everywhere.

PASTOR BURANDEL AND HIS household had been at evening prayers. They had not heard the clamor, but one of the maids, having gone outside to close the garden gate, saw the blaze and told her master, "There is a big fire in Vidy."

By the time Fernand Burandel arrived, the heat was so intense that we could not come near. We three sat outside, still calling, "Father, Mother," though we knew it was useless.

"My God, but it's unbelievable," Burandel said. He too was seized with immobility before the disaster, shivering and weeping, as was Valentin.

"Father, Mother, they're inside," I said to him.

"God have mercy on their souls," Pastor Burandel said. Around us all was mute; it was as if the whole village had gone to sleep. "Murderers, cowards," Pastor Burandel shouted into the silence. "Be assured that you will be punished for this monstrous crime!"

Masterfully he walked to the first house and pounded on its door. "Open," he said. "It is I, your pastor. In the name of Christ, open."

And Dormaz, the weaver of baskets, who lived there, opened slowly; he was one of those who had brought the torches and piled the logs. "Your wife," Pastor Burandel said peremptorily, "she will go with the children to my house. You, Dormaz, will assemble all the men of Vidy. Immediately. I will not leave till this horrible crime is punished."

Mother Dormaz, whom Mother had tended when she had the big cough and fever the previous winter, went with us to the pastor's house. Agathe Burandel twisted and untwisted her hands; she asked Mother Dormaz, "What happened, what happened?"

"An accident," Mother Dormaz muttered. "The pastor says to take care of the children." Agathe began to weep, and searched for her hymn book. Mother Dormaz hung her head, wrapped her shawl around her, and went back into the night.

Agathe put us to bed in the rooms they had built for the children who had never come to them. She plied us with hot soup and with her questions, and we replied, and she exclaimed and wept and wrung her hands. "My poor, poor children . . . it is the will of God . . . we must pray to Him . . . aye, pray to Him tonight as never before." She thought to sing a hymn but could find only "O God behold Thy creature" and desisted. She shut the door tight upon us and left us in the darkness, but we could hear her telling her servants, and their exclamations of distress and pity.

Bea and I held each other tight; Valentin was sobbing quietly, but Bea could not touch him. It was I who put out my hand to him, and he gripped it.

Several times during that night the pastor came tiptoeing in to see if we slept, and we feigned sleep. I groped for Bea's mind, but recoiled—there was such a storm and a howling in it, hatred and rage; and so I shut my eyes, only to see Horace coming out of the stable, a great ball of fire, straight at Antoine. . . .

THE BAILIFF HELD A MEETING; the Lausanne militia apprehended a few of the village men of Vidy, including Pierre-Thomas, and put them in jail.

Father and Mother were buried together in the cemetery. The whole village of Vidy was ordered to attend; Lord Kilvaney came from Lausanne, and also other gentlemen who knew my father, and Master Chavenaz closed his forge for the day.

Their Excellencies of Berne were concerned. They had promulgated edicts against the burning of witches and wizards. A magistrate, Master Hocher, came to investigate. It was declared that Mother was not a witch—there was no evidence of witchcraft about her. Hence my parents were to be buried in holy ground, and Bea and I and Valentin threw blessed water upon the coffins as they sank into the earth.

Valentin sobbed heartrendingly. He seemed the most affected of us three. Bea remained dry-eyed, and because of her, so did I.

The women, wrapped in their shawls and hugging themselves, kept their heads bent; the men—those who were not jailed—sang the hymns louder than anyone else. Afterwards some of the women tried to come up to us, timidly, but Bea went through them like a clean and sparkling sword, and the contempt in her eyes, dark slate, made them hasten away.

"Colin, you know what we have to do."

"Yes, Bea."

"We must bury Mother in the lake. She will not want anything else."

"But, Bea, she is in the cemetery. With Father."

"I mean her Soul-Keeper. That is what she would want."

That night I circumvented the watchful Agathe Burandel, who would not let us out of the house. I opened the window shutters; I had oiled the hinges so they would not squeak. Bea and I slipped out. Valentin watched us go, sadly; but he was afraid of Bea, and he obeyed her. We went back to what had been our house and was only a mess of stone and charred wood.

Bea had with her Mother's Soul-Keeper, the one she had made that night at the Jorat. Bea found the things Mother had used that had not burnt: pins for her lace, the twisted torque she had worn round her neck.

We went down to the lake shore and there were the moored boats of the fishermen. I untied one of them. I rowed straight toward the lake's center.

"Here," said Bea. She stood in the boat, let the Watcher drop into the water, along with Mother's torque and the pins.

I wanted to ask, "Why here, Bea? And what about Father?"

I wanted to say, "Bea, why did you not stop them?"

But Bea's mind was closed to me, or perhaps I did not want to know. I rowed back. I found it long and slow walking up the slopes from the lake to Montoie. We crept into the house and no one heard us.

⌘ ⌘

❧ *Five* ❧

Anno Domini 1755–1756

ISABELLE DE THUNON SWEPT down from her coach, tragic in black furs and dress. Flustered Agathe curtsied, took Isabelle into the guest room, and served her cakes and chocolate. But Isabelle declined to sit down, looking around her with established condescension.

"I come, Madame, on behalf of Monsieur Theodore Duriez of Neuchâtel. Doubtless the pastor knows that my unfortunate cousin, Baron Jean-Francois Duriez, came from that well-known family. . . ." Her voice faltered appropriately, and Agathe cut in:

"Indeed, Madame, my husband was Monsieur Duriez's greatest friend; he confided in him. . . . Those unfortunate children . . ."

"An atrocious tragedy, Madame. Doubtless Pastor Burandel will see to it that the criminals be punished, since Vidy is under his care." Isabelle made it sound as if the deaths were Fernand Burandel's fault. She now peremptorily stated that, as a relative, she was taking us with her and would send us to Neuchâtel.

We were bundled into the carriage, and Isabelle made a show of putting a blanket round my legs.

"God be with you, my children," said Burandel, moist-eyed.

"You will stay with me a few days, till your clothes are ready," Isabelle said.

At the Tramontoire, Valentin and I shared a bedroom; Bea was on the upper floor, in a charming room overlooking the lake. Maids and servants came and went. Tailors arrived and measured us. We were to be fitted out in black, as was appropriate.

"I want to go back to the forge," Valentin said. "Colin, please ask Cousin Isabelle."

"She is not *your* cousin," Bea said sharply.

Many gentlemen and ladies came to take tea, to exclaim over the tragedy; and there was genuine grief among those who had liked and purchased Father's automata. But everyone also felt that we were fortunate to be rescued. Isabelle had Bea and myself appear to bow and curtsy and thank those who murmured appropriate condolences. But not Valentin.

"He is not a Duriez. Colin, Berengere"—Isabelle insisted on calling Bea Berengere, a name traditional in the Duriez family—"you will stay a short while when guests offer their condolences. You may weep a little. Then retire in a seemly manner."

These niceties accomplished, Isabelle prepared us for Neuchâtel. "It is a city of trade and commerce," she said. "It makes watches and cloth, which are sold abroad. . . ."

"And automata, Cousin Isabelle," I said. "The workers of Chaux-de-Fonds, Sainte-Croix, are renowned for their skill." I wanted to master the craft I had begun to learn with Father.

Isabelle gave me a crushing look and said in a restrained voice, "Colin, you are not aware of the importance of the Duriez, of whom you are today the sole heir, your uncle Theodore having no children. The Duriez are one of the twelve families in Neuchâtel who decide everything, and it is time you learned your station in life. Your uncle Theodore would not like you to mingle with artisans."

"And what will Valentin do, Cousin Isabelle?"

"Valentin is not a Duriez, not of our class. Doubtless suitable work will be found for him."

Master Chavenaz came, bent and heavy, unimpressed by the luxury of the Tramontoire. Isabelle received him in the hall, as if he were a domestic, standing, cap in hand. "I wish to adopt Valentin, Madame," he told her. "He is a good, sturdy fellow and will make an excellent master blacksmith one day."

Isabelle answered that, since my father had taken "the unwanted offspring of his wife" as his son, it was the Duriez of Neuchâtel who would decide. "My poor cousin was always kind, treating the boy as his own. This is a matter of such impropriety, that, as a woman, I do not wish to discuss it."

Lord Kilvaney came, and came again. Genuinely grieved, he inquired anxiously and repeatedly of Isabelle about our future. "I am willing to take them to England with me, Ma'am; doubtless you know they are both gifted." Isabelle, with polite hauteur, told him of Neuchâtel and the Duriez family, and of me being the sole heir to the Duriez fortune.

Lord Kilvaney hugged me. I heard his heart beat strongly, erratically, through his coat. "Colin, let me know what happens to you both. Do not forget you have skill in your hands and cleverness in your brain." He tapped my forehead.

I promised, and having been left alone with him, I gave him a letter for Jacob. I was cautious; prudence was natural to me. I had not told Isabelle about the Hirsch family in Geneva, nor did Lord Kilvaney.

MONSIEUR DE VOLTAIRE WAS in Lausanne that December, and people pressed to see him as if he were a marvelous android. Daily we heard in Isabelle's salon of his sallies of wit, of the play *The Orphan of China*, which he proposed to present in Lausanne. Lausanne's best and noblest families would take part in the play, and the first presentation would be at the Marquis of Langallerie's house, at Mon Repos. Voltaire had purchased a large house at Montriond; his intention was to spend the winter in Lausanne, the summer in Geneva.

Isabelle rivaled with other ladies to attend the reception Voltaire gave on December 16. His niece, the corpulent Madame Denis—who, it was whispered, was also his mistress—would play hostess. Isabelle's salon was filled with people intriguing for an invitation; when it became known that she had been invited, it added to her luster.

Voltaire and Madame Denis then came to a reception given by Isabelle. He wore a coat embroidered with silver and pearls, and waved a perfumed handkerchief before his nose, as if to chase away bad odors. The room was dazzling with candelabra of Venice, and women in satin and diamonds. Voltaire grinned and grimaced, everyone laughing and clapping hands when he spoke. Hidden behind a drapery, I heard Bailiff de Crozay say to him pompously, "Monsieur de Voltaire, why are you a poet, not a bailiff? It is so much safer." Everyone appeared to have forgotten that only four years previously Voltaire had written: "The Swiss are barbarians who sell their blood for money."

Now he recited verses from a play entitled *Mahomet*, which had been condemned by the French Catholic Church:

> *Les prejuges, ami, sont les rois du vulgaire;*
> *Il faut un nouveau culte, il faut de nouveaux fers,*
> *Il faut un nouveau dieu pour l'aveugle univers . . .*

> (Prejudice, friend, is king of the crowd;
> The rabble needs a new cult, needs new chains,
> The blind world seeks a new god.)

I stole away, reciting these words to myself.

A BERLINE WITH A coachman and two postilions in livery came to take us to Neuchâtel. From it, a tall thin man in lugubrious black emerged. "Baron Colin Duriez?" the man inquired, bowing to me and taking off his hat. "I am Monsieur Theodore's secretary, Andre Martin. Be pleased to enter your carriage, Monsieur le Baron."

I was the heir. Baron Duriez. *The* baron.

We said farewell to Cousin Isabelle. I had grown somewhat fond of her, for there was no wickedness in her, only a yearning to be in fashion, to have her salon furnished with the wits of the time. Bea despised her. "She is empty and wants to people her vacancy." Bea's violence overawed me. I was incapable of it, and ashamed of the ease with which I forgave, forbore, forgot, because I was vulnerable, timorous. Had not the philosopher Diderot, whom Jacob liked so much, derided people incapable of great passion, fierce hatred and dazzling love, of marvelous visions?

"Berengere, do not forget to behave like a well-bred young lady," said Isabelle, who detested Bea, as she pecked her cheek.

Andre Martin barred Valentin's way into the berline. "You sit with the coachman."

I intervened. Audacity had come when I had heard the word *baron*. "My brother sits with me," I said, mustering hauteur (learnt from Isabelle) in my voice.

Andre Martin said stiffly, "As you wish, Sir."

It was almost night when we arrived in Neuchâtel. We had eaten dinner on the way: fowl and venison, pastries, almond cake. Bea had been silent almost the whole time, delving into herself, refusing my tentative approaches to her mind.

"Bea, it will not be bad."

Her mind sneered at mine. "You are now their prisoner, Colin. The heir. They are buying you for their own purpose."

"Perhaps they know I'm a coward," I told her mind, humbly.

She stared at the landscape.

Andre Martin sat in one corner of the berline, opposite me, reading a thick book. Valentin sat in the other corner, Martin keeping as far away from him as possible. Valentin tried to talk with me, commenting on the road, the undulating land, the hamlets perched in the valleys, the huddled woods between winter-locked fields. I answered him shortly, and then I pretended to fall asleep.

In the night gloom Neuchâtel was silent. Large houses, enclosed gardens, gates of finely forged ironwork. To such a gate we drove; it opened upon a French garden, stiff with sentinel beeches exactly alike, up to a portico where two brass lamps swung from the pillars.

A mansion of stone, larger by far than that of Isabelle in Lausanne. The door was opened by two servants, in the same grey livery as the coachman's, with brass buttons and black waistcoat striped with blue. One of them was an old man, who whispered immediately, "Welcome, Master Colin," and smiled with genuine pleasure.

As we went up a flight of broad carpeted stairs, family portraits stared at us from the wall, men and women looking with speculative eyes at those who went up or down.

We stopped before a door whose carvings were the escutcheon of the Duriez, though I knew it not at the time. Everything was silent, caulked, occluded, draught-proof; not the slightest movement of air in those rooms, the long corridors flanked by ornate doors, lighted by candelabra of Italian crystal, shuttered against the outside. The house distilled its own air and light, everything in it shone with subdued satisfaction; and of this suffocating, self-righteous smugness I was the heir.

Martin opened the door to me. "Monsieur le Baron." Bea followed. When Valentin tried to follow, Martin held him back. "Wait here until you are called."

Uncle Theodore awaited us, seated in a velvet-covered armchair near a marble fireplace in which great logs burnt. He was dressed in a grey coat and grey trousers, with no lace or embroidery; his hair was tied with a small black ribbon. He watched us with eyes that were like the eyes of the portraits on the stairs.

Bea curtsied. I bowed.

"Approach." Picking up a pair of spectacles that lay on the table by his side, he watched us through them.

We came forward, stood under his scrutiny. The room seemed immense. There were many books, in orderly rows. Great sweeps of crimson velvet draped the invisible windows; large somber furniture covered in embroidered petit point sat aginst the walls.

"The brood of Jean-Francois. A cripple." Uncle Theodore's voice was thin, dry.

"He is trying to hurt you, Colin," Bea's mind said.

"I know, Bea."

"Martin. Write down what I shall now say to these two."

Andre Martin's feet glided upon the floor noiselessly. There was a quill and inkwell and paper on a table. He stood, quill poised.

"Berengere, when were you baptized, have you been confirmed, can you sew, embroider, cook, play the clavecin, read?"

Bea replied, her eyes very green, her smile pleasant and dangerously gentle. "Uncle Theodore, I was baptized and confirmed by Pastor Burandel of Montoie, and I can sew, cook, play the clavecin, read, and write."

"And you, Nephew Colin?"

"I can read, write, I know a little Latin, mathematics, and I can also make clocks and automata," I replied.

"Can you?" Uncle Theodore threw his glasses on the table. "Don't speak to me of these things. They destroyed your father. That is why he took for wife a whore."

Bea's fury. It rose, filled the room.

I said, though my voice shook, "Father and Mother are dead. God in His mercy gave their souls rest. We are their children, and we ask you not to talk ill of them. It is unseemly and un-Christian, Uncle Theodore."

Andre Martin lifted his head, gaping, the quill poised in his hand. Uncle Theodore stared at me. Then he said, still in the same dry, thin voice, "You shall be whipped for your insolence, though you be the Baron. You have both been ill taught and are wayward and willful, and I have charge of your souls. I must leave the Duriez heritage in fitting hands, and you must be disciplined. Martin, take them to their rooms. And administer to Baron Colin Duriez the whipping immediately. Ten strokes. Then bread and water for three days."

We passed Valentin, who stood waiting by the door. A valet let him into Uncle Theodore's presence, while we were taken up another set of stairs and down another corridor. I was shut in a small, bare room, in which there was a narrow bed, a commode, a table, and a jug of water with a basin. Bea said, "No, no," when she saw it, but Martin called, "Madame Hunner," and a portly woman with a big apron appeared and curtsied to Bea. "Follow me, Mademoiselle."

Such was the air and style of the house that I said to Bea, "Go with her, I shall be all right." Already my voice sounded like that of Uncle Theodore.

Martin said, "Monsieur le Baron will be good enough to uncover himself," and applied the whip. I bit my lips and did not cry out, but when he had gone I cried myself to sleep, groping for Bea's mind. And it was there.

"Bea, Bea . . ."

"Yes, Colin. I'm here. He hates us. He is a beast. We must run away, or you'll become like him. He wants you to be like him. But now sleep, little brother, sleep. I'm here. . . ."

And so I was calmed.

UNCLE THEODORE HAD MADE up his mind to break our spirit. I was repeatedly whipped by Martin, and Bea by Mrs. Hunner. They whipped us respectfully, though unsparingly, as a religious duty, convinced that this was for the good of our souls. Daily at prayers we knelt, while Uncle Theodore read from the Holy Book to the assembled household. On Sundays a pastor came to the house to hold a service; he too never smiled, and he preached long sermons. After the service we were locked in our rooms, where we had to copy, by hand, twenty pages of the Holy Book and present them to Uncle Theodore at night.

Bea grew thin. I grew morose. We were allowed to walk in the garden but never through the gate; and the iron gates became a fascination to me. I dreamt of running and bursting through them. As we walked, we would come near to them, and I would stare at the beautiful scrollwork on each leaf: a Chinese mandarin, seated, with a pointed hat upon his head. Around his chair, a world of strange blossoms. The Chinese mandarins who guarded the gates seemed to smile, to beckon to me. "Escape, escape."

As for Valentin, his plight was far worse than ours. He was a child of sin, so he became a scullion, put to polish the silver, to clean the stables. Occasionally I saw him and would smile, make little movements towards him. I noticed that his hands were sore and swollen with the red polish paste that was used to clean the innumerable pieces of silver of the Duriez family. My silver.

Two tutors came to teach me, one for religion and philosophy and *belles-lettres*, the other for mathematics, algebra, and Latin. Bea had a music mistress and practiced on the clavecin many hours a day. I grew surly and numb. Were it not for the spitting volcano that was Bea's mind, perhaps I would have given up, but her fury was unstaunched, continuous, devouring her. "Colin, Colin, we must run away from the beast."

Spring came, with sap and blossom, and the lawns were bestarred with daisies and cornflowers. I could smell the apple and cherry; we could see the lake of Neuchâtel dazzling in the sun.

Once a week I would appear before Uncle Theodore, to whom my tutors reported. "A cripple, but not a dullard," he would say. "Remember you are the heir."

The Duriez owned land and a factory. I was made to learn how much land, and how much they produced. The factory made printed indienne cloth. It was situated at Boudry, and every day Uncle Theodore went with Andre Martin to supervise the work.

Letters to us were read first by Uncle Theodore. We had one from Lord Kilvaney, announcing his departure for London, giving us his address and the name of his castle in Yorkshire. There was one from Pastor Burandel; Uncle Theodore read it out to us.

"The city of Neuchâtel is famous and prosperous in many ways," Burandel wrote, "not the least of its fame being its craftsmen, who, in the long winter nights, make watches ⅛and clocks and musical boxes even for the King of Spain. . . ."

"You will not lower yourself to know these people," Uncle Theodore said. "Write to the pastor, please: 'My sister and I thank you for your care and concern. We hope to grow up worthy burghers of Neuchâtel, mindful of our duties to the Religion and our responsibilities to the estate to which God has been pleased to call us.'

"Automata and clocks. Androids." Uncle Theodore's voice was righteous. "Baubles and amusements. But the Duriez family is in textiles. This is what you must apply yourselves to know."

The looms making cloth that brought the Duriez their wealth, I thought, were a kind of automaton. The same logic was behind them as behind androids. But I kept silent, solacing myself by dreaming of machinery. I knew that none of the hamlets of the backland, where the peasants in the winter nights made clocks and music boxes, had produced traders. It was not the craftsman and the artist, but the trader, the merchant who could sell other men's inventions in the world, who became wealthy. Now I knew that the factories of Geneva made chiefly the jeweled, ornate casings of clocks and watches; but their mechanical souls were created by hungry men, driven to Geneva from a thousand small farms, from the mountain hamlets of Chaux-de-Fonds, Sainte-Croix. . . .

I read dictionaries. Uncle Theodore had me learn not only Latin and Greek but German and English. I looked up the word *program*, which I found in the Latin and the English, and thought that it might apply to what an android was compelled to do by its mechanism. We could and did, by the adjustment of cams and springs, order a program to it, and now I dreamt of an android with many programs, from which it could choose.

"Run away. We must run away," Bea repeated, "or you will become like the beast."

"I can never become like Uncle Theodore."

"Oh yes you can. He is fashioning you to inherit the factory."

"I can't run," I said. Bea could run, and Valentin could run, but I could not. I began to make plans. Bea's fury goaded me. If Valentin ran away to Geneva, to the Hirsch house, perhaps, perhaps . . . I sought out Valentin and found him in the stable, polishing the harness of the coach horses. His face twisted when he saw me, and as he hugged me he wept, his tears falling upon my face, for he was much taller.

"Oh, Colin, I cannot bear it. The other domestics, they call me a bastard; they hit me and pull my hair, they make me do all the dirty work, emptying the commodes."

"Valentin, we must run away. All three of us."

"Didn't they tell you? I tried running away but I was caught at the gates. They beat me and said they'd put irons on me and accuse me of stealing, and then I would be hanged. . . ."

Obviously Valentin could not run away. Besides, we had no money. Uncle Theodore was destroying him, little by little.

On a blustery March night when the *bise* tore the trees, Lucien, the very old servant who had opened the door to us on our arrival, came knocking softly at my door. "Master Colin, it is I, Lucien."

"The door is locked. I do not have the key," I said.

Then I heard the key turn; the door opened; Lucien stood there beaming.

"I have all the keys to every room, to the gates, even to your uncle's desk," he whispered. "Sixty years I've been a servant to the Duriez; four generations I've served . . . and I shouldn't have the keys to all the house?"

Lucien began coming two or three nights a week, especially when I was punished for some infraction or other, such as making a mistake in a Latin verb. He would bring me cake, pastry, sometimes hot chocolate to drink in a silver three-footed jug, with a fine cup of china. "I saw your father born, Master Colin. I remember him; he was much like you. My wife, God have her soul in His keeping, was his wet nurse. Madame la Baronne, his mother, died of the birthing fever eight days after he was born, and the Baron Daniel, your grandfather, married again. Married Albertine de Thunon, and then Monsieur Theodore was born; he is your father's stepbrother, and administers the estate, but your father was the heir, the Baron, he was to inherit everything.

"But then Master Jean-Francois married your mother. . . ." Lucien's voice sank, his eyes dimmed with remembered sorrow. "It was a tragedy, Master Colin, though downstairs we secretly admired him for it."

Daniel Duriez, my grandfather, had fought for the King of Prussia against the Counts of Savoie, and been raised to the peerage, become a baron, when Neuchâtel became a principality under the Prussian sovereign. "We of Neuchâtel chose well, for Prussia is far away, and so the twelve families do as they please." Lucien chuckled. "Not like Lausanne, straight under the Lords of Berne, who are too near."

Uncle Theodore's wife, also of noble descent, was Isabelle's aunt and had gone mad; she lived with five servants in an aisle of an old house, away off among the fields. It had been my great-grandmother's original house, when the Duriez were not ennobled but stone masons and builders. "One never mentions it, of course," Lucien said, "but it means that your uncle Theodore can never have an heir. And though Baron

Daniel was very angry with your father, he did not disinherit him; so that you are now the rightful heir."

Baron Daniel, my grandfather, had traveled much. The fever of enterprise was upon him, and he had been to the Indias. That was how the factory of indiennes textiles of the Duriez, at Boudry near Neuchâtel, had begun. Baron Daniel had brought back the painted and printed cottons of India, and joined in business with some of the Huguenots, skilled craftsmen in textiles, notably de Pourtales. De Pourtales had come to Neuchâtel, and the factory had been set up. The de Pourtales trading company, founded in 1753, exported indiennes to all of Europe, and with pious integrity smuggled indiennes to France, which had forbidden the entry of Indian printed textiles.

"There is a lot of money made in this trade," Lucien said.

"You know everything, Lucien." I cajoled him. He had the keys. He might help us to run away.

But Bea shrugged. "Colin, he is old, he lives for the Duriez, and only wants you to become his master one day."

"Baron Daniel wanted your father to marry Isabelle de Thunon, who was a niece of his wife," Lucien said. "All these big families intermarry. Instead, Master Jean-Francois married your mother.

"Your father liked going to the factory, not to watch the workers but to talk with them. Many of them were women and young children, peasants who couldn't pay their taxes. That is how he met your mother.

"Oh, she was beautiful, so beautiful, and only seventeen; she was a lace maker and the factory employed lace makers too. And she was with child. The other women did not speak to her, for she came from the Jorat, which is where brigands live, and because there was no father to the child."

His voice became dreamy; I could tell that he still dreamt of my mother's beauty. Mother had left the Jorat so as not to be stoned or dragged for penance at the chapel for her sin in being raped and with child.

"Your father met her walking through the mean streets, and every day he went to see her. Baron Daniel found out. He told your father, 'She is a whore.' But she was so beautiful," the old man repeated, "and with that purity about her, and no family and no one to protect her. Baron Daniel sent two clerks to drive her out as a depraved woman, and they took her to the jail, to be publicly whipped, exhibited as a whore, but your father said he would marry her and that the child was his. It was an enormous scandal in Neuchâtel."

It was also a terrible family quarrel. The doors were shut, but of course Lucien heard everything. "All of us downstairs were in a state. Then your father came down the stairs, with nothing in his hands, not even a greatcoat on his shoulders, though it was cold, and he said to me, 'Lucien, God be with you. I am going away and I shall not come back.' And he walked out, we watched him go out through the gates, just walked away and we never saw him again."

"Lucien, I too want to go away," I blurted. "I cannot stay here. I want to become a master craftsman. I want to make fine automata and androids."

"Master Colin." Lucien's lower jaw dropped, he had very few teeth left, he was truly old, and now much agitated. "Listen to me, an old man who has served your family sixty years. Just be patient, be patient a few years, then you will be Baron Duriez; all will be yours."

"I don't want it."

"*You* are a Duriez, Master Colin; you are the heir. We have waited for you, all of us."

It was clear that Lucien would not help. He might even tell Uncle Theodore. So I said, "Perhaps you are right, I am not used to all this." And afterwards, when the old man came again, I pretended to be very interested in the factory and how much land there was.

IT WAS MARCH, BLUSTERY with sudden changes of weather, and Uncle Theodore came back from the factory with a fever. There had been a cold spell and he had been caught by the *joran*, that ferocious wind plunging down from the crests of the Jura that turned the lake water black.

The doctors came, bled him once, twice. The house was hushed as he lay in bed, and Andre Martin walked about on tiptoe, issuing whispered commands. The servants now came to ask me what food I would like; and the maids flitted round Bea.

"They think the beast might die, then you will be the heir, Baron Duriez." Bea laughed.

The doctors looked at Theodore's urine in a tall glass. He had so much heat in his body, and gravel, too, so they bled him a third time.

Bea now went out, and in the garden and the meadows with the first spring flowers and timid herbs peeping out of the earth, she picked and chose; she knew well the lore of medicinal plants, which Mother had taught her. Then she asked Andre Martin whether Uncle Theodore would receive us. Martin tiptoed in and out again and nodded: "For a few moments only."

The bedroom air was thick and rancid with the fetor of illness. Uncle Theodore, a bonnet on his head, sat up on a mound of pillows. He looked pale and was short of breath.

"Uncle Theodore," Bea said, "we have been greatly distressed. We have prayed many hours that health be restored to you."

She spoke so sweetly, her eyes upon his face, all of her so gentle that I saw him melt, his body less rigid, as he whispered, "God may spare me . . . it is a fluxion, and the gravel."

Bea came near the bed, timidly putting out a hand upon the covers. "I have learnt a little about soothing potions." She held up the pot in which she had brewed some herbs. "If you will taste of this—it is of the garden, it cannot harm you."

"Child, what do you know of the humors?" Theodore whispered.

"I learnt to gather simples, and I have seen them relieve pain," Bea said.

And, wonder of wonders, Theodore extended a hand, and Bea poured her potion into a glass, and he drank it. For many days Bea was in and out of the sick room, plying him with honey, warmed and mixed with camomile and rhubarb; with verbena and hawthorn in potions, and the juice of haws, fresh crushed; dandelion with radish and thistle, and much valerian, which she sent Andre Martin and Mrs. Hunner to find among the peasants' households. Then she had lavender and saponaria for his chest pain, and *marjoram* and thyme to ease the breathing. She gave him sweet basil and arnica for the fever that made him weak—and this every day several times; so that he drank a good deal, whereas the doctors had kept him dry and his mouth had become sore, the lips cracked.

The pains eased; he no longer sweated so much. Bea ordered Mrs. Hunner to sponge him with warm water in which she also put sweet-scented herbs, and some perfume to freshen the air. She opened his window in the morning, and made me read aloud edifying passages from the Bible, but not fear-making ones. I read to him the parables, and the Sermon on the Mount. Within a month he had passed several small stones, with much pain, but was the better for it. He began to sit, then rose, and sat at his desk and conferred with Andre Martin.

"Now we shall run away," said Bea.

"But, Bea . . ." I now almost liked Uncle Theodore, having seen him in his weakness, his loneliness. He might now allow me to make automata; and perhaps, too, I was thinking of the heritage. Even Andre Martin was obsequious to me now. As for Bea, her slightest wish sent servants scurrying and running about to obey her.

"But what, Colin?" She turned on me, fierce, her eyes so compelling that I felt myself shrink. "We *must* run away. Now that he trusts me, he will not think that we want to flee, and it will hurt him all the more."

"I don't like hurting people, Bea."

Bea looked at me contemptuously. "They hurt Mother," she said darkly. "They will turn you into what they are. . . . We run away."

Now Bea went in to Uncle Theodore several times a day; he would greet her happily, almost smiling: "What do you want now, Berengere?"

"A little money, Uncle Theodore, I want to start an herb garden. . . ."

Theodore gave her money, and more money to buy new clothes, and Bea then asked for two horses that we might ride by the lake, with a groom behind us, and this was done. The saddle man made a special stirrup for me. The tailors came to fashion our new clothes—still mourning dress but slightly relieved, grey instead of pure black. Now Uncle Theodore asked me to read out the lesson from the Holy Book to the assembled household. And our doors were no longer locked at night.

One afternoon I saw Bea speaking to Valentin. Even he was now better treated. Bea was in riding habit, her small whip in hand, gesturing a little with it, and Valentin nodding, nodding. He followed her with his eyes when she left him, something of his old smile back upon his face.

June had arrived, the trees in full leaf, and soon the summer solstice and the fires of Saint John. One day Bea said, "Colin, we leave tonight."

"Tonight!"

"There is no moon. The horses will be ready saddled; Valentin will see to it. Take only few clothes. We are going to the Hirsches in Geneva—your friend Jacob."

"But, Bea . . ."

She waved impatiently. "We'll leave when everyone is asleep."

"The gateman . . ."

"He will sleep, and all his family."

I packed a few clothes, just enough for a saddlebag. And suddenly I realized I had come to like being here. That showed how soft and pliable I was, and yes, Bea was right. I might become another Uncle Theodore. I went down to dinner when Lucien struck the gong. Bea was already there, in a new dress, and smiling up at Uncle Theodore.

We ate dinner as usual, only the three of us at the enormous table, with its trimmings of silver, and the large vases in the corners, and the smell of dogrose coming through the open windows. Uncle Theodore asked me about my studies. "I am glad to note your progress, Colin. In a little while I shall begin to acquaint you with the details of your heritage. I have looked after it to the best of my ability. Though you are still young, it is not too early to begin understanding these affairs." He then turned to Bea, his face became almost young, his eyes sparkling a little. "As for you, Berengere, I have thought of your request for Italian lessons. It is a pretty language for a woman, and I'm sure you'll do well at it."

Bea rose, smiling, and put her hand on Uncle Theodore's arm, letting her ringleted hair fall forwards, almost against his face. "Thank you, Uncle Theodore . . . you are good to us," she said. He gazed fondly at her, then blushed, and drained his wine cup and rose from the table.

We now sat together for half an hour or so after the dinner. Bea played the clavecin and sang a song or two, and then it was time to retire. "Good night, Uncle Theodore," I said, with more feeling than usual. He was, in his way, a just man, a scrupulous one.

Night; I waited for Bea and she entered my room. "Colin, let me change here. I must dress as a boy." She had cut her hair. "Few will notice two young gentlemen riding through the summer fields."

"What about Valentin? Is he not coming with us?"

"What about him? He has not mentioned it."

"Bea, he goes with us."

"Of course," she replied. She changed into some clothes of mine, and we walked out, our shoes in hand, our bags upon our shoulders. No one was about. We went downstairs softly, to the door that was usually locked; but Bea had the key, perhaps from Lucien.

In the darkness outside, beyond the porch, I saw Valentin's pale face above a black cloth coat. He held two horses by the bridle, soothing them gently so that they did not paw the gravel. Valentin helped me up; Bea sprang onto her mount. "I'm going with you," Valentin said easily. "I've taken the groom's horse." Our horses' hooves were wrapped in cloth, and under the leafy beeches the shadows were thick. The keys to the gates were with Valentin. We closed the gates behind us; I turned to look at the sitting Chinese mandarins.

Outside was another horse, tethered to a chestnut tree. Valentin removed the cloths from our horses' hooves and we galloped away.

We rode for some hours, until the night paled; Valentin confident and splendid, knowing the way. "I've got a compass in my head." He laughed. We rested awhile, as dawn came in its summer rose, and I asked Bea, "How did you do it, Bea? It was so easy." When she and Valentin laughed in reply, it was the first time I heard them laugh together. "Lucien was unwell and I gave him potions," she said. "Valentin took them to him—and took his keys. The old man sleeps soundly now, and the gateman and his family too."

"Bea and I planned it some weeks ago," Valentin said. He was excited and happy. He was, I suddenly realized, a little like Bea.

Skirting Yverdon, we stayed at a small inn just beyond it, then pressed on, resting under tree clusters and tall hedges. In summer's abundance, with the peasants busy in the fields, it was easy to ask the way. We had money with us, and bought some cheese and bread, and on the third day, with the sun rising, saw the ramparts of Geneva and its tall-spired cathedral.

ABRAHAM HIRSCH WAS SCARCELY UP, but he embraced me repeatedly, his eyes joyful. He shouted, "Jacob, Jacob, Colin is here," and I heard Jacob running. We embraced each other, and he said, "We thought we would never see you again."

We sat in the great salon on the beautiful chairs in our dirty clothes, and I told our story. Mrs. Hirsch, who came in her dressing gown, and Sarah, with her nightcap still on her head, exclaimed and cried and kissed Bea repeatedly. I told them about Uncle Theodore. And when I had done, Abraham Hirsch, who had grown more and more apprehensive-looking as our tale wound on, sighed deeply, shook his head, and sighed again.

"Children, children," he said. He got up and paced a little heavily. "But you must be exhausted. First things first. You must eat, refresh yourselves, sleep."

We bathed, slept, and in the evening assembled for dinner, as if we were one family. After dinner Abraham said, "Now we must talk."

He began gently, telling us that of course he would do all he could to help us. "But I am a Jew, and a Jew is always . . . suspect. I am glad you came, but you cannot stay here, and I do not know what to do next. The Duriez of Neuchâtel have long arms and long ears. It will go ill for all of us should they discover you."

"I'll never go back," Valentin said. "I'd rather die. I'll run away tonight, to France, they need soldiers. . . ."

Now I could see the terrible danger in which we had placed the Hirsch family. We might have brought catastrophe upon them. They had been generous, kind; but we were Christians, and children. They could be accused of having attempted to steal us, to murder us. . . .

Jacob squeezed my arm. "Colin, my father is talking frankly, but of course we shall help you. Have no fear."

"You are Baron Duriez, heir to the Duriez fortune. You run away and stay with a Jew; what do you think can be conjectured out of that?" Abraham said.

I looked at Bea. She sat in silence, her eyes glowing, all of her glowing. She had created this situation, and she reveled in it; she was like the priestesses and queens of the Celts, reveling in something that was also tragedy, disaster. . . .

I said unsteadily, "If you wish, I shall return to Neuchâtel alone. But Valentin cannot go back. And as for Bea—"

Bea said, "You will not return to Neuchâtel."

Abraham sighed again. "What must I do, where can I send you? To Amsterdam? To London? Lord Kilvaney is in Yorkshire. I must find a way."

We were not to leave the house, lest we be perceived on the streets. Abraham Hirsch could trust his servants not to babble; the horses had been taken by night and loosed far from the city by a trusted groom. The saddles were removed and buried, for they bore the Duriez baronial escutcheon.

Two days later Abraham Hirsch told us that Isabelle de Thunon was inquiring through her friends in Geneva whether we had been seen in the city. I thought then that I had been wise not to talk about the Hirsch family to Isabelle.

Meanwhile I realized more than ever the quandary of Abraham, who could be accused of holding me to ransom, of trying to convert me.

"Sir," Valentin said to Abraham, "I want to be a soldier. I know horses, and I learnt with Master Chavenaz to repair firearms; I can learn to make cannon."

"Valentin, it is easy to place *you*," Abraham retorted.

The Duriez would not care whether a mere servant was found; but if he was found, he would be guilty of stealing a horse and would probably be broken on the wheel, after having his hands cut off.

We talked with Abraham of many possibilities. What about Voltaire? "He is the last person we could trust," Abraham exclaimed. "He loves to gossip."

Many people came to see Abraham Hirsch to borrow money. They came mostly on foot, not stopping their carriages in front of his house. Hirsch had a valet at the window, forever looking out to open the door.

And one day came a tall man, dressed in the garb of a Moor. Bea and I noticed him because he did stop his elegant coach in front of the house. He was handsome, and clad in white, with a cloth about his head.

"It is Abdul Reza, my father's great friend," Jacob said. "He is a merchant and a prince, but he is also a diplomat, entrusted with affairs of state."

That evening, once again, we spoke of our problem. I do not remember why I mentioned Voltaire's play, *The Orphan of China*, which had been shown in Lausanne. "The Chinese are crazy about automata, Sir," I said. "This I have heard, even in Neuchâtel. As are also the Indian rajahs and sultans of the Ottoman Empire."

"Heaven be praised," Abraham exclaimed. "Surely my mind grows dull. Colin, Bea, of course, if you are ready for adventure, even perils, then perhaps you might go to China or to India."

"With your friend Abdul Reza," Bea said.

"How do you know?" Abraham stared at her nonplussed. "Did you hear our converse?"

"Oh no, Sir, but I guessed, when I saw him enter your house this morning," Bea replied.

"You must be able to read minds," Abraham said. "This very morning Abdul Reza spoke to me of a venture in China. To repair and build automata, and to make clocks and watches in China itself. The country has many millions, and Geneva sends clocks and England sends automata to the Court of the Emperor. They need craftsmen, however, and perhaps—"

And so it was decided. Bea decided; afterwards I asked her, "Bea, how did you know?"

"When I saw Abdul Reza, I knew he would be able to help us. Do not ask me how; I cannot explain how the certainty came to me."

Abraham told us about the factories of the English in Canton where they repaired and even constructed some clocks. Geneva had been asked to send them two craftsmen to maintain the mechanisms of the automata at the Court of the Chinese Emperor. "Till now the Jesuits did it," Abraham said. "They have been in China for a century. But they are few in number and getting aged. Now it is the companies who want trade, clocks and automata, music boxes, and other devices to attract the Chinese mandarins."

"I'm willing to go," I said. Dreams of going to China, of making a fortune, assailed my spirit. And Bea would be with me.

Some days went by. I spent my time with Jacob, for I never had enough of listening to him, and now I wanted a trove of knowledge to store in mind. I began to read whatever books there were on China in the Hirsch library, and found a good many written by Jesuits, praising China greatly, and her institutions and Master Confucius. Other reports, by the English, were not so laudatory.

We talked. How we talked. Of God and His plans for man, of Jean Jacques Rousseau, reckoned an impious man. Of the *Encyclopedia* of Diderot, condemned in France to be burnt publicly. And every night we peered again at the sky, at the planets and the faraway stars. We discussed electricity, and whether trees were sentient, and were there beings on other planets under other suns than ours?

IN THAT AUGUST, BETWEEN ENGLAND and France there was fighting over the possession of Acadia in the New World.

The Marquis de Sancerre of France was in Geneva, Lausanne, and Berne, fitting out a battalion of Swiss mercenaries to fight in Acadia for the French settlements there. He also recruited women, even of evil repute, for the settlers in the New World.

Abraham secured for Valentin the post of cornet—a command of ten men, landless peasants, each one bought with a purse of five livres to go off to the war in Acadia on the French side. He fitted the men and bought new clothes for Valentin, and filled a purse for him that he might go as a gentleman's child, albeit a penurious one. There were many penurious gentlemen from Lausanne in all the wars.

Dashing in his new suit, white hose and buckled shoes, and a plumed three-cornered hat, Valentin left, saying to me, "God be with ye," and to Bea, with shining eyes, "Bea, your dreams are strong dreams, they make the world come true." I had not known Valentin to say such things before.

Valentin hugged me. "Write to me, Colin. I do not write easily, but I shall scrawl some words, even if only to say: 'Brother, I am well.' "

Abdul Reza came again—to see us. He glanced keenly at us, then asked us to tell him our story. I told him, but he looked at Bea. "It is you, Damozel, who planned the running away?"

"I did," Bea said.

He nodded thoughtfully.

He would take us with him. He would find work for us to do, and more than work. "Provided ye be not timorous, fainthearted, you will do well."

And we replied, Bea and I, "We are not afraid, Prince Reza."

Jacob gave me many books: Shakespeare's plays, and the *Dictionary of the English Language* by Samuel Johnson, among them. "I too shall travel, soon, Colin; perhaps I shall come to see you in China," he said. "Surely you will learn much there."

Abraham gave me a set of small tools, jewel-like in their neat perfection—a clockmaker's set—and with these I could make the beautiful mechanical parts for automata. "You have a talent, Colin. Your father spoke to me about it. He said you had more talent than he ever had. Use it well. The world is going to be changed by the machine."

ONE NIGHT IN SEPTEMBER we left Geneva by berline, Bea continuing to dress as a boy, with two servants to attend us. We arrived in Marseilles within seven days, and there came under the care of Abdul Reza, merchant-prince and diplomat.

⊰ *Six* ⊱

Anno Domini 1756–1757

MARSEILLES SPARKLED BETWEEN SUN and water. In its muddy lanes, hemmed in by crowded hovels, a multitude of diverse garb and color squeezed and brawled. Levantines and Moors, Italians and French, Negro slaves and Dane whalers jostled one another on its docks. In the foul streets men walked with black umbrellas above their heads, to ward off the filth thrown from upper windows. Mariners of all lands, with tattoos on their arms and cutlasses in their belts, swaggered about, looking for women. The women huddled in doorways, calling out to passersby; when they walked, their hips swung like small boats dancing on the sea. There were processions with bells and crosses to bless the ships. Beggars and pilgrims crowded the churches; the bells of Saint Mary's upon the promontory above the city tolled frequently; and murderers on the way to the rack would kneel and cross themselves when they heard the chimes for sailors' souls.

I saw the Huguenot galley slaves, condemned to row the King's ships all their lives, because of the Religion. Files of men, heavy irons round their necks, hands, and feet, clanged past us, singing the great Martin Luther's hymn:

A mighty fortress is our God

Or the canticle of the galley slaves:

And to see them thus driven to martyrdom for their faith, all in the name of a merciful God, made me both angry and sick with pain. I wanted to sing with them, but Bea restrained me. About us, the scum of Marseilles threw filth, urine in pails, and rotten food at them.

The black plague had been brought to Marseilles in the year 1720 by the *Great Saint Anthony*, a vessel carrying silk and spices from the Orient, and it was still remembered. "I was a boy of seven then, coming with my father on a Levantine prow from Tangiers," Prince Abdul Reza told us. "The plague killed many thousands, but not our people; we washed cleanly five times a day, praying to Allah, and He protected us."

Abdul Reza was not only wealthy, of noble descent, but a learned man, speaking many languages and traveling many lands, going from one to the other as easily as though changing a shirt. He was kind with a distant kindness that put us at ease. He had many children, he told us, thirteen or perhaps more, some older than ourselves. And many wives. Each day he gave us an hour of his time, his servant Ismail attending. He made us talk, and would then teach us of the world. History, geography, and facts of wars and men, and politics and trade. All that is useful and not in books I learnt from him.

The past blurred; the sharpness of grief went. I was possessed by eagerness for the unknown, my mind yearning for those fabulous lands and all they held in store. I watched Abdul Reza, his gestures, his talk, his composed behavior, the calm with which he listened. "See," he said, "we have but to cross the wine-colored sea which begins at Marseilles to step on the road to a hundred kingdoms."

The *Cardus* was a goodly three-master, a merchantman of beauty, armed with five cannon, seemingly top-heavy with sails large and small, with rigged fixed and movable, but out at sea, like a swallow, winging at the slightest breeze. She hoisted a French flag and was run by Captain Xavier Fournier.

Besides Abdul Reza, his fifteen domestics, and two veiled girls, there were on the upper deck three Jesuits, two Frenchmen of the French East India Company, and a Dutch merchant, Heer van Tromp, who seemed to know Abdul Reza well, for he saluted him twice a day. On the lower deck was a group of French landless peasants going to the Canaries and to Africa, some Muslim traders, and some Portuguese mercenaries.

The Jesuits had numerous wooden cases with them, containing astronomical instruments, books, and other valuable things for the Imperial Court in Peking. Father Pierre Amigot, a portly Frenchman from Provence, expostulated loudly with the sailors, beseeching them not to drop the boxes, wiping his forehead, moist with anguish and heat. Messieurs Davignon and de Recasse were going as replacements to Pondicherry, where the agents of the French East India Company died of fever quickly. Thus the *Cardus* was a ship of all nations, and so were the sailors, a motley crowd, many with the marks of the whip upon their backs.

Captain Fournier was swarthy, his three-cornered hat concealing thick curly hair that denoted Negro blood. He had great handsomeness about his lithe body, and prowled the decks like a cat, ever alert. I never saw him angry, but discovered him implacable, for on the journey one sailor was to be whipped to death and two more shot off the cannons' mouths. Three quartermasters helped to rule the mariners, with whips in their hands and pistols in their belts.

The crew, sweating, brought up the gangplank many crates and barrels, sweet water and cider for the scurvy, and a consignment of squealing pigs to be landed in the Canaries.

Headsails swollen with the breeze, her cannon gleaming, the *Cardus* glided towards Teneriffe. "Let us pray that we do not encounter pirates off the Barbary Coast," Father Pierre Amigot said. Every third day Captain Fournier exercised us in the handling of pistols and pikes and axes, in case we were attacked by a pirate vessel. Bea, dressed as a boy and now called Benoit, proved an excellent marksman, far better than I.

She and I occupied the same small cubbyhole, our beds two hammocks, and beyond it was the room where Abdul Reza and Captain Fournier sat and conferred and Captain Fournier slept at night. There seemed a perfect ease between them, though Fournier was Catholic and devoutly attended the Jesuits' Mass. But on the high seas, in this new world of trade, one shouldered many races and creeds; and religion seemed not as important as courage, valor, and acumen.

Fournier's father had come from the Louisiana, sailing ships across the world for anyone who paid well. He had been twelve when his father's galleon, with gold and spices, had come to Marseilles. Abdul Reza's father had adopted young Xavier when his father had died of the plague. His mother, a native from the Antilles, had died quickly, too, of the consumption, which killed so many coming from the tropic islands to Europe.

"My father believed that wealth cannot be created without good men," Reza said to us. "He rescued many Christians and never pressed them for conversion. Xavier continues to serve me, as his father did my father."

From a distance we saw Teneriffe's volcano, a massive cloud above its cone. The houses were white-bleached and people spoke a mixture of Portuguese and other languages—the lascar tongue, lingua franca on the high seas. We took on sweet water and limes and olives, flour and goats and salted meat and cabbages; the pigs were disembarked, only five having died on the way. Bea and I tasted oranges, luscious fruit sold in baskets by women in black with veils upon their heads. We had never tasted such fruit before, and this seemed a portent of more pleasures to come.

Pleasure. Delight at discovering my own body, myself. It came upon me now, as we sailed onwards, my senses unfettered, unashamed, at last. Until then, body had been guilt; what went on in this packet of flesh was censored and blamable, and my club foot had made it worse. But now, perhaps because of Fournier and Abdul Reza, both so masculine, so at ease in their own skins, I knew that not all urges were wickedness to be expunged. Abdul Reza was aware of my emotions. "You shall become a man, Colin, and a man may be pious, but must also be thankful for the bounties of God."

And so at full fourteen I felt my body change, charged with new power. I opened my shirt to the dawn wind and felt it caress my skin. The ship's roll, far from unsettling me, reconciled me to my limp, for on deck even the able-footed trod with spread legs to keep their balance. I could now climb the mast rigging, pull at the ropes, and set the bowsprit sails. I hauled myself up to the lookout to watch the horizon, and

Fournier showed me his navigation instruments and loaned me his spy glass.

As we neared the equator, Abdul Reza had his servants supply us with tunics and loose pantaloons of fine muslin so that we were cool and in comfort; the two Frenchmen and Heer van Tromp, however, stuck to their hose and coats and sweated mightily. "It is my habit; in the Spice Islands it is a weakness to dress like the natives," said Heer van Tromp. "One must remain disciplined." For the sake of discipline, he paced the deck each morning, either reading aloud from a large Bible he carried with him or reciting verses of it by heart. He carried a consignment of Bibles sent by the Dutch East India Company to Batavia, the capital of the Dutch settlements in the Spice Islands, where Dutchmen became intoxicated with soft living, consorted with dusky women, bred many bastards, and lost their religion and their character.

The Jesuits on board, Father Pierre Amigot and Brother Laurence Shane, a Scotsman, also wore looser cotton robes instead of black cassocks, but not so Father Oliveiro, who was a Spaniard and the delegate of the Apostolic Vicariate for the Propagation of the Faith. He had been sent to combat laxity and loose living among the Jesuits in India and China, for they too, it was said, became changed, faith weakened, resolve dulled, as conversion to Catholicism no longer aroused immense ardor in their souls.

"He believes in *auto-da-fes*, burning people like you and me," Abdul Reza said half-jokingly to me.

On a ship, the hours are long, and the lulling sway loosens the tongue. Pierre Amigot, Laurence Shane, and I met every day on deck, and we talked a great deal.

At night the two veiled girls Abdul Reza had brought with him were locked in a room next to his. The Jesuits thought they were his wives, but Ismail told us, "My master rescued them from a pirate ship selling slaves in the slave market of Tangiers. Since they were blond and blue-eyed and spoke French, he took them to France, trying to find their parents, but they had forgotten their own names. He is taking them to India to marry them off to some prince. They are virgins." They came on deck sometimes in their silks and gauze, and the perfume of sandalwood and jasmine enchanted me.

"It is better than to enter a convent or to be sold in a brothel," Bea said. She too was changing, growing; unlike me, however, she spent a great deal of time alone in our cabin. "My brother Benoit feels the seasickness," I said.

I became berry brown; Ismail cropped my hair and called me Sinbad the Sailor. I never tired of watching the flying fish, in greal shoals of silver arrows, and the porpoises leaping out of the water and twisting back into it. Ismail pointed out some sharks following our ship with persistent smoothness, and one day as we went southwards we saw the spout of whales, white jets against the blue horizon.

Only one thing had marred the voyage so far: crossing the equator, the sailors had become drunk, since it was the custom to open some barrels of wine to celebrate the crossing. But Fournier cut short the revels, ordering all sails up to catch the rising breeze, for we had been somewhat becalmed. One of the sailors, drunk, heaved a knife at Fournier, and a clamor of revolt began. Fournier and his three quartermasters appeared with pistols; there were muskets in the hands of the two Frenchmen and the three Jesuits and Heer van Tromp. Ismail and the other servants showed axes and pikes. Two leaders of the revolt were shot off the mouths of cannon, and two more were whipped, one dying the next day.

BECAUSE THE JESUITS, ABDUL REZA, and we were bound for China, it was natural that we spoke much of that land. Pierre Amigot soon knew I was to put my skill in clocks and automata at the disposal of some factory there.

"Which one?" he had asked.

Abdul Reza had warned me to reply, "The English one, at Canton." It was a lie, and I blushed, but Amigot seemed satisfied.

"You'll see little of the country then, you and your brother. The Chinese do not let foreigners into the city of Canton; they are confined to a narrow strip of land where the foreign factories and docks for foreign ships are permitted."

Brother Laurence Shane was skilled at drawing, an able repairer of clocks and a musician. He was twenty-five years old, and we felt near to each other. He told me how John Knox had driven the Catholic families out of Scotland; Brother Laurence's family had emigrated to France, where he had become a Jesuit at the school for English and Scottish Catholics.

Pierre Amigot, of benevolent mien and ruthless purpose, paced the deck with me, his voice cradled by the seawind, and gave me a glowing picture of his order. Perhaps he hoped that one day I would remember his words and become converted.

The Jesuits, founded by Ignatius de Loyola, a soldier-adventurer of genius, were an organism created to enforce the sway of Catholic Rome upon the world. It had battled the Muslims, and when the Arabs were driven out of Europe, had turned its might and the talent of its men against the Reformed Church of Martin Luther. Ardent and dedicated, disciplined, obedient, and learned, the order was also wealthy, for kings and princes endowed it when it so served their political aims.

But Martin Luther's Reformed Church had been a great flood against Rome's edicts, and the Jesuits had battled hard for nigh two centuries against Protestantism, using every trick: guile and bribery, intrigue, and slaughter. They had failed in England, Germany, Sweden; but in Italy, France, and Spain, success had crowned their efforts. It was due to a Jesuit, Father la Chaise, confessor to the French King's mistress, Madame de Maintenon, that in 1688 the French King had turned against the Huguenots. Through torture, the galleys, and savage suppression, nearly three hundred thousand French men and women had died for the Religion in their own country. And it was Abdul Reza who told me how it had come about.

"The Jesuits are a crusading order, but now their days are numbered. The flame has gone out of them. For they have failed in both India and China," said Abdul Reza.

"And in Japan, Christianity has been wiped out in bloodshed. The Japanese make any foreign trader who comes to their shores walk on the cross. And some do, for the sake of commerce."

Where Amigot spoke with honeyed enthusiasm, Laurence

Shane, on the contrary, blurted out despair. "Your Prince Reza is right, Colin. We have failed.

"I shall talk to you only of China, since you are going there, as we are."

The conversion of China was a long-planned Jesuit policy. In 1599 Matteo Ricci, a Jesuit astronomer, had succeeded in obtaining permission to enter the Empire; he was received in audience and presented the Ming dynasty emperor with a watch and a clock. His skill in predicting eclipses of the sun and sundry other heavenly accidents won him the official position of Keeper of the Astronomy Bureau. And since then, for 150 years, Jesuits had in succession been the chief astronomers of the Chinese emperors.

They had thus, insidiously, begun to convert the Empire, proceeding not among the poor but at the highest level, among mandarins and ministers of state. They translated Chinese books; through them, knowledge of China and admiration for her wisdom, her government, and her sage, Confucius, had pervaded Europe and seized the imagination of philosophers such as Voltaire.

"We did everything to please the Chinese," Laurence said bitterly. "We dressed as mandarins, almost became Chinese. We intrigued, accumulated property. We made cannon and firepieces for the emperors." Laurence Shane twisted his body as does a tortured man, contemplating the deviousness of the sect to which he had pledged himself.

"And when the Ming dynasty fell, conquered by the Manchus, we abandoned the Ming and served the new conqueror. All this for the greater glory of God," said Laurence.

"But God is not mocked," Laurence Shane continued. "Then occurred the Battle of the Rites.

"You know how the Chinese venerate their ancestors; in each house is a special pavilion where the forebears' soul-tablets are housed and ceremonies performed to commemorate them. Our order maintained that this was perfectly compatible with Christian morality and that we should allow ancestor worship if we wanted China to become converted.

"And by 1700, we had some three hundred thousand converts. The Manchu emperors who conquered China in

1644 continued their favor to us, since we were able to get them cannon from the Portuguese to help them subdue their recalcitrant Chinese subjects.

"By now, Dominicans and Franciscans, ignorant of Chinese tradition, denounced us as abetting idolatry. Rome sent a pious and obtuse bigot to investigate. He came in 1704 and denounced ancestor veneration, condemned the rites; all who disobeyed to be excommunicated.

"Within six months we lost almost all our converts.

"From 1704 to today is more than half a century, and still the quarrel of the rites goes on. Our order still pleads in Rome, but we have lost. The Chinese have been thoroughly insulted by the popes and their edicts; there have been religious persecutions in China because of their denying the Chinese converts the right to venerate their ancestors.

"We are still tolerated at the Manchu Court in Peking, because we are useful at repairing clocks and automata, designing architectural pavilions and gardens, and keeping the calendar in order. But Christianity cannot be taught, no missionary work is tolerated, and no Manchu is allowed to become a Christian."

"But if you know all this, Brother Laurence," I hazarded, "why then are you going to China?"

He shrugged, not answering, but took his recorder and softly blew an air upon it. Often Laurence would entertain us with music. He played many love songs, including one from Provence, called "Magali."

> O Magali my most beloved
> The sky above is full of stars
> But the wind drops and the stars fade
> When you appear . . .

Pierre Amigot would pause to listen, smiling his indulgent Jesuit smile, and sometimes hum a little with us.

The next day I asked again. "Brother Laurence, my soul is worried, methinks it is sinful to do what one does not believe in."

"Colin, perhaps because I *know* it is hopeless, therefore do I go," Laurence replied. "I want to see how all our guile, and cleverness, and talent, has been turned into making us useful marionettes in Peking—something like the automata you make so skillfully."

For now, to while away the hours, I had made, out of wood, leaping frogs, a running large cockroach, and even a snake; when wound up these animals moved on the deck, to everyone's amusement.

"I too shall repair clocks and automata, build fountains, perhaps paint the portraits of the Emperor's favorites and teach some astronomy. And all the time I shall be in torment, in an agony of doubt. But perhaps this is what God has intended for me? It is expiation for the sins of our condition," Laurence Shane said.

As we sailed southwards the winds and the oceans became wilder. In the night the boat rocked greatly, and Bea said the stars made music.

She had dreams; I heard her mutter. But no nightmare came to me.

I watched Laurence go to Bea. He sat on deck, four arms' lengths from her, and although they never seemed to talk to each other, yet I had the strong feeling that they were talking. After all, he was a Celt too, like Mother, like Bea.

He would bring the recorder to his lips and blow a gentle music. It made my heart beat faster. I fancied I had heard it in my dreams.

I did not join them; it would have been an intrusion.

It seemed to me Laurence knew that Benoit was Bea. Perhaps it was the howling wind, the heaving sea, which made me so fanciful.

BEA STARTED WITH A chisel and pieces of wood. Her fingers, like mine, itched to work, not to lose their cunning. She made a face, two faces. One of them was Laurence Shane's. I asked her what the other one was. "Oliveiro, the Grand Inquisitor."

"Oh, Bea, he is simply a man full of anger."

"He is like Antoine," Bea replied.

THE MARINERS TOLD MANY tales of shipwreck, for it is the drowned who scream in the ocean gales. Though it was almost October in Europe, here summer began. Captain Fournier changed the flag of the *Cardus* to a Dutch one.

"From now on there will be Engish vessels and men-of-war about; and England is at war with France," Abdul Reza said. "We might be taken as war booty by the English if we hazard a French flag."

One night the long dark waves like mountainous walls before and behind us tossed our ship; the sky was low and menacing. It engulfed the ocean, and Ismail said the wicked became fish, condemned to live forever in the limitless storms. Even I had to lie in the hammock for a while, such was the sway. As for Bea, she brooded and was not well. Suddenly she whispered to me, "Colin, I need some cloth and water." Womanhood had come to her in the storm. I put my arms around her when she had cleaned herself of the blood, and both of us cried for Mother and Father and clung fiercely to each other. We had nothing else in the world.

The storm took no heed of van Tromp reciting the Holy Book and the three Jesuits singing canticles to the Mother of God. It roared and shook us; Captain Fournier was up and about night and day.

One night there was a loud crack, the *Cardus* listed badly, and we were thrown out of our hammocks. We tied ourselves to the small empty barrels by our side, as Fournier had taught us to do in case of danger by shipwreck. But now we heard screaming and crying on deck: "Man overboard, man overboard!"

Van Tromp was shouting, "No, it is no use," and then Oliveiro's great bass recited the *de profundis* for the dead.

Ismail came in, streaming wet. "It is one of the Jesuits, the young one. The mast broke in the storm and fell upon a sailor, and the Jesuit rushed to save him from being caught under the splintered beam and was carried off by a wave."

Laurence. Laurence Shane.

"Oh, Bea, Bea, why did you carve his head?"

"It was not I," she said. "But he wanted to die, he told me so. He had nothing left, no faith. He doubted God, and that was like Hell for him."

HEER VAN TROMP, PRINCE ABDUL REZA, and Xavier Fournier sat in conference to decide whether to seek help at the Dutch Table Bay settlement or carry the damaged ship farther, to Delagoa Bay. The Table Bay settlement was ruled by the Dutch East India Company, notorious for their inhospitable conduct towards any ships save their own. It was said that officers of the Company had been expelled, or even imprisoned, merely for being civil to passing ships.

Delagoa Bay was Portuguese; and the Portuguese served anyone, mingled with everyone, provided they were paid. "They have the true spirit of the seas," Fournier said.

But van Tromp persuaded them to try Table Bay. It was now named Cape Town and was a bastion of the Reformed Church. The settlers had prospered, owning numerous slaves on great farms and abundant cattle. They sent wheat on Company ships to feed the Netherlands. But all the settlers were subjects of the Company, which was as despotic as any Eastern potentiary. Even van Tromp, wagging his head ponderously, said, "The Company treats even the free burghers as its domestics. However, I know the present governor, Meinheer Ryk Tulbagh; he allows foreign ships to anchor, though the price is heavy and there are many vexations."

We limped into Table Bay, four small skiffs with armed soldiers surrounding our vessel as if we were pirates. They were commanded by Portmaster Huyghens, a truculent man who sent his soldiers into every corner of our vessel and down the hold, and would have ransacked our trunks but that Heer van Tromp produced documents, including a letter from the Company in Amsterdam requesting courtesy. Since at least five of the seventeen Company lords had signed the letter, Portmaster Huyghens grudgingly relented. Still, he took down our names, ages, religions, and destinations, and asked for a list of the goods we carried. He was looking for something on which to vent his temper and concentrated on Abdul Reza, unruffled, in his robes and turban.

"A prince—a black man!" he shouted rudely. "We know such princes. . . . He must post a surety. Know you that in

Batavia some of these Mohammedans have dared to revolt against us?"

Abdul Reza stood impassive. Van Tromp whispered to the portmaster that he was a very important man, an ambassador as well as a great merchant-prince, well thought of in Amsterdam and by the Company. But Huyghens said he could not disembark, "for, Meinheer, they are all black here, and it would be bad for their souls to see a black man as a lord."

The two Frenchmen and the Jesuits went down at Cape Town to search for the local Catholics, and Fournier went with van Tromp to find a contractor to repair the mast. We stayed on board with Abdul Reza, his servants, and the two girls.

Bea said, "I won't go down, Colin."

"Of course not, Bea."

Bea always knew what had to be done, and it was well of her to stay with Abdul Reza.

I watched the port from the deck, and noted how evilly the black men were treated. Slaves were working with chains upon them, iron collars round their necks, tied to each other like the galley men in Marseilles.

The mast was repaired. Each piece of wood, barrel of water, and pound of cordage was inspected. Fournier swore mightily and looked murderous, he too being partly black.

Fathers Amigot and Oliveiro returned to the ship, having been refused permission to stay with the Jesuits of Cape Town. Jesuits and Dominicans in the previous century had begun missions to the natives, pleading with the farmers to treat them with humanity. The Reformed Church now sent its predicants and pastors from Holland to watch over the morals of the Dutch settlers, especially to prevent them from taking black women and breeding mongrels. They brought out Dutch women for the farmers, and the remaining Jesuits were preparing to leave the country for Paraguay.

With wind-filled sails we crossed the Indian Ocean; though the wind was against us, such was the cunning of the sails that we went *vent debout*, encountering only one more ship, an English frigate.

The *Cardus* exchanged salutes with the *Sea Hawk*. Its English captain expressed the wish to visit us. The Jesuits donned their best cassocks of fine dark wool with white collars. Prince Reza wore his usual white damask gown, but his domestics looked excellent in turbans and sashes of green and gold. Messieurs Davignon and de Recasse were most uneasy, being French, but made brave countenance, and donned satin coats and plumed hats.

Captain Langley came aboard, entertained with the music of flutes, two drums, and clarinets—an air of southern India played by Reza's domestics. He made no comment and asked only for our names and destinations, and, saluting the Frenchmen, he inquired whether they were replacements for the Pondicherry settlement.

"That we are," they said, wondering that he should be so well informed.

"I shall then give you a safe-conduct," Captain Langley said.

After he left, we agreed that he was a gentleman of excellent manners. The English East India Company, although merciless to its enemies and policing its new Indian possessions with extreme care, did not indulge in useless cruelties. And giving a safe-conduct to the two Frenchmen was a noble act.

We reached Cochin on the coast of Malabar, where Abdul Reza was met by a crowd of friends, with retainers and servants, umbrellas and palanquins, and musicians; Reza had sent Ismail ahead in a small boat to warn of his arrival.

Cochin was drenched in sun that day. With its white houses, green palms, and banyan trees, its multitudes walking about in clothes of many colors, it seemed an enchanted land to me. Winter cold did not exist here. Balm was in the air, and the perfume of flowers. Such a press of people; the women lovely, with blossoms in their hair, their naked feet in sandals. We were taken to a great palace, far larger than anything I had ever seen, with inner gardens, and courtyards with fountains that kept the air cool.

Mohammed Rashid, Reza's friend, was an imposing man, with a fine beard and straight nose. He looked at us curiously as we saluted him, and then he laughed. "Abdul, you are forever rescuing Christians." We were given rooms of pale marble, with many cushions and rugs on the floors. A small courtyard, separated by a carved screen of ivory, exquisite as Mother's lace, had a fountain in its midst, dispensing coolness and the music of water. I felt humbled. Were these "infidels"? They were most kind, as the Jew Abraham Hirsch, and his family, had been. We had had more charity from them than from our own people.

That night I wrote a long letter to Jacob, telling him of the voyage and what I had learnt. "These lands are strange and marvelous, yet my heart is at ease, and I but yearn for us to meet again."

In Cochin I discarded my boy's clothes, and was dressed by two maidservants in the costume of the country—fine trousers of silk, a flowing pleated skirt, a bodice with short sleeves topped by a silk jacket, and a veil of thin gauze round my head. I looked at myself in the tall mirror, which came from Venice. For here were a thousand things from Europe as well as Asia, a profusion that only wealth could bring together.

The gauze veil about my hair and neck, studded with star sapphires, set off my eyes, and the maids sighed with pleasure at the sight. My eyes. Sapphire now, the irises changing, and deep inside that golden glint which made them green with the mood of my soul and the temper of the weather.

I dismissed the maids and sat on the cushions and my soul gathered itself, and slowly, gently, insidious as the scent of the blossoms in the courtyard, my being possessed the room. I grew into my own power, and the dream came to me that I had waited for during the long sea voyage—Mother, in her white gown, raising her arms for the mistletoe falling from the sacred oak and crowning me. "Thou art Queen, my daughter. Use the Gift well."

Colin came in, exclaiming, "Bea, how beautiful you are!" and I smiled. We are the two faces of the Oneness, he the opposite of all I am, and this binds us as day and night are bound.

Colin is rapt in enchantment. He fingers everything, picks up enamel and inlays and musical instruments that lie about for min-

strels to entertain us if we wish, and says, "I wonder how is it done." His fingers flex and unflex.

He carries with him Laurence's recorder; Pierre Amigot gave it to him.

Laurence Shane. He sat by my side, letting his soul roam out of his body and reach mine. He knew the desolation of the hypocrisy he lived. The ancient voices came to him then, and he chose the thunder and the whirling glory of water. Or rather it chose him.

I am the last of my race. The very last, I know. Perhaps there are others with the Gift, in other lands. But now I know that we shall not be able to make the undead live again; save, perhaps, if suddenly, through some dazzling encounter, our separate worlds come together— Colin's world and mine.

Mother, what shall I do with this power then? I feel it in me. I can compel some minds, I can know their thoughts. But what will happen to me? What must I become?

GREAT IS ABDUL REZA'S influence here on the Malabar coast. Men bow to him, touching their breast with their right hand. The courtyard is filled with supplicants waiting their turn to see him. Mohammed Rashid sends couriers out on horseback, and when they return, the two men confer, drinking mint tea, with narghiles kept going by deaf slaves. The Maharajah of Cochin entertains Reza in a great feast, at which only men are present. I am among them, for Abdul Reza treats me as a son. Men smile at me and hand me sweetmeats and speak to me gently, and I learn how to behave by looking at them.

Cochin's Maharajah likes new inventions. Foreigners bring quaint and curious objects to his Court. He employs men of all religions. Though a Brahmin, his minister is a Muslim. He has many clocks, but does not want them wound up, for the priests have told him it is fatal to have a sinister machine erode time by counting it.

Abdul Reza, who still gives Bea and me an hour a day of converse—though even at night he works, dictating to his

three secretaries—tells me of the trouble the Christians brought
to the Malabar coast.

The Portuguese and Spaniards came, and with slaughter
and the cross and *autodafes* they converted and pillaged. The
Jesuits were here too. Dressed as Brahmin priests, they sought
to integrate Brahmin rites into Catholicism. But here too came
Cardinal de Tournon, and other rigorous prelates of Rome,
and condemned what were called the "Malabar rites": cremation of bodies at death, the Brahmin scriptures.

Here too, within three months of the edict, the Jesuits lost
all their high-caste converts; only some untouchables remained,
who, having no other hope, clung to the new creed and its
promise of paradise.

In Cochin there was a large synagogue, and several small
ones, for almost fifteen thousand Jews had fled the Inquisition of Spain and settled here, beginning three centuries ago.

Ismail took me to see the rabbi, a small, wizened man who
looked to me exactly like a Malabari.

The synagogue was paved entirely with blue and white
tiles from China. "We have synagogues in many cities of
India," the rabbi said. He blessed me, pleased to hear of
Abraham Hirsch and my affection for him. "We are all over
the world, hunted from one place to another," he said of his
people.

Besides mosques and Christian churches and synagogues,
Cochin had a multitude of Hindu temples and shrines, with a
myriad gods, elephants caparisoned in silk in the courtyards,
flowers and incense and gold thick upon their altars. Corpses
covered in blossoms were taken to the burning sites by the
river; the funeral processions were led by low-caste men shouting and singing and dancing, for death was but the passing
through life's gate into another life, and a cause for glee. And
sometimes a widow would burn. Dressed in dazzling clothes,
with jewels on her arms and round her waist, in her nostrils
and ears and upon her head, she would throw herself into
her husband's funeral pyre.

I saw one of these, for Ismail took me. A great crowd was
attending, all holding wreaths of flowers and chanting praises
to the woman as she seemed to dance in the flames; their

singing and the noise of drums and flutes was so loud that no one could tell whether she screamed.

Watching her, I thought of Mother running into the fire after Father, and I wept, great sobs racking me, until Ismail took me home.

Reza's two wards were bestowed as wives upon a young prince. The marriage revels lasted seven days, under huge tents of crimson and gold festooned with flowers. Bea sat with the women under one great tent, and I with the men. The maidens were prepared some days ahead, washed twice daily with perfumed water, their hair combed and scented with oil, their body hair meticulously plucked, and old women instructing them in the arts of love. The astrologers determined the most propitious hour. Braziers were burnt, and all the ceremonies were performed by Brahmins, naked to the waist save for the white cord round their left shoulder.

Afterwards the young prince, clad in white and covered in jewels, sat under a dais with his two wives a littler lower than he. I glanced at their faces. Were they happy? Bea, from the women's talk, assured me they were joyous, having been captured young, knowing nothing else but sequestration, and glad at the prospect of being together, and with much company, many other women, in the harem of a good-looking young prince. "See," Bea said, "one is what one is disciplined and taught to be. Uncle Theodore knew that, Colin."

After the marriage we watched a battle between elephants, which the Maharajah held once a season in the courtyard in front of the palace. It was a cruel sight and I shut my eyes when one beast was gored and trampled and died slowly, its trumpeting filling the air.

"You have a tender heart, Colin," Ismail said. He had now become a freeman, Reza having released him from bondage, and could become anything he wanted. He wanted first of all to marry a Malabari woman, "for they are the most beautiful I know." Many sailors had wives on the Malabar coast who waited for them between sea voyages.

Father Pierre Amigot came to call on Abdul Reza. Reza received him in one of the main rooms for guests, and asked Bea and me to come. Amigot's eyes bulged when he saw "Benoit's" transformation. Bea was in pale blue-green silk that changed color as the light struck it, and a gauze veil studded with gems was drawn half across her face, a gesture of modesty she had learnt from the women here. Not only Amigot stared, but I saw Abdul Reza also look at her with surprise, and then fixedly. Something changed. The air became charged with a new and vibrant energy, which I felt but could not name. I looked at Abdul Reza's face and it reminded me of Uncle Theodore looking up at Bea as her ringlets almost touched his cheek.

Amigot began a plea for my services. "You know, my Lord Reza, of the Palace of Perfect Harmony, in Peking. Yuan Ming Yuan, the Chinese call it, and it is one of the world's great wonders. In it are innumerable buildings and gardens, the replica of all the famous landscapes and architecture and the many temples of China's diverse religions, of exquisite beauty. All manner of trees and flowers, and birds and beasts, and all manner of foreign things too are there. For the last twenty years we have been the architects, painters, and craftsmen of the Court. The Emperor commissioned us to supply him with the plans and drawings of Versailles and other famous buildings in Europe, for he has begun to build an addition to the Yuan Ming Yuan, of European style and filled with European objects—including clocks and automata, of which he and all at Court have many."

Amigot was bringing back with him a good many architectural drawings as well as some very precious and rare automata. "We hope to be allowed a Christian church within the palace, since our faith has struck root in the Chinese Empire. A mosque is also being built in the palace," he added, to placate Abdul Reza.

"He wants you, needs you, now that Laurence is dead, to repair the automata and wind the watches and clocks of the Emperor," Bea's mind said to me.

Abdul Reza blandly asked Amigot questions about the foreign wing of the palace. "I have been away in France collecting more plans, devices, and instruments," Amigot replied. "There is an Italian painter at the Chinese Court, Father Castiglione. He has been in China since 1715. Emperor Tsienlung holds him in high esteem; he is the architect-in-chief of the palace. Should you and your protégés come to

Peking, Lord Reza, we would be greatly honored. As for young Colin here, he is skilled and perhaps deserves more than to serve the English in Canton."

I blushed. The lie I had told hung heavy upon me. Bea saved me from embarrassment. "Our father's great friend, Lord John Kilvaney, recommended us. We shall certainly be well cared for," she said with some hauteur.

Abdul Reza again stared at her, in admiration and surprise. And she turned her face towards him and drew the transparent gauze across it, smiling secretly, her eyelids drooping upon her emerald eyes.

Father Amigot withdrew. He lived at the large compound of the Jesuit school of Cochin; Oliveiro, he told us, was afflicted with a tenacious bloody flux, and should he not recover promptly, Amigot would set forth with us alone. "For I dare not delay any longer. The Emperor awaits the plans."

When he had gone, Abdul Reza rose, tall and handsome in his white robes. "Damozel, you have a ready, quick mind." Bea looked at him again, glowing with the sureness of power, power over him. And I saw him change; felt a strange nerve-tingling sensation at what then passed between them. I think he began to love my sister at that moment.

That night I dreamt of Horace, a bright and fiery ram racing through the sky, his horns hooking the stars.

WE SET SAIL AGAIN in the *Cardus*, with a new crew of lascars, Malabari-Portuguese sailors of great skill and daring. We landed at Macao, that Portuguese enclave off the China coast, and there Pierre Amigot, who had left Oliveiro behind in Cochin, awaited the officials of the Court, sent to convey him and his boxes with all dispatch to Peking.

Then we transferred to a broad-beamed two-tiered Chinese junk, its sails pleated like a bat's wing. The captain, a Chinese, wore a pigtail wound round his head, but Ismail told us he was a Chinese Muslim, a Hui—this being the name given to them in China.

The junk coasted northwards, never out of sight of shore for fear of Japanese pirates, the most sanguinary of all. We

landed at C'uanchou, the port Marco Polo had called Zaiton.
Zaiton was clothed in mist; a small winter rain fell.

"Here begins China, Colin, your world and your work,"
Abdul Reza said to me.

❧ *Seven* ❧

Anno Domini 1758

RINGED BY FORESTS OF candleberry and red maples, Zaiton was a
post of renown; in its estuary a hundred kingdoms had once
anchored their merchant ships. But now it had declined. It
was slowly dying, its bay sandy, the ships at its docks no
more the proud and graceful ocean junks whose sides bulged
with silk and porcelain and spices, ivory, and rare woods,
but middling and small craft, plying the coasts of China,
venturing only as far as Manila, or to the Kingdom of Ayuthia.

Our junk threaded itself skillfully into port. The morning
mist dispersed, and the fresh sunlight lit the city's roofs of
glistening tiles, and here and there the bright pyramids of
Buddhist temples and Islamic mosques. Many foreign merchants had lived here for more than a thousand years. One-
fifth of the population had been Arabs, Syrians, Persians,
Jews, Nestorians, and Byzantines. Many religions and races
had found asylum and wealth here. So Abdul Reza told me,
waxing eloquent in praise of Zaiton.

We changed our clothing, making ourselves ready for the
inspection by the Commissioner of Foreign Vessels. Abdul
Reza donned a brocaded gown, jewels at his neck and on his
hands, a turban of white with an aigrette of diamonds and
rubies on his head. His domestics were sumptuously clad
and wore the white caps that indicated they were Muslims.

A high-decked junk, with ornate red and gold trimmings

and painted eyes upon its prow, lumbered towards us, surrounded by small craft filled with soldiers in scarlet waist-
coats and black trousers. The soldiers clambered up the junk's
ladder, lined the deck's railings. They carried sticks, and two
of them had flat swords slung upon their backs. A horizontal
wood ramp with sides of bamboo was now hooked between
the two vessels. No mandarin could demean himself by as-
cending from his ship to another one. Rather, the commissioner would walk onto our low junk from his high-prowed
one.

He was a tall Manchu in an embroidered gown with a cap
upon his head, and high black boots of cloth with raised
platform soles. His horseshoe sleeves came down upon his
hands. He had a necklace that hung lower than his belt,
indicating his exalted rank. We stood behind Abdul Reza and
bowed three times, as he had taught us to do, while the
commissioner looked around him leisurely. Two secretaries,
not Manchu but Hans, presented the inspector with a document, which he waved aside. He looked at Abdul Reza and
said:

"You are a merchant of renown, with friends in our city.
We were informed by them of your arrival and we have stud-
ied the report of what you bring with you. Your underlings
are said to be peaceful and honest; true believers of the Pure
Sincere faith." Pure Sincere was the name given to the
Mohammedan faith when it came to China a millennium ago.

"The noble words of Your Excellency fill this lowly person
with delight," Reza answered. "Your Excellency's munificence
is that of a beloved parent towards a wayward child. This
lowly person dares to inquire whether Your Excellency will
partake of some refreshments, after the arduous trouble of
coming to this worthless bark of ours?"

All this was protocol—the soldiers' threatening air, the
commissioner's majestic demeanor, the ritual of set phrases.

Abdul Reza led the Manchu into the junk's interior rooms,
whose fine screens of bamboo had been renewed, the floor
covered in silk carpets, the walls with lacquered panels. Incense burners dispensed the soothing odor of sandalwood.
Meanwhile, Reza's domestics and the sailors brought from
the hold boxes and bales; gifts for the clerks, the officials, the

soldiers. Their faces relaxed, the minor officials dexterously waved their fans, discoursing with one another and feigning not to see the growing pile in front of them.

When we were called, we walked into the reception room, standing with our eyes to the floor, as tutored by Abdul Reza.

"A brother and sister, orphans in my care," Reza said carelessly.

"Outsider devils and Christians," the Manchu replied sourly. "Christians are rowdy, iniquitously inquisitive. . . ."

"They are but children," Reza replied. "Your Excellency will extend his benevolence to them and allow them to sojourn here, where they will acquire learning and good deportment."

The Manchu nodded almost imperceptibly and then rose, saying, "We shall meet again."

Five of Reza's servants, carrying black lacquered chests upon their shoulders, followed him as he walked back to his own vessel. There was a small bustle as behind him his underlings scrambled to snatch from the pile as many of the boxes and bales as they could carry before following their master.

Reza's friends now came aboard. They looked Chinese, but they were Huis, tracing an Arab, Persian, Syrian ancestry, for many merchants of many races had settled in Zaiton and intermarried with the Hans.

I had thought Marseilles bustling; Cochin a revel of color. The beauty of Zaiton was other. Handsome men, and lovely slim women with flowers in their glossy black hair, walked on the paved streets. Most of them were clothed in silk of muted color, never gaudy. There were charming two-level houses, white with brown lacquered pillars and pale gray roofs, their edges picked out in white paint, with lattice windows and carved balconies. Here was no brawling; all seemed orderly and courteous, and as our palanquins sped onwards, carried by bearers in blue, I said to Bea:

"Voltaire was right, China seems most civilized."

And Bea smiled, squeezing my hand.

Salim Ding's house was at the end of a bifurcating paved lane. It had a black lacquered gate of no great size, but gradually the house revealed itself as we trod alleys between white and grey walls. They ended in a courtyard and pavilions, followed by other courtyards with rockery and pools. We were taken through four courtyards paved with grey-blue stones to a building for guests, and given rooms on the second floor, and maids and manservants to be our domestics.

Salim Ding was a slight-framed man, with thick eyebrows and a small black beard. He commanded two of his five sons to attend to our every want. We were supplied with Chinese clothes of silk; Bea choosing from a host of colors, from satin and gauze and organza, tunics and pleated skirts, white silk undergarments, inner collars and inner sleeves, and girdles of silk with tassels. The maids dressed her hair, which had grown longer, in the Chinese style, piling it on her head, securing it with pins of gold inlaid with oval pearls and kingfisher feathers, which swayed and moved as she moved.

Here I began to understand an art of being, a constant attention to beauty of gesture, to sound of voice, to appearance. For each gesture had meaning. Even the way a fan fluttered, was raised, shut, opened, or agitated, conveyed pleasant or hostile emotion, conveyed meaning without the necessity of words.

The next day a teacher came, named Wei, and began to teach us Chinese. He showed us how to wield the brush for writing Chinese characters; how to make the ink by rubbing solid-ink tablets upon a piece of smooth stone. We learnt how valuable these stone inkslabs were; books had been written about them and catalogs compiled. The best inks had precious ingredients in them, gold and pearl and cinnabar. The smell of ink, the sight of rare stone inkslabs, sent scholars into ecstasies. Teacher Wei was indefatigable, staying with us eight hours of the day. Bea learnt with miraculous swiftness, so that Wei was delighted with her aptitude and wrote a poem to praise our assiduity:

> *The fragrance of ink and paper fills the room;*
> *Two young heads bend in search of ancient treasure.*

The sons of Salim Ding, Faiz and Iqbal, took us in chaises to visit the city and its environs. We visited the famous Buddhist temples, and though Faiz kept muttering that these were idols, and the people heathen, Bea was enchanted, as I was. Whereas the interiors of mosques and churches demanded silence and reverence, a Buddhist temple required no such demeanor. Their gardens were a joyous cacophony of men, women, and children, praying and bowing and lighting incense sticks but also talking, laughing, and eating at tables in the courtyards, under the benign and centenary gingko trees. Such should be worship, I thought. A revel of life, not an aptitude for death.

As for Bea, "I am back in my enchanted forest," she said, pointing to the deer, the doves, the apes, and the peacocks in the frescoes on the wall, all of them come to worship the Buddha Lord of Compassion, to show reverence for life in all its multiplicity.

We visited the markets, the venerated tombs of Muslim travelers and Holy Men who had come here to teach. And there was also a Hindu temple, now in a decrepit condition.

Faiz told us that Indian mariners always asked to be tattooed in Zaiton, for here were the best tattooers in the world—so nimble were their fingers that no one felt their needles' prick.

But now Zaiton was dying. No more Indian traders, and the temple was sorry with decay. Only an old Brahmin, the sign of Shiva drawn upon his forehead with ashes, remained. He gazed at us blindly, and gestured that we should not enter for we were, to him, unclean. He longed to return to Benares, the holiest of holy cities of the Indias, to be cremated there, and his ashes thrown in the river Ganges. The thought of being buried in the earth of China, and thus his resurrection as a Brahmin forever lost, was to him the greatest of misfortunes.

Faiz and Iqbal took us outside the city walls to see the silk villages. "This is where the wealth of the land lies; and also our own."

We went across the rich plain, with its marvel of young rice, green as jade, the camphor and eucalyptus trees, and the mulberry groves clustering around the small villages. We heard the whirr and clatter of the shuttles at work. Women were weaving the moon-color tissue heaped by their looms, and the sight brought back to me the memory of Mother, weaving the linen cloth we wore. Old women gathered the raw silk and folded it after making sure there were no defects in the weaving.

"My father buys what they weave," Faiz said. "We use the small silk boats to send it out, but it is no easy trade now."

We saw the silkworm barns. On wooden shelves lay shallow trays of woven bamboo garnished with mulberry leaves. Here the worms ate themselves fat and translucent. Satiated, they spun themselves into their own death of oval white shrouds. Young girls with agile fingers gathered the ripe cocoons and plunged them into vats of boiling water before the worm could chew its way out of the cocoon, to emerge as a butterfly. In the water the cocoons were swirled by hand, the thread unwound, spun on bobbins, washed again, and prepared for weaving.

Silk making was the domain of women; they bred the worms, spun and wove. Men brought misfortune to the silk, though young boys were allowed to gather mulberry leaves off the trees to feed the worms. So it had been for many centuries, and Faiz quoted from an old poem:

> At night the noise of foreigners is deafening
> in the silk markets;
> In the morning the steps of the seaport are wet
> with the boots of passersby.

"My father tells me that only forty years ago, silk cocoons were still piled high as a mountain before each village of Zaiton. But, alas, no more so. Now many empty shuttles merely weave the wind," he added, melancholic.

"But you still buy silk and send it out in small ships, Faiz," I said.

"Yes, we do. But this is very difficult. My father or Lord Reza will tell you. I am too young to speak on this matter."

❦ ❧

The women's quarters, where Salim Ding's wives and daughters lived, were another world of tree and blossom and pool, intimate and stifling. Stifling because the women did not go anywhere, save in closed palanquins to visit other women. They told me it was because so many of them were raped and massacred when the Manchus came. Now both the Hui and the Han have been cloistering their women, as if this would protect them.

Salim Ding's three wives and seven daughters greeted me, laying a spread of sweets and sherbets on the low tables. They taught me chess, gave me jeweled pins for my hair, and necklaces and bangles. They sang and played on the pipa and the zither. Their feet were not bound, as were those of Han women of quality. Neither did the Manchu, the Mongol, or the Tibetan women bind their feet. The tiny feet on which Chinese women could scarcely hobble about were a sign of wealth and leisure.

Salim Ding's women had few distractions, save watching, from behind latticed screens, ambulant players of marionettes performing the legends of the White Snake, who, for love of a man, became a woman—puppets maneuvered with such skill they seemed alive. The shops sent bales of silk, carpets and hangings and jewelry to the noble house, for the women to choose. They could not roam the streets, as did women of low rank or the wild free females of the mountain tribes. Yet the streets were full of them. Many women were shopkeepers, and all the streets were lined with shops.

I now encountered the Old Immortal.

Dressed as a boy, in a belted robe, a bonnet covering my hair, I was out with Colin, Faiz, and Iqbal, and came upon the Flowing Principle Mountain, renowned for its old trees. And here I saw the Old Immortal.

He was carved out of one great stone, odorous of the sea from which it had come—the large head with its long-lobed ears; the eyes, which looked through space and time; the hands, holding Nothingness. He was alive, totally alive, twenty-eight cubits high, and I saw nothing else, heard nothing else.

"I know you," I said, and He replied:

"We have never seen each other, yet I too recall you. You asked me then: 'What shall I do with myself?' "

"This time I know what I will do," I replied.

"That is what you must do."

His hand was raised and cupped, the universe in it and nothing in it, large enough for me to sit on. I climbed, sat on the upturned palm.

My hands caressed Him. There was life in every grain of Him.

"Go to your success," He said. The wind sighed in the lacquer trees of the plain. "Yield to the world of come-what-may. And take what it brings, without regret."

"I have the Gift. . . . I follow something in me and I will not be merely a woman, banal, cloistered . . . I will be a queen. . . ."

"The universe is splendor, yet says nothing. Discarding love, hatred occupies the spirit; and both are the same. It is fear that makes Bea want power. Fear of love. Fear of the fire, yet love and the fire will come to you."

"Shall I succeed?"

"To succeed, one must not care, one must let go . . . let go . . . let go. . . ."

The sky took up the cry, and then I heard Colin's voice, "Bea, Bea," amid the squawk of birds.

Colin and Iqbal saw me sitting upon His hand. My brother gazed upon the Old Immortal, so helpless in His stonebound state that any child could climb Him, hit Him, deface Him.

I eased myself down. "What a large statue, Iqbal! I've never seen anything like it."

Iqbal explained, "He is Lao Dze, the Old Immortal, the founder of Taoism. It is said He was conceived of a shooting star, and became a stone when He tired of traveling the universe upon His long-eared donkey. Taoism is not a religion, yet people die for it, and the Hans are really Taoists at heart, although Confucius rules their daily behavior, and many also follow the Buddha."

Iqbal, a Muslim, had contempt for other creeds, except Taoism. "The officials say Tao disrupts and confuses; it preaches revolt, negation, inquiry.

"Some say this stone came from Heaven. Others say it rolled

*down from the mountain. Still others that it walked here from the
sea. But all agree the Old Immortal is powerful, for it is in the secret
places of the mind that He dwells."*

⤛ ⤜

ABDUL REZA WAS INVOLVED in some grand design. The languid
pacing of long-robed men with imperturbable faces; the
graceful gesturing with fans; the small laughs; the pauses to
watch a bird or a cloud; the poetic comments on the light
upon the rockeries—all this was but the minutely orches-
trated cadence of a play, masking the passion of deep-laid
resolve, of some important and perhaps dangerous conspiracy.

For long hours Salim Ding would speak to us and to his
assembled sons of the past. From the eighth century onwards
Arab and Chinese traders had furrowed the seas. Great Chinese junks, holding a thousand men, with fifty sails and
masts forty cubits tall or more, had sailed in convoys, with
silk and lacquer and porcelain, camphor and jade and paper,
aloes and ephedrine and tea, to Champa and to Ayuthia, to
Boni and Sumatra, to the kingdoms of India, to Ormuz and
Persia, to Zanzibar. Arab prows had come to Canton and to
Zaiton, bearing ivory and cinnabar, sapphires and pearls and
rubies, rhinoceros horns and live elephants, sand gold from
the Indies, cotton muslins and Burmese eggplant, pepper and
clove and other spices. Back and forth from Zaiton, for many
generations, the sea roads brought wealth and opened men's
minds to other lands.

In the twelfth century the Chinese Emperor had issued
names to the Huis, the Jews, the Nestorians, and other
refugees from persecution in Europe. The Huis were given
the names of Ma, Ding, Huang, Kuo, and Bu to choose from.
One hundred thousand Arabs and their offspring lived in
Zaiton.

Thus, Salim son of Mohammed had become Ding.

"The Empire prospered, as did the merchants. One-fifth of

the total revenue of the state came from the taxes upon seagoing ships," Salim said.

But always the officials, the court eunuchs, sought to control the trade, filling their own pockets with its revenues, especially when the emperors, remote in their palaces, became weaklings.

By 1430, only merchant ships possessing special trade permits were allowed on long sea voyages, and seventy percent of the profits went to the Emperor. "And so the great expeditions ended, and no one ventured to build large junks anymore," said Salim Ding. "But we found ways, we found ways. For we had the sea in our blood; and the people of this province are venturesome, born sailors. Despite taxes and levies and preying commissioners, we went on in the small boats.

"Many crafts depended on us. The ivory carvers needed ivory from the elephants of India and Africa and Ayuthia. We exported lacquerware to France. But silk was our mainstay—silk in all its forms, shapes, weights, and fineness. A million bales a year. The small ships keep the craft alive, keep the looms weaving, feed the innumerable villages of the province." Salim Ding rocked his body back and forth as if at prayer.

"The Ming dynasty collapsed; in 1644 the Manchus of the North conquered the land. At first they were wise and relaxed trade, but now the emperors are even more rigid than the previous dynasty. Instead of opening the country, they are closing it. Much of foreign trade must be conducted under the name of 'tribute' to the Emperor, the Son of Heaven. The Mandarin governor of our province has sent his armed junks to capture more than thirteen thousand of our small boats in the coves of islands off Zaiton, saying they are smugglers.

"All this control is weakening the Empire," Salim Ding continued. "For now the oceans are ploughed by other vessels, by men of daring, merchants whom the Manchus call 'ocean barbarians.' " He smiled in a tired way at Bea and me. "This contempt, this arrogance, is a great error. Barbarians you may be, but you are clever barbarians.

"The Portuguese, the Dutch, the Spaniards, and now the

French and the English, are all coming with lust for wealth; and the Manchu dynasty is giving up the seas to them, sending no more convoys abroad, save a yearly ship or so to Manila, and a few junks to Ayuthia. We have given up the seas, and from the seas our destruction shall come."

Abdul Reza, who sat with us, nodded agreement. "The Manchus think time has stopped, that nothing will change, and that if they keep foreigners out by closing the land, they will rule forever."

"Then what must be done?" I asked.

"Learn new things," Reza replied. "Learn from the barbarians. Learn to change, learn many things. For instance, how to make clocks and automata—and machines, and better ships, and cannon, guns . . ."

Thus I understood Abdul Reza's plan.

ABDUL REZA, WEARING A robe of pale blue silk lined with smooth black fur, bade us farewell. "I go to Tenasserim, in Ayuthia. I shall not return for another year or two. You are reasonable and cautious, and you shall be well looked after in Yangchou city where everything is ready for you, Colin, to begin work."

"My fingers itch to work, Lord Reza," I said. "In my dreams I see cogwheels spin and cams and levers move. It has been too long since I've held a cylinder with pinions in my hands."

Reza smiled.

"Great souls have wills, others but feeble wishes," he said. "May you both have steady wills. But—" He now turned to Bea and his eyes hooded a little; he wrestled with himself against the temptation it was for an aging man to find new vigor with a young girl. "I must also provide for you, Damozel, for you are a woman now."

Bea said, "I shall stay with my brother and help him in his work, Lord Reza."

"But a woman must marry, and follow her husband—have you thought of it?"

She looked at him then, and again I felt the air thicken with something that made my heart beat faster.

"I am scarce fifteen, my Lord. I have no thought to follow
. . . anyone. But when the time comes, I shall choose."

Abdul Reza stared at her, pondering her words. For all his
willed calm, his face was that of a man in torment.

"I am near forty, the father of many children; and time
stays for no man," he said. "I must therefore act towards you
with wisdom—and honor."

"Time does not grow old, only hearts do," Bea replied.
"But our affection towards you, Lord Reza, will never fade."
And she curtsied.

"Lady," Abdul Reza said, rising, "you are strong and bold
beyond your years. With the mind and heart of a ruler, a
queen. I shall be returning here, if Allah wills it; and by that
time certain plans may have prospered. Go you now both, in
peace."

WE SAILED FOR YANGCHOU, Faiz coming with us, as well as servants to protect us, and maids. An Ah Hung, an Islamic
teacher returning from a pilgrimage to Mecca and going to
the Great White Crane Mosque of Yangchou, traveled on our
junk, together with some of his disciples. The junk kept close
to the shore, and the crow's nest had a lookout day and
night. "Japanese pirates—they never leave anyone alive," Faiz
explained.

Teacher Wei came with us to continue his work. In the
evening he made music, blowing melancholy airs upon a
flute. "Yangchou music," he told us. I played on my recorder
some of the psalms of the Huguenots. I read again of the
travels of Messer Marco Polo, and the *Peregrination* of Fer-
nando Mendez Pinto, the Portuguese who had sailed these
regions more than two centuries ago.

When we entered the huge Kiang, or great river, several
leagues across from shore to shore, as Marco Polo had described
it, I addressed myself to his spirit: "Perhaps we shall find
memories of you in Yangchou, since you were an official of the
Emperor there for nigh three years. Oh let me be worthy of
you, Messer Marco, and prosper as you did."

But Teacher Wei said that, although born in Yangchou, he

had never heard of Marco Polo. "There were many foreigners employed at the Court of the Yuan dynasty," he said. "The Yuans were Mongols, and we Hans got rid of them and erased some of their records—that was four centuries ago."

"Will you get rid of the Manchus as well?" I asked.

He did not reply, but blew on his flute an air fifteen centuries old.

I felt a new order in my mind, as if the diverse elements composing my spirit, like the many winds of my native lake, had discarded their random fits and accepted a methodical array. Whether it is the motion of the stars in Heaven or the affairs of men on earth, there is a logic, a mechanism, a sequence from cause to effect.

My work with automata would now become not only a means of earning a living and enriching myself—and this I wanted—but a means whereby I would trace, perhaps understand, the Grand Design of the universe.

Meanwhile, I would serve the noble design of Lord Reza, who had brought me here for a purpose.

"SALT," FAIZ SAID, as a stream of barges, bamboo matting covering their humped loads, sailed by our junk; they were going up the Grand Canal to Peking.

We were on the man-made Grand Canal, linking South to North China, crowded with thousands of barges carrying grain and foodstuffs, cloth and salt. The South, its wealth, its clever skillful people, was now a tributary of the North.

"Yangchou is at a main junction of the canal. Here live the great salt merchants," Faiz said. "The Son of Heaven has high regard for them, since his purse is kept filled by them."

Salt. I looked at the barges creeping up the canal. Without salt men died and armies could neither march nor fight. "And because of this salt, even though the Manchus occupy half of the official posts in the Empire without passing any examinations, yet still the families of the salt merchants, who are all Hans, obtain high offices for their own sons at the Court." Faiz smiled. "Your protector in Yangchou is no less than

Marquess Fang, Vice-Commissioner of Salt. A great man, who loves his country, and understands . . . many things."

On the stone dock of Yangchou stood two people garbed in blue silk, surrounded by respectful retainers. One of them wore a beard streaked with silver, and on his head was a cap with a sapphire button.

I was now so used to Chinese faces that I said to Bea, "Look, Bea, a foreigner."

"A Jesuit, no doubt," Bea said. "Surely a Jesuit."

We landed and assumed a respectful posture, while the younger of the two men advanced towards us. He had a smooth round face and lively eyes, and Faiz exclaimed:

"Third Young Lord Fang, your worthless younger brother is steeped in shame that you should have come in person. It is too great an honor."

Young Lord Fang, the Third Son of Marquess Fang, was like polished jade, his gestures and words flawless. I yearned to make an android resembling him, moving with such impeccable grace. But now he was slightly flustered.

"Welcome, welcome," he cried; then, turning and bowing to the foreigner: "Grand Master Lang Shening has deigned to honor our miserable city with his presence, and upon hearing I was to meet you he said he too would step to this landing place."

The Young Lord indicated by a small gesture of his hands his mental disarray. Never, never had a high court official come casually stepping like any commoner to meet two unknown barbarian youths. The Canons of Confucius, prescribing a rigid hierarchy of respect between old and young, master and servant, superior and inferior, had been swept away by this Master Lang Shening, who had white hairs and a beard.

But Grand Master Lang was looking at Bea, and now exclaimed in French heavily accented with Italian, "Ah, bella, belissima . . . I should so like to paint you, Lady . . . your face, in many years I have not seen such a face."

And Bea, curtsying with the grace of Lausanne's best society, replied in French, "Honored Sir, it will be my pleasure to sit for you."

Grand Master Lang advanced and put both hands on my shoulders. "And this is Colin Duriez. I've heard of you—see how fast news travels. From my brother in religion, Pierre Amigot. He was here in Yangchou, on his way to Peking."

Third Young Lord called for the sedan chairs and palanquins. The Italian Jesuit went on beaming at us and continued to speak in French:

"His Imperial Majesty is coming to Yangchou; I have been sent ahead to prepare for the commemoration of this event. I am glad you have arrived, Colin Duriez, for on the way from Canton, Brother Amigot's precious cases were dropped, he thinks deliberately. Some of the automata and clocks are broken and no one can repair them except you."

I felt trapped. "Work is awaiting me—"

"This will be a part of it." He winked. "By the way, my name is Castiglione, Giuseppe Castiglione, Lang Shening in Chinese, Court Painter to His Imperial Majesty. I welcome you to China and hope you will be happy here."

⟿ *Eight* ⟸

Anno Domini 1759–1760

ALONG THE BANKS OF Slender Lake, where pleasure boats with music and lanterns glided among the lotuses, stretched the Yuan Lin, or Forest of Gardens. Here were the mansions of the wealthy salt merchants of Yangchou, a city where the art and poetry of gardens was a passion.

Yangchou's loveliness was a perpetual discovery of exquisite detail. Every palace pavilion and garden was an alliance of nature's harmony and of the painter's art. *Yi*, the Chinese word for the emotion and thoughts aroused by the contemplation of perfection, was given expression through a most refined aestheticism. And this was achieved not by the uninterrupted spread of majestic tree and glorious blossom, but in enclosed spaces, their smallness suggesting infinite expanse, abolishing the limits of measurement. Here one garden was many, each segment opened into another, defined not by harsh walls but by subtly leading sinuous pathways, by pools and rockeries and artificial mountains and particular trees. The buildings formed part of the garden, inevitable components of its grace as any tree or stone in it, and as carefully thought out. Graceful pavilions had delicate pillars and roof eaves pointing skywards. Each garden was a statement of the poetry of living.

"Look, Bea, look." As when the wind turned on our lake

and the lake changed color, I felt the color of Bea's mind change, a flush of pleasure.

"Beauty penetrates little by little," Bea read from the device carved on one of the pillars of our pavilion. "All the world's mountains seen in a stone," I read on its pendant. All things became possible, worlds whirling through space, and the enigma of space, which materializes the unreal, as simple as watching one's face in a pool.

"It is the Old Immortal," Bea said. "Lao Dze. He is here, everywhere, in everything. These gardens are His. Colin, I'm afraid of Him."

I put my arms around her. Once again that veil of darkness fell upon her, and she shivered. I could almost smell the smoke, the smell of burnt flesh. Her mind flooded into mine, evoking the nightmare that had been real.

As we stood watching the loveliness, we were haunted by the ghosts of old terror. We heard the singing in other woods, under other skies. And then it was gone.

"Bea, Bea, cast this aside. Nothing can harm us here."

She shook herself free of me. "You will be happy, Colin. But what shall I do with myself, what shall I be?"

Her violence hit me like a blow. I felt the garden stir. Though she and I were one, yet we were also two; and for the first time I felt the terror of uniqueness, of our coming apart one day and being lost to each other. "Bea, you have the Gift, your mind is so strong, you can do so much; why, you can be a queen."

"The priestesses led the people to war, not to slothful enchantment," she said scornfully. She turned on me with that ardent fury that was the very substance of her soul, of which I was deprived. I was holding a tempest in my arms. And the faces of Jacob and Laurence came welling up from its rage.

Our pavilion was in the "welcoming autumn" part of the garden. The painter She Tao, who had designed Marquess Fang's mansion, had placed within its enclosed emptiness the four seasons, so that time was also captive here, and the caprices and colors of the year. The autumn garden had rocks of a reddish color, gleaned from a distant lake bottom and brought at great expense. It had a pool with late-blossoming water lilies, chrysanthemums, juniper trees planted in seeming disorder, and a moon-viewing esplanade. Within the pavilion were Tali marble landscapes wrought by nature in its spasms of creation: one could see in the mottled and streaked stones mountains and gorges and waterfalls, or genii in epic battle scenes, or bizarre and splendid blossoms. From the ceiling beams of the terrace in front of Bea's room hung great rings of pewter; parrots from Szechuan, white or grey with golden crests and pink tails, disported themselves, a light chain round their legs. In a cage were green lovebirds from India. Every morning they were let out by the bird-maid to wander and came back when called.

For two days we rested, and Bea came to me each night, shivering and shaking with a premonition of disaster, and lay with me as when we were children. I could not ease her anguish, helpless against her world of night.

On the third day we were received by Marquess Fang. Third Son came to fetch us with sedan chairs, though we could have walked the distance.

Marquess Fang was a tall, exquisitely well-mannered man. He did not wear his official robes, and about him some thirty members of the Fang family were similarly at ease, in silks and satins but without official emblems. It took us many months to distinguish the one hundred seventy-odd members of the Fang family who resided within the huge sprawl of the mansion, and to understand the hierarchy of relationships among them.

"My friend Abdul Reza, closer to me than lips to teeth," the Marquess said, "whose family and mine have been connected by friendship for two centuries, has told me that you are his children by affection, and so you will also be mine."

We were instructed in the appropriate generic appellations for our various new relatives by affection. The Second Noble Lady, Fang's second wife, and three of his five concubines surrounded Bea, holding her hands, exclaiming over her beauty. "Eyes like jade, she will bewitch everyone," they said. Their voices were like the sound of birds, melodious and sweet.

"Jade with fire in it," said Marquess Fang, not looking at Bea.

After tea and sweetmeats and much inquiry of our journey, Lord Fang said to Third Son, "Since time presses, take them now to the Master of the Clocks, for many things must be made ready."

We were carried swiftly between pale walls, along narrow alleys. The walls were pierced with windows of many quaint shapes, affording glimpses into other parts of the huge garden, other seasons of the year. We passed through many small gates and alighted in a courtyard unadorned but for a single willow. Then we crossed the threshold of the reception hall, and there was Giuseppe Castiglione, standing by a man in an armchair, who did not rise.

"Enter, enter," the man called in French. He was wrapped in a robe of black silk, and his face was worn and sallow, deeply wrinkled.

"Master Wen, Master of the Clocks," Third Son said reverently.

"I am paralyzed from the waist downwards," the man said, "and my arms and hands are also invaded by the creeping disease. I am glad you have come, Colin Duriez, for whatever I know I must impart to you, so that the work may continue."

Castiglione said, "My friend-and-brother-in-religion, Johann Werner, has been ill for a long time."

"Your *excommunicated* brother," Johann Werner said, with bitter irony. "Excommunicated by the apostolic vicar, who hardly spared you, but that he dare not touch you, the Emperor favoring you so highly."

Castiglione shrugged, with sadness and that touch of impish humor that never left his handsome, youthful-looking face, with its strong nose and sensitive mouth. He bent towards Johann and kissed him on both cheeks. "You always tease me, Johann; I am but one of the Emperor's many Jesuit servants. Well, I'll come again tomorrow, and"—he turned, bright and eager, towards us—"I'll paint both of you, the resemblance and the difference."

He walked away, lithe and quick in his felt boots; behind him was a servant carrying a large roll of paper and a bag with brushes and colors in bottles.

"Giuseppe is always kind, even to those who treat him ill,"

Johann Werner said. "But come, all of this is of no interest to you. Let us go to the factory."

Two servants then lifted his chair, sliding poles into rings set under its arms. "I still have a few months, perhaps a year or two before me. My hands still obey my commands, but after that—" He looked at both of us and noticed my club foot. "After that, all will rest on your shoulders, Colin Duriez."

THE FACTORY WAS A series of paved rooms built behind the court-yard where the Master of Clocks lived. There was a small forge, an oven for smelting metals, and many tools hanging on the walls. On the floor of one of the rooms lay automata, a good many of them, some mounted with clocks, all in various states of disrepair and destruction. Some of them had been there for a while; others were those recently brought by Pierre Amigot.

"Dropped on the ground purposely when being carried from Canton to Peking," Werner said. "The eunuchs of the Court are mischievous." The majority of the automata and clocks, however, no longer functioned, because the mechanisms had rusted. "Sometimes it is the great heat and cold. Metal expands and shrinks, and we have to contrive replacements."

Six young Chinese were bent at wooden tables, repairing clocks. On the walls by them were drawings and sketches to show the repairs to be made. They lifted their heads and smiled when we entered. "I've told them never to stand and bow while working, it interrupts the flow," said Johann Werner. "These are my students. All six are Chinese who have escaped from the Philippines." The latest massacre of Chinese in Manila by the Spaniards had taken place a year ago. "They know they have to learn new things; or what happened in Manila, what happens in Batavia, will also happen here. Everywhere the Chinese work, they work hard, create wealth, and then are massacred in a great wave by the new Christian rulers of Asia."

"Like the Jews in Europe," I said.

Johann Werner nodded, his face fierce yet imploring. "How

much do you know of science, Colin Duriez? How much do you understand of what makes an automaton work? Or a clock?"

"I began when I was eight years old, with my father, Sir," I replied. "And Bea, my sister, also knows something of clockwork; she makes the faces and clothes for the androids, who are automata so smooth and well done they seem alive."

"Faces and clothes are not what I need. I need someone who understands *mechanics*, and harnessing the power of fire and water to make things move."

"The steamboat," I cried, remembering Lord Kilvaney's story. "The steamboat on the Seine River in Paris . . ."

"Yes, and many other things." He shook with the frenzy of his mind, imprisoned by his disease. "Well, but you can read, both of you. I have many books. Everything on mechanics and electricity, everything that has been published until now. And Castiglione brought me more, including the books of Father Amigot." Suddenly he chuckled. "Poor Pierre Amigot. Now we must repair the automata he brought, which were broken. That is our first task, before the Emperor reaches Yangchou, which will be in six to eight weeks. Later, we shall go on to more important things."

"We?" Bea queried.

Johann Werner smiled at her. "Some of the salt merchants, Marquess Fang among them, want the discoveries and the mechanics of Europe to be taught here. They do not want this great Empire, with its many millions of people, to stand still, to become . . . enslaved. But the civil service, the Manchu reigning caste, are obdurate." He closed his eyes, as if gripped by a spasm of pain. "The Emperor is coming. We must repair some fifty pieces for his traveling palace in Yangchou. Not only he but all his Court and his eunuchs want marvels and enchantments to amuse them during their stay here. So we shall amuse them—and perhaps convert some of them to science."

Every day before dawn we rose, Bea and I, and after a breakfast of rice broth and pickled vegetables were carried to the factory. There we worked all day, coming back when the light began to fail, for Johann Werner spared our eyes. "It is bad to strain your excellent sight."

Memory returned to my fingers, clumsiness vanished. Bea was as eager as I; she collected the small parts of the machines I disassembled, laid them on sheets of pure white silken paper, finding even the minutest screws. Some of the automata were badly smashed; others merely needed rewinding of the coiled springs, adjustment of the cams, some precison paring.

There was an eight-day pendulum clock, with a beautiful case of lacquered wood with silver inlay; it had been made in Neuchâtel, and handling it was both bitter and sweet to me. There were singing birds in cages, perched on boughs, brought by Pierre Amigot. They were studded with rubies and sapphires, in cages of gold, with fruit hanging from trees of coral and amber. The bellows were disjointed, and I contrived to reset them. I labored long on combs whose metal teeth drew music from the stubs set in the revolving cylinders of music boxes. Try as I might, some of the notes were off-key, because of a minute maladjustment between the two elements. But worst of all was trying to repair the Writer, and failing to do so in time to present it to the Emperor.

The Writer came from Neuchâtel; he bore the signature of a certain Pierre Jaquet-Droz. I cried with joy when I saw him, for I had heard something of him, and to meet this android in China, in Yangchou, seemed almost miraculous. Johann Werner laughed at my enthusiasm. "They are making even better ones now, I hear," he said. "This one can only pretend to write. He obeys only one set of commands. But now I hear they are making androids in which many texts can be prepared and incorporated into the mechanism, and that they are devising other marvels, such as a Writer who will truly write, selecting the letters himself."

"A memory, a mechanical memory," Bea said.

"Exactly. I have spent days pondering on the ingenuity of all this, wondering how this mechanism can be used in other ways."

The Writer was badly hurt. The main camshaft carried eighteen cams, whose profiles set in motion three levers to transmit the necessary movements to the hand of the Writer. The hands had been smashed, and the main camshaft oscillated unsteadily, its axle no longer fitting. Some of the cams were broken, and the coils of the spring had been removed; as for the gear wheels with their interlocking pins, some of them were twisted.

The first lever received the vectors of depth, the second those of lateral motion, and the third served to raise or lower the Writer's quill.

The simultaneous movement of the three levers enabled the Writer to light a lamp before him, seize a pen, and start writing on paper fixed in the small table at which he sat.

Werner knew of the world's first android, made by Vaucanson the Frenchman: a flute player who really played the flute.

"The day will come when we shall make a machine *almost* like a human," Werner said dreamily. "An android who will speak, obey commands imprinted in its memory, walk, and perform many tasks for man. It is said that in England they have manufacturers where long lines of men and women work at weaving mills. Androids could do their work and would never weary, if only a source of energy could be tapped to set them all in motion without having to wind up their springs every day or so."

Every day Marquess Fang came to see us work, gazing round silently or talking with Werner in low tones. And Castiglione, with his pointed face and bright eyes under the silvery hair, would bring his cheerfulness, the warmth of his sunny smile. He sketched us, sketched Bea, unashamedly admiring her. "Bella, bella, eh, what a marvel are those eyes!"

Werner told us that Emperor Tsienlung, to tease his favorite Italian painter, once asked him which one of his nine concubines was the most beautiful. "They are all beautiful," Giuseppe Castiglione had replied.

"You haven't looked at them," the Emperor said jokingly, knowing the Jesuit would not.

"No, Your Majesty, I was counting the tiles on the roof," he replied.

Johann Werner was always in the workshops in his chair, carried by two servants. He watched me refitting the cylinders, the anchor regulators of the clocks; he taught the Chinese youths to make spare pieces for the watches. An old man, a blacksmith, thin and dry as a stick, not at all like Vulcan—

Chavenaz but excellent at his craft, was trying out various alliances of metal that might be less sensitive to heat, cold, or rust than what was used in the mechanisms. "No iron, only brass, preferably steel alloys," Werner said, "if we can get the heat right."

To the factory came, silent and anonymous, porcelain makers and bronze masters, a network of craftsmen intent on learning new techniques. Werner would use a strong spying glass to look at some pieces; using the instrument, two of his pupils were able to carve characters, a whole poem, on a grain of rice. And sometimes, when I was wearied and would rest awhile, he would talk with me of the need for skill of hand and eye, but even more important, the need for reason and logic behind the perfection of a mechanical unit. It was not enough to create automata with the illusion of life; one had to reach for a set of universal laws, a logic of matter, a unified theory of movement that would really pierce the mystery of substance.

"Yes, Colin Duriez, that is precisely what Galileo did—and for which he was condemned by the Church for attempting some intelligible explanation of the phenomena of the universe." Werner's face, when he spoke of the Church, showed the furrowing of enormous suffering, though he was only thirty years old.

One of the six young Chinese who worked at clocks, Ah Ming, knew Spanish and was exceptionally quick and clever. Werner put him to work with me. "You will learn from each other," he said. In a way I needed a brother, as I had needed Jacob and Valentin.

In a fortnight we had repaired four large clocks, twenty-five small watches, and ten automata. Ah Ming and the other apprentices had watched me, and they were now able to do repairs by themselves.

"But this is not enough, merely to teach them craftsmanship, skill of hands," Werner repeated irritably. "They must be taught to think science, able to *invent* new ways." He spent his evenings dictating translations in Chinese of the books that lined his rooms. One of the translators was the Second Son of Marquess Fang.

"He is a born mathematician," Johann Werner said. "Third

Son is excellent at wheedling officials, at managing people. The eldest son is in Peking, preparing for the imperial examinations to be held this year. He must become a high official. Thus every son to his appointed niche—and the family of Marquess Fang will prosper and endure."

Werner always called me Colin Duriez. As for Bea, he did not talk to her, though she worked hard, striving to refit the broken limbs and heads of the automata. New heads of porcelain were to be made. For these Castiglione drew sketches, and she made clay models of them. She also made articulated limbs of papier-mâché. New lacquered and painted boxes to enclose the clocks, enameled casings for the watches—all these Castiglione did. Many a watch and clock now had his landscapes or figures upon its outside box. He was also busy sketching and painting the scenery of Yangchou, especially those spots where much effort and money had been expended in further adornment and beautification by the Guild of Salt Merchants, in expectation of Emperor Tsienlung's visit.

"THERE ARE ALTOGETHER NINETY AUTOMATA, clocks, watches, and singing birds to be repaired. If we can put fifty in condition before the Emperor arrives, that will be good," Werner said.

"Singing birds," Castiglione said, "singing birds for the ladies of the Court, that is very important, my friend."

At last the work was done, the repaired automata set in a room, in rows, for a final inspection by Marquess Fang and Grand Master Castiglione.

"Nothing must be imperfect in the sight of the Lord of All," Werner said ironically. "Even if his eunuchs deliberately destroy a machine, the fault is ours."

There was a dancer with a garland of flowers, pivoting, the garland waving gracefully about her while she inclined her head this way and that. And I had introduced in the mechanism a small bellows, geared to the main cylinder, and changed her rigid chest into a flexible pleated cardboard one, so that she also breathed as she danced. There were three acrobats, two swinging on a trapeze and one turning somersaults. I had repaired a pair of dancers, such as my father used to make, with a set tracery of steps. There was a miniature pond of glass, with lotuses in bud, blossoming and opening, then closing again, to the sound of music. There were clocks with small figures coming out at the hours, clocks with peals of bells ringing the hours, watches with ringing bells at stated hours. All the watches and clocks were in pairs, for in China all gifts had to be given in pairs, for politeness. There were elephant watches, made for the King of Ayuthia although it was found they sold better in China. The watch was ensconced in the elephant's side, under an enameled cover that was part of the animal's jewel-studded saddle. On the saddle was a howdah, with a miniature figure inside it, and a cornac, a skilled elephant driver, sat between the elephant's ears, prodding him to pace forwards. There was a girl playing a timbrel and dancing while a boy played a flute; a set of villagers dancing, peasants walking, one of them playing a violin. And birds, birds—sixteen birds on a tree, singing one after the other, ending in a chorus. Single birds in boxes, to be given, of course, in pairs. The lid sprang open and out came the bird. Double birds, one answering the other. There was a bird only as long as my thumbnail, which sang like a nightingale.

Ah Ming now proved as skillful as I, making miniature cogs and screws, using *courroies* of twisted silk previously boiled in a thin paste of rice water to articulate limbs. And there was the Writer. I had reassembled him to function, but now he had a Chinese face and the dress of a Yangchou poet. He wrote on a scroll in praise of the Emperor—yet the scroll was prewritten, which irked me. One day, I decided, I must make one who *really* wrote on a blank sheet.

I remembered the mandarins of forged iron, sitting in an apotheosis of blossom, the centerpieces of the closed gates at the Duriez house at Neuchâtel. Now the gates had opened; I was in the world of the mandarins, just as eager for toys, for clocks and automata as were the Europeans.

"We had a clockmaker from Zug in our order, Francois-Louis Stadler," the Master of Clocks told me. "He died in Peking some years ago but he founded a clockmaking workshop under the present Emperor's grandfather. He tried to teach the Chinese to make clocks. But the clockmaking workshop vanished with Emperor Kanghsi's death, in 1722.

"The workshops were closed by the next Emperor, Yungcheng, who suspected Christians of plotting against him. Yungcheng persecuted the Christians and many were killed. He kept us, the Jesuits, at Court, however—to wind up the clocks and automata, to compile the calendar, to predict eclipses. But teaching the Faith was forbidden. We went on teaching astronomy, but it was the old astronomy, *before* Galileo changed our concept of the universe."

And yet the Jesuits had procured for themselves all the new books on science, including those condemned and placed under the Index, such as Galileo's treatises. I spent many hours in Johann Werner's rooms, reading treatises of physics, mathematics, and mechanics.

Werner had books on the history of clocks through the centuries; drawings of a clepsydra made in the tenth century in China, with twelve figures for the twelve hours, each one ringing the hour. "Every thought has a predecessor, as every being has parents. Go to the sources, wherever they may be, in whatever language," Werner advised me. "And work from them."

Almost every day Castiglione came to see him, escaping the officials who surrounded him by pretending he needed, at his age, a siesta. He would slip into our workshop and sit there, sketching Bea and also sketching the Master of Clocks, and myself and Ah Ming at work. He would talk, in that agreeable French of his, speckled with Italian words. Castiglione had arrived in China in 1715 and had served three emperors. "And though I have talked with so many mandarins, and though His Majesty has entrusted me to paint him in so many places, and so often comes to see me paint, I do not think I have made one convert," he said, and burst out in gay, self-mocking laughter.

The painter had with him a most valuable book, the sketches Leonardo da Vinci had made of his mechanical inventions. "He thought of so many ways machines would work, he even thought of a machine in which men could fly; of movable streets, of streets atop each other, so that crowds could move more freely." He handed me the book. "For you, Colin. A mind that understands mechanics is valuable."

Diderot had written: *Le travail des mains oblige l'esprit à la tranquillité, et laisse le champ libre aux mouvements de l'ame.* (The work of hands compels the mind to rest, and gives free rein to movements of the soul.) And so it was. Bent upon the minute and many parts of an automaton, with Ah Ming by my side, whose fingers were as swift as mine and whose brain was even quicker, I came back at night to read by the light of oil lamps. My mind stretched, my soul extended, my spirit soared, as in me a finer self was honed. I read of the anxious search of so many, not satisfied with only the explanations of the past. I learnt to strive, never to be content with what was written—even in the Holy Book.

Jacob had been right. "God willed man to inquire, to experiment, to probe the mysteries of the universe," he had said.

To do so was no crime; it was to come nearer to God Himself, to the final Revelation of man, God's child.

I NOW READ ALOUD from the books, then tried to translate the concepts into Chinese while the busy brush of Second Son flew on the silk paper, transcribing my words. We had planned to begin by teaching a history of timepieces: of gnomons and sundials, of clocks of wax, of water, of sand; of clepsydrae and hydraulic clocks. Haroun al Raschid had sent a clepsydra to Charlemagne, with twelve gates for the twelve hours, and each hour a door opened and let drop a minute ball of gold upon a resonant plate. In the fourth century before Christ, Plato had owned a clepsydra that put in motion a bell, to wake him up.

Mechanical clocks; the invention of the spring; the regulatory pendulum, derived from Galileo's observations of the oscillations of a suspended weight; Huyghens, with his cycloidal pendulum; the regulated spiral spring whose pulsations were isochronic, small enough to permit the watch . . .

"When every human being carries a watch upon him, this

is what will begin to instill in all minds a notion of the Machine," said Werner. "This is what we must do."

I had made an adaptation based on the anchor escapement of Graham the Englishman, invented in 1715. I applied it to the torsion cyclinder that Father and I had put into our automata, allowing them some movements at one time, some at others, and pauses between them. Johann Werner made me explain my invention, and it was duly recorded by Second Son.

Meanwhile, in Yangchou, many scholars were preparing to take the first grade of provincial examinations before competing at the public ones held every three years. One-half of the civil-service posts were reserved to the Manchus (less than 4 million Manchus ruling nearly 180 million Hans).

The South was not trusted. Some provinces had resisted Manchu rule bitterly for nearly fifty years. Yet the South provided most of the revenue to sustain the Imperial Court. The Manchu population of Bannermen, who were the garrisons in all the main cities, all of them pensioned from birth to death, fed on "tribute rice" from the South.

"It is the *content* of the examinations that stunts the minds of the scholars," Werner growled. "The classics, poetry, not a shred of science or anything practical or mechanical. An enormous waste of talent."

Marquess Fang's First Son had passed the provincial and national examinations with excellent marks. He was now attempting the third and highest grade, which was held in Peking in the presence of the Emperor. "Should he be successful, and finish among the first three, he may become a minister of the Empire, perhaps a member of the prestigious Hanlin academy," Werner said. "But his younger brothers can escape this fate to become Chinese Newtons or Galileos." He grinned. The muscles of his face, I noticed, were thinning.

Castiglione, sketching Bea at work on one of a pair of jeweled pistols (a singing bird came out of its muzzle when fired, and a watch was in its handle), said, "Here in Yangchou there is good material, Brother Johann. Malcontents, scholars out of work . . . restless youths . . ."

Werner interrupted him. "Too many of them have been set

in the Confucian mould, Brother Guiseppe. They do not understand inquiry and invention."

Werner's disease knew no respite; now he could scarcely lift the spoon to his mouth to eat, great beads of sweat started upon his forehead when he tried. Perhaps at times he thought it God's punishment, but Castiglione's presence, his constant cheerfulness, his love and concern for the suffering man, sustained and reassured him. As for Bea, she watched all that Castiglione did. He taught her and encouraged her. "You have a talent, as well as beauty, Damozel."

There were still twenty-two Jesuits at the Court of Peking, none of them as esteemed by Emperor Tsienlung as was Castiglione. He had become a third-rank mandarin; wearing a sapphire upon his hat, a peacock embroidered upon the chest of his blue satin robe. "A true Italian, a man to fit all seasons and their vagaries, yet who never demeans himself," Johann Werner said of him. "The only one who has not rejected me after my excommunication."

I translated the books. Johann Werner listened and corrected me when needed. Second Son wrote, indefatigable. We hurried, for the Master of Clocks was dying little by little, life withdrawing from his muscles by imperceptible degrees every day, every hour. Marquess Fang sent two masseurs to rub and knead him, and servants were forever by his side. And I, seeing his fierce single-mindedness, strove hard to be worthy of his trust and hope. For now I knew that I was a small cog in the Grand Design, and this made my imagination fertile, feverish with dreams of machines, with dreams of passing on to countless youths in China the same passion.

YANGCHOU WAS IN A frenzy of preparation for Tsienlung's visit; the great houses of the salt merchants were vying with one another to amuse him during his stay, to overwhelm his eunuchs with gifts.

In Yangchou, as in every main city of the Empire, there was a garrison of Manchu Bannermen. The Bannermen exercised on the plain beyond the city walls. We saw them galloping back and forth, quivers of arrows slung on their backs, the sun flashing upon their crimson and blue vestments. And as the mounted horde came galloping down the road, their feathers ruffled by the wind, their high saddles glistening, one could imagine what had happened when they had taken Yangchou. A siege of ten days, then the city captured, and in the ensuing slaughter eighty thousand dead. This had happened less than a century ago.

The Yangchou salt merchants then rallied to the new dynasty. Yangchou had recovered, become once again a center of art, of exquisite living. Poets and painters and musicians congregated here. Gardens, pavilions, and bridges vied with one another in elegant conceits. There were many pleasure boats upon its lake and rivers. Some of the courtesans of Yangchou were renowned poets and musicians.

This was the Emperor's second visit to the city. We heard gossip from our servants, far less in awe of the Dragon Throne than were the officials about him. Gossip was the very web and fabric of this world of enclosed gardens; gossip light as gossamer threads floating in spring, yet strangely tenacious. Our maidservants, who massaged us when we came back tired from the workshop, would speak gustily of Emperor Tsienlung.

"Yes, Old Ten Thousand Years is not a Manchu. His father was one of us, from the South. Everyone knows that Manchu women are fond of Han men. They love the Cloud and Water delight, they drink, ride horseback, and have lovers. If he comes here, it is actually to seek his real father—"

"Who has become a monk at the Golden Mountain Monastery. His name is Lin—"

The Emperor was coming. The imperial barges, twenty-four hundred of them, were sailing down the Grand Canal. They were but three days' journey away. Ten leagues ahead of the barges and ten leagues behind, on each bank of the canal, Bannermen rode, and the canal was emptied of all its boats, its shores emptied of all living beings.

Rumor, gossip, incredible tales. Our maids said that on his previous visit Ten Thousand Years had observed casually that the landscape needed a *dagoba,* those white, vase-shaped structures on an octagonal base erected to conserve the precious relics of Buddhism in Tibet, in Mongolia. The salt merchants were frantic but ingenious. Within a night, they had built such a white *dagoba*—of salt. Salt in great sacks was brought by sixty thousand men—so the legend ran among our maid-servants—working feverishly all night, and when Tsienlung on his dragon barge sailed on Slender Lake the next day, his eyes saw the *dagoba* he had mentioned the day before, and he was pleased.

Present in the minds of the lords of salt at all times was the question of whether Tsienlung might choose yet another con-cubine on this second visit. Or rather, whether his Grand Eunuchs in charge of the inner palace might choose, from a list of approved candidates, some new concubine.

EMPEROR TSIENLUNG HAD ARRIVED. The dragon barges had been sighted, and Buddhist and Taoist monks determined the aus-picious hour of landing. The Confucian temple had been renovated, fresh tiles upon its roofs; the brick carvings adorning its walls and the upper lintels of its gates redone. The viceroy and mandarins, robed and hatted, knelt on the landing dock.

All along the Grand Canal, the houses of the people were closed, the windows tightly shuttered to stop eyes from peeping.

The salt merchants knelt in their regalia, behind the officials, in a floating pavilion along the side of Slender Lake. Armed and mounted Palace Guards encircled the area. The abbots of the Zen Buddhist monasteries awaited, prostrate, the Lord of All under Heaven.

In the halls of the traveling palace—red and gold, with floors of sandalwood and ceilings intricately carved and painted—Yangchou's most exquisite porcelain, lacquer, silk, paintings, and ivory carvings awaited the Emperor. The se-lected automata and clocks were placed in one of these halls. We hoped it would not be known that a good many of them had been repaired. What if a malicious eunuch, an envious courtier, would start a whisper about "used goods"? It would be an insult to the Lord of All. And all who knelt to receive the Emperor that day would die, or be exiled.

The Emperor was installed in his traveling palace. He paid his respects to his dead grandfather, Emperor Kanghsi, who had in his lifetime come to Yangchou several times. Reliquaries of gold and silver from Sri Lanka and Ayuthia and Bonin and Ava, containing the Buddhist scriptures, were placed in the white *dagoba*, which had now been built of stone. Buddhist monks, those in purple from the Lama Tibetan cult, and yellow-robed ones from Sri Lanka, as well as those of the Zen Buddhist temples of South China, clad in black and scarlet, made music and sang the sutras, and for three days there were processions led by the abbots. Incense lay thick in the air, and all the altars were lit with massive red tapers.

Live elephants sent by the King of Burma danced to the tunes of their country, then knelt before the Emperor, entwining their trunks two by two. Monkeys from Africa and gaudy parrots from Peru, white albino monkeys from the deep forests in Central China, and a Buddha of white jade for the Emperor's mother from the Kingdom of Ayuthia were presented with great ceremony.

"What is Ayuthia?" Bea asked.

"Ayuthia is the Venice of the Southern Seas," Werner replied. "It is the capital of the Kingdom of the Thai. Ayuthia sends rice and teakwood and elephants to China, and in return receives silk and porcelain and the Emperor's protection."

A great festival of lanterns in the shape of lotuses was held on Slender Lake. Lotuses of silk in a season when lotuses did not bloom, each one of them opening as the dragon barge with its one hundred musicians went past. Inside each lotus was a male child, dressed in silk, singing a paean of praise to the Emperor. There was a floating island of flowers, and from it the fairy of the moon, Chang Wo, offered moon flowers, the famous *Qiong* or hydrangea of Yangchou, and executed profound genuflections, while twelve maidens sang a hymn. And then, sustained by a cloud of vaporous white gauze, the moon fairy entered a moon barge and melted into the night.

TSIENLUNG HAD BROUGHT WITH him Clear Concubine, chosen on the occasion of his first visit to Yangchou six years previously. Lord Hsu had been salt commissioner until Marquess Fang had taken his place, and Clear Concubine's mother was a Fang, her father a Hsu. As a mark of high favor, she now accompanied Tsienlung to visit her birthplace. She had borne only a daughter, which had pleased Tsienlung's mother, the Dowager Empress. The Dowager was of Mongol lineage. Though she allowed her son to have Han women, she ruled the harem strongly. Clear Concubine was tolerated because she had no son.

"The Manchus keep their heirs Manchu, and the sons of Han concubines die quickly in the palace," Castiglione whispered, when he came to tell us that Clear Concubine would visit her mother and her relatives in the Hsu and Fang palaces on an auspicious day.

❧ *Nine* ❧

Anno Domini 1760—Spring to Autumn

THE DAY OF THE CONCUBINE'S visit dawned clear. But the hour was still unknown. Dressed before daylight, the Hsu and the Fang families waited, amidst a bustle of pages and maids. Even before the ambulant time-man had struck the hour of sunrise on his scooped bamboo cylinder, Marquess Fang and the male members of his household had donned their ceremonial robes. The women's hair, dressed by maidservants accomplished in the art, was bedecked with jeweled pins and flowers.

The First Wife of Marquess Fang, a pale, colorless woman with beautiful manners, knelt before the altar to Kwan Yin, Goddess of Mercy and Compassion. Pyramids of pomegranates adorned the altar, between burning clusters of sandalwood and arm-thick red tapers in massive pewter holders.

Second Wife once again rehearsed the female members of the family in appropriate genuflections and the correct distance of ceremonial approach. The cooks had prepared congee, pickles, sweetmeats, and buns, for no fires would be lit that day. Water was kept boiling in great brass kettles at a distance from the mansion, brought by relays of young pages. The children, dressed in their best clothes, ran about, adding to the apparent confusion.

For several leagues, all the way from the Emperor's traveling palace to the Hsu and Fang mansions, which faced each other, the road was bedecked with large porcelain pots of

Qiong in blossom. These rare hydrangea, first bred in a Taoist temple upon the distant hills ten centuries previously, had globular clusters the color of white jade. Their petals were said to confer immortality, for they never touched ground, but took wing, as do butterflies.

Blossoms of peach and cherry and white magnolia alternated in serried ranks behind the *Qiong*. Orioles in gilded cages produced sweet music; children clad in scarlet and blue satin held the cages. Clear Concubine would release the birds in a Buddhist ceremony, thus acquiring merit. More children with silk lanterns, each one a different shape, also waited, should the set hour be evening. The concubine's way to visit her family would then appear as a heavenly stream of stars.

That morning, three daughters of the Fang family came to our pavilion, followed by their maids loaded with silk vestments.

"Cousin White Orchid [Bea's Chinese name], our Elevated Relative was told of you and your brother. She was enchanted with the mechanical birds you brought from the West." The Imperial Concubine wanted to see Bea. I could not attend the meeting, being a male; no male can look upon the women of the Emperor.

They made Bea try this and that tunic and shirt, arranged her hair, and urged her to put powder and rouge upon her face. As for her shoes, since she could not wear the diminutive shoes the bound-foot Han women wore, they had brought large satin shoes with embroidered uppers.

Bea's face was smooth, as if she had known this would happen.

"Bea—"

"All will be well, Colin."

I asked no more. It was my habit to follow where she led.

Second Great Lady bustled in, in her energetic, purposeful way, to inspect Bea's attire and pronounce it adequate. She had shown us especial kindness and taught us the proper ceremonial. She now instructed Bea on the genuflections, the way to hold her hands, feet, neck, and head. In her breathlessly running way, she gabbled of the intricacies of the noble Hsu and Fang families, who had intermarried for some five generations.

Bea was escorted by eunuchs of the Court, as were the

other female relatives, to the hall specially reserved for the Grace and Favor advent, there to await, for many hours, Clear Concubine's arrival.

I stayed in our pavilion. There could be no going to the workshop today, for the two mansions, and all the streets and paths to it, swarmed with court eunuchs.

Apricot, my first maid, came to me after Bea left: "We do not light fires today, Master, we must not cook." This was to avoid a building, or room, catching fire, since all the pavilions were of wood.

I could not leave our own courtyard. I read, took out my tools, inspecting their keenness, and thought of making a great android, one who would truly be like a man. Night came. I fell asleep; in my sleep I saw great boughs of mistletoe, its fruit pale moonlight, its greenness independent of the sun, and Bea walking into their glory. They clothed her, and then swallowed her. I saw her disappear, still smiling, into their voracious tendrils, and woke shouting her name.

They took me to the Grace and Favor hall, specially built for the occasion. So many women were there, in silks and jewels, a great spread of color. The pillars were enrobed in embroidered silks with bird and flower designs; the ceiling hung with many lanterns of nacreous seashell and ivory carved like lace.

By noon came two fourth-rank eunuchs, their rank denoted by a crystal button and a feather of the horse-fowl in their caps. A third-rank eunuch with a sapphire button then strode in to announce that Clear Concubine would arrive after sunset. We partook of sweetmeats and rice congee, and the maids rearranged the dresses of their mistresses; the older ladies went to lie on their beds, their embroidered covers once more changed, and the tassels of pearl and turquoise hanging from the baldachins.

It was night when Clear Concubine's palanquin, bedecked with pearls and pale jade, with six bearers and twelve ladies-in-waiting before and behind it, stopped at the gate, accompanied by two Grand

*Eunuchs of the second rank and twenty-four secondary eunuchs. The
palanquin pages withdrew—being full males, they could not look
upon the lady who stepped out of the conveyance.*

*Marquess Hsu's wife, the wife of Clear Concubine's brother, lifted
the palanquin's door drapery. Her mother, Lady Fang, supported by
two maids, genuflected to her, but Clear Concubine raised her, sobbing,
crying, "Mother," and the sound was covered by music and the
joyful din of firecrackers.*

*After due reverence to the ancestors and weeping before the spirit-
tablet of her deceased father, Clear Concubine withdrew to a specially
erected pavilion to change her clothes, and then began the ceremony
of paying her respects to her grandmother, eighty-four years old. The
old lady had risen from her bed to dress in robes embroidered with
the cranes of longevity. A throne had been prepared for Clear Concubine to sit on to receive homage, but she would not sit. She knelt to
the old woman and wept with grace. And then the old woman
returned to her bed, her granddaughter insisting on sitting on its
edge, clasping her hand.*

*I, and the young ones of the Fang and Hsu families, knelt behind
the older women of the clan, and behind us again were lower
concubines, and still farther the family wet nurses and the maidservants.*

*Clear Concubine would now receive her maternal uncle, Marquess
Fang. Once again changing her clothes, she sat in yet another pavilion,
he standing outside the curtain-door so that he could not see her.
They spoke to each other through the heavy embroidered curtains,
and again Clear Concubine was weeping, overcome with joy and
sorrow.*

*Then, in ranks, by age and hierarchy, the women of the Hsu and
Fang families came to kneel and bow to the Imperial Concubine,
feasting their eyes upon her, hoping to become one such as she. At
the end, Second Great Lady whispered in the Imperial Concubine's
mother's ear, and she whispered to her daughter, and I was signaled
to advance.*

"Approach," said a eunuch.

*Clear Concubine seized my hand. Her hands were small, warm,
her face truly magical in its perfection, the skin flawless, the cheeks
pink, the eyes very dark and bright, the shape of apricot kernels. I
noticed she coughed a little, raising a silk handkerchief to her mouth.*

"You have come from far away, you and your brother, to serve the

Lord of All. The Lord of All is pleased; he has especially enjoyed the singing nightingales in their cages."

I bowed. "My brother and I are orphans. The kindness of Your Highness's relatives rescued us. This is because the Lord of All brings the blessings of Heaven to all His subjects." I had learnt the speech by heart, and I delivered it well.

I watched the mouth of Clear Concubine, her lips followed mine, repeating my words to herself. It was a habit of hers, a charming one, as if she drank in every word that was said to her.

"Such skill and virtue as yours," she replied, "is bound to bring good fortune to anyone lucky enough to be your friend. May happiness and good health attend you and your brother."

It was over. Her ladies-in-waiting then pressed a gift upon me, a casket in which reposed a jade pendant inscribed on one side with a poem, on the other with carved figures.

"What great honor has been bestowed on you! Her Highness has given you one of her own family heirlooms," exclaimed the wife of one of Marquess Fang's nephews, enviously fingering my jewel.

I held the jade pendant in my hand. It stirred with life and power. On it was engraved the Taoist tale of the Eight Immortals crossing the sea, a delicate compliment to my coming from afar. I sent my mind to meet Clear Concubine's and she received it eagerly.

She came into the Festive Hall, where 150 kinds of dishes were set in new porcelain of the famous kilns of the South. Her own set was of pure white jade, with silver covers. Her eyes searched the crowd. I knew they were searching for me.

⁓⧉ ⧉⁓

THE LORD OF ALL had not come merely for leisure. He had also come to levy money for the wars in the northern steppes, begun four years ago.

The northern and western regions of the Empire had always been a preoccupation for China's rulers. Thence had come all her conquerors and many of her imperial dynasties. The Manchus were also part of this movable ocean of horse-mounted nomads, who invaded the Chinese plains.

Within half a century of their conquest of China, the Manchus had become more Han than the Hans, reveling in calligraphy and painting, rigid in upholding Confucianism, and intensely conscious of the danger that their still-restless "cousins" of the Great Steppes of Siberia might bring to them. A new power, the Empire of Muscovy, was advancing across the steppes after having driven back the Golden Horde of the Mongols, and this worried Emperor Tsienlung.

Tsienlung now wanted to consolidate the fluctuant regions of the Northwest, and for this he needed money from the salt merchants of Yangchou.

Third Son, more rebellious than studious Second Son, whose mind was taken up with mathematics and science, spoke in a voice furred with controlled bitterness.

"They came in, these barbarians of the North, galloping on their shaggy horses, slaughtering all before them. They carried great pieces of meat strung to their belts or couched on their saddles. They ate the stinking meat raw. They conquered our millions with a handful of horsemen and made us wear the pigtail. Oh the shame, the shame."

Abdul Reza's grandfather, who had a house of trade in the Muslim quarter of Yangchou, had saved the lives of two sons of the Fang family, hiding them, fighting off a mob of Manchu soldiery, losing two of his own sons in the fray. "And so we shall never forget the Reza tribe of Moors, the memory of their sacrifice," Third Son said.

"The Manchus know only the steppes, care only about land frontiers. They do not watch the seas. They are afraid of our seamen, who run away in small ships, to settle in other lands. Now the Emperor will levy new taxes, on salt, on iron, on silk. He needs silver, much silver, for his northern wars. My father says that we must learn all we can from you, from the ocean people. And then one day we shall kill the Manchus, all of them."

*

OUR WORKSHOPS RESUMED. Second Son was devising a better forge, one that would turn out stronger, more flexible alloys of metal, proof against rust and heat and cold. Werner had a promise that a Portuguese half-breed from Macao, educated at the Jesuit College there, was on his way to Yangchou with designs for better cannon. "Our forts, both in the North and the South, were already bested by English cannon some years ago," Werner said.

A certain Captain Anson had sailed into the Tiger's Mouth of Canton, in 1742, on the English flagship *Centurion*, bearing sixty guns and four hundred men, and two men-of-war of fifty guns, and a sloop of eight guns. In that year, China's reputation in Europe was at its height, due not only to the Jesuits' laudatory reports but also to Voltaire, who was enamored of China.

Anson encountered the arrogance of the Board of Administration of Seaports. He forced his way up the Tiger's Mouth to Canton, and found the forts and the cannon (only twelve of them) no better than they had been a century ago, and no obstruction to his sixty guns.

"The *Centurion* alone was an overmatch for all the naval power of that Empire," Walter wrote, in 1748 in a narrative of Anson's voyage. Voltaire, in 1756, had contradicted him. And the myth of China's strength had endured.

"Voltaire was wrong," Johann Werner said to me. "It is absolutely necessary to arouse this Empire to its own weakness. It is dreaming a dream of the past, and Confucius helps them to dream it. And the Jesuits are in love with Confucius, because he was as authoritarian as they are."

One night he spoke of himself. "I was a clock craftsman, repairing and winding the nearly nineteen hundred clocks in the Garden of Supreme Harmony. Then I began to study Taoism. I wrote a new translation of Lao Dze, the Old Immortal. I became involved with Zen, the synthesis of Buddhism and Taoism. On day I realized that I no longer believed in the One and Only Truth. Excommunication. My name to be erased from the order. By order of our superior, I was to be sent in a wooden cage to Macao, thence transported back in chains, to Europe, there to lie forever in the dungeons of the order in Rome.

"My friend, a Zen Buddhist monk, saved me. Took me away, brought me to Yangchou, to this house. That was seven years ago. Since then our Company of Jesus has had greater trouble than the excommunication of a mere clockmaster. I hear the College of Jesuits in Macao is to be closed by order of the Pope. We should have let religion alone, and taught only science. We were caught in the cleft between religion and science, between blind belief and the new spirit of inquiry."

THE DAY AFTER THE Emperor left we gave our first lesson in electricity and magnetism at our "school of New Learning."

The Master of Clocks spoke. Second Son wrote down all he said with a brush on a large piece of paper affixed to the wall. There were thirteen Han students, besides the six, including Ah Ming, from the Philippines.

Afterwards, the new students crowded round us, asking many questions. Hunger for knowledge widened their eyes. I could only say, "The master is tired, and I don't know enough."

The master lay on his bed, exhausted.

"What are you thinking, Colin Duriez? Is it well?"

"It is well."

"We have lit a fire in their souls."

He paused, rubbed his hands weakly one against the other, a gesture he performed almost constantly now, as if this would restore the strength in his fingers. "The English are conquering India with their better gunnery. The French are losing their trading posts in Bengal. What will stop the English, Colin Duriez, from conquering China?"

"Guns and clocks."

"Clocks and guns. Electricity, the power of steam, boats without sails, carriages without horses. And of course, androids. The automata. They too are the future."

Werner moved his head, testing his neck, which now was a mess of wrinkled tissue.

"Soon the respect and awe for China will wane, as her rulers refuse to learn. Everyone will want their spoils, a piece of this rich land. And all their professed respect for Confucius and for Chinese wisdom will not stop them."

"Newton, Leibnitz, Huyghens," I prayed, "let me do something worthwhile, so that Jacob will be proud of me—so that there will be less carnage, and more tolerance."

WE NOW HAD THIRTY STUDENTS, five rooms to do experiments in chemistry, physics, mechanics, and the wonders of light. The Master of Clocks received a letter from Macao saying not one but two gun makers would come to teach us the science of gunnery. "Let me live till then," he said. He was a man obsessed; he could no longer sit straight, was supported with bolsters. His speech was affected, he slurred his words. Until the end, I noted down everything he said, memorized the flawed sounds that the malady imposed on him. When he would begin to mumble and drool, I would know what he meant to say.

Some of our new students were far too docile, too apt to believe that once they had learnt by rote what we taught, that was knowledge. They would *recite*, but not try to understand, to smell, to touch, to inquire. Any physical exertion, even picking up a fan they let had drop, repelled them, so strong was the division between manual labor and intellect in their minds. They did not realize that science meant the fusion of the two.

Second Son spoke to them.

"How do you know that what I say is true? In the past, did not the great scholar Yen Jochu discover that the Book of History, in the ancient text, was a forgery? Every statement must be reinforced by evidence."

The notion of the classification of phenomena, the idea of observation, did not come easily to the young men steeped in Confucian rigidism. Over-all conformism kept them mind-bound.

Ah Ming was not like the other students. Perhaps because he was a seaman's son of humble birth. Perhaps because he had been in Manila under the Spaniards. I now taught him to read French, and he would inquire as to the formation of words and their origin. Often I would say, "Look, Brother Ming, I do not know . . . I am not a scholar or a philosopher."

"I must know science," he would reply. "It is a posture of

the spirit, a perpetual search for the beyond." He breathed deeply. "I shall not rest easy, now that you have opened the eyes of my mind."

I WROTE TO JACOB, telling him how security had come, and purpose, and ease. Marquess Fang would give me great strings of copper cash and also silver ingots. As for silks, porcelain, and jewelry, Bea now had five chests full, and I too was loaded with presents and gifts.

Bea, seeing me write to Jacob, smiled a little. "Colin, setting up this House of Science—in the end, what will be the outcome?"

"In the end, Bea, I shall become a learned man, bringing in instruments and books, and who knows, perhaps also teachers from many lands who will teach here."

"If the Emperor is against the school, it will be closed."

"Marquess Fang is very powerful."

"All of us are automata in the Emperor's head."

"When the Emperor knows that science is important and useful, then he will hearken to us."

Bea shrugged.

"Do not hurt me, Bea. This is a noble endeavor."

"I am thinking of a way to make you safe," she responded. Her eyes were speckled with gold. She was so beautiful, and I was a little afraid of her.

BEA DID HURT ME. Because of Apricot.

I was sixteen, and for more than a year I had felt the urgent thrust of manhood. Surrounded by girls, women, maidservants, a universe of silk, of soft voices and the inescapable peach perfume of skins, it was agony not to touch.

Apricot was twenty-two. She had been ordered to serve me, and though there were other maids, prettier and younger, it was Apricot who massaged my leg when it hurt, who made my bed. And one evening of summer, as I returned from the workshop, she was there, holding the lamp to light me to my bed. I undressed. The other maids withdrew and she was closing the doors.

"Apricot," I called "Apricot, I—"

She came towards me. I looked at her, my face congested with desire, my body racked with yearning. And very quickly she was in my bed, and I was initiated in the gestures of love, the smoothness, the release.

She lay in my arms and my strength spent itself in her, again and again. My fingers untiringly roamed her skin, her shoulders, her spare curves; she dealt out love to me until I had no care for guilt or sin.

When I arose the next day she had gone. I thought calmly of the sin of the flesh. The memory of a wrathful God floated by, gentle as last autumn's fallen leaves, and as ineffectual. She entered, fresh in the early light, carrying a cup of tea.

"It is time to dress, Master," she said.

I could smell the perfume of the tea; it had a new sharpness. The whole world was made new. Straightening the quilt she smiled discreetly. Her face showed no distress but also no special guile. Perhaps, perhaps, it had been a dream . . . but no, her fragrance, a smell of jasmine, and another smell, that of the warm gardens of summer, of childhood, of the lake, with the snow-crowned mountains topping its glory, the smell of warm slate in the sun—all of this came back, stirred me while I drank the tea, watching Apricot busying herself putting in order what was already orderly while the two younger maids set breakfast and then withdrew.

"Apricot, oh, Apricot."

She knew instantly and came to me, all dressed as she was, with a jacket of purple and ample green trousers. I now knew that these trousers, seemingly a barrier to be taken down, were slit in the middle, so that it was possible, naturally, easily, to reach the heart of her without any shame.

HUMID SEVENTH MONTH, the air replete with scent of leaf and flower, sudden clouds dropping their overflow on calm gardens, breaking the reflections of the pavilions and the willow, juniper, acacia, and bamboo surrounding the pools.

My limbs were all ardor; my senses endowed with new alacrity. Never had the sky been more blue, the trees more full of meditative exaltation; I could hear their barks crease under the pressure of the mining sap. The magnolias shed their petals as summer struck the garden with sudden heat. Summer was long nights when we heard the owl's wings as it furrowed the darkness towards its nest in the old cedar, and the discovery of her body's treasures; the untiring silkiness of her skin, the witchery of her slim belly, leading to that moist and scented calyx. With marvelous force I would enter it again and feel the slow quiver begin in her. "Ah," she said, "ah." Never more. But both of us had now known the thousand suns of delight together, and I would hold her to me long afterwards, whispering her name. "I love you, Apricot, I love you." And she would very gently stroke my shoulders, never touching my head or face. Her hands were simple and kind upon me, and I do not remember that we ever talked much. At dawn, she would always be up before me, waking me.

"The master must go to teach," she would say.

"Do not call me master, Apricot."

"But you are my master," she said. "I am glad to serve you; I only wish to serve you all my life."

I fell asleep one warm afternoon on my books, and was awakened by Third Son pulling at my sleeve. "Colin, Brother," he laughed, looking at my face, "the pleasures of Cloud and Rain are great, but use them in moderation . . . they will not run away, but you will become an addict." So he knew. Everyone knew.

I asked Apricot that evening, "You are of the Fang household. Does Marquess Fang know?"

"Marquess Fang has given me to serve you," she replied. "It is not good for a young man to be alone and waste his strength in emptiness." Yet she insisted that no one see us, for being caught in lovemaking would make her a laughing-stock of all the servants.

And now Apricot moderated my lust, saying, "I will come to you every third day."

"But, Apricot—"

She smiled and adjusted my gown about my shoulders. "It is better than to send you to the pleasure boats. You are a foreigner and do not know how to deal with those damsels."

And then the nightmares began.

IN THE FLIGHT OF ECSTASY, suddenly, a stamping and a burning, the horror, my mother running after my father into the fire . . .

My groin weakened and faded, all that was left was an opacity, as my jutting body withdrew, without pleasure, without that final drowning in depths of grace, finding only a wall and chill failure. . . .

Apricot in my arms, odorous summer with a million blossoms, and I in the grey day, in the cold sand, embraced by darkness and horror.

"There is a fox spirit about," Apricot said when, on the third attempt, I fell onto her, slack, eclipsed, negated by the dreams I had thought reasoned out of myself. Now they were back.

"A fox spirit, jealous of your happiness," Apricot repeated peremptorily. She lit the lamp and looked at me thoughtfully; and then I remembered my foot. Perhaps the evil came from there.

"It is my foot," I said.

"I shall go to the temple tomorrow and seek help to drive out the fox spirit that wants to eat you," Apricot said.

She surrounded me with the honey of her, the springing sweetness. I was consoled, and said, "Perhaps I am tired, perhaps . . ."

"These things happen, but do not worry. Let us sleep now; I shall take care of you."

Assuaging morning came, making the night unreal. I taught as usual; found Second Son and Ah Ming immersed in a problem with charts and plans and books around them. They now carried out experiments on their own. I took out my set of instruments, given to me by Abraham Hirsch.

I laid out the screws and drills, the truing calipers and the broaches, the chisels and tweezers, the special pliers and levers.

On my table was the turn, the burnishers, and pin vises. And as I watched my hands move, I knew how I would make an android, an almost perfect one. I forgot Apricot, forgot the nightmares, and set to work—there was *another* way of putting the cams and levers, setting the central pins. . . .

That evening Apricot did not come, but Bea was with me, and there was an air of triumph about her mind, like a shining barrier, so that I could not ask her anything.

MARQUESS FANG GAVE A great feast. The painters and poets of Yangchou were invited to the sumptuous main garden of summer to enjoy the peonies in full blossom.

One of the poets had had too much to drink and ventured a line:

> *Alas that petals fall on the palace steps,*
> *To be swept away heedlessly.*

Marquess Fang had seemed perturbed by it, but the feast had progressed.

Now Third Son came to fetch us. "My father wishes your attendance."

"A message from the Court has come," Bea said as we stepped into our chairs, following Third Son.

"How do you know, Bea?"

She adjusted the summer jade pins in her hair.

In the courtyard stood eunuchs in blue and scarlet. Within the reception hall were two eunuchs with silk dresses embroidered front and back. Marquess Fang was on his knees. The imperial courier stood, carrying in his hands, rolled in yellow silk, a command from the Court.

Remembering the spring of Yangchou, our spirit is solaced by the loyalty of its people; well pleased with the attention to all the rites and virtues. In particular the harmony promoted between the various people of our Empire, and the benevolence extended even to those from across the seas who dutifully come to learn, and render service, to our people.

169

We therefore invite the artisans from the Western Ocean to exercise their skill in our palace.

We bowed low three times, Marquess Fang saying the ritual, "We obey."

"It is the wish of the Exalted Lady Clear that the woman craftsman should attend her as court lady." The chief eunuch's face was pale, long, his shoulders narrow, his buttocks large in his splendid gown. "Let the foreigners come forward that I may see them."

"Rise, rise and go forward," Apricot whispered. She was behind me, giving me a hand for rising from my knees.

We advanced, Bea and I, while the eunuch stared at us coldly:

"The boy craftsman is defective in body. He cannot appear at Court. Besides, there are already many men craftsmen. Make the girl ready to go to Peking."

Everyone knelt, saying, "We obey."

There was nothing else to say.

"BEA, BEA, THEY WANT to take you to Peking, and I am to stay here, oh, Bea!"

Bea's eyes were dancing, gold streaking the irises. "Colin, of course you will be with me."

"But you've heard him . . . my foot."

"We shall find a way. Trust me."

"But, Bea, I don't *want* to go to Peking, to be a mere puppet—always at the beck and call of the eunuchs. Giuseppe Castiglione said it, remember?"

Castiglione had told us, "We have to present ourselves before the Emperor at seven in the morning. The eunuchs never miss an opportunity to find fault with our apparel, our boots, the way we hold ourselves. They do so with expressions of such tender solicitude that though we smart under the insults, etiquette dictates that we have to pretend gratitude for their help in making us presentable. They are past masters in making their hatred of us appear as concern for our safety, our appearance, our health."

Bea's mind was a cloud filling the sky, blurring its clearness, annihilating smell and sight, the delineation of the garden, the pillars with their squawking parrots. I felt myself shrink. But Bea was there, Bea in the womb with me, Bea holding my foot in her hand, so tight that the midwife could not prise away her hand—my foot had kept the imprint of her grip upon it.

"Oh, Bea," I whispered, my throat dry. *"You've* done this. *You* made Clear Concubine ask for you—"

"Perhaps, Colin."

"You want . . ."

"Colin, everything is possible once we are there. Everything can be done. Remember what Abdul Reza said: 'Only small minds have petty schemes.' "

"You are wrong, Bea." I beat the air with my hands, those raven wings, feathers of darkness, filling my mind. I am Colin, Colin Duriez.

"Bea, I want to stay here. I have work to do; I cannot leave the Master of Clocks."

"I shall convince the Emperor. He will see that it is necessary to learn new things."

The summer faded and died around me. Outside the dark room walked once again the monsters of dread.

"You shall have all you want, Colin. Once the Emperor is convinced . . ."

"APRICOT," I CALLED. "APRICOT."

She was crouched behind the latticed screen, listening.

"Fox demon, a painted devil," she said. "Ambitious."

"She is my sister."

"She wants the Old Ten Thousand Years himself. She wants to be Empress."

Apricot adjusted my clothes; the touch of her hands, firm, cool, restored me a little. I was shaking. "Apricot, Bea and I are twins. . . ."

"Only the King of Devil-Killers can stop her."

I went to Johann Werner the next morning and found him with a man with shaven head, clad in a grey gown with grey shoes. His face, smooth as beaten gold, turned to me.

"Your sister is said to be possessed by a fox spirit," Johann Werner said. The muscles round his mouth still functioned, although his cheeks had hollowed with the palsy reaching them. "That is only another way of saying that she has a strong mind and a strong will. At one time such women were called witches."

"My parents died in a fire, burning to their deaths, because of a false accusation of witchcraft," I replied hotly.

"There is a great deal we do not know about the way our minds function," Johann Werner replied. "I think that some minds can influence others."

"We are twins; we talk to each other without words."

"You are two, and you are the antithesis of each other. Because you are lame, you cannot go to Court with her. Nothing imperfect must come in the sight of the Lord of All. Perhaps your sister is right—if the Emperor were to understand and to agree to our teaching and making machines, then all could be changed."

He turned his head with difficulty. "This is my friend, Traveler in Emptiness, who saved me a long time ago from being sent in a wooden cage to Rome. Knowing I needed him, he has returned from a walk to a hundred monasteries to be with me until I too go into the Void."

The monk's gaze wrapped me. "Your heart is not at ease, for you wish to stay and you also wish to go."

"Bea does not know how to make automata or repair them."

"Your sister has delighted the Imperial Concubine," Johann Werner said. "Clear Concubine has few friends at the Court. She hungers for a strong, self-assured spirit near her."

I felt reassured. No witchcraft, no supernatural power. Bea *thought* it was her doing, but it was not.

"Traveler in Emptiness will take you to the Temple of Major Enlightenment and see to your leg," Johann Werner said. "The Bodhidharma, who founded Zen some twelve hundred years ago, taught many exercises, and what is a weakness in a body may become its strength. Have no fear about your sister. She will try to captivate the Emperor. She has great dreams. Let her be."

Like water, polished smooth on its surface but hiding within its translucence so many animals, some of them devouring monsters, others their prey, I felt myself the lair of many devils when I had left Werner and returned to my room. I felt flayed, my skin torn away, and there was filth in my exposed heart, a stench about me.

"Apricot, Apricot," I called.

"Here, Master."

That night I used her frenziedly, wearing her out until she moaned and wound her limbs about me and said, "I knew not that the exorcism would be so effective. I shall go to the temple tomorrow and thank Chung Kwei, the Demon-Killer."

But I heard the stir of voices in the air and clutched at Apricot.

Love and hate. Hate and love. Bea. Bea.

She came to me, walking in as Apricot was dressing, imperiously motioning her away. She lay by my side. We said no word. Her mind came to mine, and it was magic. Love and tenderness and beauty.

I was again in the womb, fettered to her forever.

BEA LEFT WITH TWO peronal maids and two undermaids. Four eunuchs would accompany her. She climbed on a fair-sized junk, a potbellied craft with purplish bat sails. She said, "Within six months you shall be with me."

Courage and daring my sister had, going forth to conquer an emperor, an empire. Conquest was in her blood. She was a priestess of the enchanted forests.

Second Lady Fang suddenly turned on Apricot and accused her of having purloined a piece of brocade threaded with gold, which she wanted to send to Clear Concubine in Peking. Marquess Fang's second wife kept lists of the stores of silk and brocade, gifts and jewelry, furniture and carpets and hangings. A little slave child was always by her side, carrying bundles of keys on a tray.

"Don't cry, Apricot, don't cry."

I caressed her thick, glossy hair, done in the southern manner, a long thick plait on one shoulder.

"It is the fox spirit again," she said. "She will kill everyone she does not like."

"My sister is not a fox spirit," I said crossly and pushed Apricot away from me.

I went to the Temple of Major Enlightenment with Traveler in Emptiness. I was given a small bare room whose window overlooked many old trees. A Taoist herbalist-priest came and examined my foot, laid a cataplasm of boiled herbs round the ankle. I remarked on the multitude of birds in the garden. "We are near to the seventh of the seventh month, when birds make a bridge between the two stars, the Weaving Maid and the Cowherd, separated forever but for that one night in the year," Traveler said. "It is a tale the women love. You will see them preparing cakes and cosmetics, burning incense and candles, threading needles with silk in memory of the Weaving Maid."

Traveler's serenity made me sleep dreamlessly in the bare room.

"Teach me," I said. "Teach me."

"You can only teach yourself."

The Taoist priest, whose name was Mist in a Grove, taught me some exercises to render my leg supple.

I returned to the Fang palace after a week. I felt no different, except that the rigid cord that held my foot seemed more elastic. I called Apricot, but it was someone else who came, Little Vermilion, young and pretty, eager to please.

"Where is Apricot?"

"She has left."

"Left? Where has she gone?"

"Second Great Lady arranged a marriage for her, and she has gone. Her husband is one of the stewards and rent collectors for the Fang lands. She will have enough to eat, and many dresses," Vermilion said enviously.

Apricot. I regretted her pliant body, the honey delight of her. She had loved me. But I would never see her again.

The teaching continued. Second Son and I continued to translate the new books. A servant held Werner's head upright. Still it lolled on his neck. His tongue protruded as the mus-

cles of his cheeks died, but his brain was clear. Only I understood his mumble.

The cannon maker from Macao was named Thomas Chi.
He was a Christian. His servant Dumb Liu was illiterate, but
with a natural gift for making guns. Thomas Chi was tall,
with slightly curly hair and a brown complexion. His grandmother, he said, was from Malabar, his grandfather a Portuguese nobleman. After some few days, Second Son became
uneasy.

"The fellow wants money—he knows a little something;
but he is greedy, too greedy."

Second Son and Ah Ming constructed a boat with paddle
wheels, propelled by steam. They had heard of a clock that
needed no rewinding: merely walking on the wooden floor
near it would set up vibrations that activated its mechanism.
Now they had decided to build it with my help.

"All movement is a force, and so is steam, and so is wind,
and . . . so many other things," Ah Ming taught the class.
"And one kind of force can be transformed into another."

Mist in a Grove manipulated my leg, gave me herbs to
clear the blood, taught me rhythmic and smooth movements
like music, the body's melody. I felt life flowing into my
fingers, life and cleverness. I would make an android so perfect that everyone would believe it alive.

❧ *Ten* ❧

Anno Domini 1761–1762—Winter

Johann, dear Brother in God,

I think much of you in Yangchou, with its mild winter, and pray that the Almighty restore you to health.

His Majesty has ordered from us paintings commemorating his victories in the Northwest against the Eleuths. Having seen the battle compositions of Rugendas the painter, brought by my French colleagues from Europe, he wishes to have similar ones done. Father Pierre Amigot has sent some of our paintings to be engraved on copper plates in Paris. There will be some twenty of them, the work of Brothers Attiret, Damacene, Sickelpart, and myself.

I have also painted the feast given by His Majesty at the Palace of Violet Light, in honor of his victorious army commanders. Two thousand captive chieftains were exhibited, handsome men of proud bearing. They will be asked to serve in the Emperor's armies, now that peace has returned and the Dzungarian region has become part of the Empire.

The beautiful Bea Duriez has been appointed court lady to Clear Concubine. An audience with the Emperor's mother is talked about. At present her main occupation seems to be devising clothes in the manner of the French Court for the Emperor's women. She teaches the eunuchs of the inner palace to do the hair of the concubines in French style.

His Imperial Majesty, in good spirits, has asked me to paint a scene showing four of his ladies dressed as Europeans and playing chess. This will be used on a screen in the Palace of Enduring Spring, the Western-style annex of the Yuan Ming Yuan that we have now completed.

The victorious army commander has brought to Peking, as the seal of an alliance with the Dzungarian tribes, the famous beauty Mamsiri, wife of the Hodja King, who was slain in battle. The concubines think her uncouth. A eunuch has even remarked, "Why, the new court lady from the West is better-looking." His Majesty, however, seems much taken with her.

No letter from Bea accompanied Giuseppe's missive, which I read out to Johann Werner. But Bea did not need to write; my inner ear heard the footsteps of her approach. I would go to sleep, and she would be at my side. Her eyes sparkling, her cheeks tinged with red, she wore a Chinese dress of satin with a large border, embroidered with tiny roses, and had jade butterflies in her hair. She did not speak of Mamsiri, the Hodja lady.

JOHANN WERNER REFUSED TO take more students, though scholars in cap and robe would call upon Second Son, begging to be admitted to the New Learning.

"We must be careful," Werner mumbled. "Nothing too obvious . . . danger . . . in New Learning."

Power lies uneasy, suspicious, ready to crush what is strange and foreign. Too large an assembly of scholars; too great and sudden an interest in New Learning. Werner had decided to recruit no more. We remained with thirty students.

Every other day I went to the Temple of Major Enlightenment. Mist in a Grove stretched my ankle and taught me Tai Chi, the Taoist exercises of Supreme Ultimate. My leg tendons were lengthening, my sole now more than half on the ground.

Traveler in Emptiness was often by Werner's bed. Sometimes he looked like the statue of the Buddha, and his golden coloring increased the impression. I saw him often at the temple, standing in the courtyard, watching me while I exercised.

One day the temple courtyard held five young men, naked to the waist. Two of them were wrestling, a misleading word; the grace and swiftness of their parry and thrust were more like a dance. They seemed never to touch each other, but leapt, avoided, feinted, and somersaulted.

Traveler sat on a porcelain stool, watching them. "These novices are going to Shaolin Monastery to perfect themselves in Wushu, the martial art," he said.

Shaolin Monastery was famous. There, eleven centuries ago, the Bodhidharma had first taught Zen, union of mind, meditation, heart, spirit, and body. Zen was self-realization, not ascetic withdrawal from the seven emotions and the six lusts but a perception of their essence. Zen taught that spirituality lay through perfect knowledge of the body and its power.

Zen's art of self-defense, Wushu, was what I now saw the five young men practice. Graceful bodies become precise and wonderful objects. In total control, they had the capacity to deal death with a gesture, yet the whole point of acquiring such cunning strength was in *not* using it to kill.

As I stared at the young men I felt shaken, transported. I yearned to be like them. To soar like a hawk, swooping upon the target in perfect mastery of the elements—air, time, space, and body.

"Teach me," I said. "Teach me, Master."

Traveler smiled: "You want strength, but you must first know what strength is."

"My sister has strength. I am the weakling." Unpremeditated, this confession leapt off my tongue.

"Her strength is great, but also her pride, which is weakness. Each body fulfills itself in its own way; the snake in the way of the snake, and the lion in the way of the lion."

Traveler in Emptiness began to teach me. He taught me to make use of my internal energy, rendering it pliable as a blade of grass in the wind. Yet a soft blade of grass can cut one's hand.

Mist in a Grove, massaging my leg, said, "Your weak foot will become your strongest weapon."

Traveler could stand on two of his fingers stuck in the ground. With a flick of his wrist he could smash a stone. He leapt high in the air, spinning his body, and was behind me whereas before he had been in front.

With him and the Taoist, Mist in a Grove, I began to learn Wushu.

The Grand Eunuch is tall, puffy-faced, has pale hands. His eyes disrobe me, for eunuchs know women's bodies well. They dress the hair of the favorites; handle their clothes in and out of coffers. Bedroom curtains are their accomplices. Invisible, their footsteps soundless, they watch . . . only they, the cut-men, are allowed everywhere in the palace, by day and by night. And they take their pleasures in strange and awful ways.

Each night, or whenever the Emperor desires it, the Grand Eunuch presents him a coffer with ivory blades. On each one is the name of an imperial concubine. The Emperor selects.

The eunuchs then go to the favored woman's pavilion. She strips naked in front of them, for there is a legendary fear of a woman hiding a weapon, stabbing an Emperor in his sleep. They wrap her in a wide sheet of brocaded silk and carry her on their backs to the dragon bed. She lies prone at the bed's foot, head touching the ground, waiting for the signal from the Lord of All.

While the Grand Eunuch inspects me I enter his unguarded mind. Mamsiri.

The Grand Eunuch is not thinking of me. He is thinking of Mamsiri: This barbarian girl, and that Hodja woman . . . danger for the Empire . . ."

"*The third of next month is an auspicious day,*" he says. "*The Holy Mother will receive you. It is a great honor for someone as unworthy as you are.*"

The Dowager Empress is part Mongol, of the Balaaraisan clan. She will receive me at dawn. I kneel waiting outside the bedroom threshold for two hours in the greyness while her court ladies and maids, inside the carved amber doors, busy themselves opening coffers to choose her apparel from among her three thousand robes.

Outside, some of the four thousand eunuchs who serve the Holy Mother are conveying her breakfast, consisting of sixty-four dishes, which must pass through seventy pairs of hands to come from the kitchen.

Through the heavy brocade curtains I glimpse the bed, covered in embroidered silk, with a silk canopy, tassels of pearl and turquoise and coral. The sweets she favors, pastry stuffed with ground flesh of plum and almonds, reach the bedroom. The Empress wife of Tsienlung and the favorite, Clear Concubine, are kneeling at the bedside, presenting the first teacup to the Holy Mother.

An hour later, a secondary eunuch says curtly to me, "Go in and kneel."

The Holy Mother is sitting on a day kang. *By her side is a small table with fruit and comfits. I kneel, kowtow thrice; I feel her eyes on me, her distaste. I send out my mind, and the name comes out like the thrust of a lance:*

Mamsiri.

Two barbarian women at Court, but perhaps we can use this one against the other, *she is thinking.*

"Come nearer."

I approach in three steps, kneel, then another three. I let my head fall to the ground in prostration.

"At least you are well taught," says the Holy Mother. "Let me look at your face."

I raise my head and I see her in the bedroom's gold and purple penumbra. A Mongol face, broad and ample, a high forehead, prominent cheekbones, aquiline nose, and flying eyebrows. She wears the classic Manchu inner-room headdress—a large butterfly of black satin with jeweled pins, and a gown of pale green silk embroidered with dragons.

She has hunted and loved. She is strong. And like the seahawk delving into water her mind gropes for mine. "I know you," it says. "You want what I wanted when I was sixteen, your age. I was chosen, and bore an heir to the Dragon Throne. You are beautiful. But you will not be chosen. However, I can use you. . . ."

Loudly she speaks: "I hear you are skilled at repairing those Western baubles that are brought to us."

"The Holy Mother is too kind. This unworthy one can do only unskilled work. My brother is the skilled one."

"Your brother." Perhaps she will think how she can use him. Her hand waves and her waterpipe of gold and jade is presented to her. I hear the tobacco smoke gurgle through the water.

"Let her have those two clocks of mine that are broken," she says to the Grand Eunuch. "We shall see what she can do."

And now everyone knows it in the Forbidden City, in the Empire.

Mamsiri, the Turkoman widow of the Hodja chieftain from Dzungaria, has conquered the Lord of All.

Like a young, eager boy, devoured by a passion unbecoming to his state and his age, the Emperor's obsession shakes the Great Within.

She was conveyed, on her arrival, to the Palace of Perfect Harmony, elected to stay in the section built on the model of Versailles by Castiglione and named the Palace of Enduring Spring. Mamsiri occupies the main building, in front of which is the majestic fountain with twelve moving figures, designed by Castiglione and other Jesuits.

On the fourth day after her arrival, the Emperor, with two trusted eunuchs, had gone there and spied on her while her maids were preparing her for the bath.

And fallen in love.

Without reference to his mother or to the Grand Eunuch, Mamsiri was promoted to "Fei," Concubine of Exalted Rank. Hsiang Fei, Fragrant Concubine, was to be her name because she bathed daily in water scented with attar of roses.

"He has gone mad over the barbarian." The Grand Eunuchs and the secondary eunuchs knelt in front of the Dowager Empress, the Holy Mother, and reported on this dangerous passion that had seized the Emperor.

Her broad Mongol face with its thin, high nose remained impassive. She summoned the astrologers and the abbot of the Tibetan Buddhist temple of Peking, where her son had been born, to choose an auspicious day for the audience of Perfumed Concubine.

"It is important that all go smoothly," the Grand Eunuch, still shaking with the indignity of it all, told the abbot.

On the chosen day at the appointed hour, Mamsiri stepped down from her litter. She had not changed her garb, not dressed as a concubine of the Emperor, in a robe embroidered with phoenixes. She wore a scarlet mantle of war about her shoulders, and boots and

181

trousers under her tunic; a belt with a poniard stuck in it. No one, absolutely no one, was allowed to carry a weapon within the palace.

The Great Ancestress hooded her eyes. Perhaps dreams of her own turbulent forebears came upon her. They had ridden the limitless steppes on shaggy horses, caring not for rites and pomp, the women free as the wind, laughing and drinking with the men. . . .

The Dowager watched Fragrant Concubine with benign malevolence and said, "We hope you will become accustomed to your new surroundings."

The night she was to be carried to the dragon bed to receive the supreme favor, she refused. Kneeling and knocking his forehead upon the floor until it bled, the Grand Eunuch besought her to remove her clothes, to let him wrap her in the embroidered silk sheet.

"Mamsiri shall not be carried naked by cut-men to her wedding night. She will ride to the tent of the one she has chosen when she pleases."

The Grand Eunuch prepared to commit suicide. To spare him, the secondary eunuch, who had been his lover, strangled himself with a silken cord so that the Emperor's anger might be placated.

Mamsiri now asked for a mosque, that she might pray to Allah, for she was Muslim, as were all the Eleuths of Dzungaria. A command went to the Jesuits to remodel a small building in the Garden of Enduring Spring into a mosque.

Truly, there is perfume wherever she goes. She moves the air and changes it. Her eyes are golden brown and her hair dark; her skin glows like the skin of peaches. Her legs are long, and her feet seem to dance. Suddenly every woman in the palace, bound-foot Han or big-foot Manchu, feels awkward when Mamsiri paces like a caged tigress, yearning for the wide deserts, the snow mountains of her home.

Clear Concubine shivered and burnt in her pelisses of fur; she coughed and blood welled from her mouth to stain her garments. She sobbed and sighed. "If only the Lord of All would deign to see me, all would be well."

Clear Concubine's eunuchs come running: "Exalted Lady, the Lord of Ten Thousand Years is on his way."

Clear Concubine's gaunt face becomes radiant. Quickly we dress her, changing her into a pale pink robe with a darker pink and green motif, a new invention of gauze-patterned silk from the South. Shaking with excitement and apprehension, she asks for her mirrors, gazes at her face, finds the lines under her eyes, and laments:

"He will find me too thin, old."

I am by her side; I say, "Let me help you."

She looks at my face next to hers in the mirror and her mouth quivers.

I apply the cosmetics, do her hair in a new way. The imperial procession arrives, twenty-four eunuchs bearing the silk fans and peacock fans, and after that the Emperor's litter. Out of it strides Tsienlung, dressed in plain brown silk.

Clear Concubine falls to her knees. Kindly he extends a hand to raise her. "I have heard that you were unwell, and my heart was troubled."

Overwhelmed by his gentleness and not knowing that it is the signal of her death, Clear Concubine bends her forehead to the ground and whispers, "Ah, Holy One . . . Ah . . ." But his eyes have already gone from her to me, for I knelt by her to support her. And I see he is a man of passion, virile and strong, entering that time which comes to men when the body and the spirit gather themselves in one great rage of living, and nothing seems to count but love. He is the same age as Abdul Reza.

Oh let him see me, *I think.* Let him look. . . .

My eyes go to his, soft, joyous, and promising, and then I quickly look down again. But his face has changed—a long thin face with a high aquiline nose, eyebrows shaped like archer's bows.

He has noticed me. He wavers. He is accustomed to having his way. But he is strong-willed, even in his new passion, not giving up the early-morning audiences, the work with his ministers.

"Your foreign court lady," he says to Clear Concubine.

"My Lord, she came from Yangchou."

"I remember. She repairs clocks, like my Jesuits." His eyes slide away, rest upon Clear Concubine's hair. I see compassion, not love. "You must take care of your health, let physicians minister to you."

"The favor of my Lord has already restored me. It is nothing but the cold of winter."

"May you soon be well." Again his eyes come to me; I see him hesitate.

And then he is gone. Perhaps he will remember me, when this new passion is spent. But my dreams are stark. I have little hope. And if I do not succeed, disaster will come.

❧ ❦

THE TOO-SHORT TENDONS strapping my foot had now lengthened. The tendons of my mind also stretched. Stretch, stretch body and mind. Stretch toward the sky's deep blueness, towards earth's burning core.

There was no wrathful Jehovah waiting to punish me.

Each night, in my dreams, Bea came to me. But now she was a woman, with a woman's body and desires. And I was afraid.

THE FLOWER BOATS. Floating Houses on barges, where courtesans awaited their clients. But here was no immediate joining of bodies. It took days, weeks, to bed a sold woman, and this artifice made one feel chosen, not for the money spent drinking tea and reciting love poems, not for the long wait that sharpened lust, but for oneself.

Illusion enhances and exalts reality, is inseparable from it. And love is, perhaps, a total illusion, yet men and women need love more than anything else.

In the flower boat I courted a girl whose name I do not remember. After some three weeks she gave herself to me, appeared reticent with great art, so that I grew bold.

And then it happened.

As our bodies entwined, as the tide of lust rose in me, so that I felt—true or not—that every inch of her was palpably my own, I had the sensation that this was Bea, my sister, whom I was thus engaging. Bea in my arms.

Like an android, accomplishing with faithful precision what it was created to do, my body, an instrument devoid of sensation, became totally separated from the yielding substance that was the girl. Alien, alone, joyless, while she lay back, satisfied, and whispered:

"I have been without shame . . . you made me so." She clung to me, thinking I truly loved her.

I left, knowing that she would look to my return but I would never see her again.

SECOND SON AND AH MING went to Lake Poyang, some two hundred leagues from Yangchou, to try their invention, a steam machine boat with paddle wheels. Ah Ming had thought of it because of the paddle wheels activated by men, bringing water to the rice fields.

"The boat works," they said on their return. "But we must find a way to recapture the steam, turn it back into water. Now it escapes, and only by continually putting water in the boiler can the boat remain moving."

Ah Ming said the mechanism must be made so that the boat could shift its direction; I said this was easy. It was precisely a shift that activated the automata, using different cams to perform diverse movements. And there must be a balancing wheel, as in watches.

Some of our students were now making watches and clocks, copying and reproducing with great exactitude the models from Geneva, under Ah Ming's supervision. We set other students to the work. Of course they thought manual labor demeaning. I told them that in my country it was craftsmen—woodcutters, ironsmiths, and spinners—who spent the long winter nights devising these machines, the clocks and automata they admired. Perhaps they did not believe me. Contempt for the work of hands was strong in them.

At the temple I wrestled with Traveler in Emptiness, my teacher. He taught me well, by body movement rather than words.

"Your strong leg is the supporting pillar; your weak foot the weapon that will enable you to kill."

"I shall never want to kill anyone."

"Sometimes it is right to kill. For if you give back good for evil, then what will you give back for good? For evil, there must be justice."

I went through the hand movements, suave and rounded, innocent gestures that opened the corridors of strength within my body. I learnt to use the emptiness of space, distance between me and the target, as the conveyance of that formidable catapult which is the human body when launched with skill to the enemy's destruction.

"Your foe looks upon you as a weakling; this is to your advantage. He walks up to you. You await him hesitantly, going back a step or two, limping. He thinks he can overcome you with one blow. You do not avoid the blow, only parry it with skill so that it reaches but does not hurt you. He has the sensation of having attained his aim, but wonders why you have not crumbled. While he hesitates, you advance."

Step by step, gesture by gesture.

"You have very little time. Your blows must be lightning swift. Your mind must have envisioned each coming strike."

"My mind needs armoring," I said bitterly, remembering the flower boat.

"Mind and body must be torn apart to come together," Traveler replied. "Do not grieve that things are revealed to you about yourself that you have shirked to know."

"I wish you would cure the Master of Clocks. It is dreadful to see him die by slow degrees."

I did not want to talk of Bea and the lovemaking.

"His mind will be clear to the end, while his body disintegrates. He is fortunate to observe his own death," Traveler replied. "I shall companion him on the journey he has begun."

I sat in silence, not disrupting the air between us, and from him received energy, a quiet and flowing strength. I bowed to depart, and as I turned away Traveler said, "After the Master of Clocks goes on his journey, you will build an android that can do many things, that will be almost human."

THE ANDROID I HAD begun to build faced me in my room. He waited for me to give him a soul, a program that would enable him to do many things. But my heart, like a slack sail, shivering for lack of wind, mustered no enthusiasm to carry him to his kind of life. Perhaps because I was afraid.

Bea spoke to me, told me of life at Court.

"Colin, all is well. . . ."

All was not well. There was so much she shut away from me, and I could not compel her, because now both of us were afraid to come too near each other. Forever we would have to live with the knowledge of this yearning and refuse it.

I took my android to pieces and put him together again.

I looked at the android's face. I had given him the pasty face of a replete child.

I changed the cams, added a revolving disc. He could write "A limitless ten thousand years" on the blank sheet. I added another cam. His left hand reached for an oil lamp on the table in front of him, to turn the wick and light it. But still he could not pour water from the porcelain water holder upon the stone ink slab, seize the ink tablet and rub it on the ink slab to make the ink, prepare the brush tip to a fine point, and lift it to write—all the gestures of a true Chinese scholar.

And he could write only one sentence.

I named him the Scholar. He would be better than the Writer, which Amigot had brought.

Mamsiri rode a pale grey horse, the best in the Emperor's stables of eight hundred prize coursers. She rode among the western hills in the bleak winter. Behind her was the Emperor, and behind the Emperor, the nobles, princes, and dukes, the ministers and the eunuchs. Tsienlung still punctually attended the daily audiences, starting at dawn; he still listened to the long liturgical discourses of his ministers; to the reports of the viceroys from the provinces. But there was impatience in him, for he wanted to return to Mamsiri.

No other woman, empress or concubine, had approached his bed for near five weeks. Yet the Fragrant Concubine had not yielded, refusing to be wrapped in the embroidered gold brocade and carried to the Hall of Imperial Repose, to the bed with its gilded grinning dragons.

And Tsienlung waited, went from the audience hall to her quarters. Straight and proud, making only a one-knee genuflection, she faced him.

"The Lord of Ten Thousand Years has always liked to tame wild horses," the eunuchs whispered.

She had begun to sing songs of her land. She wanted the landscape of her home round her. The command went to the Jesuits: Recruit fifty thousand men, build an artificial mountain. Castiglione painted her portrait; she was dressed in a suit of armor brought from France, with a plumed casque.

The Board of Rites was in turmoil. The Board of Censors contemplated writing a memorial of reproof, but the white-haired censors were afraid to lose their heads.

That winter morning, with snow flurries and a wolf-howl northwest wind, Mamsiri challenged the Lord of All to race her. She drove her horse, Moon Delight, up the hills in the hunting preserve where the Emperor stalked deer and lynx. And he, leaving behind the military commander-in-chief (who lost his peacock-feathered cap trying to keep up), galloped after her and broke through the three rings of his own guardsmen.

Mamsiri turned and laughed, spurring her horse, and there were only the two of them, galloping among the frozen trees. In the mind of the Lord of All rose the memory of those marriages of the steppes, where the lover captured his woman after a long pursuit on horseback. He ground his teeth, enraged and delighted; his bay streaked and overtook Moon Delight. For a while they rode side by side, and then he bent sideways and lifted her off her saddle, and threw her in front of him, and she laughed, laughed as he halted and slid to the ground with her.

And there she yielded, among the trees, on the frozen ground. Afterwards she said, "Why, I think I shall love you, Hung Lee."

Hung Lee; his own name, forbidden to be uttered by anyone except his own father or mother.

He was delighted.

Clear Concubine is dying; fever does not leave her body. The court physicians know she is doomed.

The Emperor's favor has passed from her. No one now comes to her pavilions, once crowded with fawning ladies and eunuchs.

Mamsiri bathes in the marble pool the Jesuits have built for her. The water is heated every day, essence of rose and jasmine poured into it. The palace has been ransacked for exquisite furs; even the Empress has parted with a coat lined with golden monkey, and as for snow tiger and zibeline pelts, they are stacked in profusion in her Palace of Enduring Spring.

Although I failed to draw the Emperor's attention, the court ladies and the eunuchs run an unending substratum of gossip, praising me. They say I am beautiful, young, a virgin, whereas the Turkoman is a widow. I have repaired the Dowager Empress's two clocks, and she sends me dishes from her table, flowers brought by courier from the South. "Perhaps I have some use for you," is what her mind tells me.

I send my mind to Colin and find his like a smooth lake, glittering in the sun. He is building an android. "All is well, Bea."

I cannot tell him: I dream of you. For in this palace with its constant whispers of lust and forbidden expression of lust, there is only one man. The Emperor. And I want to conquer him. But it is for your sake, Colin, my brother. It is for you.

⤙ ⤚

JOHANN WERNER'S TONGUE LOLLS out of his mouth; he is unable to lift his head. His eyes are still alive, but the muscles holding his eyelids open will also die.

Our Portuguese-Chinese cannon maker, Thomas Wang Chi, has laid by a store of saltpeter and made a pair of cannon, boasting that even the English do not have better ones. Second Son says we must get rid of him. "He is loose of tongue, becomes drunk at night, and consorts with unsavory scoundrels." Wang Chi has found out that Werner was excommunicated and complains that he has been tricked to work for a man cast out of the Church. He threatens to write to the archbishop in Macao.

The news of Clear Concubine's illness has reached Yangchou. The Hsus and the Fangs are anxious, though outwardly unperturbed, for the Hans have a remarkable ability to conceal their feelings.

Everyone has heard about Perfumed Concubine. The maidservants are busy weaving wild tales about her and the Emperor. Lasciviousness in the Supreme Ruler brings calamity upon the country. The mandate of Heaven passes away from the dissolute.

It is New Year and the salt merchants entertain Yangchou city, lavishing money on the temples, the painters, the poets, the gardeners, and all the trades. In evidence everywhere are the deities of wealth, official honors, and longevity. I am fascinated at the mixture of derision and devotion with which the Hans treat their gods.

Second Son takes me in secret to a friend of his who has unearthed an ancient coffin. I am reminded then of Lausanne and the diggings.

The coffin is an enormous chest, higher than three men and as broad as six. It is really three coffins in one, for it has three layers. The inside layer is painted, by hand, with the tale of the Ten Suns, the Ten Ravens, and the Heavenly Archer, Hou Yi.

Once upon a time there were ten suns in the heavens, each one of them supported by its raven of black night. The suns came out one by one, in rotation, resting at night on the heavenly tree, the spine of the universe, upon which their ravens perched.

One day Chaos urged all ten suns to come out together. And men died of heat, and crops burnt, and the rivers and oceans were parched.

Then came Hou Yi, the Great Archer, who had invented the bow and arrow so that men did not have to run after deer and boar but could kill them from afar. He shot down nine of the ravens, so that nine suns fell into the limitless Nothing.

That is why there is only one sun, whose raven dominates night. And on every princely coffin, the tale of Hou Yi is painted, to remind us that day and night, light and darkness, life and death, are one and the same.

Second Son knows many such tales. They trouble me, for he says, "Each of us is sun and raven, evil and good. We cannot escape ourselves."

⚜ ❧

At the Temple of Heaven, which is the central point of the universe, the Lord of All is offering the ritual New Year sacrifices.

Here the Emperor, link between Heaven and earth, becomes the priest-king. He will plough a furrow with the ceremonial handplough, offer the five grains, the bullock, the wine. The crops depend on him. All things will burgeon into life if his conduct has been worthy. If not, there will be floods or drought.

The day is grey. Winter does not release its grip upon the land.

Hail fell in the night, presage of calamity. Hence the rites are taking place late after dawn.

The sacrificial bullock moves within the box in which it is confined, lowing softly, although its vocal cords have been cut. Upon long tables of lacquer are porcelain vessels holding the five grains and the wine.

The Emperor ascends the three terraces of the altar of pure white marble.

In the palace another sacrifice is taking place.

The Dowager Empress has sent for the living Buddha from Tibet. In the Tibetan temple of Peking the monks perform their dances, faces covered with the masks of animals. They leap and swing to the scream of long mountain horns.

The Dowager Empress holds the New Year rites within the Forbidden City. The Empress and the concubines pay obeisance to the dynastic-ancestor tablets, light tapers and incense in each hall. Sitting in the Hall of Harmony, the Dowager receives the honors due her from every female in the inner palace, from every eunuch. On a

191

throne of gilt wood, with the golden cranes of longevity at each side, she becomes the Mother of the Empire. Clear Concubine, almost dying, carried by myself and three court ladies, comes to kneel. The only absent one is Fragrant Concubine.

The Dowager sends for her, delegating not only eunuchs but palace guards, for by not appearing she is injuring harmony, ritual, order. She is Chaos, which destroys the Empire.

Mamsiri is brought from the Palace of Enduring Spring to the Forbidden City, where the Dowager Empress, robed in her dragon robes, surrounded by a phalanx of eunuchs, by the Empress, the concubines, awaits her in the Hall of Constant Harmony.

Mamsiri wears her Turkoman garb—a fur cap, a tunic over trousers, and boots. Her waist is belted, a knife dangling from it on a silver chain.

She is made to kneel before the Holy Mother.

"Barbarian woman," says the Holy Mother, "you are carrying a knife into the Forbidden City, carrying a knife upon you to harm the Lord of All."

Mamsiri tosses her head. "The women of my race, which goes far back into time, have always carried knives."

"Your crimes are so great the people cry their wrath to Heaven," the Holy Mother replies. "The Board of Rites and the Board of Censors, as well as the abbots of the temples, have consulted the four horizons, the eight points of the universe. They say that you are Chaos, you are perversity. You bring disorder to the Empire."

Mamsiri looks around. "Where is the Emperor? The Lord of Ten Thousand Years must decide."

"Heaven decides," says the Holy Mother. "The Emperor is performing the New Year sacrifices and you are disrupting them, by carrying a knife, by destroying the established order between Heaven and men."

Mamsiri looks at the phalanx of women ranged round the throne, at the eunuchs solidly lining the walls. For a moment her eyes rest on me, but I give no sign.

"Our benevolence gives you a choice—either to go into a nunnery, there to expiate your crimes, or to die."

Mamsiri spits on the floor. "I prefer to die."

"Take her away."

She is led back to the Palace of Enduring Spring. Ceremonially kneeling, the Grand Eunuch presents her with the casket, within which is coiled the silken cord.

No one knows what took place. Perhaps she struggled, like a barbarian, but the Grand Eunuch had time on his side.

❧ ☙

WE IN YANGCHOU HEARD of the death of the woman from the steppes. The people now spun a tale of love and sorrow.

While he was offering the New Year sacrifice the Emperor's favorite eunuch had whispered to him that all was not well. He leapt on his horse and rode to the Palace of Enduring Spring. But by now it was after dusk, all the gates were closed, and though he called, none answered. He then rode to the Forbidden City, but his mother had ordered the gates closed "for the Emperor's safety," or so she had said. In reality, to deny him entry . . .

And the Emperor could do nothing, nothing at all. Filial duty, reverence to the Mother, was his paramount responsibility. And the Holy Mother had saved him, saved the Empire.

In the imperial histories no such event had occurred. It was all babble, unrecorded in the archives. The Hodjas had not revolted; a Dzungarian princess, daughter of a loyal chieftain, lived long years in the harem, was named Orchid Concubine, and was never painted by Castiglione. . . .

❧ ☙

❧ *Eleven* ❦

Anno Domini 1762

SOON AFTER NEW YEAR, as the magnolias shed their wide-eyed petals upon the garden paths, Third Son told me that Abdul Reza had returned.

He had arrived in Yangchou with an embassy of Thai princes from the Kingdom of Ayuthia and awaited me in the guest house for foreign ambassadors, in the viceroy's palace.

When I saw him, he was possessed by a cold smooth fury, though kind to me. "Your sister plays a dangerous game. But she is born an emptier of cities," he said, quoting the Chinese proverb that beauty allied to ambition causes the ruin of empires and the dismay of good men.

"It is not so, Prince Reza. She has done this for you and for me."

"For me?" His heavy eyebrows lifted, incredulous.

How could I explain that Bea had visions, premonition of disaster and slaughter, and was trying to avert catastrophe, to seduce the Emperor, for the sake of Reza's grand design?

I tried, haltingly, and as I spoke his face softened. Awe, wonder, disbelief, amusement, and then seriousness. "If what you say is true, then indeed your sister has greatness . . . far surpassing a woman, or even many men. It is the stuff that makes visionaries, and prophets, and conquerors. But she is not dealing with a single man, the Emperor, though he appears all-powerful. It is the whole system, the mandarins, the eunuchs, the bureaucracy—they feel threatened by any change and will kill rather than let go."

Marquess Fang, Abdul Reza and Traveler in Emptiness talked at length together; they appeared concerned. I guessed they were talking of Bea. Then they went to see Johann Werner, who could hear but no longer open his eyes or speak. I sat away from them, not listening but thinking of Bea. The fates of great enterprises are decided by accident, a trifle, a man's whim or vision, or the lack of it, as life and death are decided in the art of Wushu by a flick of the wrist, a finger thrust at the right spot.

"We shall call upon the envoys of the Kingdom of Ayuthia," Marquess Fang said to me.

For more than three hundred years Ayuthia, the land of the Thai—which was also called Siam by the Jesuits and Chinese travellers—had had excellent relations with the Empire. Sending, with every new king, gifts of gold, trees and flowers, vases, rubies and pearls and sapphires, rice and teak and ebony and elephants. Receiving in return silk and porcelain, skilled craftsmen, sometimes a princess or two, and the five-tiered yellow silk royal umbrellas, the Empire's recognition of a new king.

Many Chinese lived in the Kingdom of Ayuthia because all the boat trade between the two countries was in their hands.

Marquess Fang and I went to call on the envoys, and I presented them with automata I had devised, dancers and of course singing birds, and clocks and watches with enameled covers, made in our workshop. These were not strange to the envoys; Ayuthia had a large and diverse population of Arabs, Persians, Portuguese, French, Dutch, English, and Japanese traders, some of them settled there for three centuries or more. Ayuthia was recorded in all the books of travelers, all the commercial houses of Europe, as the gem of the Orient, the Venice of Asia, a city of fabulous splendor and wealth. And in the seventeenth century embassies from Ayuthia had gone to France, to England, to Holland, for lively curiosity was a characteristic of the Thai nation, unfettered by Confucian rigidity.

The envoys we saw at the viceroy's palace were handsome, agile men, moving about freely, laughing and shouting and singing at will while musicians strummed a dozen instruments, in rooms heaped with a medley of objects in nice confusion. All this was very much unlike the decorous formality of the Chinese, and my heart quivered, for though discipline and order appealed to my prudent mind, yet the unfettered relish for life of the Thai envoys captivated me.

Prince Udorn, a young man about my age, spoke to me in French, English, and Dutch. His forebears had been ambassadors to the courts of France and Holland; some had gone to London, to the Ottoman Empire, and to Venice, and a cousin had even been to a great fair in Neuchâtel! Udorn was small-boned, handsome, dusky-faced with large round eyes. When he questioned me on my work in Yangchou, I told him I had opened a workshop to make clocks and watches and automata, and to teach the new science that came from Europe. He smiled and said lightly:

"May good fortune attend you."

Udorn came to see me in my pavilion, brooking no interference, breaking all protocol.

"I am bored waiting to go to Peking," he said. "You amuse me."

He was full of spontaneous happiness, irrepressible as a bubbling spring, joyous without any reason, like the brisk *morget* in faraway Lausanne, blowing with happiness because life is precious, happiness the soul of living.

The envoys of Ayuthia had come not only to bear tribute, the usual gifts at the accession of their new King, but also to ask the Chinese Emperor's help against the predatory King of Burma.

"For near three hundred years we and the Burmese have made war upon each other. Twenty-two wars in all," Udorn told me. "Our great King Boromakot died in 1758. He wanted his third son, Utumporn, to succeed him, because Ekatat, his eldest son, was incapable and weak. But Ekatat nevertheless seized the throne, forcing his younger brother Utumporn into the priesthood. King Alungpaya of Burma, knowing Ekatat was incompetent, had invaded Ayuthia with an army of two hundred thousand men, including ten thousand Portuguese mercenaries. He had come within two leagues of Ayuthia. The princes gathered, clamoring for Utumporn to return, and reluctantly Ekatat had yielded. Utumporn had organized the defense of Ayuthia, and by luck Alungpaya was killed by a splinter from his own cannon, which exploded. The Burmese withdrew. But as soon as the danger was over, Ekatat was back, forcing his brother once again into the priesthood.

"It is a pity," Udorn said, "that Utumporn did not get rid of Ekatat while he was in power . . . a great pity." Ekatat now had rid himself of seventeen half-brothers and sent his delegates to the Chinese Emperor.

It appeared, from what Prince Udorn told me, that the struggle for succession in the Kingdom of Ayuthia was always accompanied by much slaughter.

My attention was drawn to Prince Chiprasong, because of his fierceness. He daily disported himself in the viceroy's courtyard with two swords. His retainers, clad in Japanese woven rattan armor, were used as foils. He uttered harsh screams as he leapt and jumped and thrust at them, and I longed to take him on, bare-handed, at Wushu.

The embassy left for Peking, its barges sailing in stately convoy up the Grand Canal, escorted by eunuchs and protocol officials sent by the Court. Abdul Reza went with them; for him it was a question of commerce, for there were also many Muslims in Peking and in the north of the Empire. I prayed that Abdul Reza would bring Bea back safely. Though every night Bea said to me, "All is well," I could only reply, "Be careful, Bea, be careful."

"COLIN, COLIN . . ."

Ah Ming was shaking me awake. Ah Ming, dressed all in black, a queue wound around his head like a boatman.

"What . . . what?" Thick with sleep, I resisted.

"Marquess Fang has been taken away, accused of treason. We must flee. Quickly."

"But—"

"No time to talk." Roughly Ah Ming pulled me out of bed, threw my clothes at me. There were no servants, no maid about; only a faint rumor, far away, and the disturbed parrots squawking.

"But what has he done?"

Ah Ming sighed with exasperation, threw upon me a hooded black robe, and dragged me outside. A handcart waited on the path, with two men in black, two students from our workshop. "Hide your face . . . you're a foreigner."

I stepped into the handcart, then remembered. "Wait." I ran back into the room, took my set of tools, and, lifting the Scholar, carried him in my arms. Ah Ming grunted, wrapped us both in the robe, and put a cloth round my head and face. The students pushed the handcart through the back door, used to dispose of the latrine ordures, with Ah Ming going in front and carrying a small lantern.

Here was another Yangchou—narrow lanes, low-browed hovels, beggars coiled like dung heaps in corners, furtive shadows. One man raised the paper lantern he carried to look at us. Ah Ming said, "Lend us space, Brother, my grandmother is ill with the swamp fever."

We sped on, reaching the Taoist shrine not far from the ramparts, a small earth-and-brick structure. On the altar within was the statue of a Taoist Immortal, and the walls were bedecked with ex-votos. Here Mist in a Grove waited for us. His robe was bound round his waist and he was panting, as if he had run. Under the brick altar was a narrow space, coffinlike. The planked sides were shut on me.

I said to Ah Ming through the remaining opening, "What about the Master of the Clocks?"

"Traveler carried him to safety."

The plank was rammed shut. I could breathe only through cracks in the wood.

Dawn broke and the first devotees came to supplicate the Immortal. It was Lu Yueh, Grand Marshal of the Hosts Against the Nine Plagues. His warhorse was named the Myopic Camel, and he had a blue face, red hair, long teeth, and three eyes. All day one or another believer would walk in. The Taoist shrine-keeper would burn incense, call upon the Immortal loudly, throw clappers on the beaten earth floor, and dispense medicine he kept in pots along the walls.

At noon Ah Ming returned. The keeper barred the temple gate and we sat down to share his meal. Ah Ming told me what was happening.

"It has nothing to do with the New Learning or making clocks and automata. Not even with the cannon. Second Young Lord had already buried them. Remember the day you went with him to see some old coffin? That was the day we got rid of them."

"But why then is Marquess Fang arrested?"

"The poets."

Emperor Tsienlung might be a lover of poetry and painting, but only in the most strict orthodoxy.

"Do you remember, Colin, at the Bright and Clear festival, after sweeping the graves many poets gathered by Slender Lake? Marquess Fang gave a feast, and a young poet became drunk and spoke heedlessly."

"I remember:

> *Alas that petals fall on the palace steps*
> *To be swept away heedlessly . . .*

"But how can anyone see treason in such words?"

"It is treasonable. It means the Emperor is incompetent, not employing talent. He has special investigators . . . every-where."

A literary inquisition. I remembered Voltaire, Diderot—they too had suffered, in the same way.

"Marquess Fang . . . what will happen to him?"

"No one knows. Marquess Fang may have caused some-one injury, and now revenge is being exacted. Clear Concu-bine is dead, so an accusation against Marquess Fang can proceed upwards; there is no one at Court powerful enough to stop it." Ah Ming rose, sighed. "Truly, everything de-pends on having relatives at Court. . . ."

It had been Traveler in Emptiness who had first warned Ah Ming that the soldiers were coming to seize Lord Fang and his family. Traveler had gone into Johann Werner's bedroom, lifted him bodily, put him across his shoulders, and gone away with him. The Marquess, however, could not run away. He and Second Son had been caught, but Third Son had managed to escape. "They are searching for him," said Ah Ming.

"Ah Ming, my sister, my sister is in Peking."

"But she is only a woman," Ah Ming said indifferently.

Only a woman. Bea, so strong-minded, who had set out to conquer the Emperor. She had wanted to help me. Only a woman, but one who wanted a destiny of her own, like a man . . . Bea.

Huddled under the Immortal Marshal of the Hosts Against the Plagues, I hungered for the touch of Bea's mind, that pure strong fire that changed all things and made them shine with glory, with strong love and unflinching hate; that was never temperate, prudent, mediocre, not even kind.

I stayed three days and nights with the marshal mounted upon his myopic camel. The old shrine-keeper went unruffled about his work. He cooked his food and shared it with me. Ah Ming came, sometimes at noon, sometimes at night, bringing news.

"Marquess Fang is in prison with Second Son. Third Son still has not been found. The Fang mansion is sequestered. First Lady threw herself into the well in her own private garden. The servants have run away. Apricot has been tortured."

Apricot, tortured . . .

"They thought she might know where you were. They think Third Son and you ran away together. Remember, you went together to the flower boats? They are seizing men who limp. . . ."

This was a bad dream. The Taoist shrine, the red-faced Marshal of the Plagues, all, all a dream. My mind groped for Bea, to warn her. But I could not reach her. Something was happening in Peking and she shut me out. And so I felt unreal, detached.

On the fourth night Traveler came with Ah Ming. "The Master of the Clocks has stopped breathing. Come with me."

We reached the Temple of Major Enlightenment. In an outer building, where the dead waited, Johann Werner lay on a stripped bed with but a grey cloth under him. His face was no longer gaunt; death had fleshed him, restored the tissues under his skin.

The brazier was ready—a circular oven with a brick chimney, reminding me of the bread oven of Vidy. The Master of the Clocks was given to the purging fire, while Traveler knelt and said, "May you be delivered from rebirth, but if you are to be reborn, my brother, you and I shall meet again, in another life." Traveler in Emptiness had loved Johann Werner with surpassing love, and his grief was very great, though he wept not at all.

Now I stayed at the temple, in one of the many small cells hewn out of the rock cliff that recluse monks used to meditate. Upon the smooth cliff face was carved the Bodhidharma.

Traveler continued to make me exercise Wushu, putting me through my paces as if I were one of his disciples. "You must be strong—you will need to defend yourself now." A novice brought me food twice a day, rice gruel and vegetables and mushrooms. Only one meal before noon, and no more till dawn. Mist in a Grove had been questioned at the Taoist shrine; but his healing gifts were so renowned that he was not tortured. Apricot, however, had died under torture, as had other maids and servants of the Fang household.

Bea came to me.

"Colin, Colin, Abdul Reza is here in Peking. I am leaving with him and the envoys tomorrow."

"I am glad, Bea." With the envoys of Ayuthia, she would be safe. The Court would not want to do anything disagreeable in front of foreigners.

"I failed, Colin," she said.

"You tried. You were so wonderfully bold."

"I am coming back, with Abdul Reza," she repeated. Then she shut her mind to me, not wanting me to know.

I stared at the cliff. Indeed I must practice Wushu and be strong. Bea would need me, and I would be there.

MARQUESS FANG WAS EXILED to the confines of Tibet. Second Son and Second Great Lady went with him. The concubines scattered; some went to the flower boats; relatives sheltered the younger children. As for his First Son, after penning a letter of devotion to the Emperor, thanking him for his benevolence, he had committed suicide by drowning himself, fittingly in the same river where, two millennia before, a great and ill-used poet had drowned. First Son had left two sons behind him, so that the ancestral rites could still be performed, as they must be, by the eldest son of an eldest son.

All the scholars of China would understand the classical dignity of his death, a protest against injustice.

The Guild of Salt Merchants of Yangchou went on, outwardly unruffled. Third Son continued in hiding. Some said he had become a monk.

TRAVELER, AH MING, AND I left Yangchou in a small junk. Ah Ming was disguised as one of the boatmen. Traveler sat on the open deck, reciting prayers. I was in the inner room, hidden in a chest piled with Buddhist scriptures. We passed the customs house and were on safe water, gliding away from Yangchou.

Summer's late effulgence clothed the land with dense foliage and tall grass. We went from one shrine to the other, protected by that invisible web of a society that had spawned a thousand folk cults and a million heroes out of the common people, whose gods and Immortals were rebels, thieves, sometimes murderers. It was a web inaccessible to Manchu power, one that still remembered that Red Lantern Chu, the founder of the Ming dynasty, had been a beggar-monk. It was a network of shamans, sorcerers, soothsayers, exorcists, close to a peasantry, which under dire misery hungered for dazzling myths and symbols and magic.

We went into villages wasted by drought, where haggard men crowned with willow danced the rain dance upon the banks of dry streams, chanting incantations to call the rain lords. They shared their mixture of grass, colza leaf, and unhusked rice with us.

Going south, south in a zigzag course. At Traveler's command I was doing Wushu until my body seemed no longer mine but a puppet I willed to go on. I asked no questions. I was pupil, student, entirely trusting.

Bea came to me at night. "We shall have to go away," she said. "Leave this country."

"I know, Bea." She told me she was now on the Grand

Canal, in one of the sumptuous barges of the Thai envoys. "Abdul Reza is taking us with him to the Kingdom of Ayuthia."

As the spill of autumn's first gold touched the hills, I saw in the distance the crimson diadem of Zaiton, a ruby crown of trees in which the city nested. And in front of me was the Old Immortal. He stood in the plain, as if he had been waiting for me, his hands open, his great ears listening to the sound of the universe. I remembered Bea sitting upon his hand.

I touched him. Boulder from the sea, rock from the sky, warm with sun. Traveler and Ah Ming saluted him, and we rested in his shadow and heard a blackbird piping its evening song.

We spent the night in the village of silk. The village elders sent a messenger to Salim Ding to report our arrival. While waiting, Traveler began to talk about himself. Soon we would part, perhaps never to see each other again.

"I was the child of poor peasants; the landlord took away our cooking pot, broke my father's back. He died, my mother sold me. I became a beggar; followed a monk, learning a little of the art, but I wanted revenge. I wanted to kill the landlord.

"Many years later I met him, an old man with rheumy eyes who greeted me politely, not knowing who I was. He prayed a great deal. My heart was distressed, but still I killed him.

"For years I roamed, standing on my head, on one hand, on two fingers. I broke stones with my wrist at fairs, earning a copper coin or two. My hatred left me restless, until I found a master who taught me that each man has a sum of good and evil to perform. Then I could accept my own evil, as every man has to do in the end.

"I became Traveler in Emptiness. Then I met Johann Werner. He taught me that knowledge is unending, and that the quest for knowledge has many pathways. This is what the Bodhidharma taught, that only through the physical is the spiritual to be known. Zen became clearer to me through him, yet he was a barbarian of the West. His search and mine were one. And so, I learnt . . . as you are learning now."

He smiled. "Let us rest now. We have journeyed many days, and more travel is in store for you."

SALIM DING'S SON FAIZ came, poorly dressed, on his face a defeated sadness, and after saying, "Colin, how you have grown," wept desolately. Things were not well with the Dings. The literary inquisition was becoming a vast and sanguinary hunt; Huis were also being killed, and the Huis of Zaiton were sore afraid of the Emperor's new ruthlessness.

"Perhaps it is the death of the Turkoman woman that has unleashed this fury in the Emperor's soul," Faiz said. "He cannot go against his mother without being accounted unfilial, the worst of crimes, by the Board of Rites, and so he vents his wrath upon his subjects."

Had Bea succeeded, I thought, she might have stopped this killing. The Emperor's mind would have been diverted. He might have learned a little tolerance, become interested in the New Learning, rather than suspect any line of verse of breeding sedition.

Many new exactions had fallen upon Zaiton. Still the small boats went on, slipping away, carrying more people fleeing from tyranny, sailing to other lands.

"You will sail to Ayuthia, there to join Lord Reza," Faiz told us. "The Thai envoys and your sister are with him in Canton; from Canton they will set sail for Ayuthia. You will leave from here."

The boatmen plying the small ships that slipped away by night from the coves round Zaiton would take us to Ayuthia. But I was a foreigner, wanted by the imperial soldiers. Should the boatmen be caught smuggling me out of China, they would be killed in a most gruesome manner, cut into pieces, slowly, as had been done to Damien, the would-be murderer of King Louis XV of France, his flesh torn off morsel by morsel, before he was torn apart by four horses tied to his limbs. And I would probably be slowly garroted to death, as had been done on the scaffold to Protestants in France.

As I was contemplating these niceties with some dread, Ah Ming comforted me. "My father was a boatman. That is how we went to Manila and worked for the Spaniards, building roads." His father had become a peddler, then a merchant, and then the Spaniards had massacred the Chinese in Manila in 1758. "Of course, it was to take the money," Ah Ming said. "We always live in the quiet interstice between two slaughters." But because his father had been a boatman, he had connections, clan affinities. "For my father's sake, because he helped many boatmen, they will help us."

Boatmen had their tight-knit brotherhoods with their own passwords, rites, oaths of secrecy. A few of them came to take us to a sandy stretch of ground where their junks were drawn up near to one another. As far as I could see the small tongue of water between the sandbanks was crowded with sailing craft, as a city is crowded with houses.

At the chief boatman's junk, Ah Ming and the headman talked; I stayed immobile. I had brought the Scholar, who awoke curiosity. The boatmen peered at him and fingered him. I made him write for them, put him through his movements, and they exclaimed, slapped their thighs, thought me most fortunate with my animated doll. The chief headman conjectured aloud that doubtless such a traveled puppet must bring good luck at sea, and so they agreed to take me.

We proceeded from the junk to a shrine, water-lapped, the small temple of Tien Hou, Mistress of the Ocean, Empress of Heaven.

Her statue in a robe of silk with a headdress of bright glass fragments was surrounded by lesser deities. The walls were plastered with ex-votos. Every boatman would come here before embarking, to pray for safe voyage. A paddle, a rope, a small sail, the bow of a junk—these lay about her altar to remind her of their calling.

Ah Ming knelt, and the headman announced to the compassionate Mistress of Waters that we would sail, and waited for the answer. The incense burned steadily; the clappers fell open three times. There was a silence, and all was declared propitious to our undertaking.

I knelt in front of Tien Hou then, for if in Marseilles so many prayed to Our Lady of the Sea, why not acknowledge the Queen of the Waters, in this shrine where She had presided over a thousand years and a myriad embarkings?

"Whoever you may be, Spirit you are. Please will you protect Bea, my sister, for she has a great boldness, and like you she is a woman, and she believes in the world of spirits."

Then Faiz paid for a feast, and we all ate, and the boatmen drank much wine. We slept on board the boat, Ah Ming and I. We would set forth when night was strong upon the moonless land. Traveler remained by the altar of Tien Hou, the Sea Queen, his face towards us till sea and land were swallowed by darkness.

❧ *Twelve* ❧

Anno Domini 1762

AYUTHIA MEANT CITY OF paradise, and its magical splendor remains, though Ayuthia is no more. There my youth ended, in slaughter and desolation. Torrents of blood drowned Ayuthia, yet she lives, a golden shimmer in the minds of those who saw her glory.

Our junk with its square prow and painted eyes moved up the monsoon-gorged waters of the *Chao Phya Menam*, the Great Mother River. We passed Little Amsterdam, a Dutch docking settlement where trade ships from Batavia disgorged and loaded, and reached the small town of Bangkok, left of the river. Here the French had built ramparts and a fort during the 1680s when with ambassadors and soldiers and priests they had attempted to gain a foothold in the kingdom against the English East India Company. Everywhere in the Southern Oceans the *farangs*, foreigners, brought with them their own wars—French against English, Dutch against both Portuguese and Spaniards.

Across the river from Bangkok lay Thonburi, a town of Chinese boatmen, carpenters, and rice traders. Here the junks from China moored for repairs, new rudders, and sails. New junks made of teakwood from the great forests of the land brought down in rafts by the Menam River were built here for the voyage back to China, where they were sold at an excellent price. They were laden with Thai rice, for Ayuthia sent much rice to China.

Our junk carried silk and porcelain and lacquerware, and in the hold, for ballast, the stone statues of generals and temple guards, or *yakshah* with demonic heads, and also statues of Dutch or Portuguese soldiers. The Thai liked to have such menacing figures in front of their palaces and their *wats* or temples to frighten the evil spirits.

In Thonburi was *Wat* Kalaya, and thither the boatmen went to thank the Lord Buddha, burning incense, buying gold foil to stick upon the base of the statues, and acquiring merit with gifts of money. *Wat* Kalaya was dedicated to Sanpao Kung, none other than the Chinese navigator Cheng Ho, who between 1407 and 1432 had crossed the oceans seven times with great fleets of up to a thousand junks and twenty-seven thousand men, visiting the kingdoms of the South Seas.

"The Kingdom of Ayuthia is rice and fish country," Ah Ming said. "Never a famine here, except when war destroys the rice fields. And gold, gold, Brother Colin—why, Ayuthia is covered with gold; even the walls, the ceilings of the King's palace, and the stables for his elephants and horses are gold-covered."

Abundance. A languid greenness. Mild and immense trees bending heavy foliage as a blessing; a green horizon of hills smothered in forest and blossom. Flowers on every terrace of the bamboo-and-wood houses, whose stilts dug into the river-banks and marched into the water. Golden-skinned people, the women walking on graceful feet, naked to the waist but for a *sabai*, a piece of folded cloth thrown carelessly about their shoulders. Their *pajong krabane* or skirt was a cloth wrapped round their hips or drawn between their thighs, the ends tucked in front and behind to resemble trousers, leaving their legs bared to the knee.

Laughter shaped their unashamed mouths, as in bright clusters they stood, throwing smiles, laughter, and flowers at the passing boats. I felt the strong surge of desire in me as the boatmen shouted pleasantries back. "Think not the women easy, my brother. They have strong wills," Ah Ming said. Sins of the flesh, but here flesh was beautiful, was kind.

Women, bathing in the river, their long hair loose. Women,

rowing slim boats alongside our junk, holding up coconuts and mangoes and plantains, clusters of red longans, betal and areca nuts. Girls in boats heaped with flower garlands, red and yellow gladioli for offerings at the *wats*, sweet-smelling champac, tuberose and jasmine.

Each place of habitation, large or small, had its spired doll-like shrine on stilts, habitation of the *Phya Phum* or Spirit of the Ground. The Earth Spirit was old, far older than Confucius or Buddha, older than the Old Immortal of Tao. He belonged to that age of man when trees and stones and water spoke.

So many legends and tales now came to the boatmen, delivered from the salt and cruel sea, sailing upriver on the large-breasted Menam. Here even the floods were kind, making the rice fields more abundant.

Bea.

The enchanted forest and its singing. Here dreams were valid and spirits manifest. "I have reentered your world, Bea," I prayed. "Now it falls into place. Here is no barrier between the world of spirits and the world of man."

Soon, soon we would be together.

For weeks now I had not been able to reach her, and I was sick and dry-boned with deprivation, a great hunger even greater than many weeks without a woman.

Up the Menam, mild wind rounding our sails, and the boatmen singing their tales.

I clasped the Scholar, my android.

"Look, look. This is where you may come alive."

But he was already alive, only waiting for my skill to come out of immobility. He was a spirit, and benign. Every day the boatmen had offered him gifts so that our journey would be smooth. They had called him the Carrot-haired Genius, because his auburn wig had turned russet in the sea wind.

Late one afternoon, the sun mellowing, the water buffalo languidly hauling themselves out of the water, it was there. Ayuthia, gleaming with its three hundred golden spires, a fabulous fairy city. I cried with delight.

"Ah Ming, I've never seen such a wonder!"

"It is a wonder, therefore much coveted," he replied, prosaic.

Ayuthia. Round it the Menam wound to meet its tributaries,

girdling the city with a great belt of water. And from her came the sound of bells, and the faint rumor of people.

"Greater than Venice or London . . . a wonder and a marvel . . ." They had not lied, those *farang* ambassadors, French, English, and Dutch, who had thus described her.

"Even if I die tonight, I shall be content, for I have seen Ayuthia," I said, holding up my android as if he too could see.

"You were ever a dreamer," Ah Ming said, and ordered slack in the sail.

WE SAILED PAST THE settlements of the *farangs* outside the city as night fell. On the right bank was the Japanese town where the families of the erstwhile famous Yamada still lived. A century ago, Yamada was chief of the elite guards of the kings of Ayuthia. Past the English town, with warehouses and factories of the East India Company. Past the Dutch town, its houses of white stone and brick, windows gleaming with the light of lamps within uncurtained rooms. Opposite them, on the right bank, sprawled the Portuguese settlement. Farther along the river's arm, on the left, was the French settlement with the Catholic Church of Saint Joseph, built eighty-odd years ago.

"All *farangs* are welcome in Ayuthia," the boatmen said.

The Chinese were not *farangs*, nor were the Arabs and Persians. These had settled in Ayuthia more than three centuries ago, and they were the mainstay of Ayuthia's wealth, so that they had old quarters within the city, and others outside its walls. Where the river divided to girdle Ayuthia was the great *Wat* Phanang Cheng, half-Chinese, half-Thai. Here we would stay the night, for now the gates of the city were closed, and the customs men had gone home.

"Your sister is surely within the city, with Lord Reza," Ah Ming said. "We shall find them tomorrow."

At a Chinese hostel near the *wat* we washed and were fed. The boatmen then went out to find women, as Ah Ming and I strolled into the *wat*. The monks here were of the Mahayana sect, as in China. They wore yellow robes and trousers, not a cloth wrapped round their bodies and left shoulder, as did the Thai *bikkus* or Buddhist monks.

The *wat* was huge. A towering Buddha figure dating back to 1320, his face lit by lamps dependent from the roof and from the high pillars around him, occupied its center. He was covered in gold, and gold foil fluttered in the wind of candles upon the hundreds of small statues that lined the walls and surrounded the main altar.

By the side of the *wat* was a Taoist sanctuary, its doors painted with the ying-yang circle, male and female, half-spirals looping eternally into each other, indivisible. And there was a small open shrine to Tien Hou, Queen of the Ocean, with an anchor, a paddle, and a coil of rope among the candles and incense sheaves in front of her.

By the shrine of Tien Hou in the darkness, a figure, immobile, waiting for me.

Bea.

She had known. She had come.

She stood, part of the magical land. I heard the singing water a few yards away, as I had heard the leaves of the oak forest in that faraway time of my childhood.

I was back, with the night, the enchantment.

I was back with Bea.

SHE HUGGED HER KNEES, next to me on the bed.

She had brought me across the river, imperiously crossing the belt of water to the inner docks. Hers was a long thin skiff, adorned with the head of some beast at its prow and four rowers.

And the Chinese gate, called the *Nei Kai*, was open to us. We sailed through it. The ramparts were pierced with gates, and under every gate was water, linking the street-canals of the aquatic city of Ayuthia to the main river. Most of the streets of Ayuthia were canals, save for a broad central avenue, esplanades in front of the palaces, and a maze of busy side-walk alleys linking water to land.

We reached the Muslim quarter, stopping at a small mansion whose terrace came down to the water. Abdul Reza waited there in the glow of lamps. "Colin, your sister said that you were safe. She announced to me that you had arrived, and I have learnt to trust her prescience."

How old he was, suddenly. Yet it was less than a year ago that I had seen him in Yangchou. In his face, the beaklike nose-thrust. A loss of substance about him. He clasped me in his arms, and perhaps because I had grown he appeared to me wizened. I think he guessed my compassion, for he straightened, and in his lordly and gracious manner motioned me to sit.

"It was a great distress for me to learn of Marquess Fang's fate," he began. "And the destruction of that great family, allied to mine for over a hundred years. The Emperor has done wrong, and ill befalls a ruler when he slights his loyal servants."

It was sorrow, then, which had aged him, and my heart smote me that during the voyage, the full extent of the tornado of suffering inflicted upon the many who had been so kind to Bea and to me had not truly afflicted me. True, I had grieved, but I had been more concerned with saving myself, and benumbed, impervious to the fate of others. Now grief seized my soul, and as if a thousand swords pierced me I cried, "Oh, indeed it was so unjust."

"The will of Allah," Reza said.

I gave him the letter I had brought from Salim Ding, and he perused it while Bea and I sat, silent. Ismail came in to clasp my hands, bringing a tray of silver with coffee in a long-stemmed silver jug. He too was older, grey hair on both sides of his face where it escaped his cap.

"I too have a letter for you," Abdul Reza said. "From your friend Jacob Hirsch." And as he handed it to me, he glanced at Bea. And I saw that he loved her, loved her with helpless and desperate clinging. She was composed, a statue. She was not his. She belonged only to herself.

"It is late, Colin. You must rest." Abdul Reza rose, clasped me as a full-grown man clasps another. "My house is yours." He vouchsafed no more but left, with a nod to Bea.

And now strangeness fell heavy between Bea and myself, undispelled by her taking my hand to lead me to my room. We were both seventeen and awkward with each other.

The lamps were trimmed bright. The bed was low on carved feet, gauze-wrapped against the insects of the night. Through the open windows came the soft river breeze. There was a smell of roses and cinnamon, for the gauze was impregnated with scent, as were Bea's clothes. "Read your letter, Colin, and sleep. We'll talk tomorrow," Bea said. I kissed her cheek, and she left.

I turned to Jacob's letter, the first one I had received since leaving Geneva more than four years ago. The letter itself was dated, so that it was strange, almost supernatural, to finger the paper Jacob had fingered at that time.

Jacob was in England to study astronomy, for in England there were great astronomers. They were speculating on the other planets circling the sun. "Voltaire has taken up the cause of religious liberty," Jacob wrote. Jean Calas, a Protestant, had been executed in France, accused of murdering his son, who wanted to become a Catholic. "Voltaire has taken up this injustice and published a treatise on religious tolerance." Jean Jacques Rousseau continued to scandalize and shock. His new book, *Emile*, had the novel idea of treating children as equals, and he had been obliged to flee from Paris because of this book. "As to the Jesuits, their colleges have been closed in France. Perhaps at last Diderot's *Encyclopedia* can be published without being consigned to the flames."

So much was going on in Europe. "In London I journey through the universe, discovering the order and beauty of the spinning worlds that lie all about us . . . how far, how large is the universe? I find my own childhood a mystery. In that first flush of life we are endowed with extraordinary aptitudes. Alas, they wither early; I find myself less apt at mathematics, now that I am full twenty years old."

Jacob twenty, myself seventeen. Folding the bulky, many-paged letter, which I would read and reread many times, I thought: *We are grown men now, childhood behind us.* And perhaps I should no longer grope for Bea's mind, for we were both adults, Bea and I. And we must begin to leave each other.

I slept among the croaking of many frogs, woke with the song of a bird multitude, sluiced myself with water from a great ceramic jar, and went into the garden. The maidservants were garlanding the *Phya Phum* spirit shrine of the house. It was of marble, raised on a pillar, and all about it were the offerings. I too paid homage to the resident spirit, a small statue. I would have to offer something to it, lest things go awry. And then Bea was there, a *pasai* of purple and gold about her shoulders and a long slim skirt of purple brocade.

"Today is purple day," she said.

In Ayuthia, every day had its color, favored by heavenly bodies. Sunday red, Monday yellow, Tuesday pink, Wednesday green, Thursday orange, Friday brown, Saturday purple.

She was slightly shorter than I was, and raised her hands upon my shoulders to kiss me. We walked into the reception hall, where low tables held fruit and small bowls of silver with many different dishes upon silver trays. A bevy of maidens knelt to serve us. After a while I saw that Bea was weeping. Weeping for the loss of our childhood innocence, for the bond that had held us together, weeping because my mind had said, "We must leave each other." We went up to my room and I held her in my arms. She clung to me. But childhood had left us, never to return.

I SLEPT UNEASILY, WAKING with the same disquiet. Bea. Love and fear of love. I fondled my android, strove to revive in myself the Colin who had thought himself a great adventurer as well as a good mechanical craftsman. I repeated as a talisman the names of those who on cockleshell sailing ships had come to these lands, seen and marveled, and perhaps, like myself when I saw Ayuthia, the City of Gold, had thought their lives complete. Or who, kneeling to strange gods, had felt their minds enlarged, and intolerance give way to a largesse of the spirit that would stay them well till the day of their death.

I meditated and grew calm. Like Traveler in Emptiness, my own life was part of the myriad things around me, undivided within the joyous pulse of matter and energy.

Ayuthia glowed gently, and the soft river wind blew echoes of music and the sound of many people.

I could face Bea now. My sister. My love and the only love in the world I would have to deny.

PRINCE UDORN CAME, WRAPPED in the saffron sheath of a *bikku*, his hair shorn, his feet naked. He embraced me, hung a garland of flowers round my neck, and would not eat or drink, since it was past noon, when *bikkus* took their last meal of the day. "No food till tomorrow at dawn, when I go begging, eyes downcast," he said, squatting on the carpeted floor. "It is our custom when the monsoon season is on and all is water-drenched, or when we are distraught by many feelings and wish to avoid the *phi*, the evil spirits preying on our minds, to retire into a *wat*, live as a monk, and meditate." He had done so on his return from China. "No man can escape birth, sickness, old age, death, thus said the Lord Buddha. Reminding ourselves of this we achieve detachment." He would now return to lay life. "Come and stay with me, like a brother," he said.

"I will." I felt relieved, and guilty because of this relief, for the atmosphere was at times oppressive here, between Abdul Reza and Bea, between Bea and myself.

"We shall be one family then," Udorn said, "for I love your sister and intend her to be my wife."

"Your wife?" My heart clutched. But I kept a smile affixed upon my face.

"Perhaps I am not good enough for her. I thought it would please you, Colin; why, I have sent away all my other wives, prepared myself. I shall make a statue to her, of pure gold, and revere it every day."

"Gold is somewhat extravagant." The words came strangled through my throat. "Bea has not told me. I am surprised, but yes, Prince Udorn, I shall be most happy if you and she are happy together."

"Gold is no extravagance in Ayuthia. All Ayuthia is gold. Have you not seen our *wats*, our gold-covered *cheddis*? In all China there is not as much gold about as in Ayuthia. Gold and rubies and sapphires and so many precious things . . .

"We are all in love with your sister. She is enchanting. Prince Chiprasong has composed love poems for her and has musicians serenading her on every auspicious day of the week." He laughed joyously. "I know that great Lord Abdul Reza is also in love with her, but he is restrained, since she is his daughter by affection, although in Ayuthia, especially among our kings, it is quite customary to marry an aunt, a niece, even a stepdaughter, and sometimes one's own daughter by mistake. . . ."

He bounded up. "But I know it will be me, Colin, I know she will choose me," he said. "For I have an iron tree in my garden that had not flowered for a hundred years. It has now blossomed, and the Chief Patriarch of the Royal *Wat*, and the Brahmin priests of the Court, have told me that it augurs well for my love."

He went on to talk of Bea. "I saw her in China as we came back through the Palace of Perfect Harmony from our audience with Emperor Tsienlung. I had escaped protocol and gone to visit the Italian painter, Castiglione, for his fame had spread, even among the Jesuits here. And I found him in his place of work, just by the main gates of the palace, and your sister was there, who had come to visit him. He was painting her portrait."

Bea had been dressed in pale grey, for she was in mourning because her mistress, Clear Concubine, had died. "I saw your sister then, and the mourning enhanced her eyes, her fair skin, her hair. Since then I have had no one else in eye or heart. More mighty than any typhoon of the Southern Seas is love, Colin."

Because Bea's mistress had died, Abdul Reza had been allowed to take her back with him as his ward. "I knew that she would be back with us on our barges sailing down the Grand Canal, and I was happy. When we reached Yangchou we heard what had befallen the noble Fangs; and that you had fled. Abdul Reza then sent his trusted messengers to Zaiton, knowing that whoever saved you would head for that city, which is renowned for smuggling people out of China. Your sister said you would be meeting her in Ayuthia. She is capable of visioning what is to come, and the Yangchou officials did not dare to arrest her, because of us."

"Lord Reza is a powerful man, a man of many talents and vast enterprises, but he is advanced in years; he must be nigh forty years old," I said.

"Forty-two. But there is no age for love," Udorn said, with that ingenuous smile of his, which concealed so much. He went on to tell me what Bea had done on board the stately galleon that had brought the Thai envoys back to Ayuthia: "She told us a storm would come and to batten and drop sails; and she was right. She reads the winds and the tides, and our ship was safe because of her. I think she is a powerful and benign spirit, and talks to spirits as I talk to you."

He went away, and I sought Bea, who was choosing brocades for her skirts in her room.

"I have just seen Prince Udorn."

"I shall marry him," Bea said, scrutinizing a piece of silk woven with fine gold. "He will not come between us."

"You do not love him, Bea."

"Have I not told you? Love is dangerous for a woman. I must not lose myself for love, as did Mother."

"We cannot be together always, Bea."

She did not reply.

I held Jacob's letter in my hands. It made me lighter, the feel of it. "I must write to Jacob."

Her arms came around me then, her head upon my shoulder. "Abdul Reza did not want to tell you, but I must. He has just had the news, through a Dutch ship from Amsterdam. Jacob is dead. He died in a massacre of Jews in Warsaw just eight months ago."

Shortly after his letter to me Jacob had gone to Warsaw to bring back his mother's sister, a widow and penurious. There had been violence against the Jewish ghettoes, despite the iron gates that hemmed them in from sundown to sunrise. One evening a band of young men had seized Jacob as he was reentering the ghetto and hacked him to death, leaving his impaled body outside the gates.

Slaughter everywhere. Rivers of innocent blood.

Why Jacob, why not me? Why him, with his great promise, and not me, merely fiddling with springs and cams and levers.

Grief would ease; the sound of Jacob's voice, his careful slow words that led to the flowering of my mind, would dim. The unrelenting dulling of sorrow in me would be harder to

bear than anything else. "Oh, Jacob, if there be another life
. . ." I prayed, as Traveler in Emptiness had prayed over the
body of Johann Werner.

IN THE BALMY AFTER-MONSOON season which was the winter of
Ayuthia, I set up a house and a factory for making clocks and
automata.

I was helped by that ample tolerance of the kingdom, for
here foreigners were not proscribed and confined, as in China.
In all the streets, on all the canals, could be seen their boats
and sedan chairs.

Ayuthia was an oval island, floating upon the surrounding
sweet water, crisscrossed with beautiful orderliness by canals,
the main ones so wide that oceangoing ships sailed up them
to moor by the trading houses. Every household had at least
one boat. And outside the city, entire villages were afloat on
barges large enough to house families.

The Thai were disinclined to work strenuously. All was
easy for them, and they glided like water upon the ease and
wealth of a land where rice grew on its own; where forests
yielded, with elephants doing the labor, wealth that the world
hungered for. Always they found willing *farangs* to do what
they did not wish to do, although they kept a vigilant eye
upon them. Thus under the *Pra-Klang*, or Minister of Customs,
Levies, and Foreign Shipping, were Dutch and Portuguese
officials; as also under the *Kalahom*, or Minister for War. All
seagoing commerce was left to the Chinese, the Dutch, and
the Arabs, for the Thai loved sweet water and were wary of
the ocean's turbulent and unpredictable moods. They levied
taxes upon all that went in or out of the kingdom. Thus grew
Ayuthia's wealth, without exertion.

And here were gathered the most beautiful wares of the
whole world. Chandeliers of glass from Venice and porce-
lains and silks and lacquerware from China; the finest leather
of Morocco, and spy glasses and clocks from England. The
shops along the small streets were riotous with colorful objects,
especially innumerable statues of the Lord Buddha. The canals were crowded with boats, gilded and carved *poluns* for

the wealthy, and plain boats loaded with fruit and flowers and fish and vegetables. Everywhere the tall and gleaming gold *cheddis*, pointing to the sky, beckoned to one's spirit. *Wats* with walls glistening of mother-of-pearl incrustations, painted and gilded and lacquered doors, reminded one that religion need not be ascetic. Such was the delight in delicate and profuse adornment of everything in common use that one remained confounded with admiration at the splendor. And because of this richness of hand and eye, the people would put on their best finery at all times, so that the streets were permanent revels. It was hard to remember that most of the edifices were of brick, stone being scarce, such was the load of gold, gilding, white silver, brass, copper, incrustations, and decorations upon them. There were rubies and sapphires and gold necklaces and armbands and ankle bracelets upon the people; gold foil, vases of gold and silver upon the *wat* altars. Were there then no thieves in Ayuthia? No one ever stole from a *wat*. The roofs of the mansions were multiple, splendid with colored tiles; seven roofs upon the King's palace, which occupied almost a fifth of the city's northwest corner, and for the nobles from three to five roofs.

From the three-hundred-odd *wats* of Ayuthia came the sound of cascades of bells hung from the eaves. And all the time there were pageants, processions, spectacles, and festivals, each one a riot of gold and silver and brocade. Gold upon the caparisoned elephants, gold trappings for the horses, gold upon the men and women carrying offerings in gem-studded boxes. And music went before each procession, music and singing.

Thus life in Ayuthia was a continuous celebration, an uninterrupted hymn to joy, which night did not interrupt, for lamps of many colors, shaped as lotuses or pagodas or elephants and lions, would be hung at every spirit shrine, or float on the river and lose themselves, however exquisitely made, in the all-devouring water.

"No wonder the Burmese covet Ayuthia," Abdul Reza said. "In one *wat* here is a statue that contains more gold—for it is fifty cubits high—than all the gold in the Kingdom of France."

IN THE DRY SEASON, after the monsoon when the countryside flooded for many miles around, my house on stilts was built within the garden of Udorn's palace. A host of workers set to it with much laughter, and though they slept through the afternoon and made music at night, the house was soon wonderful to behold.

Heer Timmermans, who commanded the Dutch settlement, came, beplumed and well dressed, in his own ornate *polun*, to call upon Abdul Reza. The Hollanders had a good service of intelligence. Timmermans had met Heer van Tromp, who had voyaged with us from Marseilles some five years ago and who had told him of Lord Reza and his two wards. Since we were of the Reformed religion, he had a good reason for calling upon a Muslim grandee.

In Ayuthia the Hollanders were amiable, hospitable, prudent, and well behaved, so that my impression of Cape Town settlement was effaced. Here Dutch ships rescued boats in peril, and conveyed Buddhist monks in embassies from Sri Lanka to Ayuthia and back. And though religious and frowning upon idolatry, they abstained from deriding Buddhism and showed much respect to the *bikkus*, even making gifts in due season to the Chinese boatmen's temple *Wat* Phanang Cheng.

Timmermans gave a feast for Bea and myself. Thither we went in a *polun*, with six rowers; we were sitting in the thronelike seat in the boat's middle, with tents of silk to shield us from the sun.

Timmermans and his wife received us with much honor. Bea was dressed as a Thai lady, save for a bodice over her shoulders and to the waist. Round her neck glittered necklaces of gold and pearls, and on her feet were slippers of brocade with mother-of-pearl trimming.

"How beautiful your sister is, most beautiful," Timmermans said to me as his wife drew Bea to meet the assembled Dutch ladies. "But she dresses as a native."

"It is more comfortable," I replied.

We talked of my setting up the factory to build automata, to make and repair clocks and watches.

"Excellent," said Heer Timmermans. "We have some craftsmen among us too, men with knowledge of metals and foundries and mechanics, though mostly to do with ships, of course.
But it can help. And whatever you need, I can get it for you
from Holland, for our ships sail regularly, and unless there is
another war"—he grinned—"all should go well."

The company had assembled, some thirty or forty men and
women, among them Scandinavians. Erik Erikssen, a tall, fair
Dane, came to speak with me. He had married a Thai lady of
good family, and when the pastor had thundered at him and
refused to marry them, he had threatened to become a
Buddhist. She had died, but he continued to live in Ayuthia,
trading in cannon and muskets, buying Thai elephants for
the Indian princes, rajahs, and nawabs, who were constantly
at war with one another and also with the English. Thai
elephants were reputed more intelligent than others.

After the dinner the men assembled to drink English port,
while the ladies went into an inner room to talk of dresses
and fans, of the heat, the rain, servants, and the latest fashions of Paris. The men's talk was of war. "The French have
lost India," Timmermans said ponderously. The English East
India Company had now conquered Bengal and was plundering it. "India is like a swirling sea in a great tempest." The
men sighed righteously, shaking their heads. The long seven-
year war between England and France had come to an end,
and now all of the New World was in English hands, save for
the Louisiana, "and surely they will also get that territory, for
the French can never agree among themselves."

War. Devastation. Greed. Plunder. Pillage. Treason. Carnage.
Death.

✥ *Thirteen* ✥

Anno Domini 1762–1764

TWO OFFICIALS OF THE *Pra-Klang* came to see me. They wore high-spired hats with circlets of gold and silver. I took them to the large reception hall carpeted with Abdul Reza's handsome silk rugs, where we sat, legs modestly tucked to one side. The officials were pleased. I had excellent manners, they remarked. I must have been a Thai in a previous life . . . certainly a man who had accumulated great merit.

I replied that my unworthy self had spent some years in China, and they nodded happily. The Empire favored Ayuthia, they said, levying no taxes upon its goods, and sending all the silk the kingdom needed in return. It had even at times entrusted Ayuthia with diplomatic missions to other Southern Ocean rulers.

I knew that never must I sit higher than an official of rank; never raise my body above his head level; never touch his head or face; never by loud voice or rough gesture disturb the prevailing harmony—so all went well. The officials greatly admired my *Phya Phum*, the carrot-haired android, the Scholar. Ah Ming had insisted on erecting a shrine for him. His fame spread in Ayuthia. A spirit that nodded its head, trimmed a lamp, and appeared to write was surely great magic.

With appropriate ceremony an astrologer and a Brahmin priest had chosen an auspicious spot in the garden for the Scholar's shrine, which was raised on a five-foot pillar of stucco-covered brick. There he sat, protected from the rain. On the ledge of the shrine platform hung flower garlands. Coconut, betel, and areca, and sweet-smelling herbs in bowls and dishes were placed before him, as well as porcelain figurines of servants, elephants, horses, and dancers. At dawn my servants, with joined hands, paid morning *sawai* to his spirit, and some visitors had even begun sticking gold foil upon him.

Within a week I received a document, written on excellent paper made of mulberry bark and imported from China:

The craftsman Keran [the Thai word for Colin] is from the small country of Vaud, which is near the Kingdom of France. Its inhabitants are hardworking and courageous, defending themselves well in war.

They produce clocks and watches and contrivances for the pleasure of many countries. Keran and his sister Didya will make these things in our kingdom, toys in no way dangerous or warlike. Hence all officials will treat them courteously, harken to their needs, allow them to import whatever is necessary for their work; and there shall be no levy upon any of the needful pieces that are brought in.

Abdul Reza was pleased. He had suffered great losses when Tenasserim, Ayuthia's important port on the Bay of Bengal, had been captured by the Burmese three years before. "But worse than the Burmese are the British, who are now conquering India piecemeal, strangling the trade of Persia and the Ottoman Empire. They have taken Pondicherry from the French and are besieging other trading posts. Whenever they see an Arab ship upon the oceans, they seize it as a pirate vessel."

And thus they were killing off all other traders to reach a monopoly in the Indian kingdoms.

Abdul Reza gave a feast to the officials to thank them, and many presents and gifts were exchanged—*pannungs* and cloths with silver and gold thread, vases and inlaid boxes and trays.

"How can we ever repay your kindness to us, my Lord?" I said to him.

He looked at me, amused, and said, "Colin, I am an old man; I have many sons who help me, and daughters, well married. And wives. But somehow my heart has gone out to you. I shall always try to look after you well."

In Ayuthia Abdul Reza kept two wives who never ventured out, for they were in Muslim seclusion. Bea brought them sweetmeats and would make conversation with them. Two of his sons, burly men with big noses, traveled between Tenasserim and India. They were trying to save not only the wreckage of their own commerce but that of many of the Muslim merchants who were established in the Kingdom of Ayuthia. India's Muslim rulers, the Moghuls and the nawabs, were foundering in internecine conflict; the French were using some of the Indian rulers to withstand the British.

The Chinese Empire's resolve to close itself, forbid its coasts to foreigners, hoping thus to be left in peace, now seemed to have some logic behind it. Seeing what was happening in India, one could understand the mandarins of Peking. However, closing the country to greed and plunder also meant depriving it of those new inventions that, I now could perceive, as Abdul Reza had seen so clearly, were changing the world.

AH MING COLLECTED CARPENTERS, forgers, and goldsmiths from among the Chinese settled in Ayuthia. The Hollanders also gave us craftsmen. Heer Timmermans obtained from Batavia six sets of clockmakers' tools. I searched for and found in the Muslim quarter fine leather from Morocco, leather pounded and stretched as thin as silk, and also got *baudruche*, the internal tegument of the intestines of newborn lambs. This, stuck with fish glue, I would shape into bellows; it was satisfying to produce the musical sound needed for the singing bird automata I made.

We now made clocks and watches that worked well, using the anchor escapement I had learnt from Johann Werner. The casings, of gold, jewel-studded or enameled, were most pleasant, for here goldsmiths and jewelers were as skilled as in Geneva. I also made music boxes in a new way, using a comb of metal teeth of diverse weight and length to impinge upon a cylinder with protruding *goupillons*. I varied this theme, sometimes using two combs, sometimes a harplike cylinder that turned and struck one or several fingers of pliable brass to produce chords. I could produce any music I wished, and now turned to Thai tunes and melodies.

I then built automata, dressed as Thai musicians, for each of the instruments played: the *pinai*, or oboe, the *ranad ek* or gamelan, and the *yongwai* or gong. I assembled several musicians, tuned them, and harmonized their mechanics. The result was what sounded and looked like a small Thai orchestra, which caused great astonishment and pleasure in Ayuthia. Many nobles and wealthy traders came to buy such pieces, and we prospered.

Yet all this, I thought, was far from what a real android would do. An android should play himself, not pretend to play with a music box hidden within him. And although everyone was delighted with the new toy I had invented and even more so when I mounted a clock above the orchestra and tuned the mechanisms so that the music played of itself at stated hours, I was not satisfied.

I began work on a new android. The idea for it had come to me in China and floated, a nebulous cloud, in my mind. It now coalesced, began to assume a shape, dimension. An android capable of not only one set of gestures (there were seventeen in the Carrot-haired Scholar), but one who would have a true soul, a memory within him, albeit mechanical; capable of certain choices in his actions, so that his movements would vary as if he had a will of his own animating him.

This android must not pretend to write; he must truly write, and have within him the potential of an unlimited number of sentences to write. I began to build one with one hundred twenty cams, inscribing forty different signs; three cams for each of the twenty-six letters of the alphabet, the punctuation and other marks, and some capital letters. As in a trance, because I was happy, I worked and saw how I could extend his area of motion with pivot poles. I made a selector disc, a revolving wheel that enabled me to prepare some texts for him. Through a mobile camshaft with interchangeable pegs of fine steel, he could select the letters from the store within him and write out different messages.

But I wanted more, much more. I wanted a true *android*, which would have "senses," the capability to see, to recognize me, his master.

And why not hear? Voice displaced the air about one, as a blower displaced air, producing music. Montesquieu in France had studied the echo; others, in England, in Holland, had studied sound. It might be possible to have a machine that talked, or to set one off by issuing commands to it—for what was sound? And if clocks could be set in motion by slight displacements of the floor upon which they stood, could I activate an android merely by walking near him?

I pondered on this and so many other things. Seeing the paper windmills of the children in China and also here in Ayuthia, which the slightest puff of breeze set off, stirred something in me. I must think, must think of a way. If I could activate an android to respond to the wind of my breath, to the sound of my voice . . .

I had now learnt to preserve the parts of the machine from the weather in Ayuthia, the moisture-laden air in monsoon time, by soaking them in the fine oil that the Hollanders obtained from Batavia to grease their barometers and naval instruments. I used spy glasses and the skill and eyes of my young craftsmen to make rivets and screws, studs and hinged pegs, small as a grain of mustard. And I thought of sinking the screws into jewels, sapphires or rubies, which did not shrink or stretch with heat or damp, to make the mechanism proof against heat or cold.

The unease and distemper between Bea and me faded and we were happy together, because my happiness was a barrier to disquiet. I thought much of Jacob; every night I would say to his spirit, "See, Jacob, I want to become worthy of you, of your great mind, which set mine afire." All this, and my work, was deliberate restraint, so that my inner ear to Bea was blocked. Better this than the womb world in which we had grown together. Better this than the truthful marsh with a thousand hidden demons screaming destruction.

UDORN CAME EVERY DAY with minstrels to serenade my sister. The musicians sang the love poems he composed in her honor, and other lilting tunes of the musicians of Ayuthia, a place famous for its music. And he had dancers perform in our garden, all to amuse her.

Bea was being courted by other nobles, both young and old. The daily throng of bearers of gifts in front of Abdul Reza's residence was a wonder to behold. Gifts brought in sedan chairs, in elaborate boxes—of silver inlaid with coral and turquoise and pearl; boxes holding scented water for lustral blessing; boxes for betel and areca nuts; cosmetic boxes; bolts of silk, fine shoes of silk; combs and jewels, jewels, jewels . . .

"Your sister enchants us all," said Abdul Reza.

Bea went out in the *polun* with the tented chair like a small throne in its middle. When she appeared, men would bow their heads and avert their eyes out of respect, for to look boldly at a woman was a mark of contempt. She now had six women to serve her as if she were a princess. Even the *bikkus* liked her, for she would visit the *wats* and make offerings to the Buddha statues with their faraway golden faces.

Mrs. Timmermans spoke to me about it. "Your sister—"

"My sister believes in respecting the customs of the land."

"But our religion forbids—"

We went to the church of the Dutch settlement and then Bea sang; her voice soaring sweet and pure, so that every head turned towards her, and the hymns were loaded with new beauty. There was no more talk against her then by the *farang* women, especially when it became known that she would marry Udorn. They were glad she would be married soon, hoping, perhaps, that she too would be secluded.

She was learning to dance, with teachers of *Khon, Lakhon,* and *Piphat.* Bea was dressed as a dancer, naked of foot, and on her head was the bejeweled spire like a crown, and jewels round her arms, her ankles, her neck.

"Bea, I did not know you could also dance."

She looked at me, a little flushed. "Colin, I want to learn everything you do. I do not want to be merely a woman. . . ."

"I know, Bea."

"Everywhere, in China, in Europe, women are deemed secondary." She took a deep breath. "Oh yes, I know that I could hold a salon in Lausanne, where clever men would eat and drink; the pleasure I would create for them would make their converse more brilliant. Or I could have famous lovers, and inspire them, become famous *through* them. But this would not be myself; this would be . . . merely becoming a clever android, the main pulse of my being in someone else's hand."

"But, Bea, a woman needs love, a husband, children."

Her eyes were blue with amusement, with indulgence. "Do not men need love, a wife, children? Does this mean subordinating what I can be, my soul, my life, to love a husband, children?"

And seeing me bemused, she said, "Colin, we are knit together, and also we have parted somewhat, and this is right—so let me be myself, find myself."

HERE IN AYUTHIA WOMEN appeared far more free than in other lands. Except for the King's wives, women went about unhindered. They owned houses and land and money; they worked and owned boats, and they could divorce a man if they did not like him. Udorn had told me of an aunt of his who had left her husband because she said he had smelly feet!

"It is men who decide how much or how little education and liberty a woman will have. But I want to decide for myself. I want the same power, because my strength is the same," Bea said.

"What power, Bea? What is power?"

"Ability to decide, Colin; to choose, why, even to change the world, as men do. To be listened to, as a man."

"As a woman, Bea, you have great power over men."

"As a woman . . . But I want to be somewhat different."

Talking with Bea of such things strangely discomforted me. There was always such turmoil, such frenzy in her.

She had begun to collect herbs and now visited the city's Chinese herbalists to instruct herself in the use of plants of all kinds, both benign and lethal.

Everyone in Ayuthia admired and praised her, and when she doctored the sick with grace and generosity, they called her a reincarnation of some great and noble princess of yore, whose skill and wisdom had saved many lives and acquired her boundless merit.

"He who knows the male, yet cleaves to what is female, becomes like a ravine, receiving all things under Heaven. He knows a power that he never calls upon in vain."

Traveler in Emptiness had taught me this saying of the Old Immortal when he taught me the intricately tender gestures of the Wushu, those that led one's opponent to death.

What was power? I sat and meditated, strongly willing my soul to be quiet, to accept Bea and myself now that childhood innocence had gone from us.

Gathering my spirit, I let the strength flow into me, slowing my breathing. Soon my joints were light. I rose, going through the sixty-four postures, prolonged and instant, losing sense of time and otherness, filled with all that was around me, void as the sky above me. Thoughts and faces floated through me like unattached clouds.

Thoughts. And beings.

Voltaire. He was present in this Thai garden, no longer a grimacing figure, but a man whose words held greatness. "Man makes his own gods, forges forever new chains for himself," he had written. Voltaire fought for man's right to be—himself. And women? Voltaire wavered, dimmed, withdrew . . . he had not thought about women.

"It is too early," he muttered as he melted away.

Jacob. Jacob was there, too. He was not dead. He would never die.

"Women, too," said Jacob. "They are our equals."

I returned. Everything became solid again. It was always so after meditation; reality had a sharper, keener taste, a crystal freshness.

And Udorn was standing there, smiling at me.

"Brother, I have watched your Wushu. Now you must also learn our Krabong," he said.

Krabong was the Thai art of martial defense; it involved manipulating weapons. I shook my head.

"I prefer my naked hands . . . and my club foot," I replied.

"A pity. Chiprasong would have loved to show you his mettle. He goes everywhere looking for a fight. Why, he went to a village the other day, to a boxing match, and knowing he was a prince they let him win." He roared with laughter. Nothing seemed to alter Udorn's good spirits.

"News I have for you, Brother Keran. Tomorrow my cousin *Phya* Cham has an audience with King Ekatat, and I must go with his retinue until the third courtyard. Will you come with me? You and I cannot go into the audience hall, but I can show you the White Elephants."

"I would very much like to see them."

"*Phya* Cham is sorely troubled, for His Majesty does not listen to the *Kalahom*, nor to the *Pra-Klang*, not even to his *Chakri*, the Prime Minister," Udorn said, sitting tailor-wise as I did. "He is besotted with his women, of whom he has over seven hundred. And now that he has married three of his sisters . . . Yes, Keran, do not be surprised. Our kings always have many wives, with many children, brothers and half-brothers, sisters and half-sisters. And so much plotting, intrigue, poisonings . . . Some kings marry their sisters, their nieces, and their aunts, and yes, even the wives of their father when he dies, and the wives of the half-brothers they have killed."

"But, Udorn, this, this is . . ."

"I know, it is called incest," Udorn said. "But—" Whimsically he raised a hand in the Buddha gesture of "no quarrel in the family."

He went on about King Ekatat's foolishness. "Our hearts are uneasy. If the Burmese attack us again . . ." For a moment the cloak of joy he kept wrapped about him slipped; I saw another Udorn, a man much concerned with the danger to Ayuthia that royal misdemeanor might bring.

"Let us go to see the White Elephants," I said, and he laughed, shrugging away worry.

UDORN'S COUSIN, PHYA CHAM, was round-faced and dyed his hair. He had the reputation of loving women and wine, but he was also a warrior, having led a sortie against the Burmese in the last war, slicing with his heavy saber at least two men on horseback and producing an enemy retreat that day. We went to his palace to join the retinue accompanying him to the King's audience. Two *bikkus* chanted prayers, to make the audience auspicious and rid us all of any *phi*, or evil spirits, who might linger about on our way to the royal presence.

As *Phya* Cham dressed, waiting for the propitious hour to leave, he told many stories of the King's house. Getting rid of one's relatives seemed a habit of the kings of Ayuthia. Only the week before, two princes, cousins of the King, had been cut into pieces and the pieces given to the crocodiles for having committed the act of flesh with Ekatat's concubines. And the women, their hands and feet cut off, had been left to roast over a slow fire.

"The Burmese have not given up their dream of destroying Ayuthia," Cham said, adjusting his tall-crowned spire hat with three gold circlets indicating his rank, his tunic, his belt of heavy gold, and contemplating the effect in a large mirror from France. "The King of Burma, Manglok, is now assaulting our northern cities, Chiengmai, Luang Prabang. I must mention the danger, though it cost me my life, for King Ekatat wishes to hear nothing unpleasant, and his wishes are Divine commands."

The kings of Ayuthia were the incarnation of Indra, the Hindu God of War, who rides on a three-headed elephant. The Court followed Hindu rites, and the palace priests were Brahmin. "Even the Chief Abbot of our Buddhist faith, the *Sangharajah*, is not listened to," Cham said. "Yet our people are Buddhist, and only listen to the *Sangharajah*."

In solemn procession we went to the palace. It had its own walls, like the Forbidden City in Peking.

We entered the first court of the palace. Twenty elephants of war, with gold harnesses, their *mahouts* in purple brocade, and two hundred palace guards with sabers watched us.

"There should be fifty elephants," Udorn explained, "but King Ekatat is lazy; he never hunts wild elephants, the usual sport of kings. A special elephant *kraal* is by the side of the palace, where *mahouts* tamed the wild elephants into submission; but now elephants of war are few in number."

The second court, paved with bright marble, held a regiment of one hundred turbaned Moors on horseback. Horses and horsemen glittered in gold brocade and gold. The horses' hooves were gilded, and the sheaths of the Moorish scimitars were of pure gold.

The third courtyard again had elephants and the palace guards, with tunics of gold brocade. Among them I discerned some *farang* faces—Portuguese and other fair-haired mercenaries. And some were Japanese.

In the fourth court were the King's special barge rowers, their arms painted red, and Persian guards, the most trusted, and eunuchs, *khanti*, who were Persian. The Persians had been in Ayuthia for many centuries and had brought the practice of eunuchs with them, but the Thais did not take to the custom, and so the eunuchs were few in number.

On to the fifth court, where officials lay prostrate on carpets. Here was a gilded stairway leading to an upper floor, the King's audience room. Its walls were covered in gold, with gilded pillars, polychrome chandeliers, and five-storied umbrellas of gold brocade. The stairway was guarded by two elephants completely covered in gold, whose tusks were studded with rubies, emeralds, and diamonds, and six horses with saddles and harnesses of gold worked with pearls, rubies, and star sapphires.

Phya Cham went on to ascend the stairway, while Udorn and I retreated, crawling backwards on our hands and knees until we had again reached the third court, where we could raise our bodies, there being no one there of a higher rank than we were.

The agility with which officials—even old ones—performed these prostrations and crawlings made me think that such might be good for one's body.

The Brahmin priests began intoning their liturgic chanting. Music played, signifying that the King was on his way. He would ascend his elevated throne, framed by an opening, seven cubits above the audience hall. The frame round the opening was of pure gold, inset with precious stones; the

King was clad in shining vestments, covered with jewels, and shone like the sun.

The stable for the White Elephants was no stable but a palace on its own, next to the King's. It had its courtyards, four hundred attendants, and servants who cured and combed and fed the animals, fanned them on hot days, and bathed them in tanks full of clear water.

In a roofed reception hall with gilded walls stood an elephant of lighter color than usual, with pink eyes and white spots on his forehead. Udorn knelt before the beast, who looked at us gently, curled its trunk, and accepted the bunch of plantains we had brought. His tusks were ringed with gold and jewels. Hanging on the walls were his harnesses and strappings and vestments, of which he had thirty, studded with emeralds, diamonds, and rubies. He ate and drank out of gold salvers, in which were placed water and grass and young bamboo shoots.

The White Elephant was the incarnation of Lord Buddha, and his presence confirmed the authority of the King. "All our wars with Burma, twenty-two of them until now, are for the sake of owning White Elephants," Udorn said. "Two hundred years ago Burma took Ayuthia for the sake of the King's seven White Elephants. Today Ekatat owns three, white, russet, and round-tailed. The kings of Burma will wage war again. . . ."

There were two other elephants, more darkly tinged, in the next halls, and a corps of musicians at their service now struck up a lively air to amuse them.

I thought but did not tell Udorn that it was the gold of Ayuthia, its wealth and its craftsmen, which the Burmese coveted, and not the White Elephants. Abdul Reza, who did not believe in the White Elephants, had told me that Burma had much land but few people. "What is needed to make a kingdom rich is many people, and skilled ones, to cultivate the soil, to feed the cities, to produce trade and commerce. The Burmese make war to enslave people," he had said to me.

We returned to the Royal Esplanade and saw *Phya* Cham standing, talking with other noblemen. Udorn hastened forward, leaving me behind, and I halted; it was clear that *Phya* Cham was in serious converse, speaking of matters of state. I watched the group. Udorn joined them, making obeisance; he was amicably embraced by Cham and began to talk eagerly.

Of the nobles with *Phya* Cham, one had a round head and square features and was of paler cast with slanted eyes, clearly with Chinese blood in him. And then Udorn looked around for me and waved at me to approach.

And thus I met Sin, later to be known as Taksin. It was a very brief meeting then. But the face with its bright, glowing eyes, the high forehead, a certain air of resolute strength, was not easily forgotten.

Phya Cham now said that he must go, and Udorn took me away.

"Let us go to Bang Paket across the river. Prince Chiprasong has asked us to an exhibition of boxing and Krabi-Krabong. He wants you to come."

Our *polun* glided on the canals, then on the river. When we reached the main stream, and as we were in safety, Udorn said, "Cham may have to go into a *wat* to become a *bikku.*" This meant Cham was trying to avoid being killed.

"What happened?"

"The King."

Ekatat had taken his place on his throne of pure gold, encrusted with jewels, high above the prostrate ministers and officials. He shone in his clothes; covered in rubies, sapphires, and diamonds; crowned with a spire of gold studded with nine kinds of precious stones—diamonds, rubies, emeralds, sapphires, zircons, amethysts, topazes, jade, and pearls. The chanting Brahmins had recited his many titles:

> The Most Holy, seeing everywhere, He who guides the rains of the world, makes the water rise and flow, the Godlike Lord of the Thais, of the white, red, and round-tailed elephant, who is Indra, Lord of War, chiefest of all the gods.

To his ministers groveling on the floor before him, the King had said, "We hear that someone is troubled by the fall of Chiengmai. Speak, whoever has this sore in mind."

And *Phya* Cham, crawling forward, joining his hands above his head, had said, "High and Mighty Lord of me Thy slave, Thy Royal Word is upon me. Thy slave desires to fight the vile enemy, who have dared to attack Chiengmai."

And Ekatat had replied through his Minister of the Right (the *Kalahom*), "Is it of the cur Manglok, so-called King of Burma that you speak?"

The Minister of the Right, his limbs shaking, had bleated, "It seems so, oh Lord."

Ekatat had laughed, a high falsetto. "Then know ye, ignorant slaves, that Manglok has died, just as his father died in the siege of Ayuthia two years ago. His armies have withdrawn, as did those of his father. Whoever dares to challenge us will die."

There had been a general murmur of praise, of pleased surprise. "The most Holy, seeing everywhere, in whose hand is the power of Indra . . ."

Phya Cham had remained prostrate.

Ekatat had said, "There is no need to reinforce the army. Ayuthia cannot be conquered, for We reign here Supreme, protected by Heaven itself."

Neither the *Kalahom* nor the commanders or governors of provinces knew that King Manglok of Burma had died. Yet the King knew. "A palace intrigue. Ekatat listens to two men, one called the Magician, the other his brother-in-law, the favorite minor queen's half-brother—and they say her lover. He is part Burmese."

The couriers to the minister had been intercepted. Udorn whispered this to me and then resumed his carefree demeanor. "Do you understand now, Keran, why a happy man must play the fool? And why fools are happy men?"

THE MATCHES WERE TO be held on the small plain of Bang Paket across the river, not far from the French settlement and its square-towered stone church of Saint Joseph. A large, happy crowd milled round the flat tamped field. The boxers and Krabi-Krabong swordsmen were ready. Chiprasong was already there, in a plain *pannung* or loincloth, his skin glistening with sandalwood oil. I think he wanted to be popular, to be known to the people as a simple man, perhaps to emulate the regretted King Boromakot, who often went among his people, clad as a commoner. Udorn and I sat down among the crowd, and the boxing began.

It was then, looking up, that I saw her, on the terrace of one of the stilt houses that lined one side of the field. She was with two older women, their hair shorn, and in black. She had turned her head to speak to one of them, and then she was looking at the crowd, as if looking for someone, and she saw me. I stared until I remembered that this meant scorn, and lowered my head, bringing it back to the boxers. Chiprasong had lifted his leg high to knock his opponent to the ground, but the latter, a limber young man and a fraction swifter, took a flying leap to bring Chiprasong to the ground. But Chiprasong stepped sideways and the young man missed.

I looked again, quickly glancing up. She was no longer on the terrace, and my heart began to pound wildly, as if I had lost an immense treasure. Oh let me see her but once again, oh let me see her . . . and then I did see her, she was on the outer edge of the circling crowd just opposite me and she was looking at me.

I did not know that I was in love then; only that the earth had changed under me, that my mind was wiped clean of everything else. Her face, her shoulders, the smallness and perfection of her. In a land where so many women were loveliness incarnate, it seemed to me that no one else but she alone was beautiful, truly so. Was she noble, was she a commoner? She wore the day's color, green for Wednesday, the *jongkra-bane* and top-tied halter as women at work did to keep their hands and legs free.

How could I approach her?

Udorn was bending over me. "Keran, Keran, are you dreaming? Chiprasong would like to have a round with you."

The sun was westering, its pink glow filled the sky, rose of a pearl. It touched her hair, her mouth. She wore a pink hibiscus in her hair.

Chiprasong strode up to me, assumed a boxing stance, calling out something that made the crowd laugh. I felt hot all over.

"You cannot refuse; this is a friendly match. Better let him win quickly, so you will not be hurt." Udorn's voice was a little anxious. He replied gaily, however, and I knew that he was trying to make the crowd laugh at something else.

But the crowd really wanted some clowning now, to finish the day. Perhaps to see Chiprasong knock down a *farang*. There would be no dishonor in losing to the Tiger man, Prince Chiprasong.

No dishonor. Except that she was there. I could not be made a mockery of. I could not let Chiprasong beat me. She would see that I was lame when I stood up to fight.

Darkness fell, and men were bringing torches, great hunks of light.

I took off my tunic, keeping only my silk trousers that I wore as the Chinese do, with a belt round my waist. I had grown accustomed to this garb. The Thai *pannung* still seemed to me precarious; I was afraid it would come unstuck.

"*Lok Ching, Lok Ching,* Chinese, Chinese," the crowd shouted happily. It delighted them that a *farang* should dress as a Chinese. They again exclaimed when they saw my skin, so pale in the torchlight. I was glad that I was not hairy, for they would have shouted, "Monkey, monkey," as I had heard them shout when some well-furred *farang* mariner exposed his torso.

With great good nature they pressed forward, discussing my hair, my hands. Now as I took off my padded shoe, they saw my foot. "Aiyah, *Tsikung,*" they called out my infirmity loudly. I remembered what Traveler had taught me. Balance the body on your good leg, loosen, let the mind go like water, sending strength into your maimed foot.

"Udorn. Tell Prince Chiprasong he fights his way, I fight my way."

Udorn announced it, loud and clear, and Chiprasong swung his head.

"The *farang* way, of course," he shouted.

As before any match, there was a short invocation, a gathering of the forces of the spirit and body, and then Chiprasong danced towards me, light on his feet, his knotted fists beautiful, almost caressing the air. He meant, I knew, to knock me down a few times, in as ridiculous a posture as possible, to draw laughter. He was grinning in a friendly manner. I hated him.

Watch his feet. He always feints with his right fist, kicks by wheeling his left foot. His big toe is lethal.

He came, lunging a deft right, a quick left, but I had already turned, letting his punch slide on my raised shoulder, and with my club foot hooked his ankle, while he was carried forwards by the momentum of his blow, and I whirled away from the impact of his body.

He stumbled but caught himself, and from a half-bent position swung once again towards my belly; but I had turned round on myself, and I was now behind him while he went forwards and fell on his back as I slammed his left arm backwards.

A long *"Hai, hoyoa"* came from the men in the crowd, and suddenly they were clamoring, shouting, and I also heard the piercing voice of women. I looked round to see where she was, whether she had seen.

And found myself on the ground, felled by a terrible blow to the groin. For what seemed an eternity, I lay panting, but it was only a few seconds. I was faint; but Udorn was there, reviving me. "That's enough, Keran, enough, lie still now, lie still."

"Oh no." I took a deep breath, clambered to my feet, but before I could straighten out was felled again, this time by a kick to my jaw which sent me spinning backwards, reeling.

Now a demon of cold fury possessed me, fury and cunning. I had fallen on my good side. I coiled my good leg under me as Traveler had taught me to do. Chiprasong was lunging forwards again, and I knew he meant to do me some hurt, perhaps break my nose.

I thrust my body up like a spring, but sideways, so that his blow went awry, glancing off my shoulder, while at the same time I used my hand, slicing at his arm just above the elbow, hitting the nerve. He screamed and his fist dropped. I had unnerved his wrist, not enough to break bone, however. But he now launched his left and caught me in the kidney. Folded within the silk belt, wrapped in leather, were my watchmaker's tools, and by good fortune they were what he hit. The blow projected me forward, and I would have fallen but somehow succeeded in keeping my balance.

Unconsciously following Traveler's words, I sidestepped, and again I hit him, this time with my other hand, a horizontal sweeping blow at his throat, which grazed him. Already he was using his left knee to hit my groin, but missed by a fraction because my blow had displaced his head. And as he missed, my club foot came into action, kicking his left arm upwards and then hooking it downwards and forwards, against his knee joint. He reeled and I seized his drooping wrist, twisting it hard and twisting him with it. Then with my good leg as a solid pillar I used my club foot to kick the back of the other knee. He fell then, and as he fell I chopped him in the neck with my free hand, a murderous blow.

He would not be up again for a while. I had tried to kill him. I had forgotten what Traveler had said: "Only self-defense, not to kill . . ."

She had seen that I was lame.

Udorn was handing me my tunic and my shoes, wiping the sweat off me. He was beaming, for I had won. "I did not know that you possessed the mastery of Zen," he said. "You keep secret many a thing, Keran."

I put on my cloth shoes, the one with a solid inner sole higher than the other first.

Men and women were pressing around me with joined hands, girls garlanding me with flowers. And she was there, smiling up at me; softly, shyly, her hands placed a garland round my neck.

The drums began. Double-headed *Tapone, Song-Na, Klong-Thad*, with their recall of hooves in the forest, of echoing tiger roar. Calling to the feast. The people of three villages had gathered, they squatted on palm leaves or on the ground. Men in black went about with pitchers of palm wine, carried vats of steaming food. The food was supplied by the Chinese, as was customary. The latter paid for every feast, a small tribute to amicable relations with the hospitable Thais of Ayuthia.

There were piglets, turned on spits, golden brown, with hot spices and honey, the flesh melting under our fingers; chickens in curry with the ubiquitous *prikeenu*, the small hot chili that had seared my mouth until I got used to it and could now swallow with the best; prawns and crabs fried in ginger and garlic, and coconut milk; fried bananas and fish, in lemon grass and coriander and spices; fish of eight kinds, all from the Great Mother River, *Chao Phya Menam*; and then the kings of fruit, mangoes, and the abominably smelly durians, so good to eat if one pinched one's nose.

Such a feast. Men coming to salute me, to ask me where I had learnt my fighting.

"Truly, tonight you are the *wang*, king of the feast," Udorn said exultingly.

Two women fanned me zealously throughout my eating, and on rattan trays in front of me were laid many bowls. I drank and ate, drank the hot palm wine. And then the dancing began.

The musicians arranged themselves in a circle, and the drums now went sweet, precise and soft, like the pulse of night, like the beat of blood, a night so soft it was almost painful to be alive, to know that such nights are not given forever. The men rose to dance, and also the women, and she was there too, in the ranks of the women, until the thickening press of dancers hid her from my sight.

Drums. The night throbbed with them, and with the sound of the *pinai* flutes rising like nightingales, throaty and shrill and calling to the forest to listen.

Dancing—long weaving files of men, and across from them on the other side of the field, the women almost immobile save for the slow, ritual movement of the arms, the hands, the necks; meditative, weaving the spell of the enchanted night. Offering praise to the Lords of the Spirit for the goodness of the evening, the feast, the dance.

The tempo quickened. The men began pacing, slowly, weaving in front of the women, who remained in place; more and more the men's gestures broadened, took on strength and might. Suddenly one, then two, more, left the ranks and began dancing alone, dancing dances of war and love. Dancing the loves and hates of the immortal gods, who in their passions are human, who betrayed and killed and lusted as ordinary men do.

The women now began to move—a slow and wonderful wave of water, the marvel of water. Their line rippled, advanced, and withdrew. They were now dancing almost together with the men, but never truly with them, never touching, never looking at them. Yet their movements created a rhythm, a tide, and I thought of the love poem that Udorn had given me to read:

> *Oh catch a rainbow in your arms*
> *Tread your way among stardust*
> *My heart is shimmering water,*
> *Shimmer that dies when the moon grows cold . . .*

"Catch a rainbow in your arms . . ." Now the women were bold, coming up to the squatting men who had not joined the dancing, giving a small wave of the *sabai* over their left shoulder. And each man thus beckoned rose and joined the dance.

Udorn was chosen by a tall, ample woman, whose arms seemed boneless as they wove from the shoulder to the fingertips, a wave of motion that made one lust for her, merely watching those arms that held all the desire of the world.

A matron with shorn hair waved her *sabai* at me to dance with her. She too was a skilled and beautiful dancer, the first dancer of her village. I rose and performed somewhat gauchely, thankful that in Thai dancing one did not have to hop, skip, jump, and hold a woman in one's arms, which now appeared to me a grotesque way of dancing.

"The *wang* must choose a maiden to dance with," Udorn said.

And because of the palm wine emboldening me I made my way through the ranks of women until I found her, and folded my hands and bowed my head in front of her. We danced, five feet away from each other. She did not look at me, nor I at her; I kept my eyes down. Only my hands, my arms, said: I love you, I love you. The world has suddenly become a rainbow, become fragrant, delectable, because of you. Oh let me but love you, my hands said, weaving the air.

"Her name is Jit," Udorn told me when we were back in our *polun*, the rowers calling out the strokes. We were through the *Nei Kai*, the Chinese gate, which could always be opened, even at night.

"I shall die, Udorn, if I can't have her," I said. "Not my body, but something within me will die."

"Ah, the thunder and lightning of love is worse than any typhoon," Udorn said. "She is the daughter of a small official; she has Chinese blood in her, as well as Thai."

"I love her. That is all."

"Let me arrange it. You are not secretive, Keran. Everyone could see you were in love. Even Chiprasong saw it. He recovered from his faint and he was watching. I think he is angry because you shamed him. But now he should understand that it was because of love. You could not lose in front of her."

The rowers' oar blades whisked the water, pulling smoothly, beating time. Time, in slow oar beats, in slow heartbeats. Time had brought me here. I heard the croaking of the night frogs delighting in the watery night.

"Udorn, if she but come to me, I shall be the most blessed of men."

⇨ *Fourteen* ⇦

Anno Domini 1763–1764

⇨ ⇦

I married Udorn at an auspicious hour in January of 1763. The ceremonies lasted three days. I changed my clothes twenty-one times, each time with a new set of jewels. Abdul Reza's generosity was unstinted; Udorn covered me with gifts. I now had five large chests of China lacquer with hinges and locks of pure gold, filled with jewelry and gold-threaded garments. And salvers and vases and boxes of gold, silver, enamel, ivory, and mother-of-pearl, enough to fill seven large cupboards.

Udorn is handsome. He has proved himself skilled and courteous as a lover. Since I do not love him I can all the more appreciate the pleasure he gives me. I keep intact the weather of my soul, and move towards my own freedom, undeterred, sovereign.

I think of the strong and bitter woman sitting in the Forbidden City of Peking: the Mother, Empress Dowager, who killed her son's love because she would not let him betray the Empire.

Perhaps she sometimes thinks of me.

Colin. Between my brother and me is a bond we must both maintain and resist. We have to shut our minds away from each other, since now we both have lovers; and we shall have to live with this interdiction all our lives. Perhaps others do, who bury deep within themselves their lust and hunger for a sister, a mother, to be more than sister or mother. With my brother and me it is a shallow grave, in which part of ourselves must lie forever.

Colin's love is a maiden shy and gentle, whose uncomplicated mind, like a rose, emits a wordless happiness. Whose body is slight, pliant, beautiful. She sees a bird and thinks: This is a bird. She goes no further, but to her the bird is all delight, marvel, joy. She will never grow weary of everyday small miracles. She has neither ambition nor malice. She wants only to serve Colin, to love him. This is her destiny.

Colin and I now speak words to each other, engage in philosophical discussions. He argues that time is a function of the universe; and that Newton has proved that time goes on, even if no one is there to make clocks, to measure time. I say that time shrinks or stretches according to the grip of our souls and the desire of our bodies. "Then you don't believe in my watches." Colin grins, looking young and boyish because he is happy.

In Newton's world are no spirits of tree and fire and enchanted forest. But here in Ayuthia are spirits everywhere, potent and powerful.

"Colin, the android you are thinking of making, he must be a king. He must have a king's face."

"The King?"

"Not Ekatat. Someone else. As yet I do not see his face. When I do, I shall make the face for you."

On the tenth day after our wedding I tell Udorn to bring back his other wives. "They will grieve without you. Your heart is mine, so I am not jealous."

Udorn is delighted. A nobleman with only one wife is a pitiful thing in Ayuthia. Three of them are back; their speech the twitter of sparrows, their manners charming. "Three is enough," I say, and Udorn laughs, and calls me an enchantress, the queen of his heart.

The Gift is strong within me here, for Ayuthia is both dream and reality, fusion of everything contradictory, diverse, wayward, mutable.

"There will be war again, Udorn. The Burmese will come again."

"I know it, most beloved." He sighs. He and his cousin Phya Cham are anxious and so is the Kalahom, for the ramparts of Ayuthia are in a poor state. Its many forts need repairs. There are no cannon balls for the cannon installed by the Portuguese under King Boromakot, Ekatat's father, some twenty years ago. Ekatat refuses to release the cannon and ammunition stored in the royal armory to strengthen the defense forts. The muskets of the palace guards have not been fired in many years.

King Ekatat is besotted with shamans and exorcists who feed him philters, love potions, and quicksilver to make him invisible and invincible, so that, it is said, his teeth are beginning to drop away.

Udorn sighs. And nothing is done.

I go to see Abdul Reza in his house in the Muslim quarter with my retinue of maids and women fighters, Amazons trained to protect other women. I order them to withdraw. "I have important matters to talk over with Prince Reza." Now they know that I can do all I want—I am not fettered as other women are—and they leave me alone.

Abdul Reza sits, dignified, tormented. A man. A man with the smell and savor of a man. He reminds me of the Chinese Emperor Tsienlung. He is the same age, with a body seasoned and inured with living and many women. I feel the stir of lust in me.

"I am yours, Lord Reza, if you so wish. For now I am no longer your ward, and I can choose the men I wish to make love with." His lips go pale. He moistens them.

"Lady, I cannot cheat."

"Udorn does not own me. I own myself."

His hands grip the small knife he wears always at his belt.

"You are wicked, immoral," he says, in a measured voice. "You play with people . . . you are cruel, Lady Bea."

"Wicked, cruel, immoral? Because I please myself, as a man pleases himself with women?"

A week later, he becomes mine, and pleasures me greatly, for he has a wonderful body, spare, undiminished by age; passion and anger make him fierce, indefatigable.

"You have taken my manhood from me," he says afterwards.

245

"But we shall always remember this hour," I reply. "For we were truthful with each other, were we not?"

⇝ ⇜

JIT WILL BE MY WIFE.

Udorn and *Phya* Cham called on her father, *Khun* Panat. He is a minor judge, traveling through the villages sacked by the Burmese in their 1760 war. There are many harrowing cases to deal with. He has but this one daughter. His wife is a pretty woman. I sit in their house, drinking tea from China, while Udorn talks. I am a *farang*, but perhaps they will accept me. *Khun* Panat is an upright man, and not wealthy.

Every three days I may sit with Jit in the reception hall. She is flanked by two aunts and three cousins. I may speak with her. I keep my head and eyes lowered, to show my respect for her. She says, "I am very young. You must teach me how to serve you well."

There is about her an innocence that twists my heart. She is perfume, the color of the sky above me. She inquires of the clocks and automata I make, and when I tell her how I worked with my father, she nods. I feel she understands everything I say.

She plays music, dances, and reads; her father wanted her educated, and she was taught to read and to write by her aunt, a learned Buddhist nun. "I shall learn my lord's language so that I may serve you well," she says to me.

I have translated, with Udorn's help, the old Provencal song of Magali, remembering Laurence Shane, who played and sang it with me on the ship *Cardus* so many years ago, Laurence who drowned in the nameless ocean.

> *O Magali if you become*
> *The moon serene,*
> *I shall become the mist of night,*
> *To wrap you in my arms . . .*

I sing it to her. Later I make a music box with the tune. She looks at me with those eyes of hers, so dark, velvet quiet, the quietness of earth, of water. She sings Magali in her own language to me.

I PASS BANG PAHAT and the handsome Saint Joseph's Church, with the bishop's stone house next to it. Here is Saint Paul's, the Jesuits' church. Perhaps there is in me some nostalgia. To hear French again, to think of Laurence, and Castiglione.

A man dressed as a Thai comes out of the bamboo house by the church. He wears a beard.

"Welcome, Colin Duriez," he says in French.

"You know me?"

"Who does not in Ayuthia? Maker of clocks and automata . . . and your sister is Princess Didya, whose beauty enchants everyone. Come in."

The house is small, bare; the reception room, save for a large crucifix, has only a table and chair and some cushions on the floor. A middle-aged woman with a long tunic over her skirt—the Christians wear such gowns to cover themselves, unlike the Thai women—comes in, bearing sweets and tea.

Father Jean Allard speaks perfect Thai and is working on a Thai-French grammar. We talk of Pierre Amigot, of Giuseppe Castiglione. He is affable, gentle, with that typical courtesy of the Jesuit, a velvet glove over steel. "There are few converts, only thirty-six hundred of them, in Ayuthia. The Thais cling to their own religion, and it is difficult to move their souls."

He is full of stories. Of how in the 1680s King Louis XIV sent the Duke of Chaumont as ambassador to Ayuthia with fourteen Jesuits, astronomers, and mathematicians. Some of the Thai princes were much troubled, especially when they found out that the aim of the French was conversion to Catholicism. They told the King that Catholic priests went into the *wats* and laughed at the statues of the Lord Buddha.

It all ended, as usual, with slaughter. The French were thrown out. "However, our order was allowed to continue to preach and to teach."

He mentioned that the French King Louis XV was now

confiscating the properties and closing the schools of the Jesuits in France, and that in the Vatican the Pope was thinking of abolishing the order. . . . "If it is God's will to try us sorely, His will be done."

In Saint Paul's Church, muskets, well furbished, lined the wall. In the sacristy were pistols and pikes. "We were asked to help defend Ayuthia from the Burmese some three years ago, and we did. The Burmese had Portuguese officers who promised to spare us as fellow Catholics. They burnt some of the Dutch quarter, though not the factory. They burnt down the English settlement and took many people away as slaves."

"I hope there will not be another war." I shivered, thinking of Jit.

Jean Allard smiled noncommittally. "By the way, Father Oliveiro is here. You know him, I think. He has gone out to administer the sacraments to a dying man."

Oliveiro the Inquisitor, his nickname on the ship. "I shall see him next time I visit you," I replied. Jean Allard laughed a little, his eyes twinkling. Of all the crosses he had to bear, perhaps Father Oliveiro was one.

I HAVE ALMOST FINISHED building my android.

I have set his movements by a clock, which is in his stomach, set in motion by a circular selector disc in his belt, with another disc concealed under his tunic. The clock runs for eight days. His movements vary according to the clock's time. He will walk, whistling a tune activated by blowers, his cheeks and mouth the resonant cavity for the sounds he emits. He sits in a prepared chair. Picks up a book placed on the table in front of him; opens it, ruffles through some pages, puts it down, seizes a quill from the inkwell, writes on a sheet of paper. Bar his walk, his movements are smooth. What he writes also varies. I have constructed his "memory" in such a way, placing enough material in it, that he may write many sentences, himself picking out the required letters to write them. By varying two mobile master cams, shifting them alternately on the selector discs, he also chooses a course of action—either writing or walking.

While writing, he breathes. This is done by blowers that inflate the jointed chest, connected to the clock. I have timed them on my own breathing. When he has finished writing, he puts down the quill, looks about him, lifting his head, rises, and begins to walk. His hands and arms go behind his back as he paces, as a man does in cogitation. His feet are weighted, and I have introduced a shifting weighted wheel that spins within his belly and maintains his balance. Alas, he has as yet no knee joints. Therefore his equilibrium is precarious on a slanted floor and his walk jerky.

The length of time he walks is also a knotty unsolved problem. He should be able to stop when confronted with an obstacle, but since he cannot see, I wonder how I can introduce into him sentience of surrounding objects. I shall now make him able to sit on the ground, gathering his legs in the lotus position as do the Thais, and appear to meditate.

We worked many hours on the android, Ah Ming and I. Every part—screws and rivets, cams and joints, alternate gears and cogwheels, and the intricate "soul" joined to an inner clock—was made and remade by us. When my sister gives him a face, I shall add other parts, so that he may open his eyelids and close them, and move his lips as he whistles. Ah Ming is now overawed.

"Colin Brother, suppose a forlorn *phi* without a home comes into this thing and inhabits it?"

"It is only a machine, Ming. No *phi* can run a machine."

"We could make soldiers," Ah Ming says. "Many soldiers—no one could kill them."

"That is true."

I watch the android perform. I have worked hard; introduced precious stones, rubies and diamonds, sinking the finest screws and pegs and rivets into them.

"When he has a face . . ." Ah Ming says.

I have named him the King. I have put him away in a chest of white metal, proof against termites and insects of all kinds, and moisture. The monsoon season is a deluge of water, flooding the land, water insinuating itself into every corner, swelling the wood of houses. But the King will keep dry.

SONGKRAN. THE NEW YEAR OF Ayuthia, which is April. Streets and canals a riot of color, pageants and processions, tens of thousands of boats on the canals, on the river, with red and gold pennants flying. Gaudy paper kites in the sky, and firecrackers everywhere.

Courtship boats, the girls in some, men in others, singing to each other of love, playing flutes and drums, throwing flowers. Blossoms everywhere; and the splashing of lustral colored water. Every Ayuthian holds a bowl of water with which to splash everyone he or she meets. The more drenched one is, the more blessed.

Bea holds a silver bowl, petals floating in it, and splashes me like a little girl, laughing happily. She throws water at Udorn and says she will splash Abdul Reza. We step into our *poluns*, our rowers handsome in blue and saffron, to visit Udorn's relatives and friends, to visit Abdul Reza. Then I leave them, and with Ah Ming go out of the city. Ah Ming does not like being wetted. Soon he and I are dripping as boatloads of young girls sail by and throw water upon us, because we are two men alone and therefore must be teased.

We reach *Wat* Phanang Cheng, where the huge statue of Buddha sits in majesty. Fairs are held in front of the *wat*. Chinese boatmen and their families congregate here. The Chinese are showing an opera. The music is high falsetto, very different from Thai music. The actors wear embroidered robes and painted faces; tiaras of tinsel, gilded or silvered, with pom-poms and feathers, adorn their heads. A tragedy of love and war and final retribution is enacted. Inside, the *wat* is thick with incense smoke and crowded with thousands of believers. Ah Ming can scarcely push his way in. I wait for him outside by the riverbank.

Two gilded barges glide by, with swan necks and snake heads and red pennants, their oars streaked with copper-gold. Royal barges. The Burmese destroyed over two hundred of them; but many are left. The Chinese boatmen comment on the barges in their dialect; I picked up some knowledge of it during the sea voyage from China.

"Number One is fetching himself another woman." Thumb raised skywards, meaning the King, whose name one never pronounces.

"That . . . crab from the cesspool . . . has married his own father's sister. . . ."

Ah Ming comes out of the *wat*. He has prayed for Marquess Fang and his family, for the soul of the Master of Clocks, for Third Son, for his own clan and village in China.

"Colin Brother, here is Monk Teo, from my village in China."

A smiling Buddhist monk, pale of skin. Monk Teo has come over from China to compare the scriptural texts of Buddhism here with those of his own monastery. "Long have I heard your glorious name," Monk Teo says to me. He has been at the *wat* ten years.

We salute him, then climb back into our *polun*. Jit is waiting for me, her village more than a league westwards. We shall go together to the fair held in the Chinese quarter of Ayuthia; doubtless a bevy of aunts and cousins will be with her.

We are to be married in another two weeks, before the heat of May. Timmermans and his wife will come to the feast. The pastor will also consecrate our marriage at the Hollanders' chapel. The pastor is now resigned to blessing the mixed marriages in Ayuthia.

All of Ayuthia seems to be on the water this day. Our progress is slow. With the jam of boats, with shouting and laughter and water throwing, at last we reach Jit's house. In front of its terrace are a few moored boats. I call out to the rowers as we step onto the terrace; they call back, "*Sawasdee*," welcome, but do not throw water. They squat low in their boats, their caps down over their eyes.

The terrace floor is red with flower garlands and with betel juice; red splashes are everywhere. I give a cheerful call, and Jit's aunt comes out. I respectfully throw some rose water from the silver bowl and I hold on to her skirt.

"*Khun*. Keran, Sir, do not be angry," she says.

She is pale. Terror pales her face.

"What is it? What's happened?"

She crumples, sobbing, falls to the floor. I look up. Crowding the entrance to the house are women, afraid, not coming forward to greet or garland me.

"Where is *Khun* Panat? Where is Jit?"

"*Khun* Keran, Jit . . . has been taken. . . ."

"Taken, where, by whom?"

Silence; then all eyes turn towards Ayuthia, its shining multitude of golden spires, towards Ayuthia the glorious, and the aunt prostrates herself, putting her hands above her head.

"The palace . . ."

I run into the house, calling, *"Khun* Panat, what's happened?"

Jit's father, Panat, lies, eyes still open, staring at the ceiling; red upon his garments, red wet with the blessing of water.

The barges. The royal barges I saw. They have taken Jit away. . . . The King.

Ah Ming now holds me down by force, for I struggle as one possessed; rushing to the *polun*, ordering the rowers, "Row to the palace, quick, row! I want to see the King!"

"Colin Brother, he is Divine, a god, no one speaks against the King."

"I'll kill him," I shout. "I'll kill him. . . ."

"Hush, Brother, hush." Ah Ming clamps a hand on my mouth.

Jit's mother comes out of an inner room; she has torn her hair, scratched her face . . . out of her mouth come only muffled syllables.

The rowers in the other boats remain immobile, removed from what is happening before their eyes. They do not want to know. They will not know, not see.

"You've let them take her," I roar. "You've let them. . . ."

Back on the bountiful Great Mother River, the rowers rowing hard, shouting one-two-three-four at the top of their voices, using their voices to deaden the sound of my sacrilegious words. Brightness, laughter, girls throwing flowers, singing, fireworks . . . the sky is full of colorful kites.

"Jit, oh, Jit."

Back in my room, Ah Ming pours the colorless, strong Chinese liquor he brought me as a gift this morning—two red-ribboned stone bottles. He whispers to one of the frightened servants, who disappears, returns with some amber liquid. "Drink this."

"Ah Ming, let's go to the palace."

"The guards won't let us in. You'll be killed; then how can you save Jit?"

Ah Ming, strong, quiet, his brain working.

"Colin, we must plan. You must be strong. Drink."

I drink and go into a stupor. I hear whispers, shapes are around me. Udorn and Bea are back. Bea's cool hands are on me, her mind holds mine.

"Colin, I am here."

"Bea, Bea." My strong sister. She is right. Nothing counts but power. Power to take, to kill, to hold.

Foolish, timorous me. Always eager to please, to be safe, smiling, prudent. Now I shall be crafty and ruthless. "I'll kill him."

"It was Chiprasong," Bea says. "The King's chief exorcist, the Magician, says that four virgin maidens must be brought into the palace to ward off evil. To bring good luck to Ayuthia. Chiprasong suggested it to him."

"I'll kill Chiprasong. I'll get Jit back."

Bea looks at me steadily. I feel her contempt.

"I am not like you, Bea." I want to hurt her. "The fire that burnt our parents has not charred my soul, as it has charred yours. I have no Gift to protect from love. I love Jit, and I will get her back."

"Little brother," Bea says, and puts her head upon my shoulder. "I'll help you. Trust me."

UDORN AND AH MING keep me stuporous with opiates. I can scarcely rise from my bed. Servants restrain me as time and again I throw myself out of the house, wanting to go to the palace. Abdul Reza has recruited four Muslim guards, stalwart men, who keep watch on me. "Colin, be quiet. We are doing all we can."

The women in the palace are secluded. There are guards everywhere. Of course, some bold pages at the Court, some of the King's male relatives, have attempted his concubines in the past. Their deaths were atrocious. Commoners are hanged by the chin on hooks to die. Princes are squeezed to death between logs of sandalwood.

Udorn keeps up a facade of music, singing, games of chess with friends. "We must, Colin, pretend to be happy."

The King's Magician has been interrogating the stars to determine the fate of Ayuthia. A great Thai king in the past, when hard pressed in war, had sworn to put to death the first four women he met, and done so. Now, the Magician promises that if four virgins are immolated when and if the Burmese attack Ayuthia, the Burmese army will be defeated and Ayuthia be triumphant.

I scream with horror, but my intrepid sister smiles. "We have time, Colin. Several months before us. The Burmese will not start a war until after the monsoon . . . we have four months in front of us to save your Jit."

I START TO WORK again at the factory.

I do my Wushu exercises; I learn Krabi-Krabong too.

Abdul Reza has found an old man, a Japanese *takeo* or teacher of martial arts. His ancestors came with the famous Yamada, captain of the King's Japanese guard, in 1620.

When he hears the story of Jit, the *takeo*'s heart is touched. He comes every day before dawn and imparts to me some secrets of his art. Then, being an ordinary *bikku* holding his begging bowl and his *tarapet*, or fan, in front of his downcast eyes, he goes from house to house for food.

The monsoon begins with spurts of rain; it thickens and now the sky itself seems to fall upon the earth in great sheets of water. Even the crickets are muffled, and the damp is unrelenting.

I think of Jit and become very thin; Udorn is much concerned.

One day *Phya* Cham's friend Sin, whom I met fleetingly on the Royal Esplanade the day I went to see the White Elephant, comes to visit Udorn. He is to be governor of the province of Tak, in the northwest. Hence he will now be known as *Phya* Tak, but everyone calls him Taksin, and it suits him. He sits quietly, saying little, but enormous vigor radiates from him. He talks in a low voice with Udorn and with *Phya* Cham, who has come out of the *wat* and has stopped being a monk, as the King has agreed not to kill him. At least not yet.

Taksin's father came from China and prospered in Ayuthia, where he married a Thai woman of good family. He died when Taksin was four, and the boy was adopted by the *Chakri*, for it was predicted that he would one day be great—he had some of the features of a Buddha upon his face.

Taksin has many friends among the Thai princes. He was educated with many of them, in the royal *wat* by the Buddhist monks, and then he became a page at the Court for some years.

Inevitably he and Udorn and Cham talk of war; King Ekatat has repeated that Ayuthia needs no cannon or musketry, neither from Batavia (the Hollanders have offered them) nor anywhere else. Even if the Burmese besiege Ayuthia, they would have to withdraw when the rains came. No army can withstand the flood that surrounds Ayuthia, several leagues wide. No army can stay with its feet in water for so many months. So says King Ekatat.

Taksin growls. "It is those magicians and fake priests. . . ."

No one speaks of the four maidens, but Taksin's eyes are upon me, full of compassion. He questions me about automata. I explain the mechanism; I show him some of the models. He nods. "Tell me, do you believe that machines can be made to enable man to go under the sea, to fly in the air?"

"It is not impossible, *Phya* Taksin." I tell him of the vapor machine to speed boats on water without sails. And of Leonardo da Vinci, who had already made drawings for a flying machine. And I remember a quotation that Jacob and I found in a book, an ancient and curious prophecy. It wells up in me now.

> *When pictures look alive with movements free,*
> *When ships like fishes swim beneath the sea,*
> *When man outstripping birds shall skean the sky,*
> *Then half the world deep-drenched in blood shall lie . . .*

"Drenched in blood," Taksin says slowly, dreamily. I think of Jit then, and tears well up in my eyes, and Taksin notices it and silently puts his hand upon my arm.

After he has gone, Cham—who still flits in and out of the

wats, sometimes declaring his intention to become a *bikku* and sometimes resuming his life as a nobleman—says, "Taksin is a good man; there are many like him. But all of us are paralyzed, unable to take any action."

"All things are in the hands of fate, Karma," Udorn says.

BEA RETURNS, AND WITH her is Ah Ming. Bea, I know, has been inquiring, through the women, into what is happening at the palace.

"Jit has been allowed to go to a ceremony at *Wat* Phanang Cheng. It is the hundred-day ceremony for her father's death—in three days' time. You will see her, Colin . . . and this is a beginning."

MY HEAD WAS SHAVED and my eyebrows. Monk Teo rubbed some dark brew on my skin. "You look almost a Thai . . . perhaps a half-Portuguese."

In *Wat* Phanang Cheng's immense hall, the corners are sunk in shadows, despite the great number of tapers and lamps. Behind the high columns the novices kneel, and I am one of them.

The hundred-day ceremony for the soul of *Khun* Panat, Jit's father, is taking place in the chapel for souls, draped in white, with white banners and hangings and white flowers. Jit and her relatives, in white garments, assemble.

Outside, the monsoon is pouring water in great sheets upon Ayuthia. Thus it has been all day. The *wat* as well as the Dutch factory farther down the river are on high ground and therefore relatively dry, but the massively swollen river rubs and tears and grinds against the steps of the Taoist sanctuary, fearful to behold.

Now I hear the monks chanting in the funeral chapel. In the *wat* itself, the devotees pray, throw clappers, kneel. Monk Teo moves about softly, to see that all is well. And after what seems many hours, and is many hours, there is a sound of silk, and a small crowd of people press into the *wat*. They have changed their clothes, not to offend the *wat* with the color and odor of death. Jit and her attendants then arrive; they come to offer gifts of robes to the monks.

Jit. I feel her presence even before I see her, dressed plainly, with no ornaments, hands joined, her face lifted to the great Face towering on the altar. She is not alone, but I see no one else. Only Jit, Jit, the tapers flinging their golden light upon her. Now she takes from a box presented to her the flowers of silver and offers them. Incense rises, and the sound of invocations, and Jit kneels, then rises. I dig my nails into my hands, not to scream, not to rise and run to her. . . . Jit, Jit, I call in my mind and she looks about her, as if she has heard me, as if looking for me.

Jit holds incense sticks, separates some and places them on the main altar, then begins to walk along the side, putting a few sticks in the incense holder before each statue. "She will pass near you. You will see her . . . but if you make any sign she will be killed, and you, and I too. . . ." Thus Monk Teo has instructed me.

Down the aisle, along the hundreds of representations of Compassion and Mercy, along the Learned and Benign and Peaceful manifestations of the Lord Buddha, Who teaches how to escape the pain of rebirth after rebirth, how to attain Nirvana . . . kneeling, bowing, rising, folding her hands, bowing . . . slowly she comes, and my eyes, which have hungered for her, stare, stare at her, and I see as she nears that her eyes search every bowed head. She sees me. I have my head raised, and Ah Ming, by my side, firmly pulls my sleeve, to warn me to lower it. But for a brief moment our eyes have met, have clung to each other, and she has stopped. . . . Almost, almost, I fear she will cry my name.

But Monk Teo is already presenting her with more incense sticks, and starting another prayer, leading her away.

"May Thy blessing be on me the unworthy one, and on my family. . . . I take my refuge in the Buddha, I take my refuge in the Doctrine, I take my refuge in the *Sangha*. . . ."

"YOU SAW HER, COLIN Brother. You saw she is well. She is untouched." Ah Ming was pleased that I had not betrayed myself.

"Ming, I cannot, cannot wait any longer. I must get into the palace."

"Childish, Colin. You are neither a prince nor a eunuch nor an Amazon."

"I'll get in." I hit the wood bench of the *polun* with my fist.

"Perhaps as a White Elephant." Ah Ming shrugged. "Your sister is trying—through the women in the palace. She is clever, your sister, and persistent. All of us are trying. . . ."

He looked up into the dark sky, where no star shone. Another deluge of water would pour upon us after a brief respite. "Another three months of rain," Ah Ming said.

❧ Fifteen ❧

IN SEPTEMBER THE MASSED cloud cohorts of the ebony monsoon began to scatter. Timid stars peered through the night, and frogs once again resumed their colloquies in the water-logged gardens. Sleepy birds shook their feathers and twittered over damp nests. The swollen Menam's swift current ran Chinese barges and rafts of teak logs to Bangkok.

Five months without Jit.

The agony I endured in those months I cannot put into words; the molten dumbness, which like lead I carried within me, still comes over me when I recall that time. I know that Bea kept me in a state of stupor, with potions concealed in my food, so that I tossed, half-awake, half-drowsy, and woke from restless sleep in a daze, thinking I heard Jit's voice.

There is an essence in the hot and steamy lands which infects the senses, so that the sharpest ransack of pain is somehow blunted, partly dissolved in the unwearying sound of rain, the ever-present heat, the almost monstrous lushness of tree and flower. Perhaps it was that torpor, an enchanted lassitude, which afflicted all of us in Ayuthia and kept the City of Gold from vigilance, from making those preparations for defense which might have saved it.

Obtuse, the days went by, while I thought of a thousand ineffectual ways of rescuing Jit, and daydreamed, and lay for hours staring at the painted ceilings of my room; and at other

259

times felt that I should rush the palace gates, and die . . . yet did not attempt to do so, knowing it folly.

Abdul Reza left Ayuthia to return to Tenasserim on the western seacoast of Ayuthia's domain. "I must go, for I have many things to attend to, many people to care for. The Burmese armies will be back, and we, the Muslims of the seaports, will have to sail to India for safety.

"Come with me," he said, entreating both of us, but his eyes were on Bea. "Ayuthia will be unsafe for you."

"Tenasserim is not safe for you," Bea replied in a troubled voice, her eyes clouded with apprehension. "I fear for you in Tenasserim."

Abdul Reza stared at her and lost his composure. "Come with me, Bea, you who have my heart in your hands," he begged. "I love you, and all that I have will be yours. Leave Udorn. I can give you so much more."

Bea shook her head, and looked at me. Had Abdul Reza forgotten Jit? He had, in a moment of passion, for now he said, "It is madness for me to say these words. Forgive me, Colin."

"Do not tarry in Tenasserim," Bea repeated. "Leave quickly."

"I blame myself," said Reza. "Nothing has gone as I thought. The times are out-of-joint, new powers are on the march, and all my plans have gone awry."

"You were not wrong, Lord Reza," I replied. "Yours was a noble endeavor, a farsighted one, and I am glad I was part of it."

Abdul Reza wept then, as he embraced me, and, taking Bea's hands in his, held them to his forehead in a token of love and submission.

The wives of the Hollanders of Ayuthia and their children prepared to leave. The pastor, who disliked Ayuthia and was timorous, went with them. Heer Timmermans and Erik Erikssen remained, with some half-breeds whose mothers were Thai, or from Batavia, to look after the interests of the Dutch East India Company and the factory. Erik still hoped that the King of Ayuthia would accept his offer of Dutch cannon.

"The Burmese will indeed invade Ayuthia soon," Timmermans told me. "Should you and your sister wish to depart, we shall take you with us. We are going to Little Amsterdam, our trading dock some leagues from Bangkok. You will be safe there."

"I shall tell my sister, but as for myself, thank you, Sir, I remain here."

"I shall pray for you both," Timmermans said. "And for the lady you love. But remember, only the One True God can really help you." He said this because the pastor was telling everyone that Bea and I were becoming idolators.

The Jesuits were not leaving. "Should the Burmese attack again, we shall fight them," Jean Allard said. "I cannot leave my flock."

I now went often to Saint Paul's and sat in the glow of color from the church window, praying for Jit. "O Lord Jesus Christ, whether Catholic or Protestant, please, please save her."

Jit's mother had left Ayuthia—no one would tell me where she had gone—after the hundred-day funeral ceremony for her husband. Perhaps, being still pretty, she had found a man to marry her and had followed him.

While I grew wan, Ah Ming became sleek and prosperous. He owned a house and two wives, industrious women who helped in our factory. He was now also a trader in silk. "My father traded in silk in Manila," he told me. "We smuggled the silk out of China, and from Manila Spanish galleons carried it to Acapulco in Mexico, and to Peru. In those lands all the church vestments and the bishops' ornate robes are made of Chinese silk and brocade, the best."

He comforted me time and again. "Colin, nothing will happen to Jit unless and until the Burmese are under the walls of Ayuthia."

"Do we have to wait until then to save her?" I sometimes flared up.

"How impatient you are. Your sister and Prince Udorn and I are working to help. We know the *Sangharajah*, the Great Patriarch, is hostile to human sacrifice. It is against the Buddhist creed. But the palace only listens to the Great Magician, so we must find a way to him. . . ."

Old, very old was the notion of ritual sacrifice to propitiate the gods. I, who had wanted to forget the spirit world, dreamt often now of the oak forests and blood making the stone

261

scarlet in honor of the Sun God. And here too it was present, that world of the undead, under the beauty, the joy, the splendor.

In India, whenever a bridge, fort, or palace was built, the blood of a child had to be spilled to make the foundations secure. And had not even God tested Abraham with the sacrifice of His son Isaac?

At times I felt on the verge of accepting the notion of sacrifice, so all-pervasive and so hypnotic was Ayuthia's spirit world. And this filled me with horror at myself.

Udorn discomfited me with mad schemes, all devised to kill Chiprasong. I would have killed him myself, but this would not save Jit.

I prayed. I would pray to any and every spirit. I almost sought out exorcists and astrologers and soothsayers, but in the end some pride prevented me from doing so.

ONE OF UDORN'S THREE wives gave birth to a son, which seemed to please Bea mightily. She cared for the mother and the child in a charming and tender fashion, and had a cradle, like those of our land of Vaud, made for the little boy. Many of Udorn's friends congratulated him that Bea should be a person of such wisdom and detachment, even if a *farang* woman.

Women now came to her, the wives of nobles and merchants and commoners, to beseech remedies to heal a sore, curb a fever, whiten their skins. They also brought their children, for Bea could heal many a child's complaint.

"What if you bear a child, Bea?"

Bea was amused. "I shall not have a child." The Chinese herbalists of Ayuthia all knew the way to her gate. She had collected the lore of the women of the North, who use mango and papaya fruit not to conceive. She could discourse on the virtue of chrysanthemum petals from China, or tiger-bone wine, rhinoceros horn, and black-footed cock's elixir.

Bea spent an hour a day being massaged. Lying on the silk carpet in her room, she was pummeled and rubbed and kneaded by Nee. Nee had a flat face and slant eyes; she had Shan and Assamese blood in her. Captured as a slave, she had learnt massage in the family she had served. One of its daughters had become a royal concubine, and Nee had followed her to the royal palace, where she was now the best among seventy masseuses.

Nee wore necklaces of coral and turquoise in the barbaric mountain manner, silver anklets and rings on her toes. Her feet were as agile as hands. She trod on Bea's spine to keep it supple.

"Are your bones sore, Bea?" I asked.

Many people in Ayuthia suffered from sore bones during the monsoon.

"No, Colin. But it amuses me."

Nee grinned. Then she and Bea squatted on the floor, chewed betel, and afterwards lit cheroots. I had never seen Bea smoke; she had got the habit from Nee.

"Nee knows all the women in the palace," Bea said casually. Then my heart started thumping, as always when I heard something that brought me hope about Jit. I squatted next to Nee and smiled at her. Nee rolled betel leaf and lime and areca for me to chew. I hated chewing the stuff—it made one's mouth look full of blood—but I would do anything for Jit and chewed valiantly. Nee smiled at me insistently.

When she had left, Bea laughed. "Colin, Nee wants you to make love to her."

"Oh no, Bea, not that!"

"I have told her that you are under a vow of religion, like the *bikkus*. But she has so few opportunities in the palace, despite the number of pages about, and a very strong appetite, both for men and for women."

Bea continued her wooing (for such it was) of Nee; and Nee began to love her. The adoration in Nee's face, the way she followed Bea with her eyes and her hands, her deft hands on Bea's body. Bea let her worship, and sometimes would not be there when Nee came, so that Nee would squat in a corner with the expression upon her face of a submissive dog waiting for its master.

So many of the hundreds of women in the inner palace were deprived of love and lovemaking and yearned for the indispensable contact of skin with skin, the thousand discoveries of the body's several score of gentle places. Not the

forceful and sometimes brutal invasion between the legs, re-
pellant when not preceded by a total adoring, but the soft-
ness and sweet art of everything stroked and silkened and
sighed over—this the women craved, and turned to one
another, everything a pretext for assuaging this hunger of
skin and hair and eyes. The shading of a brow, the widening
of an eye with kohl, sweet odors in small dabs all over the
body, the perfuming of clothes in chests with a medley of
herbs and flowers, steaming slowly, new clothes, the feel of
them, the wearing and pleating of the *sabai*, jewelry, jewelry,
adornment pretext for *attouchement*, a fingering of a thousand
and one delights, languorous hands and fingers and tongue.

And thus, from deep roots of sensuousness, came the beati-
tude from woman to woman. The silk of hair wrapping a
face, the knowingness of feet. And massage, massage, so
necessary and fulfilling when a woman's body contemplates
itself, renews intimacy with its own bones.

All this I learnt as I watched Bea being massaged by Nee. I
too had learnt something of women, their need for a total
atmosphere of erotic adoration, in the flower boats of China.
I knew now what a deep and disfiguring assault upon a
woman is the act of love, unless it is desired by the woman
herself, the undulation of her hips, that tremor inside her
belly, patiently coaxed by a thousand caresses and words.

Now Bea entered this empire of women, and she did it for
me, because of me. Because she loved me, she set out to
captivate the harem of King Ekatat.

"Pages have at times access to the royal concubines, provided they know how to dispense pleasure and lavish it upon
several, not one alone," Bea said casually.

The pages. Those handsome youths, always about the
palace. My sister would contrive to enchant them too.

I kept silent, in my heart already acquiescing to everything,
to anything. I would even make love to Nee to get Jit out of
the palace.

IN OCTOBER OF 1764, the new King of Burma, Mangra, attacked
the borders of Ayuthia. Instead of sending one army, he

dispatched two: one marching towards the northern provinces of the kingdom and one towards the southern.

Mangra seized Chiengmai in the North, there established his troops, and sent them to capture boats and force the people to build barges, a flotilla to sail down the Menam towards Ayuthia.

As for the southern army, it captured the western ports, Tavoy, Mergui, and Tenasserim, in the cool dry months from January to March of 1765.

Unlike in the previous invasions, the Burmese now laid waste every village, city, or town they conquered. They turned Tenasserim and Mergui into pillars of fire. They spared no one, not even the Christians. The Catholic Bishop of Mergui was taken in chains to Burma. The Burmese sent men and women and children, like cattle, in great droves to their own land of Burma, to till their fields and work as slaves in the cities.

I worried for Abdul Reza, who had gone to Tenasserim, and so did Bea. She could not tell clearly what his fate had been. All we knew, from the fleeing people who now came to Ayuthia, was that some merchant ships had cut their cables and sailed on to India when the Burmese came into the port.

IN FEBRUARY OF 1765 the old *Kalahom* died, and Cham was made *Kalahom*, Minister for War. Udorn became his deputy, and Bea, as his wife, now had open access to the Court.

"Colin, we must do something to save Ayuthia."

"Save Ayuthia—and also Jit." My eyes begged her.

"Your world has narrowed down to just that one little girl," said Bea.

"I cannot help it. I love her. I was never carried by great dreams and visions as you are, Bea."

Bea softened. "Yes, Colin, this is the time to get her out of the palace."

THE HEADMEN OF THE Chinese clans of Ayuthia—representing one-third of its population—held council in the Taoist temple abutting *Wat* Phanang Cheng. They were worried by the lack of any preparations for defense.

The fate of Ayuthia was also that of its Chinese population. Not only the seagoing trade, but the building of junks and barges, the floating of teakwood rafts, the foundries, the silk that clothed Ayuthia's people, the raising of pigs and fruit orchards, and lacquerwork and furniture making—in all this the Chinese were the mainstay of work, and therefore of Ayuthia's wealth.

"In their last expedition three years ago the Mien barbarians, the Burmese, burnt down two hundred forty-one of the royal barges," said the head of the boatmen, powerful among the nine great councillors of the clans. "This means that they have grasped the importance of water. They are building boats to attempt Ayuthia by river and land. . . ."

The scribes who kept the archives of the clans had noted down the number of royal barges to be rebuilt, the number of barges being constructed by the Burmese northern army. On their abacuses the young merchants calculated the cost of these, the cost of replacements, the cost of defending the river. . . .

Ah Ming sat among the young merchants. He was now a man of worth, one who knew a *farang* making movable dolls of great magic, a *farang* whose sister had married a Thai prince, now deputy to the *Kalahom*.

He spoke. The senior councilman, who had made a fortune out of gilding the *wat* spires, summarized the discussion.

"We must . . . persuade some of the advisers of the King. We must . . . diminish their influence. Then perhaps other advisers will be listened to. Let us try."

UDORN WAS UP AT DAWN, training soldiers, deploring the state of their muskets. "They are dangerous to handle—it is impossible to control their aim. The powder cannot keep dry even in fair weather." Erik Erikssen was allowed to bring in a shipment of cannon and cannon balls from Batavia, ten pairs of good stout cannon, as good as the English used on their warships. And many cannon balls. I was to examine the cannon, see that they worked without exploding in the firing.

It was April of 1765, and again the New Year festival. A year since Jit had been taken away. Fairs and a riot of color, garlanded boats by the tens of thousands. And no one, seeing the vibrant and splendid city shining in the sun, its 360 golden spires needling Heaven, its million people dressed in the most beautiful silks of the world, would have thought that two armies, altogether a hundred thousand strong, were already installed in its provinces and marching to its conquest.

Bea was at the palace with the royal ladies, attending the audience of the chief queen. Ah Ming came to salute me, throwing water upon me for good luck and I on him. We sat, desultorily talking; he knew I had no heart to go among the joyful crowds. I had begun another android, one whose movements would be set off by the sway of a boat. But I worked only fitfully. Ah Ming, however, wanted to see my latest invention.

He fanned, gently, and then he spoke. "Colin Brother, Monk Teo and I have a plan to discredit the Great Magician. You alone can do it. You will make a woman figure. A goddess, the Lady of Mercy, Kuanyin. She must raise her arms, utter lamentations. We shall place her in a *wat*. All who see and hear will know the Compassionate One does not want a blood sacrifice."

He paused. "The time is ripe. The Great Patriarch of the *Sangha* does not like the idea of human sacrifice. We must produce confusion in the palace . . . then the Magician may be . . . persuaded to change."

My heart became light. Hope soared in me like a skylark. When Bea returned, I told her about Ah Ming's plan. She nodded. "It is a good plan, Colin, though perhaps not enough. But if it fails, we can try other ways."

MY BODY ENGAGED NEE while my heart cried Jit, Jit. But I would neglect no chance, leave nothing undone.

In Nee's northern tribes the young lived together in communal houses, and the joining of bodies was usual, teaching them fidelity when marriage came.

In the King's palace were a thousand corners of night, despite watchful eyes everywhere, pages and Amazons. There were few eunuchs, some of them *khanti*, loving in unnatural ways. There were three score of noble youths, pages, from sixteen to twenty-two years old, in the King's service. And Amazons, women trained to watch the King's women. There would always be encounters, despite the guards, the watchfulness, the danger of discovery, the atrocious deaths.

Nee now tended the Magician, for he had a swelling of the legs. He wore a veil upon his face and carried a fan of iridescent silk, as the *bikkus* carry *tarapets*, black fans streaked with gold, when they go in solemn procession to eschew vision of this world, to center upon their own illumination.

The Magician was an intimate friend of the King's brother-in-law, all powerful since his sister was the King's favorite. He dispensed incantations that the King believed would make him invisible. For Ekatat suffered from a disfiguring disease in one of his cheeks; once maggots had crawled out of its purulence.

All this Nee told me while I coupled with her, her body eager, pliant, her mouth the source of an endless stream of words. I took her again easily, pleasuring myself and her. Her face might be flat, but her body was astonishing, the kind of body one does not forget. Boneless, all warmth and obedience, silk and honey.

Bea told her, when she readied herself to leave, not to come again. "Now you must do what I tell you, Nee. You will not be forgotten by us."

I felt somewhat guilty, being thus used, using Nee. But it was for Jit.

"We must get to the Magician. Nee is the best way to get to him."

THE SOUTHERN BURMESE ARMY established its base camp at the junction of two rivers in that April of 1765. It raided the villages, carrying off the livestock and the women.

Cham petitioned the King again and again. "I have asked the King to send troops, but it would be best to have Taksin here to help us. He could rally many of the Chinese in the southern lowlands, being part Chinese himself. And he is an able commander, probably the best one we have."

Taksin would come to Ayuthia. King Ekatat, always vacillating, had half-heartedly allowed him to return from the province of Tak, where he governed well.

While here, he came to see Cham and Udorn. As he stepped into the reception hall, his eyes, with their strangely intense glow, rested lightly on me. He was not tall, but somehow all eyes would converge on him. He brought with him a sense of surprise, and of strength. Bea walked in from the garden holding Udorn's little son by the hand. She had pinned a champac, the passion flower, in her hair.

Taksin did not look in her direction, keeping his head lowered out of respect, but Udorn exclaimed, "Come, let us do as the *farangs* do. My wife is a warrior at heart, as you are, Taksin, so you must greet each other."

And Taksin raised his head briefly, greeted Bea with joined hands, and looked away again.

The men conferred about the war, and Bea sat, listening, the little boy playing by her side.

The Burmese were advancing towards Bangkok, meaning to hold the mouth of the Great River. The Burmese had seized rice boats. The Burmese . . .

Taksin rose. His movements were swift and light, but made one think of a much heavier man. I saw his eyes take in the room, all of us, before he turned away. Bea continued to sit, as if dreaming, while I went back to my room to work upon the automaton that would become an animated goddess.

MONK TEO HAD GIVEN us the exact measurements of the statue. Bea carved her face. Bea, who was painting the ladies of the Court in the manner of Giuseppe Castiglione, was accustomed to Chinese and Thai mouths and eyes. The likeness to the original statue was striking.

"Tears from her eyes," Ah Ming suggested. It was not

difficult to scoop out the insides of her porcelain eyes and fill them with oil. A valve flap shifted as the lids opened, connected by a cam to the one raising the arms. The eyes tipped upwards, letting the liquid glide down the cheeks.

Monk Teo and Ah Ming placed the figure in the *wat*, removing a statue given by a benefactor a long time ago and fallen into forgetfulness. No one thus could come to claim that the statue had been changed.

Monk Teo prayed that his sin might be forgiven. "Lord Buddha, Thou who art all Compassion and Understanding, Thou knowest we do this to save life. Forgive us then for not fulfilling the rites."

Meanwhile, the northern Burmese army quartered at Chiengmai sent advance guards to take some of the cities down the Great River. Some of the governors yielded without any resistance. I was in a frenzy; when, oh when would we be able to get Jit out of the palace?

With command of the upper waters, the Burmese general now controlled the timber rafts floating downstream. His flotilla was of more than three hundred barges, and he would make another five hundred.

"We should block the river, throw a cordon of boats across, and behind and in front of it pile log rafts linked by chains. On both sides station troops with elephants," said Bea, who sat in council, like a man, with Udorn and Cham. "We could hold the advance and meanwhile seek to attack them from the rear."

"Well thought," Cham replied. But the governors of the provinces were no longer reliable. King Ekatat, King Mangra—it was all one to some of them. Over the last two and a half centuries, the provinces had changed hands so many times. "Twenty-four invasions," Udorn reminded me, "in two hundred fifty years."

King Ekatat spoke to the *Kalahom* of massing elephants and men round the city itself.

"Ayuthia does not have many war elephants," Cham replied to the King. The elephant *kraal* was almost empty. Capturing and training new elephants had been totally neglected by Ekatat. "His father, King Boromakot, went elephant hunting and pony racing, but Ekatat never leaves the inner palace.

And what is the point of defending only the city? It is in the provinces, Taksin says, that we must stop the Burmese."

The Chinese clans had offered to help in boat building to repel the Burmese sailing down the river. "We should bring boats up from Thonburi, large and small ones. We shall need many, and with the next monsoon coming we could use them against the Burmese flotilla," Taksin had suggested.

Cham petitioned the King, in audience, to build boats and asked the King to send orders to the governors in the provinces to muster men and raise armies. But the King was afraid that, with too many armed soldiers under their command, the governors would revolt against him and he might be overthrown. "We shall see," was all he would say.

In the inner palace, the favorites and the minor queens would surround Ekatat. The chief favorite would murmur to Ekatat, "Thou art He whose dignity is beyond compare, Lord of the fairest city in the world, Lord of the White Elephant, before whom many thousands of elephants bow and fall upon their knees, no one can defeat Ayuthia's King." The Magician would appear. He had just walked on fire, unscathed; two noblemen, suspect of treason, had been grievously burnt, and, having failed the ordeal, would now die, squeezed between boards of sandalwood. The Magician brewed noble philters for the King, which made him feel powerful, mighty, so that he refused to arm the provinces.

Again the monsoon began. Soon the surrounding villages would become flooded, the inhabitants living on their boats. The flood waters would surround Ayuthia, and the Burmese would be halted. Ayuthia was impregnable, and the King, reassured, refused to levy troops. Even the plan of massing war elephants around Ayuthia was abandoned.

WHEN KUANYIN, LADY OF Mercy, Goddess of Compassion, raised her arms, her eyes opened and tears streamed down, while she uttered a low, prolonged moan.

The devotees offering her gifts of fruit and flowers were terrified. They screamed, or fainted, or beat their foreheads on the ground.

By nightfall an enormous crowd had gathered at the *wat* to see the miraculous Kuanyin. Twice again the statue wept and uttered low screams. The Chief Patriarch came, witnessed the miracle, and prostrated himself on the ground before the statue.

Unending processions, lasting all night in the steady rain, wended their way to the *wat*. The *bikkus* knelt, uttering supplications to avert catastrophe.

Each house now affixed gate and door talismans to ward off evil spirits; lit incense and tapers. Every *wat* was crowded with people seeking to acquire merit by gifts. Some families gave away all their property and entered monastic life forever.

In another small *wat*, the Goddess of Mercy spoke through a woman in trance. Spinning like a top, prostrating herself and then again spinning with amazing rapidity, the woman shrieked in a voice not her own:

"Shed no blood, shed no blood . . . Ayuthia shall not be saved by shedding blood . . ."

Similar trances and spirit possession occurred among other women in other quarters of the city. Coiled snakes were seen in the canals. A dead crocodile was washed up in front of the second palace, occupied by a half-brother of the King.

The rumor that a sacrifice had been contemplated spread. The Goddess of Mercy was against it—the Lord Buddha must be against it. Both the Mahayana and the Theravada sects of the religion now joined against the Chief Magician.

NEE POUNDED AND RUBBED, kneaded and pinched, softening the Magician's dry skin with oil of sandalwood, stroking his legs from the ankles upwards to diminish the swelling. She pulled his toes one by one to release the knotted lower humors of the body. Meanwhile she babbled. "The whole city is astir. They say in all the *wats* that the gods are angry. . . ."

When she had done, she squatted, gathering her unguents and the bottles filled with ground essence of flowers and sandalwood oil. Another maid now prepared the usual mixture of sweet herbs and crushed almond that the Magician drank after his massage.

Through the muslin veil that covered his face, the Magician

looked at Nee. She was placid, her fingers steady. Always she talked, telling him of everything that went on, in and out of the palace.

He would speak to Prince Chiprasong, who had suggested the sacrifice. Perhaps it was not wise to slaughter the girls, though it had seemed a very small matter at the time. After all, none of the girls was of noble blood.

※ ⁂

"I have told the Magician. I hear he has sent for Chiprasong," Nee whispered to me as we met in the secrecy of the folding screens in the inner palace.

Usually Nee and I pretended not to know each other, and took great care not to be seen when we met.

"Thou knowest what must be done, Nee."

"Yes, great and noble princess whom I adore."

"Udorn, dear husband, you should invite Chiprasong to a feast, a small one, with only a few friends."

"Invite Chiprasong? He may not come. He must know how aggrieved your brother is."

"Let us tell him that my brother has already forgotten the girl. He will come—out of curiosity, I think."

Chiprasong did come a few days later. But he was suspicious, and under his tunic wore an armor of Japanese woven rattan.

Udorn, Cham, and other nobles had gathered for a feast. Soon there was much laughter; the musicians and dancers were outdoing themselves. Then Udorn, pretending to be drunk, asked me to honor the guests by appearing and singing for them. My voice was strong and sweet, and I sang melodies of our land of Vaud, and Thai love songs. I looked at Chiprasong, giving him those sideways glances the Chinese called "autumn waves," signals of desire. I offered Chiprasong a cup of wine. "In memory of those days on board ship from China. Sadly, Prince Chiprasong, you seldom come to visit us."

Chiprasong could not decline the wine, and to show him that there was no poison in it, I drank some from the same stone bottle. "It is a pity my brother is so busy, or he would have come," I said. "He is quite smitten with a Portuguese beauty, recently come from Mergui, a Christian."

Many such girls, fleeing from the Burmese army, had come from Mergui, some indeed strikingly beautiful. But they had fallen into evil hands and were compelled to become prostitutes. Now the nobles began to talk about the new maidens for deflowering. "Your brother may keep one for himself, but not the others," Cham shouted, as if drunk. "Come, Chiprasong, let us go and visit them at the Portuguese settlement; there are still a few young virgins among them."

"I must go home."

"Afraid of your wives," Udorn jeered. "Come, it is only a stroll to look at the new ones."

Drunkenly, helping each other, Udorn and Cham entered a polun, *taking Chiprasong with them.*

When Chiprasong went home, he remembered my glances at him. He also remembered the new, pretty girl, a Christian from Mergui, who wore a cross between her breasts and was only fourteen years old.

I KILLED CHIPRASONG THREE nights later. He was with the Portuguese Christian girl whom he had deflowered. Bea and Ah Ming had paid a good deal for her, and though she wept, she knew that otherwise she would starve.

Chiprasong had two hundred yards to walk to reach his *polun*, but I stood in the way.

"Chiprasong."

He recognized me, recognized my voice.

"Ah, you too are here," he said. "Your sister told me that you like Christian flesh."

"I am going to kill you," I said, conversationally.

He laughed. "Lame man, lame man, I'll also take this girl from you if you are not careful."

It was dark, and he had wine in him, which made him less

swift. The knife upon him made him too sure. I broke his arm in the next three passes, and then broke his neck.

Ah Ming came out of the shadows with a canvas bag. Matter-of-factly, he put the body in it, and threw the bag over his shoulder. "Let us go now, Colin."

"You go first. I shall be back later."

I walked in the night, walked to Jean Allard's house. I wanted to talk with him.

Through the open window I saw him sitting at a table, and with him Father Oliveiro.

I wanted to tell Jean Allard, "I have just killed a man." But Oliveiro was there. I could not confront Oliveiro. I must carry this freight of sin alone.

Bea was waiting for me when I returned.

"It is done, Bea."

But there was no content in my heart. No relief. Only this enormous weight within my chest. I had done what had to be done. And now it would be Bea's turn. Jit, Jit, my heart cried, till black night had thinned and it was another day.

⤞ ⤝

The Magician looked at me through his muslin veil. He had sent a messenger to me as I sketched and painted one of the eleven minor queens.

"I have heard of you—who has not? And of your brother, a powerful maker of machines that sing, dance . . . and even weep."

He knew. Or had guessed.

"You are clever, Princess Didya. It is you who planned the weeping goddess."

"Not I, Great Lord. In truth not I."

"You. And the Chinese. And Prince Chiprasong is not to be found. Doubtless he is at the moment feeding the crocodiles."

"I know nothing about it."

"Prince Chiprasong and I had in mind this ritual sacrifice, because it is potent," the Magician said. "Chiprasong told me about one of the maidens. It was of no importance to me who were the chosen

275

*ones, so long as they were virgins and commoners. Had you come to
me, I would have released your brother's love and asked only that he
procure someone else in her stead. It would have been easy for you
and for him to buy another girl. . . ."*

"My brother would not have accepted, though the idea did cross
my mind," I replied calmly.

"I would have struck a bargain with your brother. Asked him to
make me some of his magic dolls, and in return—and for another
girl—he could have had this Jit. But now the King has decided that
there shall be no sacrifice. For the Sangha is against it, the bikkus
are against it . . . oh yes, you have indeed stirred up the city,
Princess Didya."

I felt the malice seeping through his veil.

"His Majesty has now decided that the four maidens will become
his consorts. They are then sacred, and no other man can touch
them. Your weeping goddess will be pleased, I daresay, and your
brother too."

The Magician laughed. He had bested me. Jit would not go free.
But I smiled, my eyes clear, my face almost radiant.

"I am sure this will make my brother happy. My brother will be
sensible of His Majesty's kindness, and of yours."

IN SEPTEMBER OF 1765, as the monsoon began to slacken, the
southern Burmese army advanced towards Bangkok. In
late November, Bangkok was besieged. Meanwhile, the northern army occupied Sukhotai, and its boats began to sail towards Ayuthia. And a third army crossed the western border
and began marching towards Ayuthia.

IN EARLY DECEMBER, the Magician died suddenly.

Nee had massaged him as usual. Then he had drunk the
mixture of cinnamon and chrysanthemum flowers that he

affected. Now he prepared it himself, for the death of Chipra-song had made him very cautious.

Some hours later, in his sleep, his heart suddenly began to beat fast, fast, faster, faster, until it exploded in his chest.

At the same time, and while servants were running about in great dismay, exorcists and priests were called to attend to him, and the inner palace was thrown into turmoil. As the King, frantic, shouted, "What has happened?" and gave contradictory orders, some twenty guards broke away from the palace, killing two eunuchs.

Three pages and some six women also fled.

Among the six women, one was Jit.

AH MING HAD ASKED me to come to his new house in the Chinese quarter. Amid a maze of small alleys, so narrow they seemed to touch each other overhead, and overflowing with people, children, plants in pots, flowers, and clothes strung out to dry, Ah Ming had his new house. It was a small honeycomb, with many doors and diminutive courtyards. "A clever rabbit has three burrows" was Ah Ming's favorite saying.

"I'll send my chaise for you," Ah Ming had told me. "Your chaise bearers wouldn't find the way."

When I entered the house, Ah Ming was alone. He said in that matter-of-fact voice of his, "Jit is here."

"Jit—don't tease me, Ming."

"How could I, Colin Brother? She is upstairs. Your sister has succeeded."

Bea had not said anything at all. When I had left the house, she had been busy with Udorn's little boy, preoccupied with women wanting love potions.

"There was a breakaway from the palace only four hours ago. It was well plotted. Jit will tell you."

I bounded up the narrow wooden stairs. And there was Jit, in the windowless upper room, a room meant to store goods, but safe, no one could peer into it.

She was in my arms, we clung to each other, her thin body pressed hard against me.

"Keran, I never doubted. I knew you would deliver me."

Bea, not I. Bea, and Nee, and whatever they had done, which was complicated and yet simple, but which I did not want to know, because I was aware that there was killing. I did not want to know that Bea had killed.

"Keran, Keran . . . I am so happy."

We were together at last. And though we had to be careful, so careful (for should she be caught, she would die a terrible death, and also Ah Ming, and I), she was here, she was with me. Nothing else mattered. That night we were together. I held her, so slight, to my body. I would never let her go.

AND NOW A PRECARIOUS existence began for Jit and myself. She dressed in Chinese clothes, passing for one of Ah Ming's women. I would go to her every night, but in the daytime I had to be at the factory, had to show myself in my house, built next to Udorn's mansion.

The guards and the pages who had run away were never caught; nor the five other women of the King's harem. They had succeeded in leaving Ayuthia. And because of the Burmese threat, King Ekatat could not send soldiers to scour the countryside for them.

Bea's face was smooth, tranquil. I tried to speak to her about our danger, but she only looked at me, her eyes blue, then green, as when we were children. "Well, little brother, do not worry too much. Nee has helped greatly. She may want a reward."

"I cannot make love again with her, Bea. I cannot."

Bea laughed. "Luckily for you there is at the moment a page, a very strong one, who contents her. And for the rest, I shall manage. Gold and silver and jewels. I have enough in store to satisfy her."

❧ Sixteen ❧

AYUTHIA. THE ENCHANTRESS had never been so lovely. Blue skies, lotuses on every pond, pink and white and yellow. Her people went about as if in fairyland, boats bedecked and gilded, fairs and festivals riotous with color.

And Jit, her presence abolishing time, time no longer the regular stitching of a clock but eternity. Every moment immortal.

She taught me the unending shores of love, because she never taught. Every moment of her living, her face, her golden face, her limbs and body, all given to me. She was a universe of tenderness and never wanted anything but to be herself; and herself was to be with me. Jit, my shield against fear, against guilt. Through her, I became whole. And this is the greatest boon, that a man, infinitesimal speck in the great universe, comes to acknowledge his own self and is content.

Ah Ming's house was our home. Even the soldier-rowers of the King, their arms painted crimson, their armors worked with gold, would not come to the Chinese quarter without some trepidation. The peaceable Chinese could be utterly ruthless toward venturesome marauders.

Ah Ming made a partition, giving us two rooms besides the windowless attic. His clamorous courtyard with two wives, four children, and a host of relatives was protection.

The Chinese ability to create communities, associations,

kinships, and brotherhoods was our safeguard. Should a spy stray into the narrow alleys, he was immediately detected. Even the monks belonged to a brotherhood. Monk Teo was a kinsman to Ah Ming because they came from the same ancestral village in China.

"Why do you do this for me, Ah Ming? I am only a *farang*," I said.

Ah Ming did not like to discourse on intimate feelings. "You are Colin Brother."

"You are taking a great risk. You know the danger."

Ah Ming looked for an explanation that would sound rational for what was an impulse of the heart. "You have helped my ancestors' country. Tried to help my people. We never forget."

In the councils of the Chinese clans of Ayuthia the words "Down with the Manchu" were uttered at the induction ceremony of every new member. Patiently, over the centuries here and in other places of the Southern Ocean, would be forged a renewal of China.

Ah Ming was part of it. It was a dream, a vision, but men live by dreams and visions, by love and hate.

IN DECEMBER THE BURMESE southern army reached Bangkok, and Cham extracted from King Ekatat an order to send troops for its defense, some three thousand men. Raw recruits from the North, to them Bangkok was more foreign than were the Burmese, who had invaded them so often.

On December 10 the Burmese burnt Bangkok from the port to the suburbs in a fire that lasted ten days, also destroying the Catholic seminary and the church.

On December 17 their Portuguese-manned cannon subdued the last French-built fort. Their boats crossed the Menam to seize Thonburi. And encountered an unexpected adversary, an Englishman.

Captain Pawney, with two ships, had come up the river to claim twenty-eight bales of cloth. He set himself, single-handed, to fight the Burmese army. He loved a battle as others love a wife, and trusted his stout cannon to bring down any fortification. Roaming the seas as others do a garden, Buccaneer Pawney had brought on his vessel a lion, an Arab horse, and a Peruvian bird of many colors as gifts to the King of Ayuthia. He was angry because the Burmese had fired at his ship. "At them, men," he cried, and started firing back. The disheartened Thai soldiers were infected with battle fervor at the stout Englishman's courage, and perhaps Bangkok would have been retaken had Ekatat sent to Pawney (who pleaded for more ammunition, his having been spent) some cannon balls and muskets. But the King vacillated, as usual, and then refused. Two of Pawney's English sailors who had joined the remnant Thai defenders were killed, and Pawney sailed away, wrathfully taking with him some of the barges moored off Thonburi in payment for his services.

The southern army of Burma marched northwards from Bangkok, and in February encamped on high ground within ten leagues of Ayuthia. The northern army, sailing down the Menam, reached Ayuthia in March. Razing the *wats*, pillaging their treasures, and using their bricks to build high cannon towers to hoist their guns above the ramparts of the city, the Burmese now began the siege.

From the sacked cities, the burnt villages, people streamed into Ayuthia. They camped in the narrow streets, huddled below the ramparts and outside them, setting up shacks of matting and bamboo.

"Udorn, how shall we feed all these people?" I asked.

He grimaced, made a graceful gesture of despair with both hands. "His Majesty is waiting for the next monsoon to drive the Burmese away."

"But now the Burmese have boats. . . ."

"The Lord Buddha, in His Compassion, will perhaps save Ayuthia," Udorn replied.

LED BY THEIR VILLAGE elders and the *bikkus*, who discarded their saffron robes and armed themselves with home-made cutlasses and clubs spiked with nails, two hundred peasants from a village outside Ayuthia attacked a Burmese advance camp at Bang Rabhan, killing a hundred soldiers. And the news spread, swift as lightning; the peasants around Ayuthia rose, organized militias, and assaulted the Burmese.

But no soldier from the King's armies within the city went out to help them; and when they asked for weapons, once again Ekatat refused. In June, the unfortunate and valorous peasant militias were decimated. Their leaders were impaled, and their women and children taken into slavery.

"Such a sovereign deserves no loyalty," Bea said aloud when the news reached us.

"Hush, Didya," Udorn said gently. "No one must speak against the King."

In July the monsoon began in earnest, but the Burmese did not leave, for indeed they had many boats and barges. They were now within two leagues of the city, and as the flood water rose, the soldiers lived on the boats, dry-footed and safe.

By that July all the 120 *wats* around Ayuthia had been looted, their statues hacked to pieces, the gold and jewels concealed within the bodies of the statues taken away. The bricks of the temples were used to build cannon towers, and the Burmese forced their new slaves to build them.

Taksin, who had petitioned the King for the peasants, saying, "Let me go out, even single-handed, to lead them," now again petitioned the King. But Ekatat only ordered two ineffectual sorties, and once again the boats were lost.

And Taksin was ordered to stay within his house as punishment. Bea became restless and increasingly irritable. "Taksin has arranged for the Chinese barges to bring rice in at night, at great peril to themselves. The city has only enough rice for four months," Cham told us. And Bea said, "Only Taksin can save Ayuthia. Why does he submit to the King with such docility?"

"He does not want to die," Udorn replied, with surprise in his voice. "No sane man courts death unless there is good reason."

OF EKATAT'S HUNDRED OR so half-brothers, a good many became suspect of plotting against him and were now disposed of, either in monasteries or by being squeezed between beams of sandalwood. Only the powerful few round his brother-in-law and his favorite consort could now approach the King. As for Utumporn, his younger blood brother, from whom Ekatat had wrested the throne, he was not allowed to leave the *wat* to which he was confined.

The rains were heavy. The water in the city's center rose to the edge of the canal banks, and the streets became quagmires. Vagrants camped in them by the hundreds. Ayuthia, once so clean, was now plagued with rats. Refuse piled up, no longer taken outside the city. It could not be burnt in the unending rain. All around Ayuthia was water, grey and flat, spreading far out beyond eye's reach. Invisible beyond the rain curtains were the Burmese armies. "Perhaps they *will* go away," Udorn said doubtfully, as he and I, having climbed the ramparts, peered at the grey blankness. Returning, we saw the beggars hunched under the rain; crowded around the *wats*. So many beggars. The *bikkus* making their daily rounds, their heads bent, umbrellas above their heads, begging bowl in hand. They were sometimes assaulted by the beggars and their food taken away.

IN UDORN'S HOUSE THERE was enough rice. Bea had started rearing hens and ducks in the garden. She measured out the portions of food to each one, and a servant was flogged for having stolen some eggs.

Bea. Her beauty flawless, but something stringent, taut, in her, a ravening of the spirit. And at night, lying with Jit in my arms, I would strain to "hear" Bea, and my inner ear discerned a faint and distant anguish. She was tormented, and therefore I too was perturbed. What was it which made her so anguished, remote, removed from me?

The plantains and coconuts deposited in front of our resident spirit began to disappear. The beggar children stole them.

"Bea, things may go ill, if the siege continues," I told her.

The sudden fury of her eyes stripped me.

"Are you frightened, Colin? Yes, of course you are."

"Ayuthia is a mousetrap, and we the mice, Bea."

"I am not leaving."

"Of course not, because of Udorn."

Again that look of hers, now scornful. "Not Udorn, nor Abdul Reza, nor any of my other lovers for a time." Her mouth softened, all of her suddenly smooth. "Colin, would you kill again for Jit?"

"Yes, I think I would."

"And would you die for Jit?"

"Of course." But I felt a hollowness within me. Would I die for Jit?

Bea laughed, a small sound, rage and dismay and helplessness but also joy. "Perhaps you and Jit should leave then. But I wait—"

"Wait?"

"For the King. The real King. Who will save Ayuthia."

NEVER DOES LIFE, EVEN at its most fulfilling, give us total perfection, absolute felicity. Always there is the shadow, and it lengthens as our happiness intensifies. Thus it is for kings and emperors, for great and powerful empires, even for someone such as I, neither hero nor genius; a boy grown into manhood and loving a woman, fearful to lose her.

Oh the mirages of the mind, I thought. The excellent and marvelous mirages of love. And Bea too, her vision stretching beyond herself. A king, she had said. Who could it be? Not Ekatat, nor Mangra, the Burmese sovereign. Who?

Heer Timmermans, in stolid Dutch fashion, reiterated that he was not leaving Ayuthia. He would hold the factory, which belonged to the Dutch East India Company. "My Company has asked me to negotiate with the Burmese. King Mangra of Burma is at present heady with success. But will he destroy the Company? Our Portuguese couriers have an assurance. Have you seen how the Burmese have placed their boats in groups of ten round each cannon tower they build, so that it is not easy to surround them?"

The bustling Chinese markets were now silent. There was very little to buy in the stalls, and the prices were high. Some boats would still smuggle through at night, but gangs of marauders waited beyond the gates to attack them.

The Catholic churches were crowded with converts from Mergui and Bangkok, and Father Oliveiro was joyful. With shining eyes he preached, extolling the glories of martyrdom, the bliss in Heaven that would await those who died. I saw him once kneeling in front of the altar, his arms outstretched. Doubtless he wanted to become a saint.

In the *wats*, too, I discerned the same reckless fervor for death. The faithful were more convinced than ever that prayer and merit-acquiring would make the Burmese army melt away, but if it did not melt, a better incarnation awaited them.

I told Jit that I wanted her to be safe. To go away to the *farang* settlements beyond Bangkok. She looked at me in her trustful way.

"Jit stays with Keran. Jit will never leave Keran. There is no life for Jit without Keran."

And so we stayed, in that strange, hypnotic trance that had seized upon us all in Ayuthia, even Erik Erikssen, who said that he might leave, but remained. We went on making cannon balls, hoping they would be used.

AT LAST IN AUGUST, as the Burmese did not leave, Taksin was asked by the King to help defend the city.

Ekatat was at the time much perturbed about the one of White Elephants, who seemed ill. He insisted that court ritual go on as usual. The sacred elephants must be fed, though this meant many men in boats looking for food, mowing grass for them, running the gauntlet of advance parties of Burmese.

Taksin came to meet with Cham and Udorn, the *Pra-Klang*, some ministers, Erik and myself, and the nobles who were for "resistance." He proposed to strengthen and raise the walls and ramparts of Ayuthia. "Have you seen the cannon towers the Burmese are constructing?" Taksin spoke in a terse, measured tone, each word heavy as gunmetal. "They are higher than our walls. They can shoot their cannon inside the city. There is yet time to raise the walls and to have our own guns in position to shoot back. But first of all we must get the useless mouths out of Ayuthia."

The *Pra-Klang* said, "*Phya* Taksin, no one can leave Ayuthia. The King has ordered that everyone must stay."

Taksin remained impassive. Udorn told him about the cannon balls Erik and I were making, and he nodded, his heavy-lidded eyes glancing at me and then at Bea seated quietly, with two maids in attendance, a little lower than the men. Power came from him, an emanation, which changed those around him. We waited for him to tell us what to do.

Bea's face. Gooseflesh came upon my arms, the fine hair quivering. Bea was looking at Taksin. Looking at him, and her eyes—then I knew.

The King. King to be. A man of strength, of vision, and ambition. Here he was. He was of that breed of men who change men, bring down kingdoms and empires or build them. And Bea, Bea was in love with him. I felt pity, dismay, a fierce need to protect Bea. For in the man Taksin there was no place for love, love as Bea would want, as Bea would need. To him it would be surfeit, excess, an obstacle in his way. He had no time and no space in his heart for love of woman. . . . Oh could she not see it? She, who was so strong and wise?

I heard the drums of the rain, drumming the pulse of lost time, of derision and despair. What was it Jacob had said to me: "In another century, or perhaps two, we shall go to the stars, probe the far corners of the universe, and life can be felicity for all mankind." Yet Jacob had been clubbed to death at the gates of a Jewish ghetto in Warsaw. "Jacob, can you help?" I prayed. And no longer knew whether I prayed for Bea, or myself, or Ayuthia . . .

"And so," Taksin's quiet voice was saying, "we must commandeer all the bricks in Ayuthia. The brick kilns must be set to work, and the bricks stored in the *wats*, and the wood. We must train militia patrols for the ramparts, and everyone must set to work."

KING EKATAT HAD TWICE ordered disastrous sorties. He now ordered a third: a flotilla under two leaders, one of them Taksin.

One hundred sixty boats were fitted out; altogether six thousand men. Taksin shared the command of the war boats with the governor of Petchaburi, who had fled to refuge in Ayuthia when his city was captured.

The sortie failed. The governor had pressed forward, firing away, but the recoil from the guns on the boats had pushed these backwards and the governor was killed.

Taksin's boats, which were behind those of the governor, did not fire. Taksin retreated into Ayuthia. And King Ekatat was angry, accusing Taksin of cowardice, upbraiding him for not trying to rescue the corpse of the governor to give him an honorable cremation. Without a proper funeral, the governor's soul would join the *phi*, who roam at night, uttering lamentable screams.

"But Taksin was right," Bea argued. "The whole scheme was madness, a sacrifice of good boats and guns."

Once again Taksin came briefly to the house, for the King appeared to have forgotten the previous command that he stay within his own rooms. "That foolish man," he said, alluding to the governor. "He went forward and fell into the trap. . . ."

"He was a brave man," Cham replied, for he too, being a nobleman, felt that the governor's body should have been recuperated.

Taksin's eyes flared, an odd menace in them. "Foolishness is not courage, *Phya* Cham. We have lost sixty-three boats and half the soldiers in them." He stalked away, leaving us diminished by his absence.

Bea's eyes followed him, and Udorn said, "Taksin is able, but he is not a born prince, and of course, being half-Chinese, he is too practical."

She walked away.

Despite the King's anger, however, Taksin remained in command of Ayuthia's defense, perhaps because even Ekatat felt the power of his presence and his ability. Under his orders, Erik and I constructed movable platforms for the cannon of the ramparts. Taksin and Cham again petitioned Ekatat to obtain from the arsenal two hundred cannon only ten years old to replace the rusty ones, which were dangerous to use.

Ah Ming sent his wives and children away, smuggling them out of the city to Rayong, a port city of the South. They took with them my chests, containing much of my gold and other wealth—one held the King android I had made. Meanwhile Jit and I remained in Ah Ming's house in the Chinese quarter, where the inhabitants had organized their own patrols and we were safe.

Eighty Christians, five hundred Muslims, and two thousand Chinese manned the ramparts, each of them protecting only those walls enclosing their own settlements. There was never any concerted action by all the people to defend all of the city.

SEPTEMBER. THE MONSOON SLACKENED. The massed three Burmese armies seized five of the great *wats* outside Ayuthia. They now attacked the Christian and Portuguese settlements on the right side of the Menam and the Dutch compound on the other side.

From the ramparts, where I too took my turn, I could see the Burmese boats in regular files, never more than four abreast. They would land a party of their soldiers, then build pontoons.

On September 17, the Burmese cannon began to fire at the Catholic churches at Bang Pahat and at the Portuguese church. The Christians fought valiantly, climbing to the belfry towers to fire upon the assailants. But they were less than one thousand fighting men.

The Chinese clans were approached by Cham and Taksin. Would they help to defend the Dutch and Christian compounds? Within two days, six thousand Chinese volunteers went out to defend the main point where the river unfolded its two arms to embrace Ayuthia, quartering themselves at *Wat* Phanang Cheng and at the Dutch factory.

"Tell us what you need; we shall get it for you," Erik promised the Chinese volunteers.

Timmermans mustered his servants, training them to shoot. He would read aloud from a Bible, and in the morning make them chant hymns.

And all the time, there was for me an unreality about the

siege, as if it were an uncomfortable dream from which I would presently wake up. As if in the end, all would be well.

The Christian and the Portuguese settlements went on ringing the bells for Angelus and Vespers. The Chinese made lightning raids upon Burmese boats, sinking some and killing many men. Even the women who sold their bodies now came to do battle, to nurse the wounded and bury the dead. The monks of the *wats* carried water and fruit and whatever rice there was to the soldiers.

Father Jean Allard went into battle with the name of God upon his lips, and counted at night the men he had killed. He built more stockades and stone walls, and drew diagrams for battle plans.

And then one day Cham asked me whether I could make some automata soldiers to place on the ramparts. "About one hundred would suffice," he said doubtfully. "I know you once made a trumpeter and a drummer, Keran, you told me so."

"In memory of my father, who was making them when he died. I have them stored in my house."

"Then finish them, and others like them. We shall place them on the walls; they will help to give an impression of many, many men manning the ramparts. The Burmese will shoot at them, and when they do not stir, the Burmese will believe we have an invincible army, with great magic. . . ."

I doubted that this would work, for the Burmese had Portuguese officers with them, who after a time would realize that these were clockwork soldiers. But hope was also magic, and illusion and outrage certainly worked. And therefore, recruiting twenty workmen of my factory, Ah Ming, and Erik, we set to and fashioned trumpeters and drummers, who at stated hours would clarion out tunes and thump drums; and also mechanical soldiers who moved along a set path made in a wooden base, as if they walked from one place to the other. We painted their faces and gave them purple hats, and they looked fierce enough. We made about twenty, and placed them on the ramparts. The Burmese did shoot at them and could not bring them down. "Build some more," Cham said. So we set to, trying to make a hundred automata soldiers.

Because now, many of the defenders were becoming weak, they had not enough to eat. . . .

Meanwhile, Taksin was refurbishing and repairing the cannon, and still trying to persuade the King to release more guns from the arsenal.

When two *bikkus* burnt themselves alive, chanting the praise of the Lord Buddha, that Ayuthia might be victorious, this redoubled the fervor of the people, and though food was very scarce, the *wats* were still full of devotees. Some gave their last pieces of gold and silver to the monks, and then lay down quietly to die of starvation. Sorcerers sold pills for invisibility. King Ekatat also had a store of such pills. Bea planted cassava, which grew quickly, quicker than rice. Many women were growing food, wherever there was space. But when the *bikkus* came around with their begging bowls, the portions for them were very small.

Taksin had now raised and strengthened the ramparts, and had placed the available cannon. The Burmese, with twenty brick towers with gun platforms, were now near enough to fire right into the city. Taksin walked the ramparts every day checking the soldiers. He nodded grimly at my automata. I knew now that the idea had been his, relayed to me by Cham.

Taksin had placed ten cannon near each other to concentrate his fire on one target, the southwest gun tower, which threatened the royal palace. "Order the men to fire," Taksin said to the Portuguese Chief of Cannoneers, Miguel de Souza, who was in charge of the gunners.

De Souza was a middle-aged man, ten years in Ayuthia. He was also drunk on palm wine most of the time. He had taken no part in the preparations made to defend Ayuthia. Now he folded his arms majestically, ignoring Taksin's order. "Only the King can order cannon to be fired," he said.

Taksin scowled, and ordered the gunners to fire, while Erik, who knew something of gunnery, adjusted the aim of their cannon for them.

The aim was good, the guns roared, the tower was hit, and part of it tumbled. When we saw Burmese soldiers run away out of the wreckage, we shouted and clapped for joy. Then Taksin ordered the guns wheeled to another point of the ramparts, opposite another gun tower. But as we were heaving and pulling the cannon into place, up came two officials with ten of the royal bodyguard. "An order of the King!" they cried. Down we went on our knees and hands, while the order was read out:

"No cannon is to be fired without the King's consent. Taksin is to report immediately to the palace."

Taksin's face became thunderous. The veins in his neck were swollen with fury. But he followed the messengers. He waited at the palace all day and then the King scolded him. "You must not fire the guns. One of my queens cannot abide the noise. It makes her ill. The cannon must be dismantled."

Once again Taksin was in disgrace. And now we feared he might lose his life. The idea flitted across my mind that we should get rid of the King. But if Ekatat died, who would take power? There would be the usual succession struggle—and the Burmese would win. Cham and Udorn went to the palace to intercede for Taksin, while Bea angrily paced in her room. . . .

Taksin came once more to Udorn's house. By then every cat, dog, bird, and many of the horses had been eaten in Ayuthia. The lotus ponds had no more lotuses; even the roots and leaves had been eaten. Now every day on the street there were corpses, mostly errants from other provinces who had died of hunger. Bands of wild men were about, and it was said that children had disappeared to be eaten.

Taksin saluted Udorn and said brusquely, "I am going away. Some of my friends will follow me. We cannot fight from inside Ayuthia. We must organize another stronghold, create a real army, reconquer the lost provinces."

"But Ayuthia . . ."

"Ayuthia is a city. I speak of a kingdom, a people."

"The King will not let you leave."

"A king who places his women's ears above the lives of his people is not fit to reign." His hands were cupped, as if he held the future in them. "I shall go to the southeastern provinces, which the Burmese have not reached, to Rayong, a good port, with many good men. From there, with an army, I shall come back to relieve Ayuthia."

Bea knelt in front of him. "*Phya* Taksin, I shall follow you. Women, too, can fight."

"No women, no children." Taksin looked away from her.

"In Ayuthia women, even queens, have fought alongside the men."

Taksin continued to look away, stolid like a great block of stone, immovable.

Udorn stared at Bea. Then I saw his face change. He turned to Taksin, and at that moment the man's nobility came shining out of him, unforgettable. "*Phya* Taksin, both of us will follow you to save Ayuthia," said Udorn.

Then it seemed as if they were all waiting for me to say something.

Jit. I would not leave Jit. Jit could not follow, for although I had not told anyone, she was with child.

Taksin seemed to know. He turned, smiled grimly at me. "Keran, thank you for building these indestructible soldiers. The Burmese are still wasting ammunition on them. And I have not forgotten what you told me. One day men shall fly. Would we had wings now—"

He took Udorn's hands in his, not looking at Bea. "We shall leave soon. Be prepared. Both of you."

OF THE FIVE HUNDRED who followed Taksin on January 2, 1767, ten were women, among them Bea and Nee, whom Bea took with her. Udorn had managed to smuggle his son and the boy's mother out of the city. Taksin's pregnant wife was left behind, and also Taksin's old mother.

The five hundred could not have left Ayuthia had not the foolish Ekatat again ordered a sortie against the Burmese. Taksin volunteered, and out of the gates on the east side of Ayuthia they rode on the last horses of the army. They did not return. They broke through the ring of the Burmese, thinner at that spot, and galloped out into the night, pursued by the Burmese. But although a few of them were caught and killed, the bulk managed to get into the forests and away.

Of the riding they did, going east, going south, fighting through hostile governors, battling the Burmese pursuers, I know little. But I do know that in the villages they crossed, men and women rose to follow Taksin, for he had this power, this magnetic draw, to fill a man's soul with ardor and a woman's, too. When he spoke of Ayuthia, the people followed him.

He was stern, yet always careful of his followers' lives, never giving battle without preparation. Soon there were stories about him. Through that intangible web of words among the people even in beleaguered Ayuthia we heard of Taksin. He would not allow rape. He was merciless on treacherous nobles and governors. Before taking a city, he would tell his soldiers to throw away everything they carried. "Then you will be light-stepped, and take the city with good heart; for in the city you shall feast."

Legends are always created by the people around a man who lifts their souls, who kindles in them heroism and valor. Taksin was such a one.

Meanwhile, in Ayuthia, we continued, in a fatal torpor, as if entranced, to wait. . . .

THE CHINESE CLANS NOW sent Ah Ming as a delegate to Taksin; they knew that Taksin's new army was beginning to grow in Rayong. "I do not wish to leave you, Colin Brother. Truly my heart smites me within, but I have to go. I too believe in *Phya* Taksin. He will return and save Ayuthia."

"Go cheerfully, Ah Ming. I shall take Jit back to my house, which is next to Udorn's. Erik will be coming to live with me—we shall be safe."

THE CHILD IN JIT animated her, made her even more beautiful. Her skin grew lustrous, her breasts fuller. She now took care of the hens and ducks that Bea had left behind, or what was left of them, for with food scarce, we were compelled to eat them. The servants of Udorn, though now reduced in number, obeyed Jit. I had to close the factory, for the workers were weak with hunger, and some died.

Jit and I stayed together in the house, not going out except when I went daily to the ramparts to repair the automata. I too was becoming weak, light-headed at times. But I said I was not hungry, wanting Jit to eat more. . . .

Now I knew the locking in, the total obsession of passion, of love. My soul and body fulfilled, the siege of the city seemed to us a distant thing, which no longer touched us. And though we had less and less food every day, yet we remained, enchanted, in the Enchantress.

Meanwhile, the Burmese continued their merciless attacks.

Throughout the next three months, from January to early April of 1767, they still had pockets of resistance to subdue outside the ramparts. And the people fought. How they fought! Much later I was told that a French priest would write a memoir, calling the Thai cowardly, unable to fight. But I saw them fight, even when they were so weak with hunger that the weapons fell out of their hands.

The Burmese cannonade was relentless; daily the guns barked, daily something was destroyed, and the King's palace was not spared.

In mid-January King Ekatat sued for peace, offering to become a vassal of Mangra. But the Burmese King would accept only unconditional surrender, and so Ayuthia's people went on fighting.

Daily, I dragged myself to the ramparts, and once again met the Portuguese de Souza, watching the Burmese army with a spy glass. "Are you looking at their cannon?" I asked him.

"No, Colin Duriez. Their cannon . . ." He shrugged. "Extremely efficient. Better than I've ever known. No, I am looking for my friend, Paul Coelho. He and I came out here together to fight for anyone who would employ us. And he is with the Burmese. What will you? We are soldiers of fortune."

A few days later, when I met him again, he was waving and shouting through a cone, an amplifier for the voice. "I've found Coelho." He turned to me, beaming. "When all this is over we'll share a good bottle of wine together."

THE WOMEN OF AYUTHIA cropped their hair and tucked their *pannungs* as trousers. They too began to man the ramparts, as many men could no longer drag themselves up the flights of stairs.

And now began a plague, the cholera, because of the corpses. Corpses floated on every canal, swollen, livid, with an unbearable stench. The water was filthy with the smell of putrefaction. The worst was to see the corpses being eaten by the huge rats, which grew bold as the people became weak, and would even eat babies.

Men and women died, collapsing in their houses, on the streets, in the boats, in their own excrement. Funeral pyres were built everywhere to burn the dead, and the odor of burning flesh and the smoke fell like a pall upon the city. Because of the crowding embers, ten thousand houses in the Chinese quarter were burnt to the ground. Many *bikkus* now allowed themselves to die of hunger. It was said that one of the sacred elephants was dead.

Father Oliveiro reached the martyrdom he had extolled when the Burmese cannon in March destroyed Saint Paul's Church and set the houses and the surrounding stockades on fire. The Christians had to come out of the stockade. Father Oliveiro, unarmed, holding a crucifix, led them out singing. But the Burmese soldiers were enraged by the long resistance of the heroic Christians. Oliveiro had his hands and feet hacked off, his eyes put out. Meanwhile, he went on singing the praises of God, until an impatient soldier decapitated him.

The Christians were being put to death in a most gruesome manner when a Portuguese captain in Burmese employ, arriving on the scene, stopped the hideousness. They were then chained together, all their clothes removed, to be sent off into captivity.

The Burmese general had written to the bishop, promising not to harm the Catholics if they surrendered and not to touch their belongings and houses. But he and his men burnt down the area, after plundering every house. And the women they used, and many of them died under the repeated assaults of the soldiers.

While on the way to the coast, among the lone files of prisoners, Jean Allard managed to kill the Burmese guard and to flee into the forests with a few men. They remained about four months in the jungle, finding a lumber camp and its working elephants.

As for the Chinese militia, their fate was even worse: the Burmese surrounded *wat* Phanang Cheng and the Chinese defenders were starved and killed to the last man. Timmermans, loaded with chains, was also sent as a captive to Burma.

"Why do you stay, Erik? Erik, you must save yourself." I shook Erik. He was like an ambulant skeleton.

"I do not want to betray Ayuthia," Erik said. So he too was entranced, as we all were. . . .

The end of March brought blistering hot weather. Erik now spent a great deal of time singing Nordic melodies to us, with verses of his own composition. He sang of the Vikings and their great ships who conquered the seas, and of the halls where dead warriors wassailed, of the fabulous citadels in the dreams of men "who are forever, because they are no more."

And I talked of the undead, of Bea, living between that world of night and this one. My love for her returned, strong and bright, and Jit understood when I talked of my sister. We were dying piecemeal, and we felt light, and sometimes very joyous, and had vivid dreams. Jit said, "Keran, we shall be together forever. In the sky are two birds, sharing a wing; on earth two trees, branches twining. . . ."

"If this is death," I said to Erik, "then it is not bad."

Our hearts were luminous in the watching darkness, bathed in the twilight ecstasy starvation bestows. We felt our souls leave our bodies without regret, and were content.

And then one night brought the rowers of the King, the men with arms painted crimson to the shoulder.

⟿ ⟿

~❧ *Seventeen* ❧~

THE ARMS OF THE KING'S soldiers were throwing a brocade blanket over Jit (even then they did it squatting down, courteously, for she was the King's woman), were trussing up Erik, and holding me down. Well-nourished men, though I knocked the first one down, they had me with a chain around the neck, arms and legs tight bound. And then the Amazons were there, six of them carrying Jit, who fought silently, without a sound, even managing for a fleeting moment to escape the enveloping drapery. They put her in a boat with a gilded swan's head; Erik and I were tumbled in another. Jit was taken to the palace, while we were taken to the *Pra-Klang's* dungeons for *farangs* who had committed crimes.

The narrow cell had a mud floor; crawling and slithering things immediately attacked us, and soon we were both rubbing our faces against the brick walls to get rid of the insects. We were there all night, for when they came again for us it was dawn, and we were dragged across a courtyard into an open room.

Cham was there, kneeling, though ceremoniously provided with a servant to fan him; and also the Portuguese, De Souza, very pale but not tied up, squatting painfully in his tight hose. Two officials with pointed hats sat under a dais, and some five or six brawny executioners, with whips and sharp prodding sticks, surrounded us. A brazier in a corner with

297

glowing soft embers, and a few instruments of torture, such as I had seen in my own land of Vaud, pincers and spikes, lay about. I wondered whether here, as in France, they broke men on a wheel, and then remembered, without much comfort, that they had no such contrivance, but preferred impalement.

The officials began questioning Erik, but he merely shook his head and asked to drink some wine, for he was very thirsty. And water carried the plague.

While he drank I spoke: "Don't ask Erik Erikssen. He knows nothing. He came a few days ago to live with me. Neither does *Phya* Cham know anything. Everything was done by me."

They wanted to know how Jit had fled from the palace. How the breakout of the six women had been contrived. That was why De Souza was present, for two of the pages were Portuguese.

"I know nothing," de Souza said. "I am a gun master. I was on the ramparts, never in the palace."

"It is I, I alone," I insisted. "I did it all. Punish me, not the others. And let Jit go. She is innocent."

They struck me on the mouth, several times, because I had said Jit, the name of the King's consort, instead of calling her by her title. They asked me about Bea and Udorn. "They too know nothing. I lived in the Chinese quarter. Only after Prince Udorn left did I move into his house, since the Chinese quarter was burnt down." They flogged me then, with whips of leather studded with small brass pikes, the punishment for anyone who had carnal commerce with a King's consort. Then they would tear my flesh off with red-hot pincers, and rub salt and vinegar into my wounds. I saw the brazier being stirred and they told me what they would do to me. Erik Erikssen shouted in his own language, cursing my torturers. They bound me on a kind of wooden trestle, and I was so afraid that I thought I would dirty myself, but I thought of Jit and cried, "Jit is innocent, I took her away, I seduced her."

And as the pincers were heating, some King's guards rushed in, their clothes in disarray. "The Burmese have breached the rampart, they are coming into the city." With one accord the soldiers, the executioners, the officials ran out, leaving us just as we were.

De Souza fell on his knees and made the sign of the cross: "God be praised." He unbound Erik, and Erik unbound me, while de Souza helped himself to the jug of wine on the table. "Now we'll deliver that fellow to the Burmese," he said, pointing to Cham. "He's the *Kalahom*, they'll be happy to kill him."

"You scoundrel," said Erik.

De Souza drew his dagger and would have stabbed Erik, but with my remaining strength I whirled round and fell upon him, hacking at his shoulder to paralyze his arm. The dagger fell from his limp hand and Erik picked it up. De Souza shook me off, spat, and said, "You vermin, I'll leave you to the Burmese," and strode away.

We walked out of the dungeon. There were no guards about, but many prisoners shouting and thumping, shaking the doors of their cells. Now we had to find Jit. Cham, who knew the intricate hive of buildings within the palace, could guide us. We set off along the Elephant Avenue towards the palace, and everywhere there were men and women running, many looked dazed. A rumor like the sea came from the western side of the city—that the Burmese army was marching through the breached walls into Ayuthia. Terror-stricken, the people were running away. The army would now head for the royal palace to capture the King.

The canals were crowded with boats. People in them fought one another for space, and some boats foundered under the press. The Burmese were killing their way through the streets. Distraught runaways formed a tidal wave of bodies, engulfing us as we tried to reach the palace.

Cham's house was next to the palace, and he insisted that we go in first to weapon ourselves. The house was empty but for his mother, who knelt in front of an altar bedecked with yellow gladioli, praying for her son. When she saw Cham, she uttered a cry of joy. "We must haste away, Mother," he said.

"I am old, let them kill me," she began. But when she saw my wounds she hastened to a coffer and took out some balm to pour on them. "I was once a court lady and I know the women's country arts. Let us go."

We seized some weapons and proceeded through narrow alleyways to the Elephant Hall.

The Elephant Courtyard was deserted. The *mahouts* had run away with some of the ordinary elephants, hoping to force their way through the Burmese soldiery. Only one White Elephant was left in his golden room. He looked at us, his ruby-studded tusks gleaming. Two attendant priests knelt, chanting in a low monotone to soothe the Elephant. They did not look up. Thence through a maze of courtyards, with people running here or there. Palace guards in panoply were looting the objects in the many halls and carrying them off in sacks upon their shoulders. Weapons that had been thrown away lay on the ground.

Thus we reached the audience room and entered the inner palace, the King's apartments and those of his harem. Though it was daylight, lamps were lit, and the profusion of gold ornaments, gold-studded furniture, cupboards with vases and boxes encrusted with diamonds, sapphires, emeralds, rubies, the fans, the draperies of gold cloth, were such that at first we did not notice that everywhere were women, hundreds of women, squatting on the floor.

Jit, where was Jit? "Where is the Father King?" Cham asked.

"He . . . he . . ." A wail came up from several hundred throats.

Three or four pages with bundles on their shoulders, obviously ready to flee, were crossing the rooms. One of them jeered, "The fellow has run away. In a small boat."

We almost trod on women. Women huddled near one another, all the several halls covered with their bodies, passive, waiting and wailing.

"The queens and consorts," Cham's mother said. She raised her voice. "We are looking for Jit. Is she in the place of punishment?"

One of the minor queens stood up. "I will take you."

Behind the inner palace, beyond the places for bathing and relieving one's needs, was the place of punishment, a staircase down into the ground, a dungeon.

"Jit, Jit!" I shouted, running down the steps.
The glow of fire. Suspended over it a body. Jit.

SHE HUNG FROM A chain fixed in the ceiling. Below her a spiked
iron grid, under the grid a glowing charcoal fire. Sooner or
later she would have fallen, unable to hang on any longer,
fallen on the grid of spikes.

"Oh, don't let go," I cried.

I could not reach her; no one could. Cham's mother said,
"There are water jugs in the bathing rooms." We ran, taking
the jugs used for scooping water, and inverted them upon the
spikes. An uneven platform of jugs was now below Jit, and
the fire sputtered and hissed as we ran back and forth, throwing water upon it. The minor queen, clever and helpful, came
back with an armful of wet clothes, which she flung upon the
jugs. Erik and I climbed upon them.

"Jit, Jit, let go now. I'm here." I raised my arms to catch
her. But she had twisted her arms and legs into the chain so
as not to fall. Cham and Erik hoisted me upon their shoulders.
I reached her and undid the coiled chain, already very hot,
that was wound round her body. She was still alive. She
breathed—a rasping sound with long intervals between. Her
mouth was open, her tongue and lips cracked and brown.
The slow fire had taken all the water out of her body. She
would die soon, for she burnt to the touch, unless—

"Water!" I screamed.

"Oh no," Erik said, "water carries the cholera plague."

The minor queen and Cham poured a jug of water over her
body, and then I saw the wheals. She had been whipped
mercilessly, across the back, the breasts, the belly.

"It is wine-vinegar and honey she needs," Cham's mother
said. "When I was at Court, we kept a stock of it for after the
whippings." Briskly, the old woman ran out with the minor
queen. They returned with two medium-sized stone jars, one
of mild palm vinegar, one of honey. I smeared Jit's tongue
and the inside of her mouth with the mixture. The minor
queen took off her *sabai*, dipped a corner of it into the vinegar,
and squeezed it into Jit's mouth.

I noted a mechanical swallow in Jit's throat. "She's alive."

The faint seashell noise from Ayuthia now swelled into a roar. A sudden blaze of drums startled us. It was the triumphant Burmese army, which had reached the great square in front of the palace and was preparing to march into it.

"Hurry," said the minor queen. "This way."

I picked up Jit. I would let no one else carry her. The minor queen led us through a narrow alley to a postern door onto a small brick dock, where some flat black-colored boats were moored. These were the refuse boats. A small canal, with foul water, meandered onwards. We climbed onto a boat, and Cham and Erik poled it away. Within a half-league we had reached the gate in the ramparts below which the canal water ran out into the girdling river. The boat glided below the gate, for it was the dry season of low water.

Now we were on the circular stream around Ayuthia but could not proceed, as we would inevitably fall upon the Burmese barges. Instead we cut athwart the river, for its other side was a marsh. The smell of waste and rot came up from the cloacal mud, and a million insects in a thick dense cloud swooped upon us, even into our noses and eyes. Round us now grew tall reeds and bulrush grass. I helped to pole. It was hard work, pushing the boat across the soggy marshland until it finally scraped bottom, spreading into a nauseous expanse of mud.

Cham and Erik stepped into the stinking green ooze. "We must cross the marsh to the forest beyond," Cham said. I remained with Jit and the two women, squeezing honey and vinegar into Jit's mouth, a few drops at a time, whispering to her, "Jit, Jit, I'm here Jit, it's me, Jit, you're safe now." I felt her body move, twitch a little, her breathing became easier. Night fell and I heard Cham and Erik return; Cham seemed able to see his way in the dark.

"There is a clump of trees where the woods begin a mile or more from here."

The frogs and toads came out to play their night concert. The mud squished under my feet. There were the sudden wings of a disturbed owl, and Cham stopped. "Look, Ayuthia is burning." There, on our right, the sky glowed, a somber dull red.

WE REACHED THE FOREST. Thickets tore at us, bushes hindered our advance, but at last there was the usual denuded ground at the foot of a banyan tree, for nothing grows in its shade. And there we rested. And there the minor queen whose name was O Mie, began to wail, crying for Ayuthia.

I went on giving the mixture of acid palm wine and honey to Jit. And tore down and crushed leaves from the banyan and pasted them on her body as I had seen Bea do for burns. She seemed a little better, her breathing more even, no longer gasping. I held her in my arms, and while the others lay down, trying to sleep, my soul sang to her. Some magic strength inhabited me, because Jit was safe. I turned towards Ayuthia, saw the sky smeared red with the fires that were burning, burning down Ayuthia the Enchantress.

DAWN STIRRED US WITH birdsong. Jit breathed evenly but was still only half-conscious. I covered her body with mine, for there was some freshness about. Her body was cooler now. I had fed her all through the night and the jugs were empty.

Cham had wrapped his old mother in his own garment and wore only a loincloth. He stood up and said, "We must find something to eat." He and Erik went off into the forest in the hope of finding some fruit-bearing tree, perhaps a stray plantain or coconut palm. But there was little hope of finding anything, unless we went much deeper into the jungle, for many people must have already come here, searching for food, gathering anything edible. They were lucky, however; they found two coconuts on a palm tree, near a village that was totally burnt out. Erik, who had kept the Portuguese man's dagger, broke them open, and we ate and drank of the white flesh and liquor of the blessed fruit. But I kept my share for Jit, and using the piece of *sabai* cloth of Mie squeezed the coconut juice into her. Jit began to suck like a baby. And then she moaned and opened her eyes. They were bloodshot and there was white sticky matter at the corners.

"Keran . . ." she whispered.

"Yes, Jit, we are safe."

"The baby . . ."

She had hung on to that chain, many hours. And fortunately the torturers had run away, leaving her, so that the fire had not been replenished; otherwise she would have died.

We now took counsel. Where could we go? Cham said, "Many people must have fled and are in hiding in the forest. The Burmese will be too busy looting Ayuthia. We have a chance, if we go deeper into the trees." This cheered us. We would walk into the heart of the forest. There would be fruit, perhaps. We had some weapons, to kill predatory animals. . . .

Shouting. A human sound from afar, winging in the air, came to us.

I had picked up Jit, ready to flee, but Erik said, "Wait, wait, Colin." He had marvelous hearing. We listened. Very faint, the sound came again, a recognizable up-and-down calling. "Someone is calling your name," Erik said. "Co—lin, Colin, I hear it."

"You are mad, Erik. Who would call my name?" The sound came from across the marsh; the sound of a voice, and distinctly now it yodeled. I recognized the yodeling. It was as in my native land. Perhaps it was a spirit calling. Perhaps we were dead and did not know it, and the spirits of that far lake were calling me now.

"Co . . . lin . . ." Nearer now, and quite distinct; the singing up and down, that particular way of throwing one's voice to the sky and having the echo bounce back.

Wildly, I thought: *It is someone I know. Perhaps it is Jacob, calling me from beyond death.* I put Jit down tenderly, carefully, upon her bed of leaves, and walked back the way we had come, towards the sound. Whoever was calling continued to sing my name: "Co . . . lin." It could not be a Thai or a Burmese, because they would have said Keran, and anyway they did not yodel. When I had lost sight of Jit and the others, I raised my voice: "Colin here . . . Colin here . . ."

I walked into the ooze of the marsh, and there, coming towards me, was a man, carried by four bearers in an open chair, the conveyance of noblemen.

The man stepped down as he saw me. He was tall, with a blond beard and blue eyes, a hat with many feathers upon his head, a gaudy brocade jacket, and hose of fine white silk and shoes.

"Colin—" He ran towards me. "Colin, don't you recognize me? Valentin, Valentin, your brother."

Valentin, majestic and plumed, who now embraced me rapturously, hugging me with such strength that I nearly cried, for my wounds were very sore. He towered above me, a handsome giant. His four bearers and the eight soldiers with him wore green cloths, helmets of woven rattan, and carried lances and muskets. Burmese.

"Valentin, you are with the Burmese."

"Of course, Colin." He laughed, immensely pleased with himself. "They needed a good cannoneer, and I am the best gun maker in the world."

"How did you know I was here?"

"The automata, Colin, the automata on the ramparts of the city. I saw them and I thought: Now who can be making automata soldiers? I asked questions, but no one knew. But yesterday de Souza came over, he now serves under me with his friend Coelho, who assists me. Yes, he said, Colin Duriez had made the automata. I set out to search for you, ordered any *farang* caught by our troops to be spared and sent to me. I went through the palace, and the women told me you had been there. I followed your track, found your boat. . . . I'm hoarse with calling your name."

Valentin brought us back, not to Ayuthia, which had been delivered to the soldiery, but to a place two leagues north of the city, where the Burmese King, Mangra, had established his camp, which was known as the Three Pagodas.

FOR FIFTEEN DAYS THE Burmese raped, slaughtered, and looted Ayuthia. They spared none of the three hundred or more *wats*, nor the *bikkus*, whom they tortured again and again to make them reveal the hidden treasures of the *wats*.

And so Cham, Erik, and I saw all the beauty and splendor of Ayuthia destroyed.

Jit was cared for. Slaves washed her, put balm on her wounds; hourly she was fed. Valentin threatened the doctors: "She lives or you die." He threatened everyone around him all the time. They squatted down before him, bowing humbly, for he was the Conqueror, the Great Master of Cannonry.

Because I was Valentin's brother, Cham and his old mother and O Mie and Erik were also safe. I said Cham was my servant; he acted like one, and no one questioned it. He avoided the Portuguese tents, where De Souza caroused nightly. His mother wept seeing the Buddha statues hacked, hearing the screams of the tortured *bikkus*. She whispered that she wanted to die. As for O Mie, she was now one of Valentin's many women; for he had, as did the Burmese commanders, the pick of the maidens of Ayuthia.

Jit was recovering. Her eyes speaking, speaking her love, but also her distress. Often she would stroke her belly, fearful that something had happened to our child. "I hung on because I knew you would find me, Keran. I did not want our child to die before being born."

The child moved, only too perceptible under her scarred, streaked skin, marked by the whip, the burning chain. "I was brought before the King, and his face was awful to see. He stared at me; there were so many of his women about, he had never touched me. I was flogged, and then condemned to the slow fire. I do not know how many hours it was, not too long, since they only came once to put more charcoal on the fire; and one of them swung the chain, to see if I would fall. Then they did not come again." It was the Burmese breaching Ayuthia that had saved her, as it had saved us.

Valentin talked of the booty, of which he had his share. The Burmese were methodical. They made lists; Valentin and the Portuguese were ordered by the King to inspect and make records of the armaments and weaponry captured.

Of the weapons of all kinds of the royal armory, none of which had been used to defend Ayuthia, there were two thousand war boats and a hundred ten large ornate royal barges. Ten thousand ordinary muskets and a thousand encrusted with gold and silver. Cannon, those for dismantling city walls and towers, some of which Taksin had tried to obtain for the ramparts, and other guns—in all some three thousand. Five hundred thousand shells and cannon balls of various sizes. Elongated shells that on bursting cast one hundred to two hundred pellets of cast iron far and wide. The arsenals of Ayuthia were full of weapons. None of them had been used, because King Ekatat did not trust anyone, and also because his favorite could not bear the sound of guns.

Valentin roared with laughter when I told him the story. He was curious about Taksin. I told him that Taksin had gone away and that Bea and her husband had followed him. He shrugged. "What can he do? Ayuthia will never rise again."

His own share of the booty was one hundred chests filled with gold and silver ornaments and precious stones, fifty chests of gold cups and bowls and salvers, two chests of gold bullion, ten chests of cloth worked in silver and gold, a beautiful howdah encrusted with gold and rubies and sapphires, one of the seven used by the King of Thailand, given to Valentin by King Mangra as a reward for his good cannonry.

More important even than treasure were the people the Burmese took away. Of the queens, four major queens and twenty-nine minor queens. Eight hundred sixty-nine consorts of various degrees—all would be sent to Burma. The queens were placed on elephants for the journey; Mangra would add them to his own inner palace. There were thirteen sisters and half-sisters of Ekatat, his three sons and four daughters, and twenty-eight grandchildren. Two thousand other members of the royal family, and eight hundred noblemen, among them the unhappy *Pra-Klang.* No one of the royal family was to be left behind to rule, except one prince, who had run away and could not be found. The Burmese did not trust even the traitors, who were also taken away to Burma. As for Utumporn, the King's brother monk, he was taken from his *wat* and sent to Burma, where he lived a prisoner for many years.

Of the consorts and queens, some would be redeemed by their families with much gold, families that came from other provinces, now subject to Burma. Of the near million people in and around Ayuthia, four hundred thousand had died; another four hundred thousand were taken away by the Burmese.

The Burmese took away skilled men, for they knew their worth. Some one hundred six thousand families were thus transported. Musicians and dancers, carpenters and carvers and turners, blacksmiths and gold- and silver- and copper-smiths, masons and decorators and furniture makers, cutters of gems and stones, barbers, exorcists and magicians, herbalists and medicine men, persons skilled in caring for elephants and horses and training them, weavers of all kinds of cloth, from cotton to silver and gold brocade.

I sought out my workmen, those who remained. Only three out of twenty-odd were alive. Valentin gave them money to reach other provinces, and the Burmese let them go. We did not tell them they were skilled in clockwork.

About ten days after our rescue Valentin said, "King Mangra wants to see you. He wishes to inquire about this fellow who ran away, and whom Bea followed."

"Taksin."

"What can have made Bea want to leave even you for this man? To follow a bandit who will soon be caught?"

He walked up and down, always in great finery. "Bea, our sister, she never liked me."

I did not reply. Outside, the vultures that followed the armies were feeding on the corpses the Burmese had not managed to burn—great mounds of piled corpses. They made the Thai slaves gather them and burn them with quicklime. But the vultures swooped upon them, and bits of human bodies were strewn around.

KING MANGRA HAD AN ornate tent of purple and gold. Within, on both sides, upon shelves of lacquered wood, were piled the choicest treasures of Ekatat's palace. Outside the royal tent with its tall gold spire were grouped the tents of his ministers and commanders, and of his sons. Elephants ready harnessed stood by, howdahs upon them. By the King's tent was another one, as sumptuous as his, for the White Elephant, whose own court of priests and keepers had been spared, to care for him. Further on, on the plain that once had been villages and fields, great files of people waited—the captives, waiting their turn, chained to each other, to begin the long journey to Burma.

The King was seated upon the golden throne, encrusted with nine kinds of gems, which had been Ekatat's. Everyone squatted or crawled in front of him; there was little difference in protocol between the two courts. Mangra's face was square and somewhat heavy. He spoke to me through an interpreter after having nodded kindly to Valentin, who knelt by my side. "You are Wanang's brother"—Wanang being Valentin's Burmese name. "It was you who built the machine men upon Ayuthia's walls. For a while they deceived us, until we found out what they were."

I bowed my head and raised my joined hands: "I thank Your Majesty for saving our lives."

"We would be pleased to have you in our service. But first, I must ask you. You know this man called Taksin, a highway bandit. What can you tell us of him?"

"Very little, Your Majesty. I met him very few times. He seemed to be a good soldier."

Mangra scowled. My answer had displeased him. "He is a commoner, half-Chinese, adopted by a former Thai minister. Why did your sister follow him?"

"My sister followed her husband, Prince Udorn. At the time, Taksin promised to save Ayuthia."

Mangra laughed. Scornfully. "There is nothing left to save of Ayuthia, it is only a pile of rubble and corpses . . . it will never rise again. Even its memory will be effaced from the minds of men."

He was in good humor now. "Perhaps you will join your brother in serving us. We can be generous, much more so than Ekatat ever was."

EKATAT. WHERE WAS EKATAT? Mangra sent forays everywhere, deep into the forest, into the marshes, torturing some of Ekatat's ministers to find out where Ekatat was.

No one could find him.

And then two corpses were found that bore upon their faces the disfigurement that had been Ekatat's—the spreading wine-colored ulcer.

One of them was dead of starvation, near a *wat*. Twenty-six of the harem women recognized him as Ekatat.

The other was a corpse found at the west gate, near the postern for refuse whence we had escaped. Another twenty women said it was Ekatat.

The Burmese chose to recognize the second corpse. They put it in a ceramic jar, as was the custom, folded upon itself like an embryo. They pierced the bottom of the jug to let the corpse's liquors run through, and left him thus, half in the ground, half out.

VALENTIN HAD DECIDED TO go back to Europe with his treasures. "I am a wealthy man now. I can do as I please. Do you remember, Colin—" he began. We had wine and fine dishes before us. We were alone. He wanted to tell me his life story, wanted me to know him, wanted once again to be my brother, for he felt my reticence, and it wounded him. So he talked, wanting to be loved, understood. And I felt I had no right to judge him harshly. He had left Geneva as a mercenary. War was a trade like any other. And Jit and I owed our lives to him. Now he said, "Do you remember"—wanting to return to that time when we were children.

He had been to Acadia, a wonderful country, an enormous land, with lakes like seas, immense forests, the trees taller than anything imaginable. He had fought with the French against the English, but the English had won. "They won because they had better cannon, they were more disciplined. There was a great battle at Quebec and the French commander, Marquess de Montcalm, was killed. A noble gentleman, but he could not get the weapons or the men he needed. The French King did not care about Acadia, nor about the French settlers there."

The English then shipped great numbers of French settlers out of Acadia, dumping them on the coastlines farther south, and sent in their own settlers from England. "Oh, it was a sight to see them hunting down the French farmers, transporting them to faraway coasts in the holds of their ships, not caring whether they starved or not."

He had deserted when the remnants of the French army and many Acadians began walking south, south to the Louisiana, a French settlement, going by the Great Lakes and down the Mississippi River. He had gone over to the British, and reached a town called Boston, which was full of English Puritans. "And guess who was commanding the English garrison in Boston, Colin?" He slapped his thigh, ran his fingers through the golden fleece upon his head. "None other but a Kilvaney, the son of Lord Kilvaney who knew Father so well! He saw my name, Valentin Duriez, and that I was from Lausanne. 'My father spoke of a Duriez who made splendid automata.' 'That was *my* father,' I replied." Valentin chose to ignore that Father had adopted him. I did not contradict him. He had loved Father.

He had served under the English, learnt a good deal about guns, both for men-of-war and for land forts, and then decided to strike out on his own. "There's always a war somewhere. And always a good man who knows cannon is needed." He had sailed off to India and served under a nawab who was with the French, battling the English. Then he had left the nawab and hired himself out to the King of Burma, who was known to pay extremely well.

"Now what have you done?" he asked.

"My life was not as colorful as yours, Valentin. I was making automata and clocks, and though I did not fight, yet round me too people were slaughtered, for one reason or another. And now I have Jit."

"The little girl?" That is how Valentin saw her; Jit was so small, so frail. "But she's another breed, Colin. Surely you cannot think of a life with her when you go home."

"Go home?" Home was a pile of ashes and a torque thrown in the sea. Home was . . . everywhere and nowhere now. "The world's a small place."

"You are still a true Vaudois, never saying yes or no." He threw back his shoulders, straightening his tall frame. He was very handsome, and the Thai women talked of his physical attributes, saying he was built like a bull.

"I shall go back, Colin, and build myself a mansion, the largest in Lausanne. And have the best master masons and forgers, tapestry men and spinners. I have seen many fair houses, and I know what I shall have. Servants, and horses . . .

"But I shall also buy a plantation in the New World. In the Louisiana, where the land is large, and cotton is planted. Many men are making great fortunes, planting cotton. There is such a supply of black slaves, the boats are bringing them in almost every week from Africa.

"Come with me, Colin. Let us be rich together. You can claim your barony—Baron Duriez of Neuchâtel. In the New World you could establish factories, make watches and clocks and musical boxes."

"You will succeed, Valentin," I told him. "But I . . . I am waiting."

"Waiting for what, Colin? For Bea?"

"I am waiting for my child to be born. Then I shall decide what to do."

THE BURMESE ARMY DESTROYED the ramparts, the moats, the bastions of Ayuthia. Nothing remained of the proud and beautiful *wats,* ransacked for gold, the statues melted for their gold. And then in June, suddenly, the Burmese army prepared to leave.

"The Chinese are attacking Burma, Colin. In the North."

"The Chinese?"

"The Chinese Emperor is angry with King Mangra because Ayuthia has been destroyed without his being informed," Valentin said.

King Mangra left first with six hundred elephants and thirty thousand soldiers. Another twenty thousand, leading a great many captives, left a month later.

Valentin was wroth. "I do not want to fight another war. The North of Burma has treacherous and savage men, who kill from the deep forests, shooting arrows with poisoned tips. I do not want to fight the Chinese there. I shall leave as soon as I can get a ship."

The Burmese named a man called Thugyi, who had been

loyal to them, as ruler over the devastated land. Ayuthia was uninhabitable; its charnel-house odor still persistent. Now bandits and malefactors of all kinds, both Thai and Chinese, were tearing down the remaining *wats,* and even melting down the brass covers of the spires, and digging for treasure. Thugyi with twenty thousand Burmese soldiers remained at Three Pagodas.

Erik left with Valentin. He would set sail to the coast of Coromandel where the Danes had an old settlement, in Tranquebar. O Mie went with Valentin. She did not know that she would be left behind. She thought Valentin would take her to Europe.

Jit said, "Keran, you are waiting for your sister, are you not?"

"No, Jit, I am waiting for our child to be born."

"Will you too go away one day?"

"Wherever I go, Jit, you will be with me."

She smiled then. "I am glad. Yes, I shall always be with you, Keran."

In August Jit gave birth to a male child. Her labor was arduous, for she had not recovered from her ordeal. She was small and narrow, and the birth took a very long time. But our son was beautiful and bawled lustily. Jit said, "When I was hanging over the fire, I prayed he should not come to harm. Is he well?"

"He is well, Jit, a beautiful child, our son."

I placed the baby in Jit's arms. She was very pale, covered in sweat. Outside, the monsoon sent its lances of rain crashing upon the roof; the whole earth seemed to groan under the load of water from the sky.

"Jit, I love you, love you."

"Keran . . . take him . . . to your lake. . . ."

"With you, Jit. We shall go together."

She looked at me then, with ineffable mildness and wisdom, the eyes of an all-seeing child.

I wiped her forehead again. Cham's mother and the midwife had plucked scented herbs, for Jit loved the fragrance of jasmine and champa, and *phikun,* which had perfumed her clothes in her old life. We burnt some to please her nostrils.

I drew a mat near the bed on which she lay. She complained of being cold, and I went to get some covers for her. The baby lay in his cradle, content. Cham's mother had given him a little tea brewed with honey. Two maids were to watch Jit; it was the custom for a woman just delivered to be watched through the first night. I watched too, but must have dozed off. Suddenly Cham's mother was there, saying, "Jit, Jit," in a frightened voice.

I sprung to Jit's side. Her lips were blue. "Quick, fetch the doctor. . . ." But it was too late. She opened her eyes, smiled at me, and the next moment she was dead, even in death quiet, silent, uncomplaining, as she had lived.

⁂ Eighteen ⁂

Anno Domini 1767–1770

⁂ ⁂

He will not look at me. Never does his glance turn my way. Everyone thinks it is courtesy, praises him for this puritanism. He puts an
arm around Udorn, chuckling over battles won and battles to come,
ignoring me.

It cannot be otherwise. I could not love a man without passion or
vision. He is a difficult man of strong power, with no space in mind
or heart for love of a woman like me. I am his born enemy. And I
love him.

"I am afraid of you. I do not want you in my life. Between us the
struggle would be to the death." This is what his averted face says.

I follow him in battle, with rage and love. He endures it, knowing
he cannot rid himself of me.

At Rayong, whose docks hold many barges of rice and salt, men
and women flock to Taksin with food and gifts, his name ringing like
a bell upon their lips. "Phya Taksin, lead us to battle."

Taksin replies, "I shall lead you to reconquer your land."

This vision lifts them out of despair, out of shame and humiliation
into hope and pride. Surpassing themselves, they storm the cities
and conquer them.

The women crop their hair, tie their pannungs *like the men's, their* sabais *as halter tops, leaving their arms free to handle swords and spears and muskets. The Chinese boatmen bring weaponry from the Malaccas and Batavia, and do not want payment, for Taksin's father was a member of their fraternity.*

Taksin storms Cholaboon city, forbidding loot or plunder. A soldier who raped a woman is flogged to death. "Not a hair of the people must be touched. For we must build a greater and more mighty Ayuthia—in the way of the Lord Buddha."

On the day that Taksin is thirty-three years old, Ayuthia is conquered by the Burmese. Colin is in danger, but I know the danger will pass. When my mind gropes for his, he is carrying Jit in his arms, running away from the burning city.

"Ayuthia fell last night," I tell Udorn. "I saw it in a dream." Udorn believes in my dreams. Later the runaways, coming south, confirm it.

Ah Ming, who has come as a delegate of the Chinese clans of Ayuthia, pledged to Taksin, is greatly worried about Colin.

"He is alive," I tell him, and he believes me.

"He would be here, with us, were it not for the girl," he says.

"I know it." That pale, effaced, no more than water, shadow in water Jit . . .

But who, of Colin and I, is the more foolish through love? And what is love, that makes us see another being as the enchanted, the unique? That possesses us with such frenzy? My heart screams its fury in the night, its fury never slaked. For I love a king, but he will not have me.

Taksin lays plans to win over the city of Chantaburi. Although he sends couriers and gifts to its governor, the governor is in two minds. The Burmese King Mangra has also sent him gifts, for with Chantaburi his, the whole of the South would be Burma's.

Four bikkus *arrive from Chantaburi to Rayong, with garlands, and flowers of silver and gold, emblems of vassalage, asking Taksin to come to Chantaburi, promising him support.*

"Do not go, Phya Taksin. It is a trick," I say. "Chantaburi has also received Burmese messengers. And now the governor sends you four bikkus, *knowing you are pious and must believe what they say. But it is a trick."*

Taksin keeps his head lowered, thinking. I feel his strength, a fierceness that fills the air about him. Then he gives orders, crisply.

The army will march and take Chantaburi that very night, before dawn. It is from that day that Taksin begins to suspect all bikkus, all priests. He has always been impatient with ceremonies, incantations, the tricks of magicians and sorcerers.

Chantaburi is taken. Taksin then calls a council of war. He will seize Bangkok and Thonburi, to control the Great Mother River's mouth. In Rayong a fleet of ships is readied for the enterprise.

And then the news comes as our ships are readied with guns to assault Bangkok. The Burmese army is going home! Going home because the Chinese Emperor, Tsienlung, has marched into North Burma. To punish King Mangra.

The Chinese boatmen and bargemen and traders are exultant. The Empire has manifested its displeasure! Now all of them rally to Taksin. Taksin now prepares to sail for Ayuthia, and gladly the nobles of the land flock to join him.

Among them are two brothers, descendants of the noble house of Kosaparn, who was ambassador to France in 1680. The younger, Surasit, once a page at the palace, has brought with him his brother Yodfah's homage, two rings and a sword. And Yodfah has also rescued Taksin's old mother and is now sending her to Taksin.

Taksin is overjoyed. "They are both my childhood friends," he says to us. "They shall be my right and left hands when we rebuild Ayuthia."

"Take care," I want to say to Taksin. "They are able, too able for you, and you are but a commoner." But I remain silent. Taksin elevates them to be his closest helpers. And now I am afraid, for the Gift is leaving me, as it left my mother. Or perhaps I do not wish to probe too deeply into the future, do not want do know what is to come. . . .

In September Taksin takes Thonburi and conquers the forts of Bangkok. In November, with his flotilla, and an army on elephants and horses, we move upriver to surprise the Burmese garrisons at Ayuthia.

Thus Ayuthia is freed, in November, six months after its destruction. Many nobles and ordinary people, herded into camps, waiting to be transported to Burma, are released by the armies of Taksin.

With Ah Ming I search for Colin. We go to the great wat Phanang Cheng, the only wat left standing, though grievously battered. Here the Lord Buddha's statue is almost intact save for the

317

right arm, which the Burmese have tried to saw away. But the statue is too powerful, too enormous, its spirit too strong; when they tried to burn down the edifice, a sudden squall of rain damped the fire.

Colin would be here. And Monk Teo, if still alive. We find Colin in the small room the monks have given him. He is building an automaton. Around him are his tools; on the trestle table before him the parts of the machine he is putting together. He does not even raise his head as I enter the room.

⁂

BEA HAS COME BACK. My inner ear once again functioned; I heard her footsteps before she entered my room.

After Jit had died I remained in a stupor for many days. Not wanting to live. Monk Teo, who had survived, took me to *Wat* Phanang Cheng, while Cham and his mother rode away to find Taksin, and to serve him. Everyone waited for Taksin, the Liberator, the man who had challenged the might of Burma. And now he was coming to Ayuthia, to restore her to her former splendor.

In *Wat* Phanang Cheng, over two-thirds of the monks were dead. And many of the Chinese boatmen. But those who remained began once again to organize, to plant food and to man barges. Here I had seen Jit pray, and her spirit was still about. Often, in the evening, when incense rose and the monks chanted their prayers, in the mist of tapers I saw her golden face, her velvet eyes, the eyes of a trusting child, the guileless joy of her world of innocence.

Monk Teo had found a sturdy Chinese woman, whose baby had died, to give breast to my son, and he thrived. I would take him in my arms and speak to him of his mother, seeking in his features those of Jit.

And I waited for Bea. Jit had been right. I was waiting for Bea.

Meanwhile, I began an android of Jit. Her face, her fluid

body, moving as she had. Perhaps one day, because I would pray hard, and fiercely, Jit's spirit would come and inhabit the waiting shape I had made.

The undead . . . I yearned now for that belief which had been Mother's, and her mother's, and also Bea's. There is no finality in death. Oh, let Bea show me the way to bring Jit back, let her fingers fashion the Keeper of Souls. Let us return to the forest, and perhaps Jit's soul would come back to me. . . .

I roamed the night calling for Jit. Surely she was about. I felt her.

I had refused to have her body cremated. It lay in its large pierced ceramic jug, half-buried, waiting. I remembered that flaming, splendid night when all the rescued spirits had gathered. When my grandmother, Grisolde, had joined them, that dream which had been Bea's, and through Bea, had also become mine.

Let Jit come to me. Let me but once again see her face, her smile.

BEA STOOD IN FRONT of me. The woman warrior, superb, her beauty stunning, her hair short under the pointed hat. In the thick gold chain at her waist was thrust a dagger.

"Colin, Cham has told me about Jit. You knew I would return, did you not?"

"Yes, Bea." I stooped over my work. I would not look at her. Always between us this pull, this wanting to be everything to each other, which could never happen.

"Colin, Jit was . . . water, fluid, beautiful, unchangeable, adapting to you in all ways. You have a son. The world goes on. We must rebuild Ayuthia—a new, a better land."

I put in a screw with loving care. A cam and a hinged lever to raise a hand, to flex the fingers of a Jit-to-be.

I faced Bea. "Bea, remember, when we went with Mother that night to release the Soul-Keeper? Now I want you to make a Soul-Keeper for Jit. I want her, one day, to live again. That is what you believe, is it not? That the undead live again?"

"Colin, oh, Colin, I no longer know what to believe, except that yes, beyond this world of doing, there is a world of believing and dreaming—and that sometimes, the two come together."

"Then do this for me. Make Jit come alive again, or at least protect her wandering spirit so that it may rest in peace."

Light fell on Bea, made her gleam, become substance. She possessed the light, too. "There is such a price to pay, Colin. For dreaming . . . for believing . . . it's too big a price for some."

"Bea, do this for me, before it is all gone from me."

And then Bea looked at me with the eyes of her tormented soul, a soul in the fires of Hell. Yet she would always prefer that fire to the nonentity and the ease of nonbeing, which is how most men and women live. "Colin, your Jit was nothing but a mirage, a reflection in water. She was water, fluid, elusive, pliant to everything. You loved water, Colin. You and I cannot bring her back. And if you try, all your life you will be in love with an android you yourself created."

This hurt me, for it was true. My hands were still on my creation, holding the android I was making, but now life had gone out of them, I was holding inert wood.

"Bea, once you said you could no longer reach my mind; it was not true, was it?"

"Colin, it was and was not. The Gift . . . I am losing it."

I nodded. Yes, I knew she would lose it. "And you killed. You killed the Magician, Bea."

"Not only the Magician. I had to spread the poison, so that Nee should not be suspect. Several pages, two of Ekatat's cousins . . . The guards slept, some never to wake again."

Jit had been Bea's gift to me. I would never be free of Bea. "In the end, we shall only have each other, however many others come between us," Bea said.

IN NOVEMBER OF 1767, with his commanders behind him, Taksin rode through the ruins of Ayuthia to see what could be salvaged. His soldiers caught bandits still looting what remained of the *wats* and their treasures, and there were many executions.

People took heart, coming out of the forests, out of faraway hiding places.

But Ayuthia could not be rebuilt. She was shattered beyond man's power to resurrect her. There was famine. Everywhere, it dominated the land. The monsoon was very poor that year, the little rice that grew was meager and could not feed enough people. And so banditism, which always thrives on distress, continued, and there was even more destruction and killing.

Taksin sent delegations to China, asking for rice so that his people could be fed. And when the rice came, it was distributed, so much per person, which angered the hoarders and some of the nobles, who had controlled the selling and buying of rice. He set up very severe laws, punishing robbers and murderers. The country was plagued with rats and he began a campaign to catch and kill them. Even the Buddhist priests were compelled to kill rats, though they protested that this was taking life.

The late King Ekatat's jar with his body was given solemn cremation. Taksin followed the enormous funeral chariot, as Ekatat's heir. This displeased some princes, half-brothers of Ekatat who now laid claim to the kingship. But Taksin would be king by right of conquest, and because the people loved him.

King Taksin then moved the capital to Thonburi, opposite Bangkok, to become the first King of Thonburi. There he began to build a great *wat*, *Wat* Arun, Temple of the Dawn. As successor to Ekatat, he married all the late King's remaining wives and consorts, aunts and cousins and sisters, all those who had not been transported to Burma—altogether there were twenty-nine of them.

Taksin poured money into building public granaries to feed the people; he bought seed rice in China to restore the fields. He strove to rebuild the trade, but to curb hoarding and other practices, and this displeased some noble profiteers. In the provinces many claimants to the throne arose, and there were sporadic wars. Taksin also set himself to purify the religion, for the priesthood, he said, was corrupt, and there were false magicians and sorcerers among them. He planned a rewriting of the sacred texts and made new rules for the priests. Many of them were submitted to the ordeal of trial by water and by fire, to test their purity. And some died, which again created malcontents.

Taksin was a puritan, a reformer, harsh and unyielding to human frailty. But he honored and trusted the two brothers, Yodfah and Surasit, who had saved his old mother and joined him in the return to Ayuthia. Yodfah became the *Chakri*; while his brother, Surasit, became the supreme commander of the armies.

And to make the bonds between them more complete, Taksin married Yodfah's daughter as his Chief Queen, while he gave his own daughter in marriage to the *Chakri*. Thus the *Chakri* would be anchored as "second king"—virtually Taksin's heir. All this Taksin did to consolidate the kingdom and to unite the resentful nobles, who sneered at him for being half-Chinese, even if his Thai mother was of relatively high birth.

I REMAINED ANOTHER TWO years in Thonburi, where Udorn built himself a gracious palace of many rooms. Bea sat in her new house, beautiful, a princess, but there was something vague and lost about her demeanor. She no longer went to the palace, for Taksin would have no women meddling in affairs of state. She sat, or walked, or rode in her ornate barge, and there was some frozen quality about her, which perturbed me. She had walled in her spirit, and I could never reach her. She still helped other women, but she did it in a lifeless, wooden manner.

There was nothing for me to do, for Taksin's Court was not luxurious, and he frowned on foreign merchants, making it difficult for them to import baubles such as clocks. And because he did not use me, a deep nostalgia for my own land of Vaud came upon me. I yearned to return, once again to see our lake, so vivid and so varied, an endless pageant of color in every season.

"You must go home, Colin," Bea told me. "So many new

322

inventions in Europe. You must go back and meet men of science, for this is what your mind needs."

"But, Bea, you—"

"I shall stay here. Am I not Princess Didya, wife of Prince Udorn?" She smiled, a little bitterly, and then her hands, tender, came out to touch me. "Little Brother, you must go. . . . I shall wait and I know you will return one day."

And so it was arranged. I would leave with my son, John, now almost three years old.

JEAN ALLARD, WHO HAD returned from captivity to settle in Thonburi, had rebuilt the Catholic school. Money was scarce, and he informed me of an obstinate rumor that the order of Jesuits would soon be dissolved by the Roman Curia.

"What will you do then, Father?"

"I shall continue to serve God, my son, as I have served Him all my life."

I thought then of the French Jesuits in China, who, because the French King had confiscated all their property in 1762 and expelled Jesuits from France, subsisted on the bounty of the Chinese Emperor. Where was Pierre Amigot now? And that amiable genius, Giuseppe Castiglione, was he still painting for Emperor Tsienlung?

These men had also pursued a dream, an immense dream of harmonizing the different cultures and their philosophies into the Catholic Church. They would have transformed the world, had they been listened to.

Scrupulous as ever, Heer Timmermans, who had been released by the Burmese after an intercession by Valentin and without paying a vast ransom, gave me back some treasures of mine that I had left with him. I had also recuperated my treasure and gold chests that Ah Ming had sent to Rayong, before the fall of Ayuthia. Among those chests was one containing the faceless android I had built. Now, although not as wealthy as Valentin with his war spoils, I had a goodly stock of gold and precious stones.

As for the likeness of Jit that I had begun to make, I could no longer go on pretending to myself that it would satisfy me. True, all men seek to re-create their dead loves. But if I could not make Jit live in my mind, if the startled effulgence of my heart when I thought of her disappeared, if the recall of her voice, of her eyes, of her movements, of the liquidity of her (she *was* water, the infinite blessing of water), if all this left my mind, then I would have partly died. And to make an effigy, a portrait—surely this was not love but only betraying the trueness of love. This was substituting an automaton to mechanically stir the dead embers of passion. I would not do this. Jit would always be with me, a constant underground source of joy, and whenever I would hear the singing of water, I would remember her. And so I burnt the image I had begun to make, on the day Jit was at last cremated.

I had asked Valentin to inquire of Abdul Reza and his family in Tenasserim, and had considered going myself to find out, but in the end did not, as the Burmese were still holding Tenasserim and other coastal areas, and there was my son, John, to care for.

Only years later would I know that Abdul Reza had died suddenly on reaching Tenasserim, so that he did not witness the great slaughter. His sons had been able to sail for the Golconda before Tenasserim was taken. Perhaps one day I would meet them again.

Timmermans put me on board the Dutch ship *Prince of Orange,* and Ah Ming held a great feast, inviting members of the boatmen clan, among them some of those I had traveled with from China who had survived the wars. Ah Ming. Traveler in Emptiness. Marquess Fang and his sons—how could I leave these memories, this largesse of a world of men?

"You will return, Colin Brother," Ah Ming said as we put our arms about each other. He would write to me if he heard anything about Marquess Fang, about Third Son.

Our voyage home was uneventful. Uneventful in that I no longer felt anything as sharply as when over ten years ago I had set out, a young boy, wide-eyed, my mind recording everything I saw. Now my eyes were opaque, my soul blunted. I was, after all, almost twenty-eight years old, a seasoned man in his prime. The sunlight that fell upon the ocean waves no longer aroused any wonder in my heart. Avoiding excessive emotion, I was no longer enchanted, enthralled by the mere blessing of life. I had John, however, and now I had to make a life for him.

❧ *Nineteen* ❦

Anno Domini 1770–1785

THE PRINCE OF ORANGE reached Amsterdam on a day of cold mist, and John sobbed, screaming the sun had died. I had brought out with me two Portuguese-Thai women, widowed and childless in the war, to care for him, and a young child named Pok, about John's age, whom I had found bone-starved in what had once been a street of Ayuthia.

In Amsterdam I sold some of my gold and precious stones. The gem merchants were Jews, and they gave me a good price. From them I inquired of the whereabouts of the Hirsch family, for Abraham had mentioned relatives in Amsterdam. I was told that Abraham's wife and daughter were living here; Abraham had died soon after the murder of his son, and their house in Geneva had been sold.

I paced by a canal, which reminded me of the canals and waterways of Ayuthia, though the cold weather tempered my recollections to a wry acknowledgment of the hunger with which we cling to fetishes of remembrance. Water and Jit. Inseparable in my mind. Jit, a source of pure water, a spring forever to quench the thirst of my soul.

Going to the Hirsch house, I seemed to have Jacob pacing by my side, and found his mother, her hair grey-streaked, diminutive now with the shrinking of aged bones. She recognized me at once, and embraced me, weeping with joy and sorrow mixed.

And then Sarah came in, her cheeks glowing. "Oh, Colin, Colin!" she cried, and dropped the great bouquet of late roses she carried to rush into my arms.

I held her fast to me. She smelt of roses.

Sarah and I were married in Amsterdam. I did not require her to change her religion; and though there were to be many mutterings in Neuchâtel and in Lausanne, I stayed firm and was wealthy enough to have my way. Money is a balm for petty ailments of conscience.

We drove from Amsterdam to Lausanne, and there was the lake. And a host of memories. I went to Neuchâtel. Uncle Theodore had passed away. According to his secretary, Martin, he had not recovered from our flight, or, as Martin, being a true Neuchâtel man, put it, "When Monsieur le Baron [that was I] decided to go on his travels."

Martin was stiffer, more like a scarecrow in his black garb, but insisted on giving me a strict accounting of the money and properties involved. This sublime honesty was his pride, and I maintained him, even enlarging his allowance, knowing I was lucky to have such a man by my side, one who had administered even his whippings with scrupulous care.

SARAH AND I WILL be happy. I have decided that it will be so. I know how to reassure her, and her exuberant, constant cheerfulness makes light weight of small irritations. Her mother has come to live with us in Lausanne, and both women care well for my son, John, who is growing into a tall and handsome child, with fine bones and a touch of gold in his skin.

My factories are expanding; I have also bought a clockwork and mechanics factory in Geneva, where cabinotiers make exquisite watch cases. I am allied to men of substance in London and Amsterdam; we look not only to Asia but to the New World as a growing market for music boxes, clocks and watches, and textiles. The settlers in America rebelled against the British yoke in 1776 and proclaimed their independence. Their delegates are now in Europe, among them a certain Benjamin Franklin, whom I long to meet, for it is said that he is much interested in the power of electricity. Already ships crammed with men and women from the countries of Europe are leaving for the new United States of America, with its promises of wealth to come.

Voltaire has returned to Paris, welcomed with rapture, with extravagant adoration, as extravagant as the persistent malice from his countrymen that he suffered previously.

Those who like myself have traveled and made fortunes return to their native land with wondrous tales. But I merely smile and say that I have been to China and to the Kingdom of Ayuthia. My reputation suffers. I am a *taiseux*, tight-lipped, and therefore accounted miserly.

"He grows more and more like his uncle Theodore, who never wasted a word," is the comment.

Lausanne's high society is eager to receive Bea, for it is known that she is the wife of a Thai prince. But Valentin will not be received, and he, angered not to be taken in by those who create the fashions and opinions of the city, has gone away to the Louisiana, vowing never to return. "In the New World no one cares about birth, only about merit, and work well done."

Isabelle de Thunon, somewhat raddled, has decided to be our dear cousin and to make us her cherished guests at her receptions in Lausanne.

Sarah has given me two daughters. At night I tell my children tales of the splendor and glory of Ayuthia, the Enchantress, the fairy city destroyed by Evil but which will always live in memory.

Udorn writes that all is well, but yet war goes on. For nearly thirteen years now the kingdom has had to continue warring to consolidate itself, to repel more Burmese invasions. All these wars have been successful; the kingdom's territory is larger than before. Yet I discern in his letters a fretting. "The people are tired of war. We Thais are an easygoing people; we do not like strenuous effort. It's been too long that we have been on the warpath. We want more gaiety. . . ."

ONE NIGHT COMES THE dream, the vivid nightmare. Bea is calling me. She is in torment. I wake up covered with cold sweat, while Sarah sleeps. "I must go back to Bea," I tell Sarah the next morning. "Bea needs me."

"You have been worried about Bea for some months," Sarah replies. Am I so transparent?

"John must also see again the land where he was born."

"Of course," Sarah says. "India—the Spice Islands." To Sarah, Asia is one vast splendid and mysterious smudge.

"I shall go with you," Sarah says. "I remember Bea well. She was so beautiful. Perhaps she will return with us for a visit. Mother will look after our daughters."

We embark with John, his two Portuguese-Thai nurses, and the boy Pok. I have taken my tools and the android-king, for so Bea wills it. I know not why.

The android. He has lain in his chest all these years, but I have overhauled him from time to time, made him walk, write, sit. I have refined and added to his movements, inserted the needed cams for his eyes and mouth, though his face is still blank . . . waiting for Bea to carve it.

Meanwhile other craftsmen and artists have appeared, and the Jacquet-Droz brothers of Neuchâtel have continued to make superb androids. In 1774 they showed a lady playing the harpsichord, and a Writer; the lady truly plays, breathing as she plays, and the Writer truly writes. I went to see them, among a press of noblemen and ambassadors jostling one another to admire them. I saw that the Jacquet-Droz have had many ideas similar to mine, for invention is no one's monopoly, and what one man discovers may be discovered again, or at the same time, by another. But I was glad to note that my android is as good if not better than those pieces now exhibited from royal court to royal court throughout Europe.

WE EMBARKED ON AN English four-master in March of 1781. There was no longer any fear of scurvy, or *mal de terre*, for an Englishman, Linden, had rediscovered what the Arabs already knew, that juice of lime and oranges keeps sailing men healthy. I remembered Abdul Reza and Ismail, and the crates of lime they had brought aboard the *Cardus* to keep us well through our first voyage, more than twenty years ago.

329

John and Pok ran about the decks, and I rediscovered the marveling eye of childhood through them. I had taken many books with me and taught them every day. "If only Jacob could be with us." Sarah sighed.

"He is, in spirit," I said. In my first daughter I had discerned a passion for the stars and bought her a spy glass. Women must be educated as men are. In this I follow the much-reviled Jean Jacques Rousseau and his theories on education. Great changes are coming, and we must move with the times.

We dock at Bangkok in the good season of October and are permitted to anchor, though the customs are now most severe to prevent the smuggling of gold and statues, which still continues. People who discover treasure must turn it over to the state. The levies are heavy; even the Chinese boatmen are angered, for King Taksin wants to control all the trade, and their profits are greatly lowered.

On the Bangkok side of the river are houses for the *farang* companies and their factories. I inquire of Erik Erikssen, of Timmermans. Timmermans is in Batavia, and Erik has not been seen; he is still in India.

Scarcely have we landed than messengers come running announcing my sister, Princess Didya. "She must have seen our ship sail in." Sarah is surprised. "How did she know we had arrived? Doubtless she saw the ship." I cannot tell Sarah that always, always, Bea will know where I am, what I do. A woman cannot endure the thought that at any moment, day or night, someone else's mind can come groping, come between her and her husband, her lover.

Bea walks up the garden of the hostel where we have taken rooms, waiting to cross the river to Thonburi. Walking between the palm trees and the plantain, she is beautiful as ever, and I feel Sarah stiffen at her approach, aware of Bea's power to move others, to move me. But she goes forward to meet her, affectionate and joyful, perhaps a little too much so, to curb her own dismay. She kisses Bea and pushes John forward to show him to her, expecting Bea to say, "What a handsome child," and compliment Sarah on her care of him. But Bea is silent.

We cross in my sister's ornate and beautiful barge to Thonburi, to Udorn's new palace, with splendid roofs and pillars. Around it is a garden whose rocks and trees and ponds are reminiscent of Marquess Fang's exquisite garden in Yangchou. But here everything is florid, untamed, and the sensuous, full-blown beauty pleases the senses rather than the mind, with the elegance and symmetry of art, which is man's way of imposing his own nurturing upon nature.

Udorn is more portly. Many children by his wives are about. He greets Sarah with courtesy, and she becomes at ease. "A very fine gentleman," she says, "he speaks French so well."

"He spent three years at a Jesuit seminary, and his father and grandfather were ambassadors to Europe," I reply.

I have already taught Sarah and John and Pok the manners of the country, for Sarah, I know, will feel at a loss, searching for her own place in that space now restored which was my past, which was myself and Bea.

Bea wants to talk with me. A certain haggardness, invisible to all but me, flits at times across her beautiful face. That night I go to her, where she waits for me in the garden.

The darkness, with its sound of bird and water and sleepy insects, is a womb about us. I can hear in my ears that sea-shell sound of the sea we swam in our unborn days, inside our mother's belly.

"Taksin," she said.

"Tell me, Bea."

"They say he is dangerously mad, Colin. They say he does vile and ugly things." She shivers.

Wars. One after the other. Many campaigns, so many. One to defeat the evil priest-prince of Fang in the North, who wanted to set up a separate kingdom. Others, many others—to reconquer Laos, to subdue the Khmers of Cambodia. And against the Burmese, who continued their onslaughts. Never did Taksin yield, and any governor or official who yielded was instantly punished.

"Taksin's mother died during a campaign against the Burmese, when they again invaded the South. Taksin had no time to go to her bedside," Bea said. "I think the priests, the *bikkus*, are poisoning him. Udorn advised him to be more indulgent, to let go, for the people love their small knaveries, their petty corruptions, the magic of feasts. They want to laugh, but Taksin always replies, 'I have little time left. . . .' And now he has visions and dreams, and spends much time meditating, trying to fly, to achieve levitation.''

"Flying?"

"Do you remember, Colin, when he asked you whether you thought men would fly one day?"

"I remember." The scene comes back to me. Bea, playing with Udorn's first son, and Taksin asking the question of me.

I had told him of Leonardo da Vinci's flying machine, and of the prophecy: "When men outstripping birds shall skean the sky."

"What do you want me to do, Bea?"

"I do not know, Colin. I perceive danger for the King. And in my dream I heard your name. 'Colin . . . Colin can save him.' "

Her whole body is in a tremor she cannot overcome. She has sustained great agony all these years, loving a man who never looks at her. As a galley slave is chained to his ship, so is Bea chained to her love.

"HE IS BECOMING . . . STRANGE," Ah Ming told me.

Ah Ming was now a well-settled merchant of Thonburi in command of a fleet of barges for teakwood from the forests, an important personage in the Chinese community.

"When a man has great power, Colin Brother, he loses self-knowledge. He feels like a god. The King now believes that he is a Buddha and therefore can do no wrong. And he has round him sycophants, who tell him many lies."

Taksin had done many things, said Ah Ming, many of them were good. He had even written books himself to try to revive the theatre of Ayuthia. For in Ayuthia's destruction her immense accumulation of books, of historical archives, of musical instruments—all had disappeared in the fires that had destroyed her.

"But people are fickle, short of memory, Colin. They forget

easily the good done. They are getting very tired of austerity, very tired of severity."

Of course. The Chinese community was also irked by the customs' rigid controls. Their profits had come from contraband, smuggling that Taksin had curbed.

"But it is the *farang* priests and traders who have begun to say he is mad," Ah Ming went on. "He is not entirely mad, but very lonely, and some princes. . . want him to die."

JEAN ALLARD WAS IN BANGKOK, in charge of the Catholic mission and seminary there. He received me with rapture, hugging me many times. And when we spoke of the King he sighed and looked gloomy.

"The King has tried to force the Christian officials and nobles to swear loyalty to him by using only one rite, the drinking of lustral water blessed by the Brahmin priests of the Royal Court. Yet it was the custom for Christians to swear loyalty in church, knee bent, head raised, led by the officiating priest. And now the King spends much time trying to fly."

"I told him about flying," I replied, struck with guilt. "It was I who told him that it might be possible to make a flying machine one day."

Jean Allard looked at me blankly. Then, like a true Jesuit, he turned to a smooth conclusion. "The King meditates, believing he is a reincarnation of his idols. He feels his spirit leave his body and soar above it, roaming through the land. We have to condemn this, my son, for it is demonic—and so, we believe that he is not sane."

I knew then that even Allard wanted Taksin to be got rid of. It was true that the *farangs* in Bangkok disliked him. The Jesuit order had indeed been suppressed by the Pope in 1773—and Allard possibly depended now on some charitable nobleman, an enemy of Taksin.

From Udorn I learnt another aspect of the matter. The princes and nobles had greatly resented his treatment of two of his wives, who were princesses of noble blood.

"It was really all due to Nee," said Udorn.

"That is regrettable, of course, but—"

Nee, following Bea, had been one of Taksin's supporters when he had left Ayuthia. She had returned, as had Bea, with Taksin's victorious armies. And had married a man called Sanga, also reputed loyal to Taksin, who was now the commander of the King's arsenals, Keeper of the Royal Armory.

It was Nee who, going in and out of the palace at will, had whispered to the King that the two princesses were wanton and had made love with his Portuguese pages, one day when Taksin had ordered the pages to hunt for rats within the inner palace. For rats were still a plague, years after the fall of Ayuthia, and had left the ruined city and thrived in Bangkok and also in Thonburi.

"And Taksin believed Nee," Udorn said. He had put the princesses to death, hacking off their hands and feet and flogging them till they died. Although previous kings of Ayuthia had indulged in similar punishments, or even worse, yet what was shocking to the nobles was that Taksin was an upstart, a commoner, and Nee was also a common woman, who had once been a slave. "And so some of us have taken this ill," Udorn concluded.

"But after he had killed his wives, Taksin was much aggrieved and filled with remorse," Udorn continued. "He has sought to expiate this sin by becoming very religious. He retired into the *Wat* Arun to meditate. His two great friends, the noble *Chakri* and his brother Surasit, commander of the armies, run the kingdom while he is withdrawn into his meditations."

It was very clear, through Udorn's charming innuendoes, that all was set for a change. Which, of course, meant murder. And I felt that Taksin was not completely mad, but was being driven to madness. Perhaps it was true that he was fed slow poison. Bea would know.

"BEA, I CANNOT DO anything. The King must die."

Bea, gaunt with worry and grief, slapped my face.

"Colin, how dare you speak like this? Do you not know that Udorn is with the plotters against him?"

I wiped my cheek. Bea's anger did not arouse my ire. So often in childhood we had slapped each other, and then had embraced.

"In his heart, even if not in action yet, Udorn is with the princes against Taksin. And so is Nee. Nee has become most ambitious. She wants her husband, Sanga, to be king," Bea said. "She is poisoning Taksin."

"Bea." I held her, as always astir with varied impulses as her body came next to mine. "Bea, listen, there is nothing we can do. Leave this land and come back with us, just for a visit. Udorn would agree to it, and you will be safe."

Bea stared at me, and I stopped. She always had the power to make me feel paltry, and now I felt diminished, mean, in her eyes.

Udorn. His eyes knowledgeable, his face smooth, a man seasoned in the twists and turns of fortune, acknowledging pain and grief. He looked towards his garden, feasting upon its festival of blossom, as we spoke.

"Keran, you know that your sister has loved the King for many years. I have not interfered, for she has not cheated me in the way one accounts cheating, but yes, yes, take her away with you now, before—"

I understood. Before Taksin was dealt with. By the princes, the nobles, because it had now been decided. He was a danger to the kingdom, and therefore he must be removed in the only way kings can be removed.

MY SON, JOHN, TOOK well to the life in his mother's country. His Portuguese-Thai nurses, reunited with their families, were happy. Pok had looked with troubled eyes at his own people, but he was young enough to adapt, playing with Udorn's children, and soon was as one of them. I decided to leave Pok with Udorn; he needed to be with his own kind. But as for John, he would have to live in my land, with me, although I knew he would likely remain troubled many years by his double heritage.

Sarah became friendly with a great many wives of the *farang* Company men in Bangkok. Though she and Bea talked amiably with each other, never could Sarah be anything but afraid of Bea, and seeking ways to defend herself against Bea's power. And Sarah guessed—in that unworded, unconscious way in which we feel within ourselves things we never dare to utter— that I had had other lives, other selves, beyond her ken. And that the husband she knew was but one of those selves, trapped in an armor of sameness to her so as not to bewilder her. She gave me tenderness, striving to keep me in the image of me she had fashioned for herself, Baron Colin Duriez. But are we not all prone to loving but the persona we know, eschewing all others?

IT ALL BEGAN WITH what appeared as a small rebellion in Ayuthia. Ayuthia, now wasteland, derelict stones, its canals occluded, and even the King's palace only a few crumbling brick walls.

But smugglers of gold and treasure seekers still went on searching, amid the ruins, for buried hoards. The new governor had imposed a draconian rule that all treasure found would be confiscated. And this irked the treasure seekers, and also the small traders and merchants remaining around Ayuthia, whose livelihood depended on smuggled statues, and gold and silver. And one night when the moon was dark they stormed the governor's residence and killed his wives and children, while the governor fled to Thonburi.

The governor was the brother of Sanga, Keeper of the King's Armory, husband of Nee. Thus he had audience of the King, and Taksin sent Sanga to deal with the rebels of Ayuthia.

Sanga went, and a delegation of the rebels met him, but instead of quelling them he rallied them, raised a small army, and marched back to surround Taksin's palace at Thonburi. And since he controlled all the weaponry, it was impossible for the King's guards to obtain ammunition for their muskets. Especially when Sanga rallied a mob of malcontents in Thonburi itself to storm the palace.

The news reached us by messenger: "The King's palace is being attacked by an army under the Keeper of the Armory, *Phya* Sanga."

Bea rose from her seat, pale to the lips.

Udorn, unmoving, said quietly, "Sit down, my beloved."

"Udorn . . ."

"Sit down, heart of mine. Let matters take their destined course. Thus has the Lord Buddha willed it."

Bea flared. "You took an oath of loyalty to the King."

"The King is mad. Taksin is no longer Taksin."

Bea ran out into the garden, ran out into the evening, and I stumbled after her. "Bea, Bea, come back. . . ."

What could she do, alone, against an armed mutiny?

Udorn sent her women to fetch her back, and they brought her, twisting her hands, her body, away from them, pleading, "Let me go . . . I can fight. . . ."

I placed my hands upon her shoulders. "Bea, listen to me. . . ."

Udorn ordered the gates of the mansion locked. We sat together, Bea and I, in her room. I talked a great deal, but I knew it was in vain. Bea sat, still as a statue, her eyes deep pools of darkness, staring sightless at the night.

TAKSIN'S PRIVATE BODYGUARD OF thirty-six Christians fought valiantly, fought almost the whole night through, but no relief came. The people of Thonburi did not stir in favor of Taksin, although they could have done so. The Christians were slaughtered to the last man.

At dawn Taksin cropped his hair short and divested himself of his kingly garments. He besought the Chief Patriarch to admit him to *Wat* Arun as a monk and was received as a lay devout.

He dwelt in the *wat* while the nobles and princes gathered in council and announced that Taksin had relinquished the kingship.

Of the meeting which took place I know very little, except that Sanga had his supporters and strove to become king. But too many were opposed to him, and he grudgingly gave in to the general demand, which was to recall the *Chakri* and his brother, the commander-in-chief, both of them away on campaigns to subdue outlying territories.

Within a week, the *Chakri* and his brother had returned to

Thonburi. Sanga was arrested, and the mobs quelled. It was already very clear that the *Chakri* would be offered the crown, for he came of a royal line, with heroes among his ancestors.

It was now the end of March of the year 1782, and we prepared to leave. Our ship waited at dock, with merchandise of silk and porcelain and spices and a goodly company of traders impatient to be away. I pleaded with Bea to come with us. "You cannot do anything to save Taksin, Bea, nothing at all. It is the will of the people." She regarded me scornfully, went to her rooms, and shut herself up in them. And I was filled with dismay.

Nee and Sanga were put to death in the usual way, which surprised no one. And one night I woke up screaming and Sarah said, "Again a nightmare," and burst into great sobs. She could not bear what she called my nightmares, though they were now infrequent. And Bea was there, calling me from outside the bedroom door. "Colin, come . . ." So I rose, saying to Sarah I needed the garden air, and joined Bea. "Udorn has arranged that we should see King Taksin, before—" She swallowed hard, her throat working, containing herself.

Our chaises took us swiftly to the *Wat* Arun, the Temple of Dawn. Behind us another chaise followed.

Monk Teo, more wizened but all smiles, greeted us, and showed great pleasure at my sight. "It is noble of you to come. I shall lead you to the Presence."

Up the paved alley, and crossing the courtyard; up the steps to the chapel with its small rooms; and there, in a bare chamber, in front of a statue of the All-Merciful Buddha, Taksin, his hair just growing, like bristles on a brush, sat in the lotus position, immobile, plunged in a trance, eyes closed.

Monk Teo said softly, "Your Majesty, visitors have come." And then went to kneel in a corner and fanned himself gently with his black and gold *tarapet*. Taksin opened his eyes, but his gaze did not rest upon us. It rested upon the golden face of the Lord Buddha. He stared at it and beyond it as if he could pierce the walls of matter, the thick substance of things, to reach past them. His eyes still held that strange, almost unearthly glow, once so compelling, and from his body still came that emanation of Being, which struck one as does a blow.

"Keran, I am glad you are here. Are you well?" He spoke in a faraway but natural voice.

"Very well, Your Majesty. We have come—"

"To see me and bid farewell before I leave this life. You are very kind."

Bea spoke, her voice fervent and tremulous: "Your Majesty, we want to save you. My brother has built this machine man; we have brought it with us. We can place it here. The guards will think it is Your Majesty—"

Perhaps for the first time in so many years, Taksin looked at Bea. He turned his head, and his eyes went to hers and lingered.

"Noble Lady, of the great soul and the mind like a shooting star, I thank you. Indeed your brother makes excellent automata—did he not build, fifteen years ago, many machine soldiers for the ramparts of Ayuthia? And indeed, should you bribe the guards with much gold, they will mistake the machine man for me.

"But what will you have saved? Only the fleshly envelope of a man who, it is said, is no longer master of his brain. Only some more years of life for that body, when perhaps the soul within it will reach Nirvana, the Bliss of nonrebirth."

Then Bea began to weep, the tears streaming down her face, unchecked. Taksin closed his eyes, returning to his meditation, and I rose, put my hands on Bea's shoulders. Then Taksin spoke to me again, his voice already disembodied, his eyes still closed.

"Keran, do you still believe that man will fly one day?"

"Yes, Your Majesty," I replied. "Yes, it will happen . . . one day." He smiled then, and raised his hand to bless us.

Bea cried, cried for all the years of her love. When we were back in the house, I brought her to her rooms, and just as when we were children, I stayed with her, holding her in my arms for many hours.

THE PALACE GUARDS CAME for Taksin. Since he had not been ceremonially ordained as a monk, it was no sin to execute him.

They carried with them heavy golden drapes, which,

kneeling, they indicated, while Monk Teo and other monks chanted the appropriate litanies for the passing of souls. Taksin stepped into the swathes of golden silk, and the guards bound them round him like a sack, with silken gold-tasseled cords. They carried the sack to the place of execution, which was in his own palace, in the funeral chapel he had prepared for his own death.

With long flat blades of the best sandalwood, gilded and seamed with gold, they beat the sack and the body within it until it no longer moved.

This was the death prescribed for a great and noble king.

The court officials in charge of funeral rites bound the body in rolls of fine cloth, swaddling it tight, folded upon itself like an embryo, and placed it into a large jar of silver. There Taksin's body waited, his body's ichors extruding through the pierced bottom into a silver basin. A year later, when the clean bones remained, he was solemnly cremated in a ceremony fit for a great and noble king.

It was April 7, 1782, fifteen years to the day since the fall of Ayuthia, that King Taksin of Thonburi left this life. He was, on that day, forty-eight years old.

Oh painful is birth and rebirth, never-ending; and happy the mind approaching the Ineffable, which has extinguished all desire. . . .

After his death the legends began; a whisper, then a rumor, then an unending texture of the air in the small maze of alleys, among the people, seeping into their minds. Now that the King was dead they remembered him. They said he had not been killed. Oh no. He was not dead. He was alive, a reincarnated, living Lord Buddha, his spirit watchful over the land he had saved and loved. His spirit listening to the people he had fed during the years of famine. His spirit over Thonburi, and over Ayuthia the Most Excellent City, the Enchantress, the very heart of the kingdom, whose glory will never end.

The people now made little clay and porcelain figures of King Taksin, and stuck gold foil upon them, praying to him. And placed flower garlands, and miniature horses and elephants, and dancing girls, in front of small shrines to his name.

TAKSIN'S BROTHERS, SOME OF his sons, and his entourage had also been put to death, some said by unruly mobs, others said by order of Surasit, the *Chakri's* brother. The *Chakri* himself now took the name *Chakri* for his dynasty, and was known as King Rama. He was too noble, Udorn told me, to have ordered such slaughter, for the *Chakri* had married Taksin's daughter, and Taksin had married the *Chakri's* daughter to seal the friendship between them. And the *Chakri* saved one grandson, the son of his daughter by Taksin.

The kingdom remained calm; the people accepted the new King well, hoping that the wars would now stop. Already King Rama had written to Macao to recall the missionaries Taksin had expelled. He lightened the levies; he would send embassies abroad, to welcome *farang* traders in great numbers. He reinforced the Buddhist *Sangha* and gave rich gifts to the *wats*. He moved the capital from Thonburi to Bangkok across the Great Mother River Menam.

WE SET SAIL IN late April; Bea came with us. She seemed to have taken Taksin's death with composure, for no trace of grief lingered upon her face, and her gauntness had vanished. A beautiful and noble princess whose presence was all grace, she was carried in her chaise up the gangplank.

As usual on a sea voyage, Bea spent much time alone in her cabin. The sea swell discomforted her, but on smooth-sailing days she paced the deck with Sarah, both women talking amiably, holding their parasols against the glare. And when I sent my mind to hers, I encountered no resistance. Only a colorless, faceless quiet, a greyness that surprised me. Always there had been much turbulence in Bea. I had known many of her moods, all of them expressed in color, varied and changeful as the colors of our lake. But now it was the lake turned quicksilver, merging with the sky in motionless invisibility.

All was well as we returned to the Duriez mansion in

Neuchâtel, and then went to my house in Lausanne for the winter months. I bought a small house for Bea, next to mine, a charming three-storied one, overlooking the lake and facing the sun. Bea added a hothouse of glass, where tropical trees and flowers she had brought with her thrived handsomely. Lausanne's high society welcomed her, for was she not a princess, and she was gracious to all, her silks and jewels and the objects in her house making many a lady pale with envy.

ONE AFTERNOON, PASSING BEA'S gate, I thought to go in. The valet who opened the door told me, "Madame la Princesse is in her boudoir."

I climbed the stairs to those charming small rooms tufted with silk and velvet that ladies of quality affect next to their bedrooms, and heard voices. Bea must have had a guest with her, though no coach was stationed outside, and the valet had not spoken to me of a guest.

The door was partly open, so I knocked upon it, saying at the same time, " 'Tis I, Bea," and pushed the door to enter.

Bea was sitting on a low stool. In front of her was a gold tray, with flowers and incense sticks in a gold incense burner. Opposite her on a platform, as on a throne, sat the android, my android, his legs crossed tailorwise. He turned his head to stare at me. He now had a face and eyes, with a strange glow to them.

"Bea . . . what . . ."

"Colin." Bea rose, dropping a curtsy to the android, then walking backwards. "Allow me, Your Majesty." She spoke in Thai. The android continued to stare at me, through me; then he turned his head, rose and walked some paces, sat at the desk placed in a corner of the room, seized a quill, dipped it into the inkpot, and began to write.

My heart beat wildly, beat with terror, with horror. I grasped Bea's hand and dragged her out of the boudoir.

"Bea, I thought it was still in the chest. . . ."

"Dear Colin." Bea, gentle, her eyes emerald, happy. "His Majesty did indeed travel well in the chest. He was in my cabin, remember? He is now accustomed to the weather here."

"Bea, please . . . he's only an android. . . . I made him, I put him together. . . ."

Amused, Bea shook her ringlets, toyed with the necklace of diamonds and rubies round her neck. "Colin, I know all this, but what is the difference? His body may have died, but his spirit, his soul, has returned, and lives in the shape you made. Is not that what you wanted, what we all want? And it's happened."

I steadied myself. This way lay madness. I must not allow this credulity.

"Bea, you told me yourself, you no longer knew what to believe about the undead."

"Did I?" She mused a little while, charmingly playful. "I was wrong to doubt." She straightened, all of her suave, silken with fulfilled love. "He goes with me walking by the lake at night," she whispered. "Many come or whisper to us, the remembered ones, the undead."

I saw behind her, through the open door, the android rise, putting down the quill, and walk to the large bay window and look out of it, look at the glittering lake lying in the sun.

"His Majesty has called me," Bea said, and went into her boudoir, gently closing the door upon me.

I heard her voice, and, may God be my witness, I thought I also heard another voice, low, deep-toned, one I thought I recognized. And Bea laughed.

"SARAH, SARAH . . ."

I had to tell someone.

Sarah came to me, a little concerned, always maternal now, caring and warm. And then I could not speak. I sat down, collected myself, and said, "Did you know, Sarah, that Bea keeps the King-android with her?"

"Yes, of course, my dear." Matter-of-factly, Sarah sat down too, smoothing her skirts, her face guileless. "All the servants know it. She has had her apartments refurnished and changed for the K . . . the android. It is like playing with a large doll."

"But it is not the same. The android I created—she believes it's alive."

"What is sanity?" Sarah, soothing, a tinge of satisfaction in her voice. She had known all the time, savoring her small triumph.

"We all believe in dreams, dear husband. We need dreams, for dreams are strong living. You remember Jacob telling you of the golem. We need the golem, to avenge the wrongs done to our race, and Bea needs the King. Dear husband, let her be happy in her own way."

I OVERHAUL THE KING and make repairs when they are needed. Bea always lets me know, not in words, but in that universe of silence peopled with knowingness, which has been restored to us, now that, with the King by her side, we need not be afraid of each other any longer.

The captive King is sometimes with us as we wander, Bea and I, when all else sleeps in the dark enchanted forest. And slowly something else unfolds in me. A hope. Jit.

Perhaps one day Jit too will find her way to me, for love is very strong. Perhaps one night I shall begin, my fingers skillful, to make an image she can inhabit.

In a universe soughing with silent words as the trees sough with the winds of the lake, Jit will come to me; already I watch the spread and shimmer of its waters, as if she might arise from them.

But what will happen to Sarah then?

Sarah. I love her. Perhaps she already knows the temptation I am enduring, for she knows me very well. Sarah will understand, if no one else can, that without a certain madness, man is no more than a corpse adjourned. Her people understand visions and dreams, and have suffered for what others have called madness. And for her sake, for Jacob's sake, I shall not call Jit back.

Sarah orders the servants to treat the King respectfully. On sunny afternoons, it is the fashion for Lausanne's society to take the air, driving in their coaches along the tree-shaded avenue to Ouchy, back and forth.

In a handsome coach and four, Bea drives, the King by her side. So splendid is her equipage that no one finds it odd.

The ladies watch for the fashions she wears, her hats and her dresses, and the colors of her parasols. Sometimes one of them, amiably, will comment on the unmoving figure by my sister's side. "What a marvelous machine! It is a Jaquet-Droz, is it not? How very distinguished!"

I never contradict. After all, I shall not build any more androids.

⤜❧ ☙⤛